I0762955

Purple State

Also by Dana Perino

I Wish Someone Had Told Me . . .

Everything Will Be Okay

Let Me Tell You About Jasper . . .

And the Good News Is . . .

A NOVEL

DANA PERINO

An Imprint of HarperCollinsPublishers

HarperCollins books may be purchased for educational, business, or sales promotional use. For information, please email the Special Markets Department at SPsales@harpercollins.com.

hc.com

FIRST EDITION

Art © kaisorn / Shutterstock

Library of Congress Cataloging-in-Publication Data has been applied for.

ISBN 978-0-06-348656-0

Printed in the United States of America

26 27 28 29 30 LBC 8 7 6 5 4

TO MY SISTER, ANGIE PERINO MACHOCK

PART ONE

Chapter 1

Dorothy "Dot" Clark sat looking out her office window in Rockefeller Center west toward the Hudson River. She rested her elbow on the desk and had her chin in her palm. She twirled a piece of her long blond hair with the manicured index finger of her other hand. The late-October sun was setting in the early evening, and she felt herself fading with the light.

She took a deep breath and sighed. It had been a long day.

The deck for a new pitch glared from her computer screen. Dot worked at a large public relations firm that specialized in tech, and they were going for a new healthcare software account. The potential client wanted a PR company to get them media attention; unfortunately, her presentation was as flat as their brand. She needed to add some pizzazz, or they'd never land the account.

Dot's eyes drifted to the arrangement of sunflowers and coral roses sent that morning by her boyfriend, Ryan Montgomery. "Just because," the card read. It was signed "Ryan" and had "xoxo" right below his name. She wondered if that was *his* doing or the florist thinking his message was a bit basic.

The entry-level staffers in their cubicles swooned as she carried them from the reception area back to her small office. She'd been given that coveted private space—a room with a door—when she'd been the first to raise her hand to work in the office five days a week. She blushed as she carried the flowers and playfully rolled her eyes at them. They had no idea that her relationship with Ryan was on the rocks.

Then again, neither did he.

She'd met Ryan six months before on a "respectable" dating app. He was half a foot taller than Dot at six feet even and considered a very good-looking guy—the kind you'd take home to Mom for dinner and show off to friends on Instagram. She was toned from running and Pilates. They made a good-looking couple.

He resembled a young, more put together Harry Styles—his brown hair had that tousled look she'd liked since her preteen years. His eyes were as deep a brown as hers were a light blue, and his chin was strong and smooth. He said he couldn't grow a beard if he tried, which suited her. Facial hair on a guy? Hard pass. If a guy's profile pic included a mustache, she'd swipe left in a second.

Ryan was athletic, though on the thin side of fit, and had broad shoulders and a flat stomach. He'd played lacrosse at his high school on Long Island, and his team made it to the national prep championship—they'd come in second. "It still hurts," he'd said on their first date. Back then, hopelessly attracted to him, she'd thought that was sweet.

His economics degree was from Boston College, and he'd landed a finance job in the city right after graduation at the firm where he'd interned. Ryan was smart but not as widely read as Dot. He read only the sports section of the *New York Post* in his office's cafeteria when one of the older guys had left their copy behind. She was more the news and opinion in *The New York Times* type. He preferred video games at night. She loved to read a novel before bed.

His typical outfit was what Dot called the finance broniform—khaki golf pants, a white or light blue button-down, and a navy company-branded vest, no matter the weather. It was a good thing he was tall, or she might not be able to pick him out of the crowd at P.J. Clarke's on a Thursday night.

They'd matched because she said she was looking for someone who loved New York, liked travel and good conversation, and wanted a long-term relationship. She'd tried to tone down the specifics of her life plan—married by thirty-two, two kids by thirty-six, and a second home for weekends away from the city—because she was afraid the details were scaring off potential matches. To seem more carefree, she'd added photos of herself skiing in Colorado and having drinks with friends at the Frying Pan on the Hudson River.

Immediately after, she matched with Ryan. His profile said that he was great on a road trip (a detail that gave her adventurous but responsible vibes), wanted to get a dog and have at least two children, and was looking for a lifelong commitment. Dot took that as a good sign that he was up for marriage . . . eventually, of course.

On their first date, Dot thought he was smart and handsome. She'd even described him as "hot" to her girlfriends. By their second date, they asked for proof beyond his dating profile pic. No one trusted *those* photos anyway.

Asking for a selfie seemed too eager, so she'd snuck a photo of him by pretending to read a message while she walked back to their table after visiting the ladies' room. Her friends and sister gave him a solid score. As a bonus, he wasn't a total creep like other guys she'd dated.

She really liked that he was self-assured but not cocky. Her dates since graduating college three years before had varied from the totally aimless to the ridiculously arrogant. Ryan seemed just the right mix of humble and confident. She believed he'd be a loyal partner and, jumping ahead as she tended to do, that together they would send their kids to private schools, take fabulous summer and winter vacations, and own a place in Sag Harbor for the weekends in between. She could picture it when she let her mind wander far ahead into the future.

But there was a slight catch. Politically, they weren't totally aligned. Well, he wasn't aligned at all. He wasn't even registered to vote. At least he wasn't a Republican, she'd reasoned. And while his disinterest in politics was a red flag, she thought she could live with that at first and convince him to vote at some point. For the Democrats, of course.

Overall, after tossing aside a few bad pancakes, she liked that Ryan had a life plan and was strictly sticking to it. Order and decisiveness had always spoken to her.

Or at least they had.

Having everything planned out was Dot's go-to move since she was a little girl. But now she was realizing that half her plans weren't panning out and the other half were hemming her in. She fretted that she'd mapped out the wrong life.

And life was coming at her fast.

In some ways, Ryan was very different from his peers. He lived by a regimented schedule, planning out his days, months, and years. One of Ryan's plans was to be married by the time he was twenty-eight, the age his happily married parents had wed. He'd just turned twenty-seven. His clock was ticking. And to Dot, it had started to sound more like a bomb.

Her intuition was firing, and she'd developed a feeling he was going to propose. And she wasn't sure she wanted him to pop the question.

Lately, the air was seeping out of the Ryan balloon. Whereas the first few months had been exciting, and she was caught up seeing how it could all work out perfectly, she was now trying to avoid him.

The problem wasn't so much him, but her. He hadn't changed—he was still the same guy—and *that* had become the problem. She realized he had no interests except making money and playing golf. He didn't have any curiosity outside of those interests. And while she'd tried for a while to get him talking about things that mattered to her, she had fallen short.

The truth was, she was getting bored by him. And it was starting to show.

At first it was little things like not immediately replying to his texts and not bothering to like his Instagram posts about Scottish golf courses. But it had grown into making excuses not to go for drinks after work and strategically scheduling brunch or walks with her girlfriends so that she'd have something on her calendar that conflicted with his.

She knew Ryan had noticed her distancing but supposed he'd chalked it up to her being overwhelmed at work. And he wasn't wrong about that. Public relations was always on lists of the top five most stressful jobs in America, and she was under the gun. The business was changing, or maybe even ending—artificial intelligence threatened everyone's jobs. Plus, clients thought a PR company could just make a product go viral by using some sort of messaging mind trick on a TV show host or influencer. It didn't work that way, and the pressure was rising on everyone in the industry.

So now, to get their relationship back on track, he was love bombing her, as if that could help win back her affection. That's why he'd sent the flowers. The previous week it had been chocolates. And the week before that it was tickets to a Broadway musical, something she usually loved.

Unfortunately for Ryan, the extra attention was backfiring. Instead of being touched, Dot cringed. She had the six-month itch.

And so far, nothing could scratch it.

Chapter 2

A sudden double knock jolted her out of her office chair, and Dot toppled over her water bottle.

"Daydreaming again?" Ugh, her team's senior vice president, the SVP. He was always needling her.

"Nope, just thinking!" She jumped up and started mopping up the spill with a tissue. Her voice was usually steady and medium-pitched, but it went an octave higher when she was trying to sound extra cheerful.

"How's the pitch looking?" he asked.

"It's coming together." She feigned confidence with a cheerful smile. "It'll be ready by tomorrow."

"Good. Feel free to get them to help." The SVP jutted his pointy chin toward the cubicles where the new hires were wrapping up and laughing together. Dot felt responsible for making sure they all kept their jobs, and that meant landing this new account. "They're always chatting and giggling. It's hard to imagine what we're paying them to do."

"Actually, they've been a big help. Lots of creativity and enthusiasm," she said brightly, hoping to convince him they were pulling their weight.

"Well, we'll see," he said dismissively. He looked down at his Apple Watch. "Okay, I'm due at the Polo Bar."

Of course he is, she thought. But said, "Don't worry, we've got this."

"You better."

Dot didn't like the shift in pronouns there. Where was the "we" she thought they'd have as a team? He was the kind of boss who didn't help with a project but was quick to take credit or pass blame. Sadly, she realized, it was probably how he'd gotten so far so fast.

The SVP turned on his heel and strode to the elevator in his Deerskin Triple-Stitch Zegna sneakers, his black leather man-bag bouncing on his hip.

"What a piece of work," Dot said to herself.

She had never gotten past how he'd promoted one of her colleagues—a guy he golfed with on weekends at a club in New Jersey that both their parents belonged to—ahead of her, despite the fact she did more work and got better results. That had stung, but she'd swallowed it, fearing that complaining would make it worse for her in the long run. She was hyper-aware about being liked and tried to avoid confrontation. So, she'd just doubled down and worked harder.

When he'd disappeared, Dot sat back down and stared at the screen for a while. She had a couple of ideas that were promises the firm couldn't guarantee, but that the client would probably appreciate. She added them into the deck and left herself some room to make any additions she might think of first thing in the morning.

She decided to call it a day. As her grandfather who served in the Air Force used to say, she was running out of airspeed and altitude. Better to sign off and clear her mind.

While Dot wasn't prone to anxiety, she wasn't sure what was wrong with herself lately. More and more, at twenty-five, she was feeling out of sorts and like she was running behind everyone else. This was despite moving up quickly after joining the firm. She was one of the youngest of the account managers and had a lot of client contact and responsibility.

But she wasn't excited by her work and dwelled on why she'd been passed over for promotion in her last review. Her boss, the SVP, had just said they wanted to see more. The "more" was left undefined, which left her frustrated and grasping at straws. And regardless, she couldn't see any real opportunity for advancement at the company in the next two years. And she had ambition to get ahead.

Beyond that, she'd thought at this point there would be more clarity in her life when it came to work and love. But things felt more confusing and harder than ever. This wasn't how she imagined her life at this age.

Not wanting to dwell on worries, Dot decided to shake all that off at least for a night. She was meeting her girlfriends, Mary and Harper, at her apartment.

They'd been invited to a big conference call about next year's presidential election and possible volunteer opportunities. And George Clooney was the guest speaker to kick things off, so she had to say yes. Dot had signed them all up and offered to host at her apartment. She didn't know what the call would be like, but it was a good excuse to get together.

Dot, Mary, and Harper had met their freshman year at NYU in English Lit 101. They were fast friends and had grown close over the years. The name for their yearslong text thread was given to them one late night after an off-campus party by one of the workers at Joe's Pizza. "Check it out, guys, here comes The Crew." The nickname stuck and became the title of their group chat.

She needed to get moving to beat them to her house, but before she left the office, Dot had to go through her routine. It was borderline OCD, she realized, but she had her personal clean-desk policy to keep organized.

First, she got her email inbox down to under twenty unread messages. Then she collected her colored pens and highlighters and put them back in her Waverly Diner coffee mug. She gathered the loose papers on her desk and kept only what she really needed. Finally, she separated the trash and recycling, wrote out a fresh to-do list, and reviewed her schedule for the next day.

Satisfied that everything was in order, Dot slipped off her black high heels and put them under her desk next to the nude pair she kept at the office. This saved her closet space at home and from schlepping them back and forth to work. She put on her sneakers and a traditional tan trench coat, belted in front. She pulled a printed silk scarf from her coat pocket and tied it around her neck, Audrey H. style, to ward off the chilly draft whipping through all the Midtown towers.

Before she left, Dot glanced at Ryan's flowers. She didn't want to carry them home. She thought about posting a pic on her Instagram story to show everyone what a great boyfriend she had.

But in the end, she did neither. Instead, she turned out the light and headed for the elevator.

Chapter 3

Dot walked out of her office building onto Avenue of the Americas. She took a right toward Central Park and merged with the mob of commuters and tourists heading to workouts, dinners, first dates, or the theater.

While she waited at a light with several others, she fumbled in her backpack for her AirPods so she could listen to one of her favorite podcasts on her walk home. Next to her, a young woman was loudly making plans on her phone.

"I'll meet you at Quality B on Fifty-Fourth."

"Fifty-Fifth," Dot said at the same time as the man just in front of her.

The young woman looked at them.

"Wait. These two people just said it's on Fifty-Fifth—and they don't look like tourists."

Dot smiled at her and winked at the guy when he looked back and caught her eye. The lights changed and he gestured for her to go in front of him. Who said chivalry was dead?

They snaked through the taxis and limos in the crosswalk and went their separate ways.

"Have a great night," he said.

"You too!" she responded, appreciating how she'd probably never see him again, but they'd had a Manhattan connection. It was moments like those that kept her love affair with the city going.

As she walked, she found the *Left, Right, and Center* political podcast and pressed play. Dot grew up in Providence with politically active parents who both worked at Brown. When she and her sister, Anne, were little, they'd gone with their parents to New Hampshire to door-knock for President Obama's re-election, and they'd cried when Hillary Clinton lost in 2016.

Politics was next door to PR, and she was really into the upcoming Democratic primaries. It was an election year, and she was following the horse race closely. There were more than twenty candidates planning to run. It was so exciting. On most days she found she was way more interested in politics than her day job. Podcasts kept her informed on the state of play.

The lights changed and she crossed into Central Park, kicking some of the early fall leaves on the path she took to get to her small apartment on the Upper West Side. She passed a co-ed softball game and heard the umpire tease the woman catcher who'd just botched a throw back to the mound.

"Next time just roll it," he said, to which she laughed good-naturedly.

For the next play, the self-appointed coach screamed at the man on third base to tag and sprint home. She slowed to watch. Close call but the runner was safe, and Dot heard them cheering as she turned toward Central Park West.

Dot exited the park on Sixty-Seventh Street and could see her building, the Buckley, down the block. It was a well-maintained pre-war apartment block with big blond bricks and dark green trim on the windows. Her modest apartment, inherited from her grandmother, was on the third floor. She knew how fortunate she was to have it. And since her grandparents had paid off the mortgage long ago, she only had to cover the monthly fees—which were still ridiculously expensive, but at least she didn't need a roommate to help pay the bills.

Albert Hawkins, her favorite doorman, was outside the entrance, helping an older woman into a taxi. Once she was securely in, he shut the car door, and rapped twice on the roof, signaling to the driver he was good to go.

Dot had known Albert ever since she could remember. As a young girl, she'd visited her grandmother often on weekends and holidays and he'd always been there. He was a tall, slender black man with bright eyes and a cheerful smile. He kept his graying hair cropped close to his head. He had excellent posture he'd developed in the Army as a young man. He wore his uniform every day—black pressed trousers and a matching blazer, white shirt, and a burgundy tie. The only cheat he allowed to his usual work attire was modern dress sneakers, since he was on his feet all day. His wife had died two years before, and he'd told Dot he preferred to keep working rather than sit home and mourn. So, at seventy-eight, he still showed up every day to the Buckley.

"Miss Dorothy, welcome home," he said, opening the door with a flourish. He'd always called her by her full given name, as her grandmother had. "Will you be going back out tonight? Beautiful evening."

Dot reached up to air kiss his cheek.

"No, not tonight. But Mary and Harper are coming over. We're hopping on a call about the presidential election."

"Another election already? Feels like the last one never ended."

"I know. And I was just listening to an analyst who said this one's going to be super close, and probably the most expensive in history, too."

They walked into the foyer and Dot stopped to get her mail from the old-fashioned mailbox.

"Just a bunch of junk, as usual," she said, leafing through it.

Albert reached out his hand. "Give that to me. I'll put it in the bin."

"Thank you," she said, handing him the small stack and turning to head up the stairs. She stopped at the first one and turned back.

"So, let me ask. Do you think that the Democrats can win this time around?"

"Oh, I don't know," he said, leaning an elbow on the banister. "I try not to get too caught up in it. Nothing much changes either way."

"I suppose you're right. I'm just trying not to become a complete cynic." She batted her eyelashes a couple of times.

"You're hopeful, Dorothy, and that's why everyone loves you. Now get going."

Dot turned and took the wide stairs two at a time.

"Slow down, Dorothy! You're rushing away your youth."

"Ha! Don't worry about me, Albert!"

But she knew he had a point. She *was* in a hurry to get her life going.

When she got into her apartment, she hung her coat on the hook and put her bag in its spot. Small apartments meant keeping organized. Her phone buzzed. A text from Ryan.

"Dinner tomorrow? Just the two of us. I got a reservation at Peak. 7 p.m."

Dot's fingers paused over the screen. She was torn. Wait . . . why dinner when they already had plans for brunch that weekend? And Peak? That was just for special occasions. And the reservations were impossible to get. It was on the 101st floor and was used for . . .

"Oh no," she groaned. Did this mean what she thought it meant?

Her thoughts started to race as Dot psyched herself out. The three text message dots danced in anticipation of her response. But none came.

She set the phone down without replying.

Chapter 4

Lady Liberty glowed golden in the evening's last slice of sunlight as Mary Russo looked down at the southern tip of Manhattan from her office window in the Financial District. She pulled back her long black curly hair and tied it in a loose knot at the base of her neck with a tortoiseshell claw clip.

"What would *you* do?" she asked the statue. "You know, from one liberated lady to another?"

The usually coolheaded Mary was in a jam. She was twenty-five, a young woman in a hurry who thought maybe she'd made a bad decision with her career direction.

She was the first of her Staten Island family to graduate from college, and no one was surprised when this argumentative Russo girl became a lawyer, a year earlier than expected based on early credits. She'd immediately joined the prestigious firm where she'd interned during law school. It specialized in initial public offerings, and mergers and acquisitions, which was a lucrative path in New York. However, if she was being honest, it was somewhat boring. There was little drama in corporate law. Almost everything was settled in conference rooms not courtrooms.

After several months at the firm, a few doubts about her career path crept into her mind. On the one hand, she was good at her job and on track to become a junior partner. She was proficient with the AI paralegal software the firm licensed and tried to teach herself something new about it every day. That made her stand out, and she was often asked to join cases by partners across the firm who'd heard about her skills. They appreciated how she'd explain the new technology in a way that didn't make them feel ancient. Because of her efforts, she'd even received a surprise bonus after a big case she assisted on was settled.

Given that her salary was decent, she was able to rent a studio apartment in Battery Park City and could see a path to a corner office in several years. That was very appealing—no financial worries, and living in one of the trendiest neighborhoods in New York City.

But on the other hand, what about the time between now and that corner office? Was this *really* what she wanted to do with her life? Was there more to life than billable hours for bankers?

A message popped up on Slack from one of the office managers. "Is anyone able to walk a charger over to Henry Rickleman at district court? He forgot to take it with him. Again."

Mary responded right away. "I can do it." Any excuse to get out for some fresh air. Autumn was her favorite time of year.

"Great—thanks. Hey, bring back some cookies from Funny Face for everyone. We could use some Crumbfettis to get through the afternoon. Brutal new deadline just came in. Just expense it."

"I'll bring back the fun." She knew that as soon as she set the cookies out in the communal kitchen they'd be gone within minutes. Sugar was a heck of a drug for lawyers who didn't leave the office to eat.

Mary got up from her chair and smoothed her light gray cigarette pants over her long legs. She wore an ivory silk top with a ruffled front, a pale gray blazer, and her signature black stilettos. She could walk as easily in heels as she could in sneakers. Her medium-size gold hoops and her great-grandmother's small gold cross around her neck were her only jewelry. Before leaving, she grabbed her mid-length and well-worn black leather coat off the back of the communal coatrack and threw it around her shoulders.

Mary was five seven and model thin. She shunned exercise and loved the big Italian meals her grandmother made every Sunday.

"Mangia, Maria," Nonna teased her.

"It's not fair," her friends said, wishing her natural metabolism would rub off on them.

Mary was the beloved youngest child of Tony and Christine Russo. She had three older brothers, Gabe, Frankie, and Joey. They ran a protection racket around their baby sister, which had been a blessing and a curse as she was growing up.

Mary had always been smart and naturally stylish. She loved word games and witty retorts. She favored dramatic dark eyeliner and mascara below naturally arched brows and red lipstick that somehow never smudged. Her long nails were always manicured in a neutral color that went with everything. Her closet was filled with the latest fashions, and she had a nose for hitting the best sample sales that she heard about through following the coolest influencers and their secret network of stylists.

She picked up the charger on her way out, placed it in her red leather tote, and headed to the courthouse.

Out on the street, the wind was whippy, and the air smelled like autumn. She shivered in her coat and picked up her pace, careful not to catch the sidewalk cracks in her spiky heels.

On her way, she passed a Legal Aid office she'd never noticed before, though she'd made this trip several times. She stopped to read a sign taped to the window that read in capital letters: VOLUNTEERS NEEDED FOR FAMILY COURT.

A young man sat inside and caught her attention when he waved to her. She waved back and quickly scanned the QR code onto her phone intending to look it up later.

"Hi. Please tell me you're a lawyer who wants to do a good deed. We really need more help," said the man after he'd gently opened the door. She noticed his looks right away. He was slightly taller than she was, fit like a boxer, with broad shoulders, dark brown eyes, and very white teeth. He had on straight dark-blue jeans, stylish Veja sneakers, and a snug navy quarter zip.

"I am, but not this kind. Went the corporate route. Don't hate me." She shielded her eyes with her hand in mock shame. "Do you take volunteers with no experience in family court—beyond the class we took in law school?"

"We take anyone. Even corporate lawyers." His wide smile showed he was in on the joke. "We just need people with a pulse. And a heart. There are so many foster children who need an advocate. And there are many moms and dads who could use some help, too." He handed her a brochure. "There's a seminar this weekend for new volunteers."

She took it and skimmed the contents.

"By the way, I'm Manny Rios." He stuck out his hand.

She took it and gave it a firm handshake and met his eyes, just like her dad had taught her.

"Mary Russo." She smiled, feeling a stirring of purpose. And maybe something else.

She hadn't dated anyone since getting herself out of a terrible relationship with her law school boyfriend who had turned possessive. It got scary. Restraining-order scary. That had put Mary off men for a long while, though her family was really pressuring her to get set up and find someone. They wanted her to settle down and start having children as two of her three older brothers had. Her eldest brother, Gabe, had become a priest, so he got a pass.

"Hope to see you there, Mary Russo."

"You just might." She started to walk backward, not wanting to break eye contact with Manny, and nearly got hit by a tourist riding a Citibike on the sidewalk.

Manny reached out and grabbed her. Then he made sure she was steady before letting her go.

"Thank you." She felt the heat of his touch through her jacket.

"Those bikes are so dangerous. Are you okay?"

"Yes, I'm fine. Thank you for saving me. Not just potentially my life—but from severe embarrassment." She looked around to see if any other bikes were coming their way. "Tourists on Citibikes . . . the worst."

"You should sue."

"Not a bad idea. Know any good lawyers?" She knew time was getting on and that Mr. Rickleman would be wondering where she was. She didn't need trouble with one of the managing partners, but she liked talking to Manny.

"I might have just met one."

Okay, he was flirting with her. And she kind of liked it.

She turned and started to walk away, waving to him over her shoulder.

"Hey, Mary Russo!"

She stopped and turned around.

"Yes?"

"You were going that way." He used both hands to point in the opposite direction.

"Oh right. Right. Thank you. This way." She turned on one spiked heel and flashed him a smile as she passed him, now toward the courthouse.

"Well, that was unexpected," she thought. Meeting Manny had put a spring in her fall step.

Chapter 5

Harper Lee Adler sat in the faculty office at the ritzy private high school where she taught English Literature and Creative Writing. She was scrolling through her emails while she waited for her after-school appointment with outraged parents whose son had earned a C- on his most recent assignment.

And now the sophomore biology teacher, Brad Tam, sat next to her crunching on Corn Nuts so loudly that she thought he'd break a tooth. She couldn't concentrate, but there was nowhere else to go. The school put a lot of money into the students' experience, but the faculty lounge was a Coke machine and folding chairs.

Still, she felt fortunate to have this job. Especially given how her last year had gone. She ignored Brad and thought back on how she'd ended up here after graduating with honors from NYU.

Harper was below average height, straining to hit five feet when she stood with her best posture. A high school boyfriend had once called her "curvy," and while he meant it as a compliment, she sometimes struggled with what the word implied.

She had hazel eyes, light brown curly hair, and a smattering of freckles across her rounded cheeks. She was cuter than she was pretty, and while she knew that was her lot in life, she still wished for things she'd never have. Like a small up-turned nose and sharp cheekbones.

One thing she did have down pat was her style. She favored a Bohemian look and loved the sale rack at Anthropologie and the vintage shops in Soho. She had a collection of ankle boots, colorful chunky cotton sweaters, and patterned maxi dresses that made her unique among the black suits and turtlenecks of the city.

Harper grew up in Park Slope, Brooklyn. Her dad had worked for President Obama as a speechwriter and now he was a senior fellow in global health at the Council on Foreign Relations. Her mom was a social worker and was serving another term on the board at the Food Co-op. Harper had the classic brownstone upbringing, made good grades at Berkeley Carroll, and got into the creative writing program at NYU. She had dreams of becoming a novelist.

But her dreams were interrupted by Charles "Kai" Calhoun, a gorgeous surfer from California who came to NYU to study film. He wanted to make documentaries showing volunteer work in poor countries that also happened to be great locations for surfing. He invited her to tag along. She loved the thought of being adventurous and not tied down. Kai was her ticket to somewhere. She fell under his spell, and after graduation, followed him to West Africa. Her parents were more than skeptical. While they cautioned her against the move, they didn't forbid her to go.

"If anything happens, you can always come home," her mom had said.

"Nothing will happen," Harper assured them, believing it was true. She was wrong.

On their so-called mission trip to Senegal, they were meant to help locals build shelters and wells, and she was going to teach English, too. Kai planned to document the entire thing on his iPhone and then he'd edit it into a YouTube channel and have a million followers. After their first week there, Kai carved K & H in a heart in the trunk of an old tree outside their shack, and Harper was fully in love. Unfortunately, that was about the extent of their romance in Africa.

Immediately, Harper suffered from bug bites and the heat. Her curls frizzed out in the humid climate. The food didn't agree with her, and she fell embarrassingly ill often. A friend of hers from the NYU school of public health sent her a DM on Instagram that said, "You can always eat the fries." And so she did, ignoring the voice in her head that nagged her about the seed oils in which the locals cooked them.

Before their adventure, she'd imagined spending full days with Kai. But once they got to Senegal, it wasn't easy to get his attention. He was often with other surfers, checking out sets and breaks instead of pounding nails into new house frames. After a few months, the entire undertaking had gone sideways. Harper knew she'd made a mistake.

As had been hooking up with Kai in the first place.

Harper had been so blinded by her attraction to this gorgeous surfer boy that she really didn't know much about his background from his California days. She had no idea he'd left a bunch of girls brokenhearted on various beaches. They'd all learned the hard way that commitment, loyalty, and faithfulness weren't high on his value chain. He saved his devotion for the waves that called his name at mid-tide every day.

One day, after three months of wondering how much longer she could take it, a local woman named Faye she was teaching English to stopped the lesson and looked at Harper like she wanted to tell her something.

"What?" she asked. "What is it? Tell me."

The woman's English was not very good yet, but she didn't need to speak. She raised her eyebrows and pointed to a photograph of Kai that was hanging on the wall of the makeshift community center.

"Bad." She shook her head.

"Bad? No. Kai is good," Harper corrected her.

Faye disagreed. She pointed to Harper's heart.

"He's not good. Not for you."

"No, no, he's a good guy."

Faye shook her head and said, "Come." She got up and gestured for Harper to follow. They walked down to the beach where Faye's sister ran a little restaurant called Saly Bar. Faye peered through a side window and then grabbed Harper's hand and said, "Look."

And there was Kai, Gazelle beer bottles piled around him, and a beautiful Portuguese woman Harper knew from another aid group on his lap. They were kissing in a way that made it clear they'd forgotten they were in public.

Harper's heart imploded. She knew that Faye was right to protect her from a cheating boyfriend, but in some ways, Harper wished she'd never seen it. And though she wanted to run away, in that instant she decided to put her big girl pants on and confront him in front of everyone.

Harper marched up behind him and poked him hard in the shoulder.

"Hey!" she shouted.

"What the hell?" He pulled away from the other young woman and turned to see who'd just interrupted his good time. "Harper? I thought you were teaching today."

"And I thought you were here to do good. Not to do. . . . to do . . . *her*!" She didn't have a plan, and it showed.

"Look, Harp, chill." As Kai said this, he gently nudged his other girlfriend off his lap and she backed off a few paces, watching the scene unfold.

"I'm not going to chill. I'm going to. . . . leave!" And in that moment, she decided it was high time to get back to America and restart her life. Turning to the other woman, she said in perfect Portuguese, "Boa sorte." Her nanny had been from Brazil, and she'd learned a few phrases from her. "Good luck" was one of them.

Then Harper turned and walked out, her head held as high as possible.

What really upset her was Kai had acted like it wasn't a big deal. He didn't even try to get her to stay. He'd just let her walk away, even though she'd changed her entire life plan for him. This is what she got for that? The humiliation and the heartbreak crushed her.

Back at her hut, she started stuffing clothes into her oversize duffel. Then she picked up her phone and thought of having to call her parents to confess that her great plans had all fallen apart.

"Call Dad," she said to Siri, grateful to still be on her dad's international phone plan. She winced in anticipation of the conversation she was about to have.

He picked up on the first ring.

"Harper? Are you okay?"

Her voice broke as she heard his voice. "I'm fine. But, you were right, Dad." Those were tough words for her to say. She'd blown off her parents' concern about her decision to throw in with Kai and go to Africa without any real plans for what would happen if it didn't work out. She braced for the "I told you so," but it didn't come.

"Aww, Harper. It's okay. Come on back. We'll figure it out." He reassured her, and she was so grateful he was her dad. She knew he was glad that this adventure was over.

By the next morning, her parents had sent her details for her flight home. Coach, no upgrade.

She decided that was fair.

Her parents said they'd pick her up at JFK, and she was so glad to see their old Volvo hybrid pull up to the curb. Her dad put the car in park, and her mom jumped out to wrap her in a hug. As much as she frustrated them with her breezy impulses, they loved her big heart and felt protective of her.

"I'm sorry, pumpkin," her mom said into Harper's hair as she held her tight. "You were too good for him anyway."

When she moved back into her childhood bedroom and unpacked her duffel bag, she felt safe and like a kid again, even though she knew there was no going back. She took an unending amount of teasing from her older brother, Ernest (yes, her parents thought it would spur their kids to great heights if they were named after famous authors). Her dad pulled a few strings and helped her land a teacher aide job at the Van Buren school. She considered enrolling in an online Master of Education degree program so that she could eventually get a full teaching job.

For once, though, luck was on her side. Her teacher got a dream job at Dalton and Harper got bumped up for the rest of the school year. But still the job didn't pay enough to cover her expenses, so she supplemented her income by tutoring or babysitting. Out of some semblance of pride, she tried not to ask her parents for money. At least not every month.

Harper couldn't believe that everything she'd thought and dreamed about had turned out to be wrong. Even her goal of writing a novel seemed so rearview mirror. She wanted to write great fiction but knew that in order to do that she needed to see the actual world outside of the five boroughs. Going on this adventure with Kai was supposed to give her two things she wanted—a chance for love, and a look at the real world. But now, when would she have time to write when she was constantly working on her lesson plans, grading papers, and dealing with the parents of her entitled and spoiled students?

And now Miles Lascher's parents were demanding to meet with her. The mom had emailed Harper explaining that Miles's tutor hadn't had a chance to work with Miles because the family helicopter out East had malfunctioned. Harper almost couldn't believe that was their story.

As she sat down in the meeting room with Edith Thistlewood, the school principal, Mr. Lascher looked a little embarrassed or maybe bored, but the shiny, creaseless face of Mrs. Lascher hid deeper contempt. Harper explained why the paper didn't merit an A. The mother went through her litany of complaints and excuses, she had even tried to book the tutor a private helicopter service to get him out to the North Shore, and everyone turned to the principal.

Who didn't back Harper up.

"Can we find a way for Miles to redo this assignment, Harper?" Ms. Thistlewood asked, signaling what Harper needed to do. "I'd love to be able to tell the headmaster that this small matter has been settled."

Harper felt trapped. She didn't think it was right to change the grade because they gave money and had the privilege to complain.

But she needed the job. She looked down and agreed that Miles should have another chance to rewrite. And she knew that *that* paper would get an A.

"That's great to hear." Mrs. Lascher nodded. All her jewelry shook with her.

Harper stood as tall as she could and squared her shoulders, mustering any dignity she could find. She thanked the Laschers for their time and gave Ms. Thistlewood a fake nod of gratitude. Her poker face lasted until she got to the faculty lounge, where there was no sign of Brad Tam. There, when she was finally alone, she let a couple of tears fall. Then she blew her nose, grabbed her jacket, and walked out of the school. It was just over two miles crosstown to Dot's place, and Harper had plenty she needed to walk off.

RIGHT AT 7 P.M., Mary and Harper met at the entrance of the Buckley. They hugged each other and Albert sent them right up. "She's been waiting for you," he said.

The two of them talked at the same time and Albert wondered how either of them understood the other.

"Oh, to be young again," the doorman said to the empty foyer as he stepped back out into the crisp fall night.

Chapter 6

Dot yelled "Yay!" when the doorbell rang and rushed to open the door to her friends.

"Welcome!" she said, arms wide.

"Sorry we came empty-handed," Harper said. "I'll make it up to you when it's safe to have people over to my apartment. My roommates are so messy."

"Nonsense. We're past all that! Come in, come in." She took their coats and hung them on the coat-tree. Harper and Mary set their bags down on the bench in the foyer.

They traded hugs and air kisses all while coming out of the hall and into the living room. Dot had lit two candles on the mantel and turned the gas fireplace on low. She loved her tidy bright living room and the quirky kitchen with the tiny stove. She'd painted the walls in a creamy ivory and the moldings in a rich camel color. Her grandmother's paintings decorated the place, including a commissioned portrait of Dot and her younger sister, Anne, set at the Bethesda Fountain in Central Park. In Dot's mind, it was the perfect place to live, and she had no intention of ever moving. She loved the city and didn't want to live anywhere else.

"Sit," Dot said, gesturing to the small sofa. "Tell me everything."

"You first," Mary said. "How's Ryan?"

Dot blinked at her. "He's . . . fine."

"Fine?"

"Yep—I mean, more than *fine*. I'm just. . . ." Dot couldn't find the words.

"Just what?" Mary had great relationship-problem radar. She searched Dot's face.

"Nothing! He's great."

"Oh, now he's great, not fine?" Harper chimed in. "What's wrong?"

"Look, I know everyone says this, but it's not him. It's me. It's really just me."

"So, it's *definitely* him." Harper tucked stray strands of curly hair behind her ears.

"Wait. Are you going to break up with him?" Mary continued the interrogation.

"Oh gosh I don't know. No. I mean. I don't know." Dot wasn't ready to say those words. She pleaded, "Could we talk about this later?"

"You're killing me but . . . in your words, 'fine,'" Mary said.

"Great!" Dot said, relieved. "Let's change the subject. Harper, how's teaching?" Dot knew it had been a rough transition since her return from Senegal.

"Oh, you know—same old story. You wouldn't believe how much rich families get away with. Today it was the Laschers. I gave their kid a C-minus on an essay, which he should have flunked, but I was being kind. Then the parents came in to complain." She switched to imitating Mrs. Lascher's posh accent. "Oh, Harper, be reasonable. Our helicopter broke down, so Miles couldn't possibly have had time to do his homework."

"Wow. My parents would have killed me," Mary said. "They were old school. The teacher was always right."

"Same," Harper said.

"Don't worry, Harp. What goes around comes around," Dot said. "They'll be stuck paying his bills for forever. Then they'll probably divorce and blame one another for failing at parenthood."

"Well, I'm not looking forward to the rest of the semester. Ms. Thistlewood will be watching me with her big owl eyes. But also, have you seen this?" She held up her phone. Kai and his Portuguese girlfriend were hawking some new energy drink. They were trying to be influencers.

"Unfollow him, Harper. Here, give me your phone." Mary tried to wrestle it from her, but she hid it in the cushions.

"I will. Tonight. Or tomorrow."

Dot and Mary made eye contact. Harper was still mad about Kai.

"Suit yourself. But one day you'll tell me I was right." Mary raised an eyebrow at Harper.

"You always are!" Harper snapped back.

"Girls! Let's have a drink." Dot poured the wine. Their sushi order from

Sugarfish was on its way. Mary had offered to treat after her dad had put an extra $150 in her Venmo account when she'd told him about her evening plans. He texted, "Tell the girls I said to come see us one Sunday for a real meal! Sushi is for the birds. Literally."

"So, what's this all about tonight, Dot?" Mary took the bottle from Dot and poured a big glass. She reached over and squeezed Harper's hand. All was forgiven. "Some political thing?"

"Yep. Remember Kitty Bell from college?"

"Oh, yeah. The redhead every guy was crazy about?" Harper said. "Wasn't she president of the College Dems?"

"Exactly. She was the one who graduated early and made a big show of her move to Washington." Mary remembered liking her. "I guess she was cool. Not necessarily a girl's girl, though."

"I always got the feeling she thought she was better than the rest of us," Harper said.

"I sort of remember her that way, too. But I have to say, she's really landed on her feet," Dot said. "She has this amazing job where she has control of a bunch of money to help Democrats win races across the country. She's kicking off the campaign season with this huge conference call so that she can get people interested and recruit volunteers. And tonight, as I mentioned, she invited George and Amal Clooney as the draw."

"She's not looking for money, right? Because I'm maxed out for this cycle!" Harper joked.

"Maybe the Laschers can donate," Mary deadpanned.

"Ha! I can loop them in. That'll be my contribution."

"They probably vote Republican, though, don't you think—Upper East Siders?" Dot asked.

"Good point. That fits," Harper said.

"Anyway," Dot continued explaining what she knew, "I don't think Kitty's group is asking for money from people like us. I get the sense that big-time donors give her huge amounts of money and tell her to spend it as she sees fit. And because it's a Super PAC, the original check writers can remain anonymous. My dad was telling me it used to be just the GOP that used dark money to win races, but the Democrats have caught up. In fact, one of our tech clients just started a PAC to help elect candidates who want to build a compound on Mars. They give to both parties, because they have more money than they know what to do with."

"How about helping people get health insurance first?" Mary asked.

"That might come up tonight. Health insurance, housing costs, climate change, abortion rights. Maybe other things. Kitty reached out on Instagram to invite me. I think she needs to show a high number on the Zoom count tonight to help justify her job."

The doorbell rang. Mary jumped up. "I'll get it." Her stomach was rumbling.

While Harper and Mary unboxed the shrimp shumai and spicy tuna rolls, Dot positioned the computer in a way that all three of them could see and logged onto the call. Whoa. Over five thousand people had already joined.

"Good turnout," Dot said, making sure her microphone was muted.

Mary and Harper set the rest of the sushi out on the coffee table, and Dot got each of them a small tray to hold on their laps. The buffet was open and the call was about to get going.

"Welcome, everyone! It's great to see so many people here for our inaugural For the Win call. I'm Kaitlyn Bell, but everyone calls me Kitty. I'm the executive director of the PAC."

Disguising her upper Midwest accent, Kitty sounded elegant and mature, like she'd left her early twenties behind. Her long dark red hair was blown straight and parted slightly off center. Her milky white skin was enhanced by a glowing foundation and professional eye makeup. She wore a fitted royal-blue blazer and diamond stud earrings. She was *definitely* pulled together. Harper sat up a little taller at the sight of her.

"Let me kick things off. I know you've probably heard this before—but this time it's true: The next election is the most important of our lifetime." She paused for effect. "I'm excited to have you here. FTW has big plans for the coming year. And I'm so pleased to turn the microphone over to our honored guests, George and Amal Clooney."

The Hollywood couple beamed onto their screens, and it was almost like having a one on one with them.

"Have you ever seen more beautiful people?" Harper asked. "My gosh, she makes me want to delete every selfie in my camera roll."

Dot kept her focus on the screen and listening to the Clooneys, but her mind turned to Kitty. She knew that she'd always had big plans. She'd never been shy about wanting to work in the White House one day. She even used a photo of herself as a child during the Obama administration standing on a stool behind the press secretary's briefing podium as her profile picture on social media. So, she'd been building on this dream for nearly two decades as Dot was still trying to figure out her next move.

While Dot lost focus for a couple of minutes, the Clooneys wrapped up their introduction and turned it back over to Kitty. Their work was done.

"I wonder how much Kitty had to pay for their appearance," Mary asked.

"You don't think they did that for free?" Harper asked.

"Nothing in politics is free, Harp."

Kitty took back over, gushed about the Clooneys' dedication to the party, and gave an overview of the political landscape. She shared maps that showed the heartbreaking loss Democrats suffered in 2024 and then another with For the Win's projections of how Democrats could capture enough states to take back the White House in the next election.

"It's pretty amazing that Kitty got through all that scandal in her congressional office when she first got to Washington," Dot said.

"What scandal?" Harper didn't stay up to speed on Washington politics.

"Oh, you never heard about that? When she left NYU, she got a job working for her home-state senator—from Minnesota. And not long after she moved to D.C. to take the job, he had to resign after an influencer posted that he was having an affair with a lobbyist." Dot tried to make a long story short. "It was a mess. Kitty had to scramble to get a new job, and from what I know, she almost gave up on politics altogether."

"Then what happened?" Mary asked, intrigued.

"Well, as I understand it, that's around when she met her fiancé, Casey Morgan. He's a big shot lobbyist. I looked him up today. His firm represents everything from big oil to vaping—the new tobacco companies. He makes a ton of money and gives a lot of it to politicians on both sides of the aisle. And he connected her to these Democratic donors who created For the Win."

"And so, his name helps her get her foot in the door all around D.C.?" Mary was catching on.

"Correct. And now they're like a power couple. They have a townhouse in Georgetown and host a lot of cocktail parties. She's always posting these pictures of them as 'seen around town.'"

"Oh, that sounds awful," Harper said. She wasn't the type that wanted to rub elbows.

"But Kitty loves it. And she appears to be living her best life," Dot said, with a twinge of envy.

They turned their attention back to the call.

"Let me show you what we're up against." Kitty pulled up a county-by-county map of the US. The red states for Republican, the blue Democrat. "And the purple states switch back and forth between the two. These are your battlegrounds: Arizona, Nevada, Georgia, North Carolina, Pennsylvania, Michigan, and Wisconsin. Of all these, we believe Wisconsin is our best bet for a flip from red back to blue this cycle."

Kitty continued her presentation, giving some statistics on the slim margins of the last election.

"You might be wondering what you can do to help," she said. Then she smiled, signaling she was about to make her pitch. "I thought you'd never ask!"

The Zoom counter was now over 7,500.

"There are several ways to volunteer. Of course, For the Win will support traditional phone banks plus door knockers and convention helpers."

Harper's eyes watered after she accidentally consumed too much wasabi and she flapped her hand in front of her mouth to try to cool it down.

"I bet this is where they ask us for money!" she said through the pain.

But that's not what Kitty needed. She needed something more valuable and complex than donations.

"So, this is the new idea I'm proud to announce. I'm looking for a few good people to move to a purple state for the year—well, ten and a half months, starting in January this year. Why? Because I don't believe we have enough real-time information about what's going on in those states, and that's why we lost some very close races, including the White House, the last time around. We need more eyes and ears on the ground sending back observations and intelligence to For the Win, or, as we like to call it, FTW."

Mary gently rolled her eyes. "Doesn't she realize that FTW takes longer to say than For the Win? Abbreviations are supposed to make things shorter."

Dot giggled and then double checked they were on mute. She didn't want to offend Kitty.

"And For the Win, thanks to our generous donors, will pay for everything—housing, transportation, and living costs. This effort could make all the difference. And, as I mentioned, our top target is Wisconsin. It's *essential* to victory—without those ten electoral votes, we'll lose again."

Dot imagined that Kitty would also benefit if FTW was able to help deliver the White House to the Dems. Was this ploy part of her plan to land a job at 1600 Pennsylvania Avenue?

Dot felt another sting of career-choice regret watching Kitty make her pitch. Coming out of college, Dot had thought about following her passion, which was politics, but she hadn't wanted to leave the city, and local politics seemed too small for her. Plus, she thought she'd make more money in tech. Not to mention that living in D.C. sounded dull.

But watching Kitty command a conference call with thousands of people and being able to wield influence through a Democratic organization flush with cash made Dot feel like maybe she'd made the wrong decision. Kitty had put herself on the fast track and had a glamorous, meaningful job. It was everything high-tech PR was not.

An impulse came over Dot, and she pushed the "raise hand" button. Kitty immediately called on her.

"Dot Clark, my longtime friend from NYU, thank you *so much* for being on the call. Everyone, Dot's the best! Go ahead." Kitty was laying it on a bit thick.

Dot started to speak.

"Dot, you're on mute," Kitty said with mild annoyance.

"Oh, sorry. Hi, Kitty. You remember my friends Mary and Harper—they're here, too."

Kitty waved to them.

"Of course, Mary, Harper, you look *gorgeous*. Send me some of your secrets!"

Mary waved then collected the lap trays they'd used for dinner to put them away.

Dot continued, "Hi, everyone." She wiped her palms on her pants. "So . . . where in Wisconsin would you want people to live for a year?"

There was a clatter in the kitchen as Mary dropped the trays onto the counter.

"Dot. Are you serious?" she yelled from the other room.

Kitty smiled, like she had a live one on the line.

"Good question. We've mapped it all out—to the county level. The most important place for us is in a suburb of Milwaukee called Cedar Falls. That's a town in the swingiest county in Wisconsin. It's flipped back and forth from red to blue every election since Bush-Gore. And while in the last cycle they went a little to the left, the rest of the state went to the right. But it's a growing county, and with just a few more votes for Democrats in that area, we could have won it."

"And so, in theory, someone volunteers to move there and sends back information and works on the campaign?" Dot asked.

"Precisely. I truly believe a lack of on-the-ground intelligence held us back. The campaign last cycle relied way too much on algorithms. We lost track of what people *actually* think."

There was silence for a moment and Dot stared into the distance, as if she could see Wisconsin from her apartment. Was she nuts to think this would be amazing and maybe just the shake-up she needed in her life?

Kitty jumped back in. "And to repeat, FTW would cover all expenses. Housing, transportation, and a generous living allowance. We have the funds to do it." Trying to close the sale, she asked Dot, "Are you interested? Wisconsin is lovely in January!" she joked. "But you'd be in the heart of the country—and the ultimate battleground in the election."

Dot quickly shook her head no. "Oh, I was just curious. It's a good idea. But obviously not for me. I mean . . . I'm a New Yorker through and through!" Her voice hit a higher octave. She didn't want to be rude, but who would leave the city to move . . . anywhere.

"Well, let me know if you change your mind. It's for less than a year, and I think you'd find it much more rewarding than . . ." Kitty's voice trailed off.

Ouch, Dot thought. But she's not wrong.

Kitty kept the call going.

"Now, let's go to Skylar in Arizona. Hi, Skylar."

Dot put the computer back on mute.

"Is it *that* bad with Ryan that you're thinking of running off to political summer camp in Oshkosh? You know you can't leave the city!" Mary looked shocked.

"Yeah, you can't leave me here with all these . . . New Yorkers." Harper looked at Dot, trying to read how serious she was.

"Harper, you're from Brooklyn," Mary said.

"Exactly. And look where it's gotten me!"

"I'm not moving to Wisconsin. But I feel like I need to do *something*." Dot was restless.

"Then let's go out next weekend. We're in a rut, and we need to move with a *purpose*." Mary liked to organize nights out, and she liked the little dig at Kitty. "Let's go to the Spaniard Saturday night. I'll text Jimmy for a rez." Jimmy was the super-hot bartender that Mary flirted with every time they were in there.

"I'm afraid I'll only be able to drink water. I can't afford to go out." Harper knew that cocktails were about twenty dollars a pop.

"I've got you," Mary said. "Besides, Jimmy will get us the first round."

"You can't keep covering me."

"It's not for forever. Just shut up and say yes."

"Okay, yes."

Dot glanced back at the Zoom. Kitty was poli-girl explaining some more charts.

After Harper and Mary left her apartment, Dot dried and put away the plates Mary had washed in the sink. It occurred to her that she still hadn't responded to Ryan's text asking her to dinner.

She gathered the trash and took the bag to the chute. She listened for it to hit the bottom and then went back to her apartment, secured the lock, and decided to call it a night.

Her last thought before falling asleep wasn't of Ryan.

It was of Wisconsin.

Chapter 7

The next morning, Dot beat her alarm and woke a few minutes before six.

She brushed her teeth, put on running clothes, and to keep her ears warm, added a hot pink beanie with a hole in the back for her ponytail. Four times a week she ran three miles up and around the Jackie O Reservoir in Central Park. She listened to *The Daily*. That morning's topic was the upcoming Democratic primary and the steep climb to win the next presidential election. "Serendipity," Dot thought. She wasn't the only one thinking about the election all the time. The show's host sounded depressed, and she understood how he felt. The struggle was real.

Dot thought of Kitty's election plan to flip some of the purple states. She appreciated the creativity. At least it was a new idea, which is what the party needed.

When she got back to the Buckley, she took the stairs to the third floor and made a coffee in her Keurig dupe and added a splash of almond milk. She sipped it while she scrolled through the headlines sent out by the corporate office. Nothing unexpected, thankfully. She avoided looking at her text messages, knowing Ryan's message about dinner that night sat unanswered. She knew she was avoiding the inevitable but she needed a little time.

Dot showered and dried her hair straight. She got dressed and by 8:05 a.m., she left her apartment and entered Central Park for the second time that day. This time she walked toward the East River. She enjoyed watching all the dogs run around. The park didn't require leashes for three hours starting at six in the morning. It was one of her favorite things about the city. She smiled as she watched them play on the grass and the sandy ball fields as they raced around their owners' legs, the humans standing with bent knees so they wouldn't get bowled over.

As she neared her office, she stopped at her favorite coffee cart before going upstairs. Her regular guy, Freddy, moved with speed to prepare her latte with extra foam.

"Thanks, Freddy!" she said, tapping her card and adding a 20 percent tip. Then she flashed him a smile and turned to face the day.

"Here we go," she said to psych herself up for the pitch review.

She got to her office and finally made herself look at her text messages.

Ryan: "Dot. Call me. Are you okay?"

She responded in a flush of panic.

"Yes, I'm sorry! My call went late last night . . ." she texted, convincing herself that wasn't a lie.

He answered immediately. "The reservation was hard to get. You can make it, right?"

Dot had a knot of anxiety she couldn't ignore about the location. Peak spelled big-time occasion. And while she knew she was probably overthinking things, she asked for a change of venue.

"Rough week—work stuff. Okay to go more casual tonight—save Peak for another time?"

His three dots came up. He was obviously thinking of a reply. She kind of hoped he'd just say forget the entire thing. But he didn't.

"Sure. Joanne? I can meet you there at 7:30. I'll get us a table."

She admired his choice. Joanne was on West Sixty-Eighth, near the Buckley. Lady Gaga's dad owned the place, and aside from having a great menu with their family's meatballs and arancini, there was always live entertainment that started around nine. Once in a while the famous daughter would drop in for a set.

"Sounds great. See you then. Maybe we'll see you-know-who." She didn't use any exclamation points or emojis, which wasn't like her. She was trying to send a low-key message. She knew he'd suspect that something was wrong. But that problem was for later. The new business slide deck was the problem for the morning.

She turned on her computer and combed over the presentation one more time. Satisfied that it looked perfect, she sent three copies to be printed for the senior partners to review.

When she went to the shared office printer to pick up the copies, the printer was jammed.

"Typical," she said to herself. She yanked out the crumpled paper—a spreadsheet that seemed unremarkable. But before she threw it away, the heading caught her eye: Talent Review—Confidential.

It must have been printed accidentally or someone had forgotten to pick it up.

The spreadsheet had three columns labeled *Meets, Below, Exceeds*. She glanced quickly at the names—there were all her colleagues, including some of the junior staffers she'd helped train. Their salaries were noted in another column, and the final column determined their performance.

All of them were marked at meets or below. The only ones with exceeds were her and Arturo Rodriguez from Accounting. The note at the bottom said, "Reassign client work to Dot C."

Her eyes blurred as she stared at the page and realized what was happening. Even if she helped win this new healthcare client, the firm planned to downsize and unload all the work onto her. And she was already working twelve-hour days. But the message was clear: they were trimming the fat. And she was expected to carry the load.

Her face burned with embarrassment, shame, and worry. She ripped up the document and threw it in the recycling bin. Then she took the presentations back to her desk.

She took a few moments to calm down. So, now she knew what the score was. Corporate wins, staff loses. It wasn't fair.

Chapter 8

Good morning, Dot!" Darius Thompson, one of their new hires, said as he walked by to his cubicle.

Dot waved and smiled. She really cared for the junior staffers. She'd been one not long before, and she knew with the economy slowing it wouldn't be easy for them to find new jobs.

She thought of Kitty's conference call, and how exciting and energizing it felt to talk about politics for a bit the night before. Shaking that off, she picked up her company-branded Stanley cup filled with lemon water and headed to the conference room.

She put on her best poker face. "Fake it 'til you make it" was one of her favorite mottoes.

And it was time to go to work.

"EXCELLENT PITCH, DOT," the president of the company said. Dot appreciated the rare compliment.

"We'll see if they buy it," the SVP said. "They're a tough crowd. But, I agree, it's a *very* good pitch." He falsely flattered her in front of the boss.

Dot smiled and thanked them, with a little less enthusiasm than usual. She got through the meeting and walked back to her desk, trying to focus on the praise she'd just received. Why was it that she took criticism more to heart than admiration?

"All good?" Darius asked her.

"Yes. Great. Thanks for your help. You had some good ideas." She knew accolades went a long way for the younger staff.

Her phone buzzed with a text.

"Call me. Now." It was from one of their most important but annoying clients who was always messaging her. She knew what this was about.

Dot waited three beats for her own dignity before calling him by video chat.

"Hi, Michael." Michael worked in San Francisco. He'd created a mortgage-related tech start-up as his main project when he got his MBA at Stanford. Even before he graduated, a bunch of venture capitalists threw money at him. He was one of those guys with extra-long bangs, like a Shetland pony, which required him to keep tossing his head back so that he could see.

"Dot, am I booked on CNBC this afternoon before the market closes?" His eyes were dark beads, fitting his mood. "I need to be out there. I have to raise another round, and that jerk from LendingTree is all over *Squawk Box*. If we don't show the same kind of hustle, I could lose funding."

"I hear you." She was well-versed in language to de-escalate a tense conversation. "I have a call in to the producer. We are looking for the right time to get you on. Right now, your competitor is rolling out a product, so they have something new to say. As I've mentioned, we need you to have something new to get on the show."

"Let me ask you something, Dot." He paused for effect. "Who's the boss of you?"

"Excuse me?" She blinked, surprised by his tone.

"I asked: Who. Is. The. Boss. Of. You? Let me answer. I am. *I* am the boss of *you*. Is that clear?"

She held his gaze but didn't answer.

"Get me on the network by the end of the day. Or else, we're done." His voice was menacing.

"Understood." She knew she'd have to call in a favor to get him on TV.

She clicked off without saying goodbye. Her stomach was in knots. The SVP, the staffing memo, Stanford Michael. The uneasiness with Ryan. Nothing felt right and it was all just too much. She decided to walk it off. She grabbed her coat and left the office.

DOT HEADED OVER to Fifth Avenue. She didn't mind the crowds and liked to people-watch and look in the store windows. The fall displays had a couple more weeks before the holiday decorations took over.

Determined to improve her day, she turned north and walked up the east side of the block, passing Saks Fifth Avenue and St. Patrick's Cathedral. As she strolled, she felt a little calmer. Then, right before Fifty-Seventh

Street, she saw a familiar figure. It was Ryan. And he was going through the revolving door into Tiffany's.

Oh no, she thought, her stomach dropping to the ground.

Though her heart screamed run, her curiosity compelled her forward.

She dialed Mary and walked into Tiffany's.

"What's up? I'm on a big Zoom meeting," Mary whispered.

"Can you step out? I need you." Dot saw Ryan enter the elevator at the back of the store. She tried to hide behind a pillar until the doors closed.

Mary shot a note to her managing partner and said she'd be right back on the call. She picked the phone back up. "Okay, I'm here. What's up?"

"I'm at Tiffany's. Ryan is also here."

"Oh! My goodness, Dot. This is so exciting!"

"No, it's not. It's not what you think! We aren't here together. I happened to see him walk in. Now I'm following him to see where he's going."

"So do you think he's . . ."

"Yes, I think he's going to get it. Mary, what am I going to do?"

"Wait. Dot. You *don't* want to marry Ryan?"

"Mary, I don't even think I want to *date* Ryan."

"Oh. Well. This feels very new. When were you going to clue me in?"

"Ugh, don't give me a hard time right now. My head's a mess. This is a huge problem."

"Okay. Okay. Did you see what floor he went to?"

"I'm checking. Hang on." Dot moved through the iconic showroom and checked the directory by the elevators. She mouthed to the woman working the elevator. "Third floor, please."

"Still with me?" Dot asked.

"Yes, where are you now?"

The doors opened onto the third floor. Fifteen feet from her was Ryan, his back to her, looking down into the glass display counter.

"Oh Lord!" Dot ducked behind the elevator operator, praying her boyfriend didn't see her.

"May I help you, miss?" a smartly dressed Tiffany staff member asked her.

"No thank you," she whispered loud enough for him to hear but not enough to get Ryan's attention.

"Mary, he's looking at rings!"

"Can you get out of there before he sees you?"

Dot scooted backward to return to the elevator bank. The elevator lady who had just brought her up tilted her head in confusion. "Shall I take you back down to the ground floor, miss?"

"Yes. Thank you." Dot dived into the waiting car and pressed herself against the side wall. She was trying to keep it together. Into the phone she said, "Mary, I'll call you later."

"Don't forget a single detail. I can't *wait* to hear this story."

When the elevator doors closed, she felt like she couldn't breathe.

In just one morning, both her career and her personal life had taken major turns.

And at that moment, she truly didn't know which way to go.

Chapter 9

Mary couldn't get Manny from the Legal Aid office out of her mind. He was so handsome with his olive skin and wide, kind eyes. She could picture his tight curly hair cut close on the sides, chiseled jaw, high cheekbones, and muscled shoulders. He had a beautiful smile. Perfect teeth. He'd looked straight into her eyes, not intimidated by her like other guys.

She wished she was going out with him tonight. Unfortunately, she'd made other plans.

"Ugh, I can't believe I agreed to this!" she said out loud, walking down Stone Street in FiDi. It was Oktoberfest, and downtown was hopping. The bars were decorated for the season and packed with people her age from the big financial companies, all washing down their day and having a good time.

But Mary couldn't stop and linger because she had a date.

Mary's mother had set her up with Theresa Molinaro's son, Ricky. Mary knew Ricky all too well. He'd gone to St. Joe by-the-Sea with her brother Gabe—the one who'd put his high school exploits behind him and become a priest, forever and ever, amen. Ricky's father owned Paisano's, a huge Italian import business on Staten Island. Ricky was not in charge of that. Instead, his dad had made him manager of his indoor pickleball facility, The Dink Den.

"Mary, he's a good boy," her mother had said on the phone. "And listen, you've not brought anyone home in ages. Not since that Irish boy, what's his . . ."

"Colin."

"Who hid in the bathroom during Sunday supper because he thought everyone was yelling at him."

"They were! His family are Islanders fans, I'm sorry."

"I'm just worried about you. I'm your mother—built to worry. I'm afraid you're wasting your youth. Please, Mary. It's just dinner. For me?" Her mom knew how to press her buttons.

Hence, a 7:30 p.m. reservation at Adrienne's Pizzabar. She'd worked at the office until the last possible billable hour before heading over.

Her heels clicked on the sidewalk as she turned in to the restaurant. Ricky was sitting at the table by the window, wearing a fitted long-sleeved white T-shirt and a black leather jacket. He still had a baby face and was drenched in Drakkar. He was just like every guy Mary grew up with—fun family guys who were not at all her type. They were her people, but they'd never be her boyfriends.

Bracing herself, Mary took off her tan leather belted coat as she walked up to the table.

"Ricky, hi. Good to see you." She sat and took a sip of ice water, the cold hitting her teeth.

"Wow. Mary Russo. You look. . . . amazing." He seemed stunned by her. She was in black crepe wide-leg pants, a red silk shirt, and silver hoop and charm earrings.

"Thanks for coming into the city. I couldn't get away from the office."

"No problem. The ferry is still free, baby." He held his hands out wide.

"All the best things in life are." She kept her hands in her lap.

Mary settled in with a glass of the house cabernet. And keep 'em coming, her eyes said to the waitress.

Ricky and Mary chatted about the old neighborhood before ordering, but they were interrupted by his gearhead obsession. Every nice car that went by, he had to comment on it.

"That's a McLaren! I wonder if it's Aaron Rodgers's."

Mary smiled and nodded.

"He was the Jets quarterback for a time . . ."

"Oh, I know." Mary barely looked up from the menu, bored by cars and sports. He didn't notice.

Finally, they ordered. Salmon, medium rare, for Mary, chicken parmesan for Ricky, and a side of spicy broccoli rabe to share.

"We could have eaten better at home," Mary teased. At least Ricky laughed at her joke.

"There's nothing like our ma's home-cooked meal. But this place is all right."

They chatted about their families during the meal. It seemed everyone they knew was getting married and having children, except for Gabe. And them.

About halfway through their entrees, Ricky's phone rang. He looked at it and set it back down. "It's my ma." He rolled his eyes and ignored the call.

Two minutes later it rang again.

"Sorry," he said to Mary and picked up his phone. He answered it this time.

"I'm at dinner, what?"

"How's it going?!" Mary could hear Mrs. Molinaro even though she was not on speaker. She gestured to Ricky that she was going to use the ladies' room.

Before going back to the table, she texted the Crew.

"Please stop me if my mother ever sets me up again. Nice guy but wow this is boring."

"Let me guess: not your type, doesn't understand you, rarely leaves the island?" Dot asked.

"Exactly. It's almost like my family wants me to date someone exactly like one of my brothers."

"Want me to call and pretend to be a work emergency? Some bankers with the SEC at their door?" Harper texted back. She loved cooking up an escape route, having needed so many of her own after dates gone wrong.

"No thanks. It's almost over. But pray for me." Dot and Harper both liked the message and said they'd catch up with her later.

Mary went back to Ricky, who was finally off the phone.

"Sorry about that. My ma is a little crazy."

"Well, maybe all of them are."

"Especially the Italian ones," he said.

Mary smiled in agreement. "I know the feeling." She got the waitress's attention and ordered a double espresso.

"That won't keep you up all night?" he asked.

"I always sleep like a baby."

"I'd be climbing the walls if I had that right now." And Mary imagined him frantic in the night, checking out all the car websites and chugging milk from the carton.

Finally, a few beats after dessert when Ricky told her about what everyone on the St. Joe's baseball team ended up doing in life, Mary thought she could politely excuse herself.

"Well, this has been very nice. But I need to get going. I still have some work to do." Mary got up and started to put on her coat. Ricky sat back in his chair and placed his hands on the armrests.

"Hey now, if we worked out, you might not have to work at all." He winked at her and gestured widely with both arms. "The Dink Den is packed. And I have expansion plans."

She tilted her head, raised her eyebrows, and laughed lightly. She leaned over to kiss his cheek.

"I'll think about it."

She would not think about it.

THE NEXT DAY Mary got assigned a new case. It was tedious work, going line by line through a client's bank records looking for any anomalies that their plaintiffs could use against them. Her firm used AI software for the first look, but it was her job to double check.

Feeling the need for a mental break before she dug into the assignment, she went for a lap. She walked around the 9/11 Memorial, which always reminded her to be grateful for what she had. She wasn't born until the year after the attacks, but she grew up learning the stories of so many of her parents' friends who had died that day. Firemen and police officers, secretaries, clerks, people from all walks of life and all parts of Staten Island.

The endless waterfall in the footprint of the towers was a perfect tribute to their lives. Someone had placed a red rose over a loved one's name. Mary leaned onto the ledge, said a prayer for the departed, and looked into the water. She thought about what she was doing with her life. She had a good job, but was it going to be meaningful enough, working in corporate law?

She started back toward the office but took a detour to walk by the Legal Aid office where she'd met Manny. She thought she'd stop and flirt, while finding out more about volunteering to help foster kids. Two nonexclusive, noncompeting positive things.

She was wearing a red pantsuit and black patent leather block heels. The day was sunny and warm, so she carried her coat over her arm. Her black hair hung loose down her back, and several appreciative glances came her way.

Outside of Legal Aid, she knocked on the door and gently opened it. A bell rang. There was no one at the front desk, and the office was quiet.

"Hello?" She craned her head to see if anyone was around.

"Be right there." She hoped it was Manny.

Mary looked at the bulletin board with notices for children advocates. She'd heard of these volunteer opportunities. It was where you could provide legal aid, helping families know their rights, especially when child services was involved. Starting there could lead to representing parents or children in court as part of her pro bono commitments to the firm.

"You're back!" Manny came into the front office, smiling. "It's great to see you again. Mary, right?" They shook hands again. She hoped he felt the same spark that she did, the one that had been missing from her date with Ricky.

"I've been thinking about making my law degree worth something."

"That's amazing. Let me get Rafael—he organizes all the volunteers."

Mary felt her cheeks flush, and she did a little turn in her heels. She imagined taking him home for Sunday supper. She was getting ahead of herself, but she had a feeling he'd fit in perfectly.

Manny returned a few minutes later with a slim man in a stylish and well-cut navy suit and a white shirt unbuttoned at the collar.

"Mary, meet our volunteer coordinator, and my boyfriend, Rafael Hernandez."

"Hello, Mary. It's nice to meet you. I love your outfit." Rafael shook her hand and gave her suit the once-over. "Red is your color."

Boyfriend?! Mary felt mortified. So, that wasn't a spark she'd felt. That had just been a *handshake*. She'd cut herself off from serious dating for so long that her romantic instincts were way off.

"Oh, thank you," she stammered, trying to recover her composure and praying Manny didn't realize the mistake she'd made. "I'd love to do this—but I've just got a text and need to get back to my office. Can I come by another time?"

"Anytime. You'd be a great addition, and we could use you."

"Great. Great. Okay, um, bye. And thanks." She hustled out of the office, face now red with embarrassment.

She rushed back to the office, head down, feeling low.

Why did she keep stepping on the dating rake and hitting herself in the face?

Chapter 10

That same morning in the West Village, Harper was in the bathroom putting on mascara before work when she felt a drop of water on her head. She glanced up and didn't see anything.

"That was weird."

Another drop fell. And then another. She stepped to the side and looked up again.

"Oh no."

The drips turned into a steady stream of water as the apartment bathroom above flooded into theirs. Her sleeve got soaked as she tried to rescue her phone before it got deluged.

"I can't deal with this today!" she thought.

"Help!" she called out to her two roommates, praying one of them was home. Libby was a graphic designer into marijuana and her tuxedo cat Eliot, and Megan was a production assistant who worked overnights at CNN. Harper and Libby rarely laid on eyes on her. Megan was like a ghost roommate—the best kind.

Harper ran to get their one big spaghetti pot to catch the water. "I need towels!" she shouted.

Finally, Libby emerged from her room, taking her AirPods out as she realized what was happening. She scrambled upstairs and banged on the neighbor's door to get them to turn off the water. By the time she got back, Harper had gathered all the spare towels into the bathroom to soak up the mess.

Once Harper had mopped the floor, she replaced the pot with the large kitchen garbage pail to give her some time to think through this disaster.

"How is this my life?" she asked herself. She really needed to get it together and move to a decent apartment.

Libby looked at her. "Laugh or cry?"

"Cry." To Harper, this was no laughing matter.

Since Libby worked from home for a composting rights initiative, she agreed to call the super and try to get things sorted out. Harper thanked her, changed into dry clothes, threw her ruined hair into a bun on the top of her head, and headed to Van Buren. Her class was reading *Great Expectations.* How ironic, she thought.

"Maybe I should write *Least Expectations*—life lessons from a disappointed young woman," she thought. "Not a terrible idea." She tapped the idea into her notes app. It had potential.

During her lunch hour in the faculty lounge, Harper got a text from Libby. The super said it could be several days before the ceiling was fixed, and they were turning off water to the building for a few days.

"Great. That's just great." She put her head in her hands and imagined how much dry shampoo she'd have to use to get through the week.

The biology teacher was gnashing and chomping potato chips like an animal. "That sucks." Brad Tam chewed with his mouth open. Harper wondered if that alone would work with the jury as a reasonable defense during her trial for his murder.

The school's longtime receptionist poked her head into the room.

"Harper, the headmaster would like to see you."

"Uh-oh!" Brad Tam spit chip flecks out onto the table.

"I would say you eat like a pig, but pigs are more polite when they chew."

He threw his empty chips bag at her.

"Lighten up, Miss Adler."

She glared at him, pushed away from the table, gathered her things into her cloth tote from the Strand bookstore, and headed to her boss's office.

The headmaster's door was open, and he was staring across double computer screens. The bookshelves included lots of vacation photos with his wife and three young children. She knocked gently.

"Miss Adler! Please sit." Phil Swift was in his fifties, losing his graying hair and going a little soft around the middle. He wore thick-framed, trendy eyeglasses and expensive suits befitting a headmaster.

"Please. Call me Harper."

"All right, I will." He folded his hands and rested them on his desk.

She put her phone in her bag, crossed her legs under her maxi skirt, and gave him her full attention.

"Harper, we have an issue. Anastasia Baldwin's parents called today. They've filed an official complaint about you. They say you've been retaliating against their daughter with undeserved bad grades because you're jealous of her."

"That's ridiculous!" Harper's face burned red. "Why would I be jealous of a girl who cannot even write a complete sentence!"

"I know she can be a difficult student. But the Baldwins. Well, I don't need to remind you."

"Yes, I'm reminded by *her* every time I try to give constructive feedback. I know her family built this school, but she doesn't even try."

"I understand that, and I hope you understand that once there's an official complaint, I have to investigate. We must do this by the book." He double tapped a small stack of papers with his pen.

Harper's eyes filled with tears, worry welling up inside of her. The Baldwins were best friends of . . . you guessed it . . . the Laschers. Word had spread. And they were coming after her.

"Oh no. Please don't cry. I feel terrible."

"I'm sorry. It's just that my apartment flooded today, and this is so upsetting."

"Tell you what. You and I have never really gotten to know each other. How about I take you to dinner this evening to cheer you up, and we can talk about how best to approach working with the students and parents at this school? We can go early. Say, five o'clock at the Grand Central Oyster Bar? Then I can catch a train home. What do you say?"

"Oh, you don't have to do that," she said. "I'm sure you're too busy for that."

"No, I'd like to. It's the least I can do for one of our most promising new teachers."

It was the nicest anyone had been to her all day.

She hesitated a couple of moments, not wanting to be a bother but appreciating the gesture.

"Okay, sure. Yes, that would be nice."

"Wonderful. I have a meeting off campus at four this afternoon, so I can meet you at the bar."

"Great. I'll be there." Her mood lifted slightly.

"And, Harper, we can get this taken care of. Try not to worry. If we get this straightened out, you could be here a long time."

She thanked him and walked back to her classroom, glad to have a vote of confidence from her boss. She returned to her juniors, who were presenting their essays on their favorite family vacations. She could hardly stomach listening to all these trips to the Louvre, zip-lining in the Alps, glamping safaris in Kenya, and sailing in St. Tropez.

She scrolled her contacts to text "Climate Denier," her conservative brother, Ernest, who lived in a new building in Hudson Yards. She found the neighborhood soulless, but he said liked the new construction and walk-in closets.

"Hey. Can I stay over a couple of nights? Bathroom flooded at my place. And don't say I told you so. I know it's a dump!"

They argued bitterly about politics, but they were good to each other. He said yes, of course she could stay.

"But only if you text me Mary's number." Their running joke about how he was in love with her friend.

"Fat chance!"

AT 4:30, HARPER finished going through the last of her emails and jotted some notes about her experience with the Baldwins for the conversation she had to have the next day. She freshened up in the teachers' all-gender bathroom, putting her hair in a tidier bun and adding some under-eye concealer and lip gloss. She wore a long tan dress, ankle boots, and her signature brown leather jacket that she'd had for years. It was perfectly broken in and had just the right number of pockets. She thought her outfit said youthful and creative, part of the New York crowd who did *not* work in finance or media.

Harper had enough time to walk to the Oyster Bar to get there by five. She enjoyed the city at this time of day, before the evening rush. The restaurants were starting to fill up as tourists grabbed an early dinner before the theater. She loved Broadway and made a mental note to enter a lottery to see if she could win tickets for a show—she knew all the tricks to getting decent seats at a good price.

Mr. Swift had beat her to the restaurant inside Grand Central. He was at the bar, a martini in front of him, and an empty seat to his right.

"Harper. You made it. You look beautiful."

She was flattered but thought that was a little weird coming from her headmaster. She shook it off and ordered a glass of Sancerre, which she thought made her seem sophisticated. He asked the bartender for the special oysters of the day for them to share.

"Right away, sir." The bartender was efficient. Harper realized he probably made way more money than she did. Should she consider a part-time job after school?

They made small talk for a while. She'd been hired quickly when the previous English teacher had moved on to Dalton. He asked about her upbringing and told her about growing up on the Main Line in Philadelphia. They ended up talking about their favorite books, which was a topic she loved. She felt warm and happy. She ordered another glass of wine.

"So, Harper. Edith Thistlewood told me all about the . . . uh, other situation today—this thing with the Laschers."

"Yes. I'm sorry that I've caused you a hassle."

"It's okay. It's okay. I know how these parents can be. I understand from Edith that you handled it as best you could in the moment, but she's not sure they're completely satisfied."

"I'm sorry to hear that. What else can I do?"

"Oh, no need to apologize," he said, reaching into his pocket, pulling out a card, and setting it on the bar. The logo was recognizable: Hilton. The hotel next door to Grand Central.

She stared at it, not sure if he'd meant to get out his credit card to pay the bill before he caught his train.

"You know," he continued, "I could talk to the Laschers privately. And we can make all this go away." He looked at her over his martini. "If you want it to."

For the second time in front of him that day, heat rushed up her neck to her face. She was ashamed, embarrassed, and furious. And confused. Was he asking her to sleep with him to keep teaching at Van Buren?

Harper's brain set off in several directions at once. She needed this job, but this man was way out of line. Her instincts were firing. Her parents had drilled this advice into her head at an early age: "You're the only one who can protect your integrity." She'd made some bad decisions in her life so far, and she knew that sleeping with her boss would be the worst one yet.

She had to think quickly—the second glass of wine had been a terrible idea.

"That's a very interesting proposition, Mr. Swift." She tilted her head and didn't meet his eye.

"Phil, please." He put his hand on her knee. She flinched.

"Tell you what," she said. "Let me use the restroom and I'll meet you at the front entrance on Forty-Second?" She smiled and met his gaze. He looked relieved, his eyebrows raised in salacious expectation, believing he'd made the right call in exploiting Harper.

He dug in his pocket for cash to leave on the counter as she grabbed her jacket, threw her bag over her shoulder, and walked toward the ladies' room. Her heart was beating fast.

She ducked behind the busboys' station and peered around the wall. Once she saw Mr. Swift leave the Oyster Bar, she slipped out a west exit onto Vanderbilt Place and headed toward the Hudson, keeping her eyes forward and her pace steady. She forced herself to look straight ahead, afraid to look back in case he came looking for her.

On the street the only luck she'd had all day came through as a taxi pulled over as soon as she hailed for one.

"Where to?"

"The Oskar—Hudson Yards."

The driver nodded.

Harper forced herself to take a deep breath. She leaned her head against the back of the seat and felt embarrassed and angry at herself.

How did she keep getting into one mess after another?

Chapter 11

Dot took a deep breath, and she walked into the restaurant, right on time as always. Joanne's was hopping. It gave her a lift as she looked for Ryan.

He waved from a corner table and stood when she arrived. He looked handsome and relaxed, and Dot tried to put the Tiffany visit out of her mind. Maybe he was there helping a friend pick out a ring for someone else? That could be it.

That was probably not it.

"You look beautiful." He kissed her cheek, pulled out her chair, and when she was settled, he pushed it in for her. "I put in an order for meatballs and the calamari to start us off."

"Thank you. My faves." She tried to sound cheerful, but her stomach had been in knots since the Tiffany affair.

They settled into catch-up and chitchat. Ryan's sister and brother-in-law just announced she was pregnant; the family's first grandchild would be born in May. His work was fine, the market up, then down, but mostly up.

It all felt normal. And easy. Maybe she'd incorrectly read this entire situation.

Until Ryan suggested a weekend away.

"Hey—I got us a reservation at the Rose Hill Vineyard for next weekend. Won't that be great?"

Rose Hill Vineyard. How did she know that place?

"Oh. I . . ."

"You're free next weekend, right?"

She tried to buy herself some time and couldn't think of a convincing reason that would prevent her from going away with him for a weekend. So instead she said, "Yes. Of course. It sounds nice."

"Oh yeah. It's so nice. Super expensive, too," he said, glancing down at his menu. "It'll be my half birthday." Then he cocked his head and raised his eyebrows at her as he reached for his beer.

Then it hit her. Rose Hill was where his college buddy Jordan had proposed to his girlfriend (also named Jordan) over the summer. The Jordans were getting married this Christmas at The Plaza.

Aha, she thought. His half birthday was a sign. Ryan always said he wanted to be married in his twenty-eighth year. She wasn't great at math, but simple arithmetic she could do. Her mind raced with flashes of him shopping for rings at Tiffany. Her stomach knotted thinking about how to get out of going to the vineyard. What could be her excuse?

She didn't have to think of one. The conversation took a turn as he abruptly changed the subject.

"By the way, I think you'll be glad to know I'm finally a *little* interested in politics. We had an all-hands meeting on the trading floor with the governor from Virginia. Cool guy. Might run for president one day. He was so great. I'd vote for him."

"Wait. What?" she asked, knowing exactly who the governor of Virginia was.

"Especially with his economic policies. He'd be great for the market," he replied.

"But there's more to life than the *market*, Ryan." Dot was shocked.

Ryan held up his hands defensively. "Hey, hey—calm down. I just thought he had some good ideas."

"Oh really. Like what?" she asked, clearly skeptical.

"Well, he talked about how they have a generous state benefit for stay-at-home moms there."

Dot suddenly set down her fork and stared at him, unbelieving of what he'd just said. "Is that what you *want* for your future wife?"

"Isn't that what *most* women want?" he asked, slightly mocking her. "To be able to relax and raise the kids, not have to worry about anything."

"Oh Ryan . . . you think raising children is relaxing? My gosh, you sound like . . . like . . ."

"Okay, forget I said anything." He tried to surrender but the damage was done.

But Dot could not forget. "You sound like a *Republican*."

THE MOOD SOURED and they ate quickly as the rest of their conversation took a turn to the terse.

Leaving Joanne, Ryan fell into step with Dot toward the Buckley. As they got closer, Ryan grabbed her hand. She tensed.

"Can I come upstairs?" He searched her eyes, but she looked away.

"I don't think so, Ryan. Not tonight. I'm sorry."

"Look. I won't vote for him. I promise!" He tried to lighten the moment. "Come here."

He leaned down for a kiss, but she turned her head. He brought her head into his chest. He smelled so good. But she stayed rigid and wouldn't relax into him.

She gently pulled away.

"Good night, Ryan."

Reluctantly, he let go of her. "Look, I'm not sure what's changed. But I won't push it," he said. "Good night, Dot."

He stood and watched her head in as Albert opened the door for her.

"Mr. Montgomery. A pleasure to see you as always," Albert said, being discreet as usual.

"You too, Albert."

Dot peeked back to see Ryan standing outside, watching the door close, no doubt wondering what was wrong with her. After a few moments, he turned and headed down Central Park West to catch the train back to his apartment.

She started up the stairs, but then suddenly, she was back out the door of the Buckley and running down the street.

Just as Ryan was heading down the subway station's stairs, she called his name.

"Ryan!" She was sprinting in her flats and her hair had come out of its knot.

"Dot?"

"Ryan, I . . . I can't do this," she panted, trying to catch her breath.

"You can't do what?"

"You're a great guy. And you'll be perfect for someone someday. But that someone. . . . that someone is not going to be me."

She met his eyes and held them.

"Dot, come on, you can't be serious. Is this because I said I'd vote for the governor of Virginia?" he scoffed. "That's ridiculous."

"It's not just that. It's been building for a while. I think we were initially a good match—the apps figured that out. But algorithms don't know our hearts and our dreams. And I just think we want very different things out of life. I'm sorry, Ryan."

"Well, this sucks."

"I'm sorry. Please take care, Ryan."

"Like you care, Dot. And to think, I was going to ask you . . ."

But Dot couldn't stand to hear it and turned and walked back to her building. She folded her arms against her chest and braced against the cold. Albert had watched her run down the street. He was there with a hug for her.

"Aw, Dorothy. Did you just break up with him?"

She nodded, wiping away her tears.

"There, there." He patted her back. "You did the right thing, dear. You followed your heart. And there's nothing wrong with that." He handed her his handkerchief.

"I feel terrible."

"It would have been worse if you'd kept it going even if you knew it wasn't right. This way you can both get on with your lives and find your special someone."

She used the handkerchief to wipe away her tears. "What am I doing, Albert?" He knew she meant with her life in general, not just in that moment.

"Living." He put his hands on both her shoulders and made her look him in the eye. "You're going to be fine. You're an educated woman, living in the best city in the best country in the world. There's no need to worry about what's next. What's next will be what it's meant to be."

"Thank you." She took a staggered breath. "How do you always know what to say?"

"It comes with age. Trust me, everything will all look better tomorrow."

She smiled weakly, then slowly took the stairs up to her apartment. When she closed the door, she leaned against it and let herself cry.

Then, after a restless night where she tossed and turned in her bed, Dot thought of how Albert was right—everything *did* seem better in the morning.

Two things struck her.

First, she'd woken ready to stop worrying so much about her love life and to start focusing on her career.

And second, she had a big idea of what she wanted to do next with her career.

Chapter 12

The Crew met for dinner in the Village the following Saturday night. The Spaniard was buzzing. The weather was warm, and people were spilling out of the large windows onto West Fourth Street.

Harper got there first and grabbed the table. Mary and Dot arrived at the same time and joined her.

"Jimmy! Gonna need a pitcher of sangria." Mary called to the bartender whose arm was sleeved in tattoos.

"You should go out with him. Just one night." Harper raised her eyebrows at Mary.

"Maybe I will!" she said.

"Maybe *I* will," Dot said. They laughed and then realized she wasn't joking.

"Wait. Are you still with Ryan?" Harper asked.

"Is he going to propose?" Mary was dying to talk about Dot's stakeout at Tiffany's.

"He's *proposing*?" Harper felt out of the loop.

"He's *definitely* not going to propose." She waited a beat. "Because I broke up with him."

Harper's hand flew to her mouth. "Oh no!"

"Ah, I'm sorry, Dot." Mary wasn't entirely surprised. "He was great—for a while. Are you okay?"

"I am. I mean, I will be eventually. This morning, I had a cry and then went for a long run. I spent the afternoon just reading a novel, got my hair blown out at Drybar using a gift certificate from my parents, and came to see you. And there's no one I'd rather be with tonight than you two."

"Wow. I can't believe it. I was thinking you were going to get married one day. I even imagined our bridesmaid dresses." Harper raised her mason jar of sangria and toasted Dot. "Well, I think it was brave of you to break up with him. I mean, who knows when you'll meet another guy."

"Gee, thanks." Dot felt deflated but agreed. It wasn't like there were a lot—or any—prospects lined up.

"Harper! Have some faith!" Mary playfully admonished her. "I'm sure the app has your next special someone all lined up."

"Oh no. I'm done with the apps for a while. I deleted my accounts," Dot said. "I need to get through my identity crisis before I try again." She laughed but there was a hint of truth in what she'd said. "But enough about me—Harper, you've had quite the week."

"Tell me about it." Harper rolled her eyes and looked to the ceiling. "It's been wild."

"Yeah, Harp, how did you handle those entitled Van Buren parents?" Mary asked.

"Well, here's how I handled it: I quit."

"What?" Dot and Mary couldn't believe it.

"You quit? Wow, there you go, Harper. Good for you," Dot said. She was surprised by her friend's decisive action. She was usually rather hesitant to make big decisions.

"It wasn't just that. Believe it or not, the headmaster tried to sleep with me."

"He did not." Dot's hands flew to her chest.

"He propositioned me. Right there at the Oyster Bar." She took a sip of her drink. "And he was really open about how he'd then just take the train home to his family in Westchester."

"Holy smokes," Mary said. "You know what he did is super illegal in New York, right? It's not quite bribery, but it's clearly sexual harassment. You could sue. It's outrageous. And this guy works with children!"

"I talked to Ernest about it. He's been letting me crash at his place since the leak at my apartment. We decided that the truth is that I didn't really want to work there anyway. And beyond that, I don't even know what I want to do at all, jobwise. It's like I'm stuck between bad luck and indecision. It's not a good look." Harper could be open with her friends about how she was really feeling. "It's embarrassing. I'm twenty-five years old and crashing on my older brother's couch. I should have my act together by now."

"Hey, you're not the only one doing some rethinking," Dot said. "I've been having second thoughts about my PR firm. It's a grind. I'm not inspired at all, and they're about to downsize which means more pressure, less help, and no raise."

"Ha, you too? I was feeling the same way this week—but more about my love life, or lack thereof, than my job. The partners at my firm are great, but sometimes the job is tedious," Mary said. "And I'd like to do something more meaningful with my law degree. Even if that's volunteering somewhere."

"I know what you mean," Harper said. "It really can add up when you look at what these wealthier parents can and will do to buy their children's way out of having to do any hard work." She sipped her drink. "And the truth is, I really do want to write. That's my passion. I just don't know if I can pay the *rent* with my passion."

And with that, Dot found her opening. She rapped her knuckles on the table.

"So, given that we are all close to capsizing the 'what the hell am I doing with my life' canoe, I want to run something by you." Mary and Harper leaned in a bit. "Before I begin, promise me you'll hear me out and not interrupt me until I finish?"

"Promise," Harper said. Mary nodded.

"Okay. I called Kitty Bell about Wisconsin. I'm thinking of taking her up on her offer to volunteer for the election. Like a political gap year," Dot said. She waited a couple of beats before adding the kicker. "And I want you two to come with me."

Mary had anticipated where this was going. "Ha, that's funny."

"I'm not kidding."

"No. No freaking way," Mary said.

"Wait—you promised to let me finish."

"Fine. Go on," Mary conceded.

"Mary, your mother keeps setting you up with guys you'd never date but that she wants you to marry. That's not going to change."

"Can't stop won't stop," Mary acknowledged.

"And Harper, you need time and space to write your novel or even do the online course to get your teaching certificate. So, listen . . ."

Harper's brow creased and Mary crossed her arms in front of her chest.

"Kitty already has a place for us to live. It's a great old house in this super cute town called Cedar Falls. It's just thirty minutes north of Milwaukee, so it's near the airport . . . and restaurants."

"Cedar Falls? Are you serious—that's a real place, not a Hallmark movie town?" Mary was skeptical.

"It's in this battleground county that went Republican by just 368 votes last time around. It's ripe for a change. It could make all the difference in the election since it's expected to be so close. But beyond that—it's an adventure!"

"I can't afford to . . ." Harper always worried about money, but Dot jumped in quickly.

"It wouldn't cost us anything! I've done the math." She pulled out her phone to show them a budget she'd made. "With the money that For the Win will give me to manage the year, and free housing, plus a car, we would be able to handle everything without a struggle."

Harper stared into her sangria. "I can't take money from you, Dot."

"You wouldn't be taking money from me. The house and car come with the gig. And it has *four* bedrooms. You'd even have your own bathroom, Harp!" That perk got Harper's attention. "Come on. We can do this. It would be a break from the city. Together. Crew two-point-oh."

Mary furrowed her brow and laid her hands on the table. "You're serious, aren't you?"

"I think it'd be good for us. We can do something meaningful, as you just said, Mary, and we can all have one more year together before we finally meet the men of our dreams and settle down back here at home in the city."

With that, Dot sat back, letting her girlfriends consider the idea. Harper opened the door to it first.

"Well, what's the worst that could happen? It's not like my life is on the right track at the moment," Harper said. "Maybe I need to shake things up."

"What's the equivalent of good Italian in Wisconsin? Is it like a bratwurst?" Mary said.

"I'm sure we will find you something to eat," Dot said, taking a playful jab at Mary's appetite. "Let me ask—do you think your firm would let you work remotely for a year?"

"Maybe. The senior partner of the firm is a big Dem and often does election protection and integrity work pro bono. She might be cool with it."

Suddenly, Dot sensed a stirring. It felt like . . . hope.

Their pitcher of sangria was empty.

"Another round, Jimmy!" Mary winked as he swung by their table.

"Anything for you, Bonita," he said. "How about I add calamari and the kale and artichoke dip? On the house."

"Perfection," Mary said, rewarding his generosity with one of her big smiles.

Dot kept pushing and said, "Girls. You know me. I'm not reckless or spontaneous. I've thought this through. I wouldn't let you down, you know that." She waited several moments as Mary and Harper sat quietly, quizzical looks on their faces. "So, what do you think?"

"I'm thinking." Mary looked to the ceiling as if the answer were there. Could she picture herself in. . . . Wisconsin?

Harper tried to break the silence, but no words came out. She closed her lips again and considered Dot's proposal.

Dot held her breath, giving them a moment to digest.

"Let's say we did this." Mary leaned back in the booth, tapped her nails on the table. "If I could keep my job, and if my family wouldn't want to hold me hostage in our basement—could we make a deal that we're back next year in time for . . . let's say . . . the tree lighting at Rock Center?"

"I absolutely can agree to that. Kitty said they only needed people up until the election. We can even book our flights so that we come back on . . ." Dot paused while she looked up the date of Election Day. "November 8, 2028. The day after the election. Then we'll know that this is an adventure with a firm end date."

Harper let Dot and Mary chew on the details but was thinking about her own circumstances. "I hesitate because I truly have no money, and I can't ask my parents to help fund another year of finding my way . . . not that this is a waste of time, Dot, but that's how they'll see it for me."

"Even if you told them that by the end of it, you'll have written your novel?" Dot asked.

"I guess it's possible they'd believe that. I just don't know if I could even manage to do it," Harper said. "But I know I am never going back to *that* school, not after what happened. And my living situation is a nightmare. I suppose I could find some desperate trust fund baby to take over part of my lease at the apartment."

"And even if you couldn't, your landlord can't successfully chase you down for rent on an apartment with a giant hole in the ceiling," Mary said.

"Plus, it might be the best way for me to hit the reset button after the disaster with Kai. I could really dedicate some time to writing." She was saying all her inside thoughts out loud. "I'll be honest. I don't hate the idea. Nothing I'm doing right now is turning out the way I thought it would. Maybe a clean break is just what I need. And then I can come back in a better place."

"That's how I see this." Dot felt hopeful they'd say yes. "We all need a little push to get us over these humps. I look at Kitty and think she's really nailed it. Her life looks amazing, like she's got it all figured out. Perhaps a little time away, doing something totally different for a while, in a new place, and for something that matters, could get us to where we want to be."

Mary felt torn. "Yeah, but I want to be in the city long-term."

"Me too," Dot assured her. "I'm never living anywhere else. It's just for the year. Less than a year. I promise."

"Give me a minute." Mary excused herself to the ladies' room. Dot watched her go and willed her to have an epiphany before she returned to the table.

Harper kept wondering aloud about how she'd manage. "I want to say why not?" She smiled broadly, her eyes shining with new confidence. "But I'm lactose intolerant. Don't they eat a lot of dairy there?"

"I think that there are plenty of lactose intolerant people who live in Wisconsin and do just fine," Dot said, hoping that was true.

After a few minutes, Mary came back. She sat down and clasped her long fingers with their perfect red nails together, then said, "All right, you win, Dot."

"Really?"

"My mother is going to freak." Mary held up her glass for another toast. "So, with that in mind . . . let's go freeze our butts off in Wisconsin!"

"Yes? You'll go?" Dot's eyes teared as she looked from Mary to Harper.

"I think we'll go." Harper raised her glass.

Dot, realizing her wild idea was about to become reality, picked her glass up and met theirs in the middle of the table.

"Well! To Cedar Falls and new beginnings!" she said. They clinked glasses.

Dot picked up her phone and pushed herself out of the booth.

"I'm going to call Kitty."

Chapter 13

The next few weeks went by in a flash. There was so much to do.

In the whirlwind, Dot often pinched herself. Was this really happening? Was she really going to break up with her boyfriend, jump off her career track, and move to the middle of nowhere for a *passion* project, of all things?

The impulsivity of her decision to take Kitty Bell up on her offer felt exhilarating, which was certainly not her natural state. She'd always been so methodical—she liked to have everything planned out and *just so*. That said, the feeling of excitement wasn't unwelcome. To the contrary, she felt invigorated. She felt *alive*.

There were so many decisions to make and things to do before she, Harper, and Mary moved to Wisconsin for the year. To keep track of everything, Dot took to writing and rewriting her to-do list. It felt like every time she crossed one thing off, another two things came up.

First up—telling her parents. She agonized about this. She worried they'd think she was cracking up, losing her mind, or even worse, being *irresponsible*. She tied herself in knots going over the conversation. When she finally got them on FaceTime, she thought she might vomit from her nerves.

Her parents surprised her when they immediately said, "Good for you! This is so exciting. And a great time in your life to do something like his. We're so proud of you!"

Chalk that up to another lesson learned—she'd been so concerned about what her parents would think, and imagined that it would go badly, that she'd wasted all that time worrying for nothing.

Her sister Anne had a similar reaction. "Wow. I didn't think you had it in you to be so adventurous. It's brave, what you're doing. And maybe you'll meet some hot guy there."

"Fat chance. I'm going to focus on work completely," she replied.

Dot got a boost of confidence with her family supporting her decision. Her parents even offered to take over the co-op fees and utilities for the year, since they both loved the city, and they already had a long list of things they'd do on the long weekends they planned to spend in Manhattan. "Broadway, museums, restaurants, lectures. I can't wait," her mom said.

That done, Dot then had to resign from her job. She planned out her side of the conversation and thought it was generous to offer a month's transition, through to Christmas. She knew she wouldn't miss her clients or the horrible SVP, but she'd miss her tiny office with the view and the younger staff that looked up to her.

The managing director of the firm was understanding and kind.

"You always have a place here, if you want to come back," she said. And while Dot didn't plan on ever returning to high-tech PR, she was glad that she hadn't burned a bridge. At least with the top boss.

"This is a risky decision, Dot," the SVP said. "You know it's not likely to work, right?"

"What's not going to work?"

"The Democrats are hopeless. Their brand is toxic. Eighty percent of the country can't stand them."

Dot swallowed her initial reaction to fight back with statistics showing the Republicans were also underwater with public opinion.

"We'll see." That was her go-to answer to prevent an argument. She avoided him for the rest of the month and knew she'd never miss him.

She would miss, however, her friends, her apartment, Albert, her runs in Central Park, the neighborhood dogs, the bodega owner on the corner, and Freddy, her regular coffee cart guy. She'd miss the subway, Fifth Avenue, the High Line, and more. She'd miss all of it.

The closer she got to her departure from New York, the more she loved it. She did one last run the day before they left and stopped at the northern end of the Great Lawn to take a selfie with the skyline of Central Park West behind her.

"NYC is the best boyfriend," she captioned the picture on her story, making it clear to all she was no longer with Ryan, who'd unfollowed her soon after the breakup. At least she knew the park would be right where she left it.

Before returning to the apartment, Dot stopped by Blank Street Coffee and got an Americano for Albert, and a latte for herself. She handed it to him when she arrived.

"Cheers, Albert."

"Here's to *you*, Dorothy. You're following your dreams. Your grandmother would be proud."

"You'll be here when I get back?"

"I'll always be here."

And they clinked paper cups and sipped.

HARPER HAD SO many reasons for wanting to leave New York City, starting with her terrible, leaky apartment.

To get that behind her, Mary sent a harshly worded complaint to Harper's landlord. She signed it, "Mary Russo, Esquire." After she emailed the letter, she called the landlord to confirm he'd received it.

"To confirm, Harper Adler is free and clear of her lease?"

"Yes, ma'am."

"And you'll be issuing her a check with her full security deposit?"

"Well, I don't know. There's a leak that needs fixing . . ."

Mary cut him off. "The leak came from the apartment above hers. When will you have her full security deposit available for her to pick up? This afternoon?"

"Ummmm . . ."

"Is that a yes?"

"Okay, yes."

"Good. Because I was about to call my colleague at the city department of housing."

"There's no need for that."

"I'm glad we understand each other. Goodbye." Mary hung up and Harper high-fived her.

"That felt good," Mary said. "More fun than going through SEC briefs."

"What would I do without you?"

"Make it up to me one day—put me in one of your books."

"You got it. You'll make a great character. No one will believe you exist in real life, though," Harper said.

Aside from her landlord, Harper just had to convince her parents it was a good idea.

To her surprise, it was like pushing on an open door.

"I think it's great," Harper's dad said. "You'll see another part of the country, have time to write, and help the Democrats win back the White House." He'd stayed somewhat active in the party after his tenure with Obama. "And you'll be fine when the year is up. You'll have more of an idea of what you want to do."

Even her brother was encouraging. "That's cool. Sounds like fun. And maybe you'll meet a real man, not like the guys who live in the city."

"You live in the city," she said.

"Yeah, but I'm not one of *those* guys."

Harper rolled her eyes and tried to imagine a future sister-in-law. Poor girl, she thought.

On her last Sunday before leaving, they all met at their favorite brunch spot in Cobble Hill. Their orders matched their personalities. Her brother got a crispy buffalo chicken wrap, while her dad went for the tuna salad. Her mom ordered the egg-white omelet with veggies and hot sauce, and Harper chose the chicken Caesar wrap. They shared an order of Greek fries—covered in feta, oregano, and lemon. Endless hot coffee filled their mugs.

"We have a little surprise for you," her mom said. "Check your Venmo."

Harper picked up her phone and her eyes widened. Her mom and dad had sent her a nice chunk of money. She was shocked.

"I don't know how to thank you," she said, blinking back tears.

"Consider it an advance of an advance," her dad said.

"We believe in you, Harp." Her mom hugged her and kissed her on the head.

"Knock 'em dead, kid," her older brother said, lightly punching her on the arm. She was touched by his kindness. "By the time you get back, you'll be a Republican."

"You wish." She lightly swatted him with the back of her hand. "Maybe by the time I get back you'll have realized the planet is about to boil over."

"Tell that to the dinosaurs," he said, signaling to the waitress for more coffee.

"Exactly!" she said. He was infuriating, but she loved him.

AS MARY EXPECTED, her law firm was fine with her plan, and the head partner, a Democratic donor, was highly encouraging.

"I think it's great. I wish I'd done something like this when I was your age," Sofia Garcia said. She'd grown up in Queens and risen through the ranks to the top of the firm. She'd been in the "Top 40 Under 40" of the national law trade for ten years—until this year when she'd turned forty-one.

"I had a good run," she joked.

"And you think you can handle all of your work remotely?" she asked Mary.

"I do. I have a plan. I'll be up early and on all the calls. They won't even know I'm gone."

"I checked with the partners you report to, and they said you're hitting all your marks."

"That's good to hear."

"All right. You have sign-off from me."

"Thank you so much."

"There's just one more thing I need."

"Sure, anything."

"What's the name of that lipstick?"

Mary smiled broadly. "Big Apple Red."

"Nice."

They shook hands and Mary turned to go, feeling like she really wanted to make Maria Garcia proud.

After subletting her apartment to some tech bro, Mary's biggest test was still to come. Her family's Sunday supper was going to be brutal. No one in her family could understand why she was going on this wild adventure with her college girlfriends instead of staying home and working on getting married and starting a family. She'd been bracing herself for days in the lead-up to the feast.

She got to Staten Island at three in the afternoon before the rest of the family arrived. Her Nonna had already been cooking up a storm.

"Hi, Nonna," she said, wrapping her grandmother in a hug from behind while she continued to make meatballs. "That smells so good."

"Special gravy for you tonight, my girl."

"I'm so lucky." She looked around the kitchen. "Who else is coming—the entire island? There's enough food here for everyone."

"I made extra. Going to send you home with it for your freezer."

"But I'm leaving on a plane tomorrow, Nonna."

"I know. That's why I got you an extra suitcase when I was at TJ Maxx."

"You've thought of everything." Mary relented. There was no way she was hauling all this food to Wisconsin. She hoped her subletter liked Bolognese.

Her parents walked into the kitchen with open arms.

"Hi, Pop," she said, folding herself into his embrace.

"Hi, baby girl." He kissed her head.

"I can't believe you're leaving me," Mary's mom, Christine, said.

"I'm not leaving you. I'm going on a short-term adventure. I'll be back before you know it."

Mary kept a positive attitude the entire night as it went on like that.

"Welcome to the Last Supper," her brother Frankie said as he passed the bruschetta.

"I'm not dying," she said.

"Why do you assume you're Jesus in this scenario? You might be one of the other guys."

"Yeah, like a tax collector. The old-fashioned lawyers," Joey, her closest brother in age, said.

"Could you weigh in here?" she implored Gabe, the priest, to back her up.

"I'm the peacemaker, Mary."

She rolled her eyes.

"Do you think you'll meet any lumberjacks out there?" her sister-in-law Donna asked, biting into a roasted pepper.

"I can hope," she said, imagining bringing a burly man back to Sunday supper and showing him off to her family.

After dessert, her dad raised his glass of Sambuca.

"To Mary," he said. "You're our best girl." Emotional, he wiped away a tear.

"To Mary," everyone repeated in unison.

"Salute!" And they drank up.

Before she left, Mary spent extra time with Nonna.

"I love you; you know that, right?" she said.

"Yes, yes. You know you're my favorite?" Nonna replied.

"You don't tell all of us that?"

"I do. But with you, I mean it."

"You're my favorite, too." She kissed her grandmother's cheek and said goodbye. "I'll FaceTime you tomorrow. I'll be back before you know it."

Nonna wiped away a tear and said, "Go. And know we're proud of you, Mary."

"Thanks, Nonna. That means everything."

THE NIGHT BEFORE they left, Dot sent one more text to the group.

"Everyone all set? Got your rides to the airport planned?"

"Yes, Mom," Mary texted from her bed.

"Car coming at 10 a.m. Meet you at the gate," Harper said. "Don't get cold feet!"

"Remember, you never know who you might meet on the plane," Dot said.

"That never happens." Mary was a skeptic.

"It does happen! Lots of couples have met on planes. It's where you can sit and talk and just be yourself. It's a great way to fall in love."

"Like love at first sight?"

"No. Love at first *flight*," Harper chimed in.

"I don't have a great track record. Last time I flew, I sat next to a guy who drank six screwdrivers on the way to Las Vegas. And it was six in the morning," Mary said.

"Maybe he saw you and thought he needed liquid courage to start a conversation," Dot replied.

"I watched five hours of *Housewives* instead."

"Harsh blow to his ego."

"And to my brain cells."

"Good night, Crew. And . . . thanks." Dot was ready for bed, though she didn't know if she'd be able to sleep.

"Sweet dreams." Harper added a sleeping emoji.

"Hoping for dreams a little more stimulating than sweet." Mary was having fun now.

"Go to bed, you nut." Dot set her phone down, then picked it up one more time to check she'd set her alarm. She could hardly wait for the morning to come.

AT THE AIRPORT the morning of their departure, Harper was pacing.

"What's wrong?" Mary asked. "Sit down."

"I can't. I gotta get the wiggles out."

"Well, you're making me nervous."

"Maybe that's the triple espresso you had after we cleared security."

"Fair."

Dot was checking her bag, making sure she had everything.

"Why do you always do that?" Harper asked.

"Do what?"

"Check everything multiple times. You never forget anything."

"I guess I'm afraid if I don't check, something will go wrong."

"Maybe it's time to start letting go, Dot," Mary said. "Isn't that what this is all about?"

"Okay. Fine. I just want to make sure I have my charger and then . . ."

"Stop! Your charger is right there." Harper pointed to the white cord sticking out of the zippered pouch.

"You're right." Dot kept looking through her bag.

"Dot," Mary said. "Dot, look at me."

Dot looked up and met her friend's eyes.

Mary reached for Dot's hand and then grabbed on to Harper's, too. She looked at them both.

"This is going to be so fun. It's an adventure. It won't be perfect. Let's just roll with it, okay? We may never get the chance to be this spontaneous again. Harper, you'll be a bestselling author and traveling the world. Dot, you'll be the CEO of some major company or running the White House. And I'll be billing hours and going home for Sunday supper for the rest of my life. This is *it*. This is our chance for one more roll of the dice before permanent life sets in. Okay?" She squeezed their hands.

"Okay." Dot visibly relaxed.

"Okay," Harper agreed.

"Can I come for Sunday supper even after I'm a bestselling author?" Harper asked.

"If you play your cards right, I'll set you up with one of my cousins."

"Now that's something to look forward to!"

AS THEY BOARDED, they made their way to their seats. Each of them had a window seat on the small jet bound for Milwaukee.

Mary sent a text to their group chat.

"Wow, Dot. You were right. Sitting next to a handsome man!"

"Nice!" Dot typed.

"But he's already committed."

"Married?"

"Yes."

Then Mary sent a selfie of her and her seatmate. She looked gorgeous in her black Alo leisurewear, her hair tossed into a messy bun on top of her head. And he looked handsome in his priest's collar.

"To God."

Dot typed back a series of crying emojis and heard Harper burst out laughing three rows behind her.

She put her phone away in her backpack and settled into her seat. To her left, she could see the skyscrapers of the city in the bright blue winter sun.

The plane rumbled down the runway, and the nose tipped into the air. As the pilot climbed out of LaGuardia and banked left, Dot rested her forehead against the window and took in the city.

She gently waved and whispered, "Be right back."

They were off.

PART TWO

Chapter 14

Monday morning in early February, Dot looked in the hallway mirror and tied a teal cashmere scarf tight around her neck. She threw on a long navy Patagonia coat—a Christmas gift from her parents. She added a black "I Love NY" bauble hat and light pink fleece-lined mittens. Her outfit didn't match, but who cared when it was only two degrees outside?

"Negative 12 with the windchill!" she texted her sister, comparing Cedar Falls to Vail.

"You win again—it's going to get up to 40 here this afternoon," Anne replied, up early to take a group of winter tourists out on the slopes for the day. Dot always said she wasn't competitive, she just loved to win. Anne played along.

That morning, Dot was heading into the local Democratic offices in Cedar Falls. The first Democratic presidential primary debate was just two weeks away, and the DNC had chosen the University of Wisconsin-Madison to host—less than a two-hour drive from The Crew's new digs.

Through its D.C. office, For the Win had offered to handle the candidates' greenroom needs. Dot was the team's organizer, and she'd recruited Mary and Harper to help.

"Think we'll get to meet that handsome governor from California? What's his name . . . ?" Mary had asked.

"You mean, Cal Ashby?" Dot reminded her. It was easy for Dot to remember his name. Soon after he'd won the gubernatorial election, he ran national ads on cable and YouTube. He'd looked into the camera and winked. "Governor Cal Ashby. It's in the name. . . . *Cal*- ifornia." He so saw himself as a future president.

"Oh yeah. Cal. He's pretty hot," Mary said. She always had her priorities straight.

Before she left for the day, Dot checked on Harper. The night before, she'd fallen asleep on the sofa while they watched a favorite *Grey's Anatomy* rerun. Dot thought Harper might still be afraid to be alone in the big house at night, even though they'd been here for just over a month.

"It's too quiet," she'd complained when they first arrived. She missed the sirens, and sidewalk sounds from the Village. She downloaded an app that played city noises, but that made Mary bang on their adjoining wall and yell, "Make it stop!"

Dot pulled the blanket up to her chin and said softly, "Happy writing. See you tonight." Harper groaned and rolled over into a fetal position. She wasn't ready to get up yet.

Dot heard Mary moving around upstairs in her room. Mary always woke before dawn to get a jump on her billable hours. So far, no one from her firm had complained about her working remotely, and she was pretty sure no one would since her managing partner had approved.

"Not sure the other lawyers even know I'm gone," Mary had said after they'd been in Wisconsin for a couple of weeks.

"Just keep making them money—that'll keep them off your back." Harper wore disdain for corporations on her sleeve.

And yet, Harper was the first to gush about their plush living arrangements that Kitty had set up for them.

Their house on Maple Avenue was filled with well-kept Craftsman-style houses that were built at the beginning of the twentieth century. The town had strict historic preservation rules, so many of the homes had old-world charm but modern conveniences, like built-in microwaves and central air.

The owners of The Crew's house had kept the stained-glass windows and refinished the oak floors. That family of five had relocated to Nashville for the dad's job in medical devices, and they decided to rent it out instead of selling. For the Win had snapped up the lease immediately.

Upstairs they had four small bedrooms with spacious closets that The Crew just couldn't believe.

"I can do cartwheels in here." Harper had never had a walk-in closet.

The finished basement had a small guest room and bathroom, plus a workout area with a treadmill and free weights.

"Dot, you can have this entire spot," Mary had said when they arrived. "I don't plan ever to come down here again."

The kitchen had light gray granite countertops, white cupboards, and brass fittings. Its best feature was an island with room for three stools where they could eat a meal or work on their laptops.

A remote-control gas fireplace made the living room super cozy, and they stood in front of it to warm themselves as soon as they returned home. Harper had struggled with the cold since they'd arrived. "I am chilled from the inside out. It's all up in my bones."

They looked forward to sitting on the spacious front porch once spring came—a glider sat under a big canvas cover to protect it from the winter elements. And though the big ceramic pots were empty, they had ideas for the kinds of flowers they could plant when it warmed up.

The house was painted a dark slate blue with white trim, and stone facings decorated the columns that held up the frame. A sign on the yellow front door said "Home Sweet Home."

"A girl could get used to this," Harper said.

"Don't get *too* comfortable. Remember, come mid-November, we're outta here," Mary said.

"Oh, I could never *live* here," Harper said. "But I plan to enjoy it while I can. When in Rome!"

It was a great setup. But Dot couldn't hang at the house. She went into the office every day, just as she had in the city.

That morning, ready to step into the big chill, she pressed play on *The Headlines* podcast from *The New York Times* before she opened the front door. She braced herself for the ten-minute walk to the office.

While she had settled into Wisconsin living fairly well, she missed being able to just walk a block to get whatever she needed from the local bodega or to pop over to her hot yoga studio.

Mary, the only one with a driver's license, had offered to take her to the office every day, but Dot insisted on walking. She didn't want to be one of those people who drove everywhere just because they lived in the suburbs.

Mary scoffed. "I'd drive ten feet to stay out of this cold."

"Why don't you just wear the Uggs your dad sent?"

"They make my feet look like blobs." Mary had temporarily left New York City, but she wasn't about to give up on her put-together self.

Dot had no problem wearing her big snow boots around town. She carried her work shoes in her backpack—cute black patent loafers that gave her a little lift. She wasn't as fashion-forward as Mary, but she wasn't about to clomp around the office with hot feet either.

She took a left outside the door. Their neighbor, Kristy Gunderson, was scraping the ice off her windshield before her hospital shift in the physical therapy department. Kristy personified Wisconsin nice.

"Hi, Dot! Good morning! Want a ride?"

"Good morning! No, thanks, I'm going to get my steps in!" Dot waved a mittened hand then glanced up and down the charming street. She stopped and turned. "Congrats on the Pack!"

"Awesome night, right?" The Packers had won the Super Bowl the night before. Dot had only been there a month, but she knew what a huge deal it was. The Crew had stayed up to watch the half-time show with America's football's princess, Taylor Swift—that was *their* Super Bowl.

Dot headed down the hill to Lincoln Street. Her podcast started, and as she walked, she learned about a major natural disaster in Comoros. She made a mental note to look that up on a map.

When she got to Main Street, she hung a right and walked the winding path along Cedar Creek, a river that gave the town's founders exactly what they needed to build a mill on its banks. The wind from the latest polar vortex ran right through town and hit her smack in the face.

"Okay. That's cold." She walked faster, almost running down the street, passing A Cut Above hair salon. That reminded her to schedule a blowout for Friday afternoon—it cost half the price of a shampoo and dry in the city. "I'm down," Mary said when they'd driven by their first week in town and saw the sign in the window.

Finally, she reached her new favorite bakery, Flour Power, to get a box of pastries for the team.

"Good morning, Mimi!" She'd made friends with the young baker, Mimi Downey. Small businesses were a big deal in Cedar Falls. Major chains, Dot learned, were banned within city limits, which made rents more affordable for the locals, and small businesses were patronized enthusiastically.

A few early birds were in Flour Power already, cozy in unzipped puffer coats, their hats and gloves hanging off the backs of their chairs. Huge arrangements of silk flowers decorated the windows with corresponding small vases of flowers on the bistro tables. The customers were drinking big steaming mugs of coffee and sat reading the weekly paper, *The Cedar Falls Gazette*, or scrolling on their phones. "Wi-fi always free."

"Hi, Dot! Good weekend?" Mimi's face was flush from the warmth of her ovens. "I saved a Schnecken for you." She reached behind her for one of the cinnamon sweet buns that looked like snails.

"Oh, I love those! They'd go down well back home," Dot said, thinking Freddy would sell out of them every morning from his cart on Sixth Avenue.

In addition to her own breakfast, Dot ordered a mix of bear claws, Danishes, and chocolate croissants. She paid with an FTW-issued credit card. The PAC didn't even need receipts. "We trust you," the finance officer said. Dot knew the Super PAC was flush with cash, but she was still careful with how much she spent. There would be no red flags on her watch.

"Let's take a pic," Dot said. She snapped a selfie of herself, Mimi, and the pastries. Then she posted it on her story saying, "Flour Power—the BEST in Cedar Falls!" She added Mimi's tags and hit send.

"I can't believe how many new followers I've gained since you first posted about us," Mimi said. "I appreciate it so much. Even if most of them live over a thousand miles away!"

"You never know—Flour Power could become a national chain," Dot said, dreaming big early in the morning and putting her mittens back on her hands. Then she picked up her order, waved to the morning coffee crowd, and wished everyone a good day.

She hoped for one, too, because at eight o'clock sharp, she had a call with Kitty Bell.

Chapter 15

When she got to the office, Dot held the box of pastries in one arm and opened the office door with the other. She twirled around and landed inside the warm room. She blinked a few times, stomped her feet to clear them of snow, and shook off the cold.

The space held several desks, a couple of printers, and a few signed posters of Democratic memorabilia from all the campaign stops politicians had made in Cedar Falls over the years.

"Good morning!" she called out. She knew someone was there because the smell of freshly brewed coffee filled the office. She couldn't wait for her first sip.

"Hi, Dot. Be right there." Of course, Rose Perkins was already in the office. Rose was one of the first people Dot met at the local DNC headquarters. She was eighty-two years old yet seemed a decade younger. She'd volunteered with the Democrats since she was young and John F. Kennedy was the party's nominee.

Rose had been a widow for three years. Her children and grandchildren still lived in the area. Along with a wide circle of friends and her work for the party, she was busy as ever.

"I brought a few treats for the team," Dot said, laying the pastry box next to the coffeepot and throwing her Schnecken in the microwave to warm it up.

Rose came around the corner, dressed in black knit pants, tall lace-up winter boots, a white turtleneck, and a Green Bay Packers hoodie. The sweatshirt was a gift from her grandson who worked at an AI start-up in Milwaukee.

"You're an angel." Rose chose a bear claw and grabbed a napkin. Then she poured coffee into two of the ceramic mix-and-match cups that had collected there over the years. No one had the heart to throw any of them away.

"Brats, Cheese, and Beers Can Save Democracy" was Dot's favorite.

Rose loved the white Clinton/Gore one. She was a longtime Bubba fan.

"In politics, you only fall in love once," she'd said when they first met and were getting to know each other. Dot wasn't sure she was in love with any of the candidates yet, but she fondly remembered President Obama from her childhood.

Dot had delicately brought up President Clinton's scandal with the intern. She'd watched an entire show about it on Amazon Prime. She still couldn't believe that the women's groups hadn't backed the women caught up in the president's scandals. She liked to believe that they would today and said as much to Rose.

"I'm not so sure of that," Rose had said. "I remember that I didn't think it was handled well at the time. And it certainly hurt the party. In fact, I believe it was one of the reasons Hillary didn't win when she ran in sixteen."

"Oh gosh, don't remind me. I cried the entire next day." Dot recalled how stunned her parents had been when Hillary lost.

"Well, if there's something I've learned over the years, it's that politicians are mere humans like the rest of us. And at some point, even the ones you love will let you down."

"Kind of like influencers," Dot said.

"What are those?" Rose asked, and when Dot went to explain, she saw the older woman was kidding. "I have grandchildren, you know."

"You got me!" Dot said. It wouldn't be the only time Rose surprised her.

Rose finished making her coffee to her liking with a packet of sugar and a dash of half and half. Then she clinked mugs with Dot.

"Congrats on the Packers!" Dot had passively watched the Sunday night game knowing that all of Wisconsin was transfixed.

"What a game! My family didn't go home until almost midnight—we stayed up to watch all the interviews and the partying. Who knows how the kids will do in school today?"

"It'll be a memory they have forever," Dot said, glad that Rose was a morning person like her. It made getting the day started so much nicer.

"Any sign of Fletcher?" Dot started to arrange chairs around the Polycom for the conference call.

"Not yet. But we'll hear him coming. That boy sure can make an entrance."

Fletcher Abbott was another For the Win volunteer doing a year in Wisconsin. A native of San Francisco, at twenty-seven, he was anxious to head east to New York. But first, he was spending the election season in Cedar Falls.

Fletcher was very tall with broad shoulders and a narrow waist. He had a sharp jawline, almond-shaped hazel eyes, foppish light brown hair, and an easy, wide smile. He turned all the girls' heads. Plus, he was friendly and approachable. His parents, early employees when Facebook went public, were donors to For the Win. Given all that, he and Dot found common ground right away. They could easily talk about high tech or politics.

"He's almost pretty," Mary had said when she, Dot, and Harper observed him from across the bar at the Badger Trap the first week they were in Cedar Falls. Dot and Fletcher had proposed a FTW "snow happy to meet you" cocktail party to introduce themselves to the local Democrats who worked in the office and volunteered on the campaigns. Free food and curiosity led to a good turnout, even in the freezing winter temps.

"I don't know. I mean, he's not my type." Dot looked at her nails and pretended he wasn't hot.

"Who are you trying to convince—me or you?" Mary asked.

"Doesn't matter to me anymore. I'm swearing off all good-looking guys," Harper cut in. "From now on, I'll only date nice guys nobody wants."

"Why can't you have nice *and* good looking?"

"You can only pick one." Harper sighed. "It's the way of the world. Or at least it is for me."

Dot stirred her vodka soda. She was *not* looking for love in Wisconsin. She was still getting over her breakup with Ryan. And while she didn't regret calling it quits with him, she missed the *idea* of him. Plus, she'd put off dating until she was back in the city—her new personal policy.

The thing was, Fletcher would be in Manhattan after the election, too. He'd graduated from Princeton two years ago and knew Kitty Bell from his time working with the College Dems. She recruited him to the FTW project when she'd recognized his parents' names among the big donors to the PAC. She'd given Fletcher his choice of purple state in which to volunteer. He'd chosen Wisconsin for the same reason as Dot: It had the most potential to flip from red to blue—a high-impact opportunity.

A bit of a nepo baby, Fletcher was living large. Not only did he have the FTW assignment, but he also already had a cool job offer in New York, regardless of who won in November. He was set to join an up-and-coming Democratic influencer incubator that was trying to beat the conservative podcasting world at their own game. Big donors were throwing tons of money at the problem, hoping some of it would stick. So far, no one had cracked the code, but Fletcher aimed to change that. They'd promised him his own podcast and everything he'd need to create content and build a following.

Fletcher's near-term plan made Dot a little uneasy and somewhat envious. Whereas he had his next moves all planned out, she was staring at a blank slate. She had nothing set up for after the election. But when she tried to picture herself as a Democratic influencer, she'd laugh. She liked to *listen* to podcasts, not rant and rave on them.

When she thought about it too much, she'd start a cycle of worry that was hard to stop. She actively had to shove aside thoughts about what would come next and trust that it would all work out. Because for the time being, she needed to prove herself to FTW.

She turned on the flat-screen monitor on the wall of the conference room and made sure that the Zoom login was working. She hated to have to scramble at the last minute to find she had the wrong link.

"Yoo-hoo, I'm home!" Fletcher came in, big and brash, and gave Rose a hug. "The Pack crushed it last night!"

Rose gave him a high five.

"Are you ever going to take off that swag, Rose?" he asked.

"I'm thinking it was good luck. I might wear it every day until the election!" she replied.

"Good thing green's your color!" He winked at her. Rose blushed. He had his charms.

"Morning, Dot," Fletcher called. "Thanks for the nosh!" He grabbed a Danish and a chocolate croissant and took a seat in the small conference room.

He took a bite of pastry and wiped his sticky hands on a paper napkin.

"Did you hear that we're likely to get another candidate? And just before the next debate. Crazy," Fletcher said.

"You're talking about the tech guy from Austin? One of the bros said yesterday that Texas is fool's gold for Democrats. But if he's going to throw his own money away, who's to stop him?" Dot asked.

Fletcher nodded in agreement. "I'm sure the DNC would rather he donate to winnable races. He'll probably throw a hundred million dollars of his own money . . . at his home state."

"And still lose by six or seven points," Dot agreed. "If he even makes it that far."

She checked her phone. It was almost eight. Time to log on to the Zoom and get this campaign going.

Chapter 16

Dot and Fletcher invited Rose to join the call since she was the best volunteer the Democrats had. Her knowledge of Wisconsin election history ran deep, and they needed her expertise.

Dot turned on their camera and unmuted the microphone. Kitty was there from her Georgetown house, waiting. She always seemed to be a step ahead of them.

"Kitty, hey gorgeous! It's great to see you!" Fletcher said.

Was that kind of greeting still allowed? Dot couldn't get over the super-bold way he flirted with the woman they reported to.

Kitty did look put together, though. She'd pulled her dark red hair into a sleek low bun and wore a deep purple cashmere crewneck with a thin gold chain and crystal chandelier earrings.

"Oh, stop, Fletch," she said, pretending to brush off the compliment.

Fletch? Dot took note of the nickname. They sure were chummy.

"Hi, Rose—it's been a while since I saw you last cycle. You never age! You'll have to tell me your secret." Kitty had volunteered for the DNC during the last presidential election. That's how she'd met Rose and made so many contacts that led to her running For the Win.

Rose laughed the compliment away. "It must be the climate, Kitty."

"And Dot—how's it going? Are you settling in?"

"Everything's great. The house is huge. Harper says she'll never go back to sharing a bathroom." Dot projected optimism and didn't bother telling Kitty about their adjustments to suburban Wisconsin living and Mary's worries that she'd never thaw out.

"Good, I'm glad. I want you to be comfortable. If there's anything you need, shoot me a note or just expense it."

Dot wasn't used to this kind of financial free rein. At the PR firm, she'd watched every penny and was careful not to expense anything that would draw attention.

"We have a lot of work to do getting ready for the debate," Kitty said.

"Before we start on that," Fletcher said, "do you have any polling updates? Just so we're not flying blind."

"Glad you asked. This came in overnight." Kitty threw up a PowerPoint slide on their shared screen. Dot, Fletcher, and Rose leaned in.

"As you can see, we have a bit of a challenge. Overall, Wisconsin voters are saying they prefer Republicans to Democrats by about five points. That's the number we need to change." Kitty used her stylus to circle the polls.

"How does that compare to the last election?" Dot asked.

"Back then, at this point in the cycle, it was a little closer but not much different. So, to prevent another loss, we need to drive up the Republicans' unfavorables and increase our favorables. It's going to take some time and effort. And money. But we have plenty of all three."

"Do you have any numbers on the top issues for likely voters?" Fletcher asked, noting the delta between being registered to vote versus likely to vote. The difference between those two groups could swing a close election.

Kitty switched to another slide.

"Here's what the national polling shows. The DNC didn't do a state-specific survey yet. As you can see, the economy is number one across the board for both parties. But after that, Republicans and Democrats diverge. Republicans say they're concerned about government spending, crime, and immigration. And the Democrats mention health care, climate change, and abortion rights—in that order."

Rose scowled.

"What do you think, Rose?" Kitty had picked up on the older woman's skepticism.

"Well, I respect the DNC, but I just don't know many Democrats around here who prioritize that way. And last time, we got so caught up in what the DNC thought that we ended up losing. In my humble opinion."

"I agree," Kitty said. "That's one of the reasons I wanted to do this project. We need to listen to the people *there* and not let Washington drive."

"Exactly," Rose said. "The voters I know care mostly about jobs, the price of food and gas, the economic future for their children. That includes health care in their minds. And then way down the list is climate change and abortion. If we follow the national trends, we won't win here."

"You're preaching to the choir," Kitty agreed. "I just need to play nice with the priorities of the DNC while delivering Wisconsin by focusing on what we know matters."

"It reminds me of 2016 when we were begging for visits to the state from campaign headquarters and the DNC, because we could feel Wisconsin slipping away," Rose reminisced. "But oh no, they had their fancy data. Those Brooklyn kids believed they knew more about Wisconsin than we did."

"And look how that turned out," Kitty said. Then, moving the conversation along, added, "I promise we're not going to let that happen again. But Rose, don't be shy. Let us know what you're thinking and hearing."

"You betcha," Rose said. Dot smiled at her sweet singsong of a midwestern accent.

"Dot, I love that you found out your neighbors didn't vote last time around. Do you think they're gettable this time? They can't be the only ones who stayed home, looking at the numbers."

"You're talking about the Gundersons. Yes, I think so. If we have the right candidate. They're motivated to, as they put it, 'see change.' We're having dinner at their house next week, so I'll see what else I can pick up." Dot made a mental note to remember to buy a hostess gift.

"Speaking of candidates, should we switch gears to the debate?" Fletcher opened his tan Moleskine to take notes. "I'm thinking we need one or two volunteers per candidate?"

"Whatever you think we need," Kitty said. "My main objective is for everyone to walk away with good feelings about For the Win, so they pass good words back to the DNC and the eventual presidential campaign once we have a candidate."

Rose raised her hand. "I have several volunteers already lined up. I'll get their contact information to Fletcher today."

"Great. Dot, could you make sure to order the volunteers something nice to thank them? And maybe they should have matching T-shirts or even polos for the night? With the FTW logo? I like that idea. I'll order them. Oh, and Dot—could you organize a nice gift bag for the candidates—good local stuff that they'll love and not just throw away?" Kitty's ideas came fast.

"On it." Dot noted her assignments and was amazed again that money was no matter at all. Then, sensing an opening, she decided to throw out an idea she'd had in the shower that morning.

"So, I wanted to run something by you. Since we arrived in Cedar Falls, I've noticed that there are a *ton* of community events here. There's something every weekend—a potluck, a dinner dance, a festival, live music, fundraisers. That kind of thing." It seemed to Dot there were almost more things to do in Cedar Falls than in New York.

"What if For the Win sponsored a chartered bus that would take people from Cedar Falls to the debate and back?" she continued. "We could serve a boxed lunch on the way and have local beer and snacks on the return. And then, because they'll have signed up, we'll also have their contact info for future calls and door knocking."

"Love that. Smart." Kitty beamed at Dot's suggestion. "Let me confirm I can get enough seats for inside the auditorium at the debate. How many do you think? Fifty or so? Yes, I think so." Kitty often answered her own questions. "The DNC will *love* it."

Dot nodded and started a to-do list. She loved to please.

After they wrapped up the call, Rose went to call some of her veteran volunteers and Dot and Fletcher went over their meeting notes to make sure they'd not missed anything.

"So, you know Kitty pretty well?" Dot asked, trying to casually get some intel.

"Oh, yeah. When we were with College Democrats, we hung out with the same crowd at events," he said. "She's incredibly driven."

"Tell me about it. I feel like I have a lot of ambition, but she's next level."

"Well, she's also highly motivated to win. And not just because she wants Democrats to get elected."

"How so?" Dot asked.

"Well, for one thing, there's the money. There's a huge win bonus for her if she can prove that For the Win helped get back the White House."

"A win bonus?" Dot asked. "I've never heard of that."

"Basically, if the Democratic candidate wins in November, she gets the dough." He made a gesture of rubbing cash between his fingers and thumb.

"How much are we talking?"

"It's at least $500,000. My dad said that most of these PAC directors won't do it for less. They take a lower salary but have the potential for a big payday if they succeed."

"That's so much money. I can't even imagine that number in my bank account." Dot felt suddenly terribly inadequate and naïve.

"But perhaps even more than the money, Kitty really wants to be seen as *the* go-to Democrat on the Georgetown cocktail circuit. My mom says she's got a great gift for hosting and brings lots of people together to help make connections. People go there to network and gossip, which is the most valuable currency in Washington. So, if the Democrats win, she'll get the money and likely a job in the White House. Then everyone will want to come to be one of her guests."

"And reach all of her goals before she's thirty," Dot said, realizing the stakes for Kitty were even higher than she'd known.

DOT, FLETCHER, AND Rose worked through the afternoon and had a good plan underway for the debate bus charter. Then, as the winter sun set around 5:15 p.m. and the sky turned into swirls of pink, Dot felt her phone buzz. It was a text from Harper.

"Mary's cooking. Big scene. She's bringing Staten Island to Cedar Falls. Home soon?"

"20 mins." She added a red wine emoji. Harper gave her a thumbs-up. They'd bought a couple of bottles at the local wine shop, Pour Decisions, over the weekend.

Dot called over to where Fletcher was sitting. "Would you mind locking up tonight? Apparently, Mary's making a big dinner."

"You got it, Dottie."

Dottie? Dot's brow creased at the nickname.

"Dot-erino?" Fletcher gave it another shot, but her head tilted to the side. She didn't like it.

"Too much too soon?" he asked.

Dot nodded.

"How about we go with . . . Dot?"

"Perfect," she said, then she spent the last few minutes handling emails and tidying up the kitchen area. She wanted everyone to know she wasn't above any task.

Before leaving the office, she looked at the February picture of her Manhattan calendar—a winter scene of ice skaters at the Wollman Rink in Central Park. A pang of longing passed through her. She always loved getting Mary and Harper to join her for a skate, even if Mary was a bit like Bambi with her long legs not quite steady on the blades and Harper held her hand so tightly it cut off her circulation.

While she was putting her all into her work for FTW, she very much missed the city. Dot drew her red Sharpie across that Monday's date.

They were one day closer to Election Day . . . and their return to the city.

Chapter 17

Mary started the FTW-provided Jeep Grand Cherokee before opening the garage door.

"Four degrees. This is insane!"

She turned the heat on full blast and warmed her seat and the steering wheel before reversing into the street. She wondered how people survived before these luxuries.

That afternoon, she wore a silver puffer coat over a long, black turtleneck tunic and dark gray yoga pants with tall striped socks and her sneakers. Not her usual outfit, but she made exceptions for the weather. It wasn't like she was going to run into anyone she knew.

She was headed to the store for ingredients to make her Nonna's spaghetti and meatballs. She craved a taste of home.

As she drove, Mary sang along to Sabrina Carpenter, a flashback to the song of the summer that had shocked her mother with its lyrics. In the seclusion of the Jeep, Mary belted out the most profane line. "Brilliant," she thought.

Mary didn't mind running errands for The Crew. The grocery store was her domain. Besides, she was the only one who really knew how to drive. Dot and Harper were like a lot of city kids, just taking the train, taxis, and Ubers to get around.

Mary was the opposite. Her father had insisted she learn how to drive a stick shift in case she was ever stuck somewhere. "Survival skills," he'd called it.

She took to driving right away, especially in the city. Sometimes she'd take her dad's Mercedes sedan across the Verrazzano Bridge, along the BQE to the tunnel and into the city north all the way up the FDR, cut across from the Harlem River Drive, then snake her way south down the

West Side Highway before heading back home to Staten Island. It gave her time to think.

As a typical New Yorker, she was insanely aggressive in the car, which often gave her passengers a bit of a heart attack.

"Merge or die," her brother Frankie said the first time she navigated through Times Square.

With her combat experience in the city, driving in Cedar Falls was too easy. There was light traffic and very polite drivers.

At the store, she whipped around putting items in her cart. She bought a jar of Ragu. "Forgive me, Mother." She wasn't talking to the Virgin Mary, but to her own, who never served anything but homemade sauce for dinner.

Everyone was friendly at the Piggly Wiggly. When she couldn't find fennel seed, she asked a young man working at the store for help. He said he'd never heard of it.

"Let me go ask my grandma—she's working the register."

He came back with a cute, owlish woman with sparkly blue eyes wearing a red uniform smock. She led them two aisles over from where they were.

"Son, it's right here. Always in aisle three."

"Got it, Grandma."

"Thank you so much," Mary said to the woman, missing her Nonna. Turning to the young man she said, "Be good to her. She's a treasure!"

The boy put an arm around his grandmother and squeezed.

"Always," he said.

"He's my favorite. Just don't tell his brothers." She poked him in the ribs then went back to her post. Did every grandmother play this favorites game?

When Mary went through the checkout, the boy offered to carry her bags to the car. She nearly turned him down.

"You're not even wearing a coat."

"Oh, it's not that bad out," he said. "Besides, I like the cold."

Were they even the same species? She reached in her bag for a five-dollar bill. Her dad had taught her always to have a little cash for tips. "Makes the world go 'round," he'd said.

The boy seemed surprised.

"Thank you, ma'am."

Ma'am?

Mary snuck a glance in the rearview mirror before leaving the parking lot, vowing to use more eye cream.

ABOUT TWO BLOCKS from the house, police lights flashed behind her. Strange, Mary thought. The streets were so quiet. Who could they be after? She thought there must be an emergency up ahead.

She pulled over to let the police cruiser pass. But it pulled in behind her. What in the world?

She waited for the officer, a little unnerved. It had been ages since she was pulled over. Not since that time at the Jersey Shore after a night out at the Point Pleasant Beach boardwalk a few younger and dumber years ago. She'd been speeding on the Garden State Parkway to get home by curfew. Her high school friends were in the car with her, and all of them were still in their bikini tops and cutoffs. She'd blinked wide-eyed at the officer, and he'd sent her on her way suggesting she slow down. She promised she would. Then she raced home to Staten Island before her parents put out an Amber alert.

She rolled down the window and turned off the car. A freezing blast hit her in the face and made her eyes water. She heard the crunch of the policeman's boots on the frozen street.

"Evening," he said. "License and registration, please."

He was taller than the Jeep and had to bend down to look in the window. He wore a thick navy blue ski jacket and matching hat that said "Police" in white lettering. He had bright blue eyes, a chiseled jawline that was only slightly sharper than his cheekbones, and a small scar on his chin.

"Hello." Mary's tone was cool.

"Do you know why I pulled you over tonight?"

"Boredom?"

"Wrong. I've never been bored a day in my life."

He smiled out of one side of his mouth. She noticed a dimple in his left cheek.

"So, what did I do? Or . . . what do you *think* you saw me do?"

"Aha. Let me guess—a lawyer?"

"As a matter of fact, yes."

"Well, counselor, you rolled through the stop sign back there. And stop means stop."

"So, I've heard. And said."

She needed to pull it together. She decided not to fight. She took a deep breath.

"Okay. Let me try again." She turned toward him with a smile. "Officer, I thought I stopped. I promise to pay more attention in the future."

"Now we're getting somewhere. I'll be right back." He took her documents and returned to his car.

Mary shivered in her seat, unsure if she was allowed to restart the Jeep, roll up the window, and turn on the heat while the officer checked whether she had a rap sheet. A few minutes felt like forever. Was this a violation of her civil rights?

In the side mirror, she saw him walking back to her driver's-side window.

"What's the verdict?" She decided to try some charm, hoping to avoid a ticket.

"How's this? I'll give you a warning—this time. Take it easy. This isn't Manhattan."

"Yeah, I noticed." She tried to hide her snark, but it wasn't easy.

"With that accent, I had a hunch you weren't from around here. We'd have met before," he said.

"Hopefully not like this."

"Definitely not like this." There was that smile again. "So . . . New York. What brings you to town?"

"The weather. And the nightlife."

He laughed and patted the top of her car. "Okay, ma'am. You're free to go."

A second "ma'am" in less than ten minutes? There wasn't enough eye cream in all of Sephora.

"Thanks . . . and sorry about the stop sign." She gave him a genuine smile.

As she pulled back into the road, she honked a goodbye.

She snuck a glance in the rearview mirror. He stood watching her go.

She thought he was probably wondering how a girl like her ended up in a place like this.

If he only knew.

Chapter 18

A few days later, after finishing up her writing for the day, Harper texted Mary from a bar on Main Street.

"Found a cute spot. Come meet me. The Sin Bin. Next to the coffee shop."

"Sin Bin? Doesn't sound like your kind of place. More like one of mine! Be there in 30."

Mary closed her laptop. She'd spent hours reviewing briefs for a class action lawsuit that was brought against a banking client. She was way ahead of schedule, so she could bang out a short brief of her own in the morning before the lead partner in New York even got to the office.

Mary threw her hair in a messy bun and touched up her makeup. She stood in her closet and considered what to wear to a place called the Sin Bin. It had warmed up to twenty-five degrees and hadn't snowed in a week. Almost felt like a heat wave.

Feeling casual, she chose a navy blue silk shirt, an olive-green suede blazer, dark blue jeans, and black high heels. She threw on a long emerald brushed cashmere coat, grabbed her black sling bag and keys, and headed downtown. It took just five minutes to get there and park.

Harper was set up in the corner against the far wall, under a giant TV screen. She had on light blue wide-leg jeans, a navy turtleneck, and a hot pink puffy vest with ruffled sleeves that she'd found in a local shop called Vintage Vibes.

Harp's eyes lit up when she saw Mary. She cleared a space, putting her notebook and laptop into a giant cloth tote bag.

Mary gave her a hug and took a stool opposite her. "So, *this* is a Sin Bin? It looks like a sports bar to me. I was expecting something a little more . . . dangerous?"

"Ha! The Sin Bin is where hockey players sit when they get in trouble. It's like being sent to your room to think about what you did."

"I didn't know you knew so much about hockey."

"My dad took my brother and me to Rangers games a few times a year," Harper said and looked around the bar. "He'd love this—especially all the memorabilia. When he was growing up in Canada they watched hockey every Saturday night. He said it was a national obsession."

She pointed out the vintage hockey sticks that hung down between the exposed beams on the ceiling, the framed jerseys on the wall, and some of the most iconic moments in hockey captured in a large hand-painted mural opposite the bar. A huge mirror in a gorgeous wood frame was mounted behind the bottles of booze.

"Love that. My dad and I used to go to games together, too, but he was a Mets fan. His favorite player was Mike Piazza. We met him once at a pizza place near our house. My dad never stopped talking about it."

"Maybe in the spring the three of us can go to a game in Milwaukee. Big weekend out."

"I feel like we're putting a lot of to-do items in the spring bucket," Mary said. She pointed at Harper's laptop. "Get very far today?"

"A solid chapter and a half. I think. I keep second-guessing myself."

"Sounds like normal novelist neurosis." She reached for Harper's hand and gave it a squeeze.

A busboy walked by, and Harper flagged him down.

"Hi, could we order?"

A couple of minutes later, a tall man in a tucked-in flannel shirt, well-worn jeans, Harley Davidson boots, and with a white bar towel thrown over one of his sturdy shoulders came to their table. He had medium-brown hair pulled into a small ponytail at the base of his neck. He smiled, showing a small dimple in his left cheek. Though she'd never met him before, he looked vaguely familiar to Mary.

"Hi, I'm Tommy. This is my place. Was glad to see you working here this afternoon, but didn't want to bother you. Everything good?"

"All good. Loved the Coldplay mix from earlier."

"Bar standard. Everyone seems mildly okay with Coldplay. Where's that accent from?"

"East of here," Harper said, then fearing that was rude, quickly added, "Brooklyn, actually."

"Well, welcome to Cedar Falls," Tommy said. "What can I get you two?"

"What do you recommend?" Mary asked, looking over the menu.

"Do you like beer?"

"Not really," Harper said. "How about vodka soda with lime?"

"Tito's okay?"

She gave him a thumbs-up.

"Do you have a local beer?" Mary asked.

"Try the Spotted Cow. Only sold in Wisconsin."

"Really? Why?"

"Gotta keep enough stock for the locals. We drink a lot of beer."

"Well, how can I resist with a recommendation like that. I'll take a Spotted Cow." Now she was curious.

He rapped his knuckles on their table. "Coming right up, ladies."

"He was cute, right?" Mary raised her eyebrows at Harper. "You were flirting."

"I was not! Besides, remember . . . I'm swearing off cute!" Harper was sticking to her plan.

"Whatever you have to tell yourself," Mary said as she looked around the bar. "Guys are different here than back home, don't you think?"

"For sure. Do you think that's for the better?"

"Maybe." She saw a few potentials in the bar. "Jury's still out!"

"Do you think they're all Republicans?" Harper asked as she observed the patrons. She assumed they were.

"I don't know. Maybe. But I'm not interested in how they *vote*, Harp. They're kind of cute. In, like, a rustic way."

"They don't seem too into politics, anyway, going by their hats. They're more into the Packers and whatever animal those antlers belong to. Lots of camo going on around here."

Just then they heard shouting near their end of the bar. Turning, they saw two guys push their chairs away, toppling them onto the floor. They stood chest-to-chest, arguing about something. A couple of young women pleaded with them to chill out, but they shook them off.

Harper saw Tommy pick up his phone while coming to stand between the fighters, but the guys started shoving each other harder.

Mary pushed her stool back to get a better view, and Harper strained to see.

While Tommy jumped out of the way and spoke into his phone, the bartender hurdled over the bar and pushed his way between them to break it up. But then he got hit in the jaw and held his hand to his face, scrunching his eyes in pain.

The yelling got louder, and their girlfriends begged the men to stop. The taller of the two fighters got the other one in a headlock and was asking his opponent if he'd had enough. Several customers started moving away from the melee and two of them crouched behind the bar.

Finally, a couple of cops came in. "Knock it off. Now!" one said with authority. Each of them held one of the guys while the fighters caught their breath and glared at each other.

That's who Tommy must have called—the cops.

"Is my brother with you?" he yelled over to them.

"He's right behind us."

"Thanks. I don't know these guys. And I don't want this kind of reputation. We just opened!"

"You got it, Tommy."

Mary grabbed her keys and eased off the stool. "Let's get out of here, before another hockey fight breaks out," she said. She had to admit she loved watching the drama of a good bar fight as long as no one got seriously hurt. "We can call Dot and go get a pizza."

Seeing them preparing to leave, Tommy rushed over. "I'm so sorry. I swear this has never happened!" He looked disappointed they were going.

"Oh, it's okay—we just . . . well, we'll come back another time," Harper said. She wanted to stay but followed Mary's lead.

"What were they fighting about—run out of Spotted Cow?" Mary asked, throwing her coat over her arm.

"Had to be about a girl. They looked like a couple of bucks in rutting season," he said.

"Does that happen in here, too?" Mary asked.

"Not yet. But the night is young."

"Something to look forward to then." Mary started toward the door.

"It was nice to meet you, Tommy. I'm Harper." She stuck out her hand to shake his. "And that was Mary."

He shook her hand as he ran his left hand over his hair.

"Promise you'll come back? Drinks on me next time."

"Deal," Harper said.

As the girls walked out, a policeman was pulling open the door and bumped into Mary.

He instantly recognized her and smiled. There was that dimple again.

"New York! Fancy seeing you here. I should have figured you'd cause trouble again. They throw you out of the bar?"

"Hardly! *And* I never even got my beer," Mary said cooly. "But I'm glad you finally showed up. Maybe you can focus on the real troublemakers for a change."

"Oh, you're a troublemaker. I could tell that the moment I set eyes on you."

"Well now you can watch me walk away."

Harper had no idea what was going on. Mary grabbed her hand, looked both ways, and dashed across the street.

"That's jaywalking, New York! I could write you a ticket for that."

Mary gestured with her right hand. And she wasn't saying goodbye.

Chapter 19

Dot's chartered bus idea was coming together nicely.

Kitty had secured a block of fifty seats for their guests, right in front of the debate stage. Thirty seats were already taken.

Rose got a few of her friends from church to say yes. She'd promised them cans of Spotted Cow on the way back.

Fletcher was posting on social to get the word out and build For the Win's brand as a player. And he was beta testing a new app with ActBlue to keep track of everyone's contact information—possibly the most valuable part of the operation.

The family-owned And That's a Wrap just off Main on Washington Street was on board to make boxed dinners with a choice of buffalo chicken salad, ham on cheddar, turkey with muenster, or roasted vegetables and sprouts.

Over at Flour Power, Mimi immediately posted one of the flyers and agreed to make sweet treats for the snack bags.

"I'm thinking Wisconsin-shaped icebox cookies, frosted with royal blue?" Dot suggested.

"On it." Mimi planned to make lots of extras they could pass out in the greenroom.

That afternoon, Dot thought she'd pop into the Reader Falls Bookshop to try her luck there. She'd been meaning to visit the shop—she loved a good independent bookstore. When she was very young, she'd spend hours in Coliseum Books with her grandmother. She missed that store—and of course that special woman who loved her.

She put the *No Lie with Brian Tyler Cohen* podcast on to listen to while she walked. The topic was beating Republicans at their own game in the culture wars—as it had been for as long as she was listening to liberal podcasts. Her father teased her that she'd never have survived the Rush Limbaugh days.

"Who's Rush Limbaugh?" she'd asked.

"Oh my gosh. Google it," he'd said, exasperated at feeling older than his years in that moment.

Mercifully, the weather had given them a break from the extreme cold. The sun shone on blond-brick historical buildings that made up almost all downtown Cedar Falls. In some ways, they reminded her of the Buckley.

She stopped for a moment on the bridge to look at the frozen Cedar Creek under her and admired a mural of Wisconsin history called *Founded 1862* that covered the entire side of the best clothing stores in town, Mills and Twills.

Feeling the chill, she moved along and reached her destination. As she opened the door to the bookstore, a little bell rang, and she smelled the moldy scent of old books. The store was warm; a little stuffy, a little dusty. Thick, faded antique carpets covered well-worn hardwood floors, and the building's original tin tiles lined the ceiling.

The bookcases heaved, and the shelves weren't level; you had to tilt your head more than usual to read the titles on the spines.

The store was divided with fiction on the right, nonfiction on the left, with a special section for "state and local authors" and the history of Cedar Falls and Wisconsin near the front window. She picked up *Raft of Stars* by Andrew Graff—she liked the cover. She tucked it under her arm to purchase before she left the store.

Distressed leather couches and chairs were placed all around; seats where customers could sink in and stay awhile. A reading corner for kids was set up in the back. It had colorful beanbags and Bucky Badger held a sign for a children's reading hour, 4 p.m. Wednesdays and 10 a.m. Saturdays.

Dot noticed a local artwork display on one wall, and a big community board with ads for piano lessons, babysitting, tutoring, and a polar bear ice plunge (Never! she thought.)

She looked around for someone to ask permission from before tacking her flyer up.

A small-boned woman of about sixty with blond hair cut in a short bob and bright blue eyes was standing by the new releases moving books around. She wore a navy turtleneck under a long-sleeved plaid flannel shirt, jeans, and lace-up boots that looked like they'd been through a lot.

"Excuse me, do you work here?" Dot used her quiet bookstore voice.

"Not anymore. Spent several years and nearly half of my paychecks on books after high school here, though." The woman laughed and stuck out her hand. "I'm Grace Taylor."

"Hi, Grace. Nice to meet you. Dot Clark." They shook hands. Grace had a firm grip for such a small person.

"Are you new to town?" Grace asked.

"Yes, I'm from Manhattan and working with a Democratic group through the election."

"Aha. I've only ever been to Big Appleton."

"You've never been to the city?" Dot couldn't believe that. She thought everyone had been to New York at least once. "Oh, you must go. You'd love it!"

"Well, it's hard to get away with the farm, but I'd like to go one day." She gestured around the new releases. "And all these books seem to have a connection to it somehow. I've read so much about New York I almost feel like I know the place. Seems dangerous. And romantic. And exciting, of course."

"Oh, it is. It's . . . everything." Dot felt personally responsible to make sure everyone loved New York as much as she did. "*This* town, however, is just totally adorable."

"Yes. It's a wonderful place to live. Been here my entire life. We work hard to keep it the way it is. Outside forces are always trying to get their noses under the tent." She gestured toward the front door at the outside forces. "Anyway, was there a book you're looking for? Maybe I can help. I still know my way around."

"I'm definitely getting this book," she said, holding up the novel she'd already picked up. "But first, I'm wondering if I could post a flyer on the notice board." She handed one over. "It's an invitation for a free round-trip bus to the Democratic debate in Madison next week."

"A debate already?" She put the back of her hand to her forehead. "It's hard to believe it's that time again. We never got over the last election. Or the one before that." Grace sighed.

"I can imagine what it's like during elections season, especially since both sides need Wisconsin in order to win."

"Well, it's terrible. You can't even turn on the TV toward the end of it. But we'll get through it. We always do. At any rate, I'm sure the owners would be happy to let you do that. They're probably in the back. I'll go check."

Grace disappeared and Dot picked up a couple of titles she'd seen on BookTok and set them aside to buy with the one she already had. Buying books was one of her indulgences and she realized she could just check these out on the online library. But she loved the hard copy. And besides, she could share them with Mary and Harper. A mini book club with wine was one of her favorite weeknight events.

A few minutes later, Grace returned with an older couple who walked arm in arm. Dot guessed them to be in their late seventies. The man had a kind face with blue eyes and was mostly bald with just a little bit of gray hair sprouting above his ears and around the back of his head. His wife had a pretty shade of white hair that she wore in a medium-length pageboy cut, parted on the side. She had creamy white skin and twinkly brown eyes and wore cherry-red lipstick.

"Ted and Jeanie Jankowski, meet Dot. She's new to town."

"Dot, what a pleasure." Ted used both of his warm hands to shake Dot's. And Jeanie opened her arms and pulled her into a strong, grandma-type embrace.

"I'm a hugger—can't help it," she said in a British accent. Dot squeezed back—it felt good.

"Grace says you're working on the election for the Democrats. Ted will *love* hearing about that." She leaned in and whispered, "He's one of yours."

"And *she's* a Republican, so I give her a hard time," he said, winking at his wife and putting his arm around her waist. "You must know Rose. Great gal. Went to high school with my older brother."

Dot gushed about Rose and explained her connection through For the Win and the bus trip.

She handed Ted a flyer.

"Well, this looks interesting. Heck, I'd like to go. How about you, Jeanie?"

"Pass! I don't want to get in trouble for muttering under my breath every time they drive me up the wall," she said, elbowing him in the ribs. Dot picked up on their ease with each other.

"Wonderful! I'll put you on the list, Mr. Jankowski." Dot took the business card he offered her. "That's a tradition we should bring back," she thought. "To heck with QR codes."

"Call me Ted, please. And give me some of those flyers," Ted said. "I'll take them to my men's group. We're meeting in a little bit at the Kozy Kitchen for our weekly get-together. I bet Fred would want to go."

"You're all so kind. I should have come in sooner," Dot said. "I love to read, and your store is wonderful. Feels like it has some history."

"Oh yes. We've been here since the seventies—that's like ancient history to a young woman like yourself." Jeanie looked around the store. "It's holding together okay, but we're getting up there."

"And it's tough to compete in the book trade nowadays," Ted said. "Sometimes it feels like we're more of a community center than a business. And we love that, don't get me wrong. I think every community needs a bookstore to keep strong."

"My grandmother always said the same," Dot said. "Even in New York."

"You two don't need to worry about the store," Grace said, reassuring them. "Something will work out."

The bell rang and in walked a man of about thirty years old, six foot two and very solidly built. He had black hair and a red flush on his cheeks. He wore sunglasses on top of his head, a Carhartt coat, jeans, and workmen's boots.

"Danny Dawson, as I live and breathe!" Jeanie opened her arms to hug him. He let her do her thing, then he kissed Grace on the cheek, and shook Ted's hand. "Danny, this is Dot. She's new to town."

"Hi, Dot." He shook her hand gently. His hand was large and rough from working outdoors. So different from the guys she knew back home.

"It's nice to meet you," she said, immediately reluctant to let go of his warm hand.

"And you." He had sad but beautiful dark brown eyes. A spark ran up her spine when he smiled at her. He let go of her hand and gestured around the store.

"Jeanie, can you help me find a book for Lacey? She loves poetry but I don't have a clue."

Poetry? So, he was taken, Dot supposed. She couldn't help a pang of disappointment. Then felt silly for feeling disappointed.

"I have a couple titles that might work. Let me show you."

Jeanie led Danny to a section in the back of the store. Dot talked with Ted and Grace for a few more minutes. Then Danny checked out at the register and said goodbye to everyone, ringing the bell as he walked out the door.

Jeanie came back over to the new releases table. "I love that boy."

"Me too," Grace said.

"His wife's lucky to have such a romantic husband," Dot said.

"Danny? No, no. He's not married. The book is for the nurse who took care of his mom when he was in college. She died of breast cancer his junior year," Jeanie said.

"Oh. I'm so sorry to hear that. No wonder he looked so sad." Dot felt bad for jumping to conclusions. But noted that he was unattached.

"Unfortunately, he carries around a lot of grief," Ted said. "After playing college football over in Madison, he got engaged to his longtime girlfriend, Sadie Tibbets. She was a pistol, that one. Loved him like crazy. Went to all his games."

Dot noticed the use of past tense regarding Sadie. "What happened to her?"

"Oh, it was terrible," Jeanie said. "To make a long story short, she was killed by a drunk driver just about two years ago now."

"That's absolutely terrible," Dot said, wincing at the thought.

They all looked out the window, watching Danny get into his truck.

"Did the driver . . . ?" Dot started to ask about his fate but Grace interrupted her.

"Nope. Not even a scratch," Grace said.

"But he's serving a double life sentence," Ted added.

"Was there someone else in the car?"

"Well . . . yes. Danny and Sadie's unborn baby girl. She was eight months pregnant," Grace said.

Dot gasped.

"They were engaged when she found out she was pregnant," Jeanie explained. "They postponed the wedding until she was due. They wanted their daughter to be at their wedding."

"He always wanted to get married and have a family." Ted added, "He wanted to be a father. Never knew his own."

Grace began straightening the books on the table. "He's like a son to me. Been friends with my three boys since they were kids."

"Well, he's certainly fortunate to have you," Dot said, and with that sad and sober end to their friendly chat, she thought she better get going. She threw her backpack back on her shoulder.

"Could I buy these before I go?" She added the latest from Patti Callahan Henry and handed it to Jeanie.

"Oh, yes. I love her books. Did you read the last one? It was so good." They talked about books for a few more minutes. They had similar tastes in fiction.

Finally, needing to get back to work, Dot made a move toward the door.

"Ted, I'll see you on the bus!" Dot said, the bell ringing as she stepped outside.

"And don't be a stranger!" Jeanie called to her.

"Oh, I'll be back with my girlfriends. They'll love this place. Thanks again!"

As she went out the door and turned right to head back to the office, she didn't bother putting in her AirPods. Instead, she thought about the new people she'd just met, and of Danny Dawson and what he'd been through. She guessed that you never really knew what people were dealing with on the inside.

Something her doorman Albert had told her back in New York came to mind. "Everyone is always going through something."

Wasn't that the truth.

Chapter 20

Debate day finally arrived.

Kitty had flown in from D.C. the night before to ride with her For the Win team to the University of Wisconsin for the event. She'd stayed the night next to the Democratic offices at a boutique hotel called Maple and Main.

"Sorry it isn't a four-star," Dot said when she arrived. She wasn't sure why she felt the need to apologize. The Inn was adorable.

"It's perfect," Kitty said, though she eyed the chintz fabric with a skeptical eye. "I like quaint."

Dot wasn't sure she believed her but appreciated the effort at feigning comfort. She and Kitty had a quick drink at the self-serve bar in the hotel sitting room and caught up. She briefed her on the plans for the bus ride to Madison.

"It sounds like you've thought of everything," Kitty said.

"Team effort." Dot wanted to make sure Rose, Fletcher, and the volunteers got due credit.

"It's appreciated," Kitty said. "And if all goes well, we'll win in November."

"And you'll get a win bonus," Dot said, her hand immediately flying to her mouth in shock that she'd just said that.

Kitty froze for a moment but recovered, a softness coming over her eyes. She nodded slowly and waved her hand dismissively. "That's right. It's standard for all consultants, though. It isn't something special just for me." Her voice had a defensive bite.

"Oh, I think it's great," Dot said, trying to recover and lighten the moment. "And I sure hope we win. And that you get your bonus."

"There's a lot more riding on all this than the bonus, which isn't that much money anyway," Kitty said.

Dot tried to hide the skepticism she felt. To her, half a million dollars was . . . a half a million dollars.

Kitty took a sip of wine and continued, "After all, we have a country to save."

"Indeed," Dot said, matching Kitty's grave tone.

Kitty laughed, giving Dot's shoulder a small push. "Come on, don't be so serious."

Dot decided to embrace the moment and laughed, too.

"Tell me more. What else is happening around the state I should know about?" Kitty sat back ready to listen to whatever information Dot could share about voter preferences and local concerns. They chatted for another thirty minutes, and then they both decided it was time to get some sleep.

On her walk home that night, feeling safe in the quiet suburban town, Dot thought how awkward the bonus talk had been, but admitted how Kitty had been very open about it. "And why shouldn't she get paid what other consultants got if they turned in a victory?" Dot thought. She vowed to be more like Kitty Bell and not care so much what others thought about her.

But she'd have to do that another day. For now, she needed to focus on job one—the debate.

THE NEXT MORNING, Kitty sat with Rose at the front of the bus, looking chic in tall, high-heeled boots, a black leather skirt, and a royal-blue silk turtleneck and matching felt-wool blazer. Her engagement ring was blinding.

"Is she marrying a royal?" Harper asked, sitting next to Dot, and well out of Kitty's earshot.

"Almost. In Washington, he's definitely a princeling: a high-flying lobbyist named Casey Morgan."

"Sounds like they make the perfect couple," Harper said. "There's gotta be a catch."

"I've been looking. Haven't found one yet," Dot said.

Rose had finally taken off her Packers swag and wore an ivory twinset, blue knit pants from Eileen Fisher, and her white "dress" sneakers. A vintage red, white, and blue donkey pin she'd had since Walter Mondale's campaign completed her outfit.

"I've never been able to wear heels like that," they heard Rose say to Kitty, pointing to her boots. "They're very . . . sexy."

Kitty placed a hand on her arm. "Don't be surprised if I'm crying by the end of the night. They're already killing me."

The bus rolled along Highway 60 to Madison. The guests ate their made-to-order wraps, and Mimi's "Make Wisconsin Blue Again" frosted cookies were a big hit. She'd even thought to bring wet wipes for everyone so that they didn't smear blue dye on their clothes.

After lunch, a local struggling comic who Dot hired for entertainment led a Wisconsin trivia contest from the front of the bus with a microphone:

- *Name the cheese that was invented in Wisconsin but sounds like a European country? (It's very holey. Swiss!)*
- *In what Wisconsin city was splinter-free toilet paper first made? (Green Bay . . . Our thanks to the inventors!)*
- *These dolls became collectibles . . . and have nothing to do with cabbage patches . . . (American Girl Dolls)*

"I thought they came from Midtown Manhattan," Dot joked to Rose.

- *And the final question—name the circus that launched in the Badger State? (No, Ted, it wasn't the Democratic primary . . . it was Ringling Brothers!)*

The riders loved it. Kitty noted the smiling, engaged passengers in the large rearview mirror and turned around to where Dot was sitting and said, "This is so great."

Dot beamed. She loved to be complimented on her ideas.

Remembering Harper, she glanced back to check on her. She'd moved to sit with Ted Jankowski and his friend Fred Harkin. The two men had been high school teachers together; Ted had taught English and ran the speech and debate club, while Fred was a biology teacher and coached the football team. They were arguing about the Bucks' terrible season and their hope for the Brewers that spring.

Harper was leaning in, listening to the older men tell her stories. Her eyes sparkled. She caught Dot's eye and smiled. "They're so cute!" she mouthed. Then she reached for Ted's hand and clasped it. He beamed.

Dot could relax a little—everything was going well. So far.

MARY HAD WANTED to volunteer at the debate, so she'd worked overnight to finish the legal work assigned to her by the partners working on a big corporate merger. Dot had asked Mary to travel earlier in the day with Fletcher and their team of volunteers in a separate sprinter van.

"All good?" Dot texted.

"I saw a cow!" She added a cow emoji.

"Yeah. It's Wisconsin."

"CA gov team here. He looks like an actor."

"He *is* an actor," Dot typed. "Like he'd rather win an Oscar than an election. Keep me posted? Kitty's hounding me for info."

"Will do. Fletch is funny. Might run away with him."

"Wait until after the debate?" Dot had to hand it to that guy—even Mary was charmed by him.

"Here, show Kitty these." Mary then sent a series of photos and a video of the site showing the camera crews setting up on a platform in front of the stage decorated in red, white, and blue. The nine podiums were in position, spaced two feet apart.

"And here's a video of the greenroom. Then the last one is the spin room." She'd kept the videos short. "Oh, and here's one of Fletcher fooling around." She'd taken a photo of him pretending to be a candidate on center stage.

"Those are great. Any reporters there yet?"

"Yes—they're walking around. I even saw Bill Hemmer from Fox. He's my mom's favorite."

"Your parents still watch Fox?"

"24/7."

"Wow. It's a miracle you turned out the way you did."

"They think it's more of a tragedy than a miracle."

Dot sent a laughing emoji and said she'd see her soon. They had about ten minutes left in their journey.

With the time remaining, Dot nodded to Kitty that it was time for her to say a few words. Dot took the comedian's mic and got everyone's attention.

"Hi. I'm so glad you're having a good time. I want to introduce Kitty Bell. She runs For the Win, which is the Super PAC that organized our excursion today. She's got some key insight into tonight's debate and agreed to say a few words. Kitty?" Dot knew to keep intros short. A round of applause greeted Kitty's mic takeover.

"Well, thank you all. And thank you, Dot. This has been a terrific prelude to tonight's big event. I thought I'd give you a little scoop about the state of the race." She had their attention now. Everyone loves to feel like they know something more than their friends and neighbors.

"You're all very politically active, so you know we have nine candidates. They're all interesting people, and collectively, this is a strong democratic field. But we've done some data analysis, and truly there are only three likely to advance in the primary.

"The ones unlikely to move forward include the senator from New England. While Virgil Penfield is popular with some, and he's run several times before, this time around, he's not gaining traction. We want him for comic relief, though. He's got some great one-liners and is an experienced debater.

"You can also trust that the vegan mayor from Newark, Isaiah Grant, isn't going anywhere this cycle. Same with, I'm sorry to say it, your home state U.S. senator. Tessa Danforth's approval rating is stuck in the teens."

"Does that mean I can tell her campaign to stop calling me during dinner?" someone yelled from the back. Others on the bus laughed and agreed.

"Well, let's see how tonight goes." Kitty had them eating out of the palm of her hand. They liked feeling like insiders.

"So, who *should* we watch for?" Ted asked.

"Great question. I'd say watch for the governors of California and Kentucky—Ashby and Stone. Cal has a lot of polish, but Ramsey Stone has been elected twice in a red state, proving it can be done. He has a good track record, too," Kitty explained. "And governors have performed well for the Democratic party in the past."

"What about the rocket guy?" Fred asked. As a scientist, he was part of a Facebook group that batted around his name.

"Ah, you mean Theo Maddox from Austin, Texas. My take on him is that he's got a lot of money and some out-of-the-box ideas. But we'd have to see an amazing performance out of him tonight if he's to advance."

"What about the girl?" an older woman called out from one of the back seats. "The one from Georgia."

"I'm glad you asked. She's the one I'll be watching. Her name is Lucia Lopez. She goes by Lucy. She's a state senator from Atlanta. She's a long shot, but I like her political talent. If she has a good debate, she just might break out of the pack."

"I like her too. My granddaughters keep sending me texts with her videos. She's a real spark plug." This woman was now jointly holding court with Kitty.

"We're five minutes out," the bus driver called back to everyone.

"All right, this is it, folks. Have a great time and thank you again for coming today!" Kitty handed the mic back to Dot who gave everyone the plan for when they arrived.

Soon she could see the venue, and as they pulled up, Fletcher and Mary were there to greet them.

"Everything look okay?" she asked them when they got inside.

"We're all set," Fletcher said. "Now it's up to them." He nodded to the candidates.

The stage lights dimmed, the network music started, and the candidates were called to the stage.

Fletcher casually draped an arm around Dot. It was friendly . . . and possibly more than that. Dot noted the gesture, then set it aside and turned her attention to the debate.

"Here we go," Dot said, gently hip checking Fletcher. She felt a rush well beyond booking a tech bro on cable. Maybe she'd finally found her calling.

Chapter 21

Just before the first debate question was asked, nine candidates put their hands over their hearts as a rising senior from the University of Wisconsin's choir belted out the national anthem.

Dot and Fletcher stood offstage in the wings near the greenroom watching.

"Goosebumps!" Dot said, rubbing her arms.

"She nailed it!" Fletcher whistled loudly and started the applause. He was a good hype man.

Everyone took their seats, and the moderators kicked things off by inviting each candidate to deliver thirty-second opening comments. The candidates got off to fairly good, somewhat scripted starts, except for the tech guy who lost the crowd by stating his website name repeatedly in his allotted time.

"We got it, dude," Fletcher groaned. He shared a look with Dot and rolled his eyes.

"That's why Kitty said we could ignore him. He's more cabinet than commander-in-chief."

Next, the moderators asked for a show of hands.

"Will you agree to take a cognitive test and release the results if you win the primary?"

Everyone except the older candidate, Sen. Penfield, raised their hand. He was well into his eighties, and in that split second, he hesitated. The crowd booed.

Fletcher cringed and Dot shook her head.

The debate rolled along with questions about health care, climate change, jobs, artificial intelligence, and trade. After an hour, the moderators went to a commercial break, noting they'd cover education, immigration, and foreign policy in the second half.

The candidates scrambled off the stage for the five-minute break. For the Win's volunteers kept a close eye on them all, trying to anticipate their needs. Dot and Fletcher scanned the greenroom to make sure everything went smoothly.

Governor Cal Ashby raced to the men's restroom, beating Senator Penfield in some sort of bladder power move, and then took his sweet time in there.

"Unbelievable!" Penfield yelled. He pounded on the door, knowing exactly what his much younger opponent was up to.

Mary distracted the senator by offering him the snack-size bag of the Skittles he'd requested. He funneled several pieces into his mouth straight from the bag and chewed grumpily.

The tech bro, Theo Maddox, stood in a corner scrolling through his phone, checking his site's engagement. Dot offered him a bottle of water, which he took but didn't thank her for. He downed it in one go. "'Thirsty' described him in more ways than one," she thought.

Rushing into the greenroom, Mayor Grant grabbed his phone, checked his messages, and angrily placed a call. When someone picked up, he started yelling, unaware he was still mic'd and his words were playing over the speakers in the debate hall. He was cursing someone out for not getting his signs in the crowd shots.

"My own mother sent me a message saying no one in her assisted living facility could see my signs!" he ranted. "What in the hell do I pay you for?"

Kitty ran into the greenroom from the auditorium, frantically waving her arms and pointing at Mayor Grant. "Hot mic!" Kitty yelled, and Fletcher, quick to catch on, leapt over a sofa and muffled the mic on Grant's lapel.

"What in the actual . . ." Mayor Grant cursed at Fletcher.

"Your mic is still hot . . . sir."

Embarrassed, the mayor yanked off the mic and tried to hold his head high, smoothing down his suit as he stomped away.

In the meantime, Harper overcame her shyness and approached the young governor of Kentucky, Ramsey Stone.

"Governor, may I introduce myself?" Harper put out her hand, and he shook it.

"Please do. I could use someone to talk to."

After just a couple of minutes, Harper came away impressed. "He's got his act together," she told Dot.

"Good to know. I heard the donors really like governors in general. They have a lot more experience than congressional members. And they don't have that D.C. stink."

"At least not yet," Harper said.

In the meantime, Kitty sought out Lucy Lopez.

Lopez was under forty and striking. Slim with long black hair, she rocked a red lip and would raise her eyebrows and give a sharp nod of her chin to make her points. She was so different from the older yet more experienced candidates the Democrats had been saddled with, despite the party's efforts to move them into retirement.

The young state senator wasn't married and kept her love life to herself. She had two small Havanese dogs that filled her social media and gained her a lot of followers. She carried herself well, her excellent posture the result of years of competitive Latin dancing. She was a natural in front of the camera, speaking from the heart and without notes.

Her dad was an immigrant from Cuba, and her mom had moved from Puerto Rico to Georgia with her parents when she was a girl. Her father had spent his career in the military and her mom had raised their three children while working as a hotel maid.

Two months before the debate, she'd gone viral for a speech about how Democrats needed to get it together or they'd never win again. Her major issue was education. She thought it was criminal that kids in public schools weren't learning to read or write at grade level but being passed along anyway.

"We are robbing children of their future. It will be *our* fault when they lose confidence in themselves and don't see any opportunity to succeed. Are you willing to be guilty of that? To take away their chance of achieving the American dream? I ask you!" and then, in her signature stage whisper, "I ask you."

Kitty had picked up on Lopez's growing popularity. She had early on sent a note to the entire FTW team. "Lopez has potential. People are falling in love. And she's not afraid to take on one of the Democrats' sacred cows, the teachers' unions."

Lopez didn't come across as a left-wing Democrat or a squishy moderate. She was independent-minded and blunt when telling the truth. Her authenticity was part of her appeal. Add that to her being a party outsider, a Latina renegade, and she had a shot to appeal to the sliver of independents they'd need to win the election.

Chapter 22

At the end of the break the debate audience found their seats and a bell rang signaling one minute until they were back on air. The volunteers herded the candidates back to the stage. But their older New England senator, Virgil Penfield, was missing.

"Where's Senator Penfield?" Dot asked, her eyes sweeping the room. How could they have lost him?

Fletcher heard a pounding on the bathroom door. He rushed over and opened it. The older man bolted out of the john.

"That punk locked me in, damn it! Out of my way!" Penfield pushed Fletcher aside and sprinted to the stage.

"Wow, he can move!" Harper said.

The senator, with green skittle tint on his tongue, mopped his brow as the second half of the debate got underway.

"Please tell me someone got that on video." Mary imagined it going viral.

"I hope not!" Dot was alarmed.

Kitty would *not* have liked that.

With the candidates back in position, the moderators pressed on, and the crowd got more aggressive in cheering and booing the answers. Toward the end of the second hour, it became a free-for-all, with all the candidates pandering to dairy farmers and talking over each other, and the moderators failing to get a handle on it.

The control room finally cut everyone's mics so that they could wrest back control. It was time to wrap it up. They gave each candidate another thirty seconds for a final statement.

State Senator Lopez was passionate and gracious.

"I ask you for your vote." And then more quietly, in her deep stage whisper, "I ask you."

She flashed her smile and looked confidently straight into the camera.

"Gorgeous," Mary said.

Then Governor Stone of Kentucky explained how he was clearly the only one who could beat the incumbent Republican president.

"I'm the only one who has what it takes to beat him—and, unlike others up here tonight," he said as he glanced up and down the row of candidates, "I have a record to prove it."

Lopez gave him side-eye and a lift of one eyebrow.

"Wow! Shots fired," Fletcher said, rubbing his hands together.

The Wisconsin senator got a round of polite applause and talked about deer hunting with her boys. She hadn't lit the room on fire.

Rose shrugged. "She's nice. But even I know she's boring and safe."

Theo Maddox reminded everyone he was the only billionaire who could self-fund his race. Then he asked the audience to donate through his website.

"This guy's killing me." Fletcher put his head in his hands.

Senator Penfield told the crowd, "It's your last chance to have me as your president. I hope you don't screw it up like last time." That got a laugh.

Governor Cal—it's in the name—Ashby went last. He chose to say he was launching a brand-new website that would go live as soon as the debate finished. He gave the address out several times in rapid-fire.

As the debate wrapped up and family members swarmed the stage to congratulate their loved ones and pose for the cameras, Dot finally exhaled.

"What do you think? Who's the winner?" Fletcher asked, catching up with her.

"Well, I'd put green arrows next to Stone and Lopez."

"Not Penfield?" Fletcher pulled a face and made Dot laugh.

"Touché. He's going nowhere. Except maybe Substack," she said.

FOR THE WIN volunteers cleaned up the greenroom while they watched the spin room on the big screen.

The governor of California was doing an interview with the female host of the show with the biggest prime-time audience in cable.

"Governor Ashby, we looked up that website you mentioned in your closing statement."

"It's great, right?"

"Well . . . I'm not sure you gave out the correct website. I believe you said 'come and join us dot com' but did you mean dot org? When we searched dot com, we were taken to a . . . how do I say this . . . an 'adult content' site." The host used air quotes to make her point.

The governor's face flushed. Dot gasped, Rose's hands flew to her eyes, and Mary's shoulders bounced up and down as she tried to hold in a laugh. But soon they were all in hysterics.

Dot thought of the governor's poor press secretary who'd have to clean up the mess.

"He didn't exactly nail the dismount, now did he?" Mary asked cheekily.

"Mary Russo!" Harper pretended to be offended.

"Let's get out of here, girls." Fletcher led the way to the bus, which was warm and ready to take them home.

WALKING OUT OF the venue back to the bus, Dot pulled out her phone to check the headlines.

"Here's the snap poll results. Lopez and Stone tied. Ashby trailing third, and everyone else far below," she said to Kitty, Rose, and Fletcher.

"I'm not surprised," Kitty said. "That trio is the strongest by far."

"Lopez is a long shot, Kitty, but is she one worth taking?" Rose asked.

Kitty Bell didn't hesitate to answer. "Yes," she said, striding to the bus with purpose.

Her Wisconsin team followed quickly behind her. There was so much to do.

THE RIDE BACK to Cedar Falls was lively. Cans of Spotted Cow sponsored the debate about the debate.

Consensus seemed to be that Governor Stone had the best night.

"He reminds me of Bill Clinton." Some cheered. Some groaned.

But there was also a lot of support for Lopez.

"She comes off more factory floor than faculty lounge," Ted Jankowski said. Dot told Fletcher to write that down. It was a good line.

There was one vote for Senator Penfield.

"I've supported him for years," Rose's friend said.

"So, you're the one!" someone in the back yelled to laughter.

And there was broad agreement that the tech bro had to go.

After they got back into town, Kitty side huddled with Dot and Fletcher before she got off the bus.

"That was amazing, guys," she said. "We put For the Win on the map.

Great job. And thanks. But we need to step on the gas. This state is critical and there's a lot to do."

Dot flinched inside under the pressure, but Fletcher said, "Don't worry, we've got it." He exuded confidence, which made her feel more secure.

Kitty nodded and got off the bus and into the backseat of the car waiting to take her to the private jet terminal in Milwaukee. One of the For the Win donors had chartered a flight for her. Must be nice, Dot thought, hoping one day she could summon such a ride.

As Kitty's car pulled away, Dot let out a deep breath. Fletcher held up his hand for a high five. Dot slapped his palm weakly.

"Don't worry about her. She's just stressed." He could tell that Kitty had stolen some of Dot's good vibes.

"Somehow we pulled that off, Fletcher," Dot said.

"More than that. We crushed it!" He reached out his arms to hug her. When she wrapped her arms around his neck, he lifted her up and twirled her around. She let herself feel a little thrill of excitement about how well the day had ended, in the face of all the challenges.

He set her down gently and she tilted her head up to see his face.

"We make a great team, Dot."

"We do."

"See you tomorrow," he said. "Oh, and . . . keep an eye on Mary. She's wild!"

Dot laughed and glanced at her friends, who were waiting for her under the awning of the Democratic office on Main Street.

"She is. In all the best ways."

She waved goodbye to Fletcher. He'd really grown on her. He was good looking *and* a good time.

"Let's go home, girls," Dot said, turning to The Crew.

"So, Dot, is there something you want to tell us about Fletcher?" Harper asked.

"What about him?"

"You two looked pretty cozy together," Mary said as their shoes crunched on the light ice that had frozen on the sidewalk, and they noticed the frost on the Jeep's windshield had been cleared.

"Wow, that was nice of someone," Dot said, changing the subject away from Fletcher. She didn't feel like analyzing their relationship. They didn't even *have* a relationship. But could they? Stop it, she told herself.

As they climbed into the Jeep, Mary saw a piece of paper under the windshield wiper.

"What the heck?" she said. "A ticket. For what?!" She looked around to see if there was a no parking sign she'd missed. She got back out of the Jeep, resentful for having to get back into the chilly air if even for a moment.

She used a gloved hand to pull the ticket out from under the wiper. A box that said "warning" was checked. No fine.

She turned the ticket over.

"Strike two, New York" was scrawled on the back.

Chapter 23

Mary wondered what Dot had gotten them into.

"What are we supposed to wear to dinner on a farm?" she yelled down the hall from her room.

"I don't know. I've never been to dinner on a farm!" Dot was looking in her closet, too.

"Do you think I should wear something plaid?" Harper joined in. "I think farmers wear a lot of plaid."

"I think as long as our clothes are clean, we'll be fine," Dot called out. "Now let's go. I don't want to be late."

Earlier that week, on a cold, windy day, Dot had bumped into Grace Taylor on Main Street outside of Flour Power. It was now March, and she hadn't seen her since their first encounter at the Reader Falls Bookshop.

"Hi, Dot! Glad I ran into you. I've been meaning to invite you and your girlfriends to one of our Sunday suppers. My mother used to host but I've taken over and everyone comes. Family attendance is mandatory, and we love having guests."

"That sounds like a great tradition and a lovely invitation. We'd love to come some time."

"Would this weekend work for you?"

"Let me see." Dot pulled out her phone and pretended to check her calendar. "As expected, no plans! We don't have the most active social lives here like we did in the city."

"I bet you find it slow as molasses around here."

"Oh no, we love it!" Dot worried she'd offended her and rushed to make up for it. "Cedar Falls sets the perfect pace."

"If you like small towns and a strong community, it's just about perfect."

"I agree. And I haven't even been to one of the farms yet. What can we bring?"

"Just your appetites."

THE GIRLS MET downstairs and assessed each other's outfits.

Harper had nixed the idea of plaid and had on wide-leg khakis, a white button-down under a Kelly green cotton cardigan, and her well-worn ankle boots to give her some height. She'd put on a little "Sunday supper" makeup and her hair was held back by a scrunchie.

Dot wore skinny jeans tucked into tan knee-high boots with a flat sole, and a lavender cashmere turtleneck. She arranged her hair in a sleek ponytail and put a hint of pink gloss on her lips.

Not surprisingly, Mary was the most dressed up. She had on black knit leggings, over-the-knee kitten heel boots, a hot pink silk blouse with pearl buttons, a gray suede blazer, and her large gold hoop earrings. Red lips, lined eyes, and defined brows completed her look.

"What?" she asked, noting Dot and Harper looking at her with their heads in a dog tilt.

"You are definitely dressed for agriculture," Dot teased.

"And where did you get those skinny jeans—from the vintage store?" Mary shot back.

"Hey, these are back in! I'm glad I kept them from high school."

Mary looked at herself in the entryway mirror.

"Do you think I should change?" Mary wasn't typically self-conscious.

"No! You look . . . the part. Let's go or we'll be late." Dot grabbed the bottle of Duckhorn they'd bought as a hostess gift, and they headed out.

THE FARM'S LONG driveway was lined with sugar maples, which were just starting to bud. The afternoon sun filtered through the leaves. The gravel road to the house was bumpy, and mud flicked onto the undercarriage of the Jeep as Mary drove slowly to the house.

Mary turned off the music. They were only about thirty minutes from their house in Cedar Falls, but it looked like another world.

"Wow. It's beautiful."

"So serene," Harper said, sitting cross-legged in the backseat.

They passed several cows lining the fence.

"Look at these cuties!" Dot said, pointing them out.

The driveway curved in a loop around a big oak tree in front of the Taylors' stone and brick ranch-style home. To the left was a large red barn and several smaller shed-type buildings, about ten yards from the house. On the right, a large tractor sat just inside a big metal garage that had its doors rolled open.

"Welcome!" Grace called as she came out of the house, waving one arm high in the air and shielding her eyes from the sun with the other. She was dressed as she'd been at the bookstore, in a long-sleeved flannel shirt, jeans, and lace-up boots.

Two big yellow Labs bounded around her as they barked at the Jeep.

"Did I overdress?" Mary wondered aloud before they got out of the vehicle. "They said Sunday supper!"

"Oh, no, not at all." Dot glanced into the backseat to meet Harper's gaze and winked. "I'm sure there's a wedding we can drop you off at later."

"Puppies!" Harper had always wanted one, but her parents had never given in. She got out of the car first, excited to pet the dogs and glad she'd remembered to take an allergy pill before they left the house.

Once they were all out of the Jeep, Dot provided introductions and handed the wine to Grace.

"Why, thank you. I'll see if we have a corkscrew. Not much call for one around here!"

Mary realized they should have brought a dessert instead.

"Ray, Floyd, calm down!" Grace's voice carried authority. The dogs stopped barking immediately. "They love company."

Harper bent down to scratch their ears. "They're gorgeous!"

Grace called to her husband.

"Joe, our guests are here! Come in for a bit."

She turned to the girls.

"He *never* stops working."

A trim man, about sixty years old, came out from the barn, wiping his hands on a cloth. He wore a baseball cap, thick denim shirt, Carhartt overalls, and work boots.

He took off his hat and tucked it under his arm. His forehead was starkly white compared to the rest of a face that had been hammered by years of sun and wind. He had big blue eyes, and the skin around them was evidence that he laughed easily. His salt-and-pepper hair was still thick, and the girls would later learn that Grace had to trim it every two weeks in their kitchen.

"I've been looking forward to meeting you," he said, shaking their hands. "Come, come. Let's get you inside—it's chilly out here with that breeze."

They started in, and Joe held Mary's elbow.

"Careful, young lady. It's muddy as heck around here. Well, it's mostly mud."

Mary stepped gingerly, trying to protect her boots.

The Taylors' home was warm and inviting. The aroma of a home-cooked meal filled the air—scents of roast beef, pepper, baked apples, and cinnamon.

They hung their coats in a crowded mudroom, everyone talking at once as they got to know each other.

"Staten Island. Brooklyn. Providence. I never met anyone from those places," Joe said. "I'm afraid I've not traveled too far afield from this farm. It's hard to get away."

"I'd never leave if I got to live here." Harper turned on the charm, and Dot gave her a grateful look. She wanted them to have a good time, and she was also interested in getting to know more people in the community so that she'd have better intel to send back to the insatiable Kitty Bell.

Grace led them into the family room. A large sofa and three recliners surrounded a big television screen. Iced teas were passed around along with a tray holding small bowls of mini pretzels, peanuts, and cheddar cheese Pringles. Harper sat on her hands to avoid snacking and ruining her dinner.

"How long have you lived here?" Dot asked Joe.

"All my life. I was born in Cedar Falls. Went to school with Grace and her younger sister, Mercy—the preacher's daughters. You know what they say about dating one." Joe winked.

He leaned back and crossed his wool-socked foot over his knee.

"I knew I wanted to marry Grace from the get-go. Thankfully, she did me the favor of becoming my wife, even though she knew I'd only ever be a farmer."

Grace reached for Joe's hand.

"Growing up next to the church, we didn't farm ourselves. But we spent a lot of time at friends' houses helping with chores. So, it wasn't hard to convince me this would be a great life."

"We raised three sons here," Joe said. "The oldest, Mike, farms with us. He's married to a great gal named Kelsey. She's an art teacher at the middle school. They've given us our two grandkids." He pointed to a framed photograph of two blond kids, a boy and a girl, sitting on top of a black pony with a white mane and a stripe down its nose. "They're at their other grandparents' tonight. We trade off Sunday supper with Kelsey's parents."

"And our younger two sons are twins. Fraternal but they look a lot alike. Neither of them is married yet, so they've not given us grandkids—just several heart attacks over the years," Grace said. "One is a daredevil and served in the military. And the other one was on track to play professional hockey, but he broke his leg in college and decided to start his own business in town. They're good boys."

"It sounds like a pretty perfect family," Dot said.

"Well, no life is perfect. But I wouldn't want to live any other way." Joe reached for some pretzels and sat back again. "Enough about us, tell us about you!"

AS THE GIRLS told Joe and Grace about how they became friends at NYU, they heard a car pull into the driveway.

"That'll be the twins," Grace said.

"Ma, we're here!"

"In the family room. Come meet our guests."

They walked in with their stocking feet, having taken off their muddy boots.

Mary looked up and did a double take. She recognized the taller of the two men immediately.

And he recognized her.

"*New York*? What in the heck are you doing here?" It was Mary's cop.

"You two know each other?" Dot asked.

"Oh, yeah. She's the new troublemaker in town." He jutted his chin toward Mary and winked at her. "Serial offender."

"Hardly!" Mary's cheeks grew immediately hot. She rarely let anyone get a rise out of her, but there was something about this man.

Just behind him, his twin walked in.

"Harper?"

"Tommy!"

"Mary!"

"Hey, Tommy."

"Wait. How do you all know each other?" Dot was confused.

"I love writing in bars, and he owns the Sin Bin—the bar that's just down from your office."

"This is amazing," Dot said.

"Wow. What a coincidence!" Grace loved a small-world story.

Soon they were all talking. The conversation flowed easily.

"You two really do look alike," Harper said, looking back and forth at Tommy and his twin, whose name was Jake.

"They both have that dimple that melted my heart the first time they smiled at me," Grace said.

"But I got the height," Jake said, needling his brother.

"That's all right. I got the hair," Tommy gave it right back to him. Jake's hair had receded so much that he'd just shaved it all off.

"Seems like a fair trade," Mary said, thinking Jake had made the right decision not to fight the inevitable.

"Boys, enough. You've been harping on each other since the womb."

Joe then stood up and suggested that they all get the chores done before supper.

Jake said he'd do the chickens and challenged Mary to go with him. She accepted, not sure what "doing the chickens" meant.

That left Tommy to handle the cows. Harper offered to join.

"Boys, get those girls some muck boots and old coats from the shed. They can't walk out there in . . . that."

Jake and Tommy left to retrieve the more appropriate footwear.

"Dot, why don't you join me in the kitchen," Grace said. "I just have a few things to warm up."

"Happy to," Dot said, grateful her assignment didn't include going back into the cold. She watched Harper and Mary waddle out the front gate, huddled in their borrowed coats, and snapped a picture. She sent it to her sister. "At a farm. Check this out."

"This ought to be good," Anne responded right away.

"I'll let you know if they survive." Then Dot tucked her phone back into her jeans and joined Grace in the kitchen.

Chapter 24

"So, New York. . . . What *actually* brought you to Cedar Falls?" Jake led the way to the chicken house, grabbing an empty basket and a bag of feed from a shed on their way, his broad shoulders and narrow waist grabbing Mary's attention.

"It's kind of a long story." Mary went on to explain as best she could.

"So you left your job and your family to come here to help the Democrats win an election. Do I have that right?"

"Yeah. Well, Dot came to work on the election, and Harper and I help her whenever she needs it. She convinced us to come along for the ride. You know, one last big adventure before we all settle down and can't do wild and crazy things anymore," Mary said, watching where she walked. "I still work for my law firm, just from my bedroom. But it's only until the election, then we go home. Back to the city."

"So it's like a gap year—but one you do *after* college?" he asked.

"That's a good way to put it," she replied, nodding her head.

They stepped into the fenced-in chicken area. Several chickens squawked around their feet and pecked at their boots. Mary squealed and kicked up her heels in fear.

"They won't hurt you. I promise."

"They're kind of scary with those red-rimmed eyes."

"Any worse than the pigeons in Manhattan?"

"Fair point. There's a woman who feeds them near my apartment. I get so mad at her, but she seems to love them. Like they're her best friends. So I just stay out of her way."

"Around here, these birds we actually *have* to feed. Here, you can help. Just take this bag and scatter handfuls of this food into these trays, and I'll get them something to drink."

Mary stuck a gloved hand into the bag of tiny pellets of corn, barley, and oats and did as he instructed.

Jake refilled the chickens' water tray from a pump. "Here's something. You know this chicken coop is haunted?"

"It is?"

"Yes. We have a poultry-geist."

"You're an idiot." But she giggled.

Then Jake ducked into a henhouse that smelled sharp and unpleasant. He came out with several eggs in a basket.

"Here's breakfast," he said. She winced. The eggs were dirty.

"Oh, come on. Where did you think eggs came from?"

"Trader Joe's."

"Who's that?"

"A guy I see a lot back home. He's got a killer frozen food section."

Mary pointed to a stump with a large red stain. The blade of an axe stuck out of the top. "What's that?"

"That, New York, is where your dinner came from."

Mary paled and swallowed.

"Come on, now. Do you think your grandma got chicken from a lab?"

"Well, no," she admitted. "To be honest, I've never really thought about it."

"Well, now you can tell everybody back home that you saw where real food comes from."

"They'd never believe this." She looked around at the scenery and took a deep breath of the fresh air.

"I think you look great in my mom's boots and that barn coat."

She threw her arms out wide and looked down at her outfit.

"Think I'm pulling this off?"

"Wow. You move fast. We just met and you're talking about pulling your clothes off?"

"You can dream. But I'm keeping all my clothes on."

Jake laughed, taking off his gloves and stuffing them in the back pocket of his jeans. Then he stepped closer to her and tipped back her chin with his free hand, which she didn't mind at all.

"Oh, New York. I have a feeling you can pull anything off."

She met his eyes and for once was without words. He held her gaze for a few beats.

"Come on. Let's go eat." Then he reached for her hand, and she followed him back to the house.

MEANWHILE, TOMMY TOOK Harper into the dairy barn. The animal smells were pungent and caught Harper by surprise.

"Oh my," she said and put her hand over her nose.

"You get used to it," he said, but she had her doubts.

Tommy grabbed a bucket and some gloves for the one remaining cow waiting to be milked. She noticed how he wore his hair long and how he favored his left leg a little bit. That must have been from the hockey injury Grace had mentioned.

"Ever milked a cow before?" he asked.

"Definitely not."

"Want to try?"

"Definitely not sure."

"Come, I'll show you." He pulled on a pair of disposable gloves and grabbed a stool. He set it next to a large cow that stomped her back legs in anticipation of being milked. Harper jumped.

"She won't hurt you. Just stand to the side, though." He put his hand on the cow's haunches. "Easy there, Bessie."

"Her name is Bessie?"

"We call all of them Bessie. Makes it easier." Tommy sat on the stool and showed her how it was done. "First, we clean her all up to get rid of any dirt. That helps get the milk flowing, too. Then you hold the udder between your thumb and finger, give a little squeeze, and then try again."

Suddenly and smoothly, the milk started to stream into the bucket.

"Want to give it a try?" He offered her the seat and crouched beside her. She put on the gloves he handed to her and reached for the teat. On her first attempt, she missed the bucket and squirted milk right into Tommy's face.

"I'm so sorry!" She was mortified, but he just laughed and wiped it off with the back of his gloved hand.

"Nice shot. Try again." He put his hand over hers and showed her how to get it just right. "Try to breathe easily. If you're nervous, she'll sense it, and then we'll be here all night."

Harper willed herself to chill out. And then, slowly, she started to get the hang of it.

"I see. There's a rhythm to follow," Harper said.

"Exactly. See! You're a natural."

She was almost disappointed when it was over.

Tommy added some feed to Bessie's trough and grabbed the bucket that was nearly half-full. He poured a bit into a large cast-iron skillet.

"For the barn cats." Harper saw a couple of skinny cats and a few kittens come out of their hiding places.

"They're so cute!"

"Good mousers, too. Everyone's got a job around here."

They walked to where a big machine was churning the milk. Joe had already dumped his bucket in and gone up to the house.

Tommy dipped a ladle in and said to Harper, "Here, have a taste."

"Oh, I don't drink milk. I think I might be lactose intolerant."

"Ah. That's just something TikTok has told people. I promise; we've drank milk all our lives. Trust me?" Tommy motioned her to try it. "I promise you've never tasted cream like this."

"Is it safe? It hasn't been cleaned or anything."

"You literally can't get milk fresher than this. It hasn't had a chance to get messed with. That's what they do at the factories before they ship it out to you folks in Brooklyn."

"Manhattan. I grew up in Brooklyn but moved to Manhattan."

"Is there a big difference?"

"How much time do you have?"

"Clearly not enough," he said. "Here. Drink up!"

"Okay. But if I get sick, you'll owe me . . . something."

"I'm confident you won't get sick."

She decided a little couldn't hurt and brought the ladle to her lips. A sweet cream that felt like velvet coated her tongue. She swallowed and was surprised by how good it tasted. "Okay, you were right. That's so different from back home." She bent her head down for one more taste.

"I've always loved it," he said, removing his gloves and taking Harper's to put in the bin. "In fact, I have a dream of starting a little ice cream store on one of the back roads of the farm. Like a special destination with an Instagrammable setting. But my family thinks I'm crazy."

"I like the idea. It's like that movie about the baseball field in Iowa."

"Yes, you get it! Build it and they will come," Tommy said. "I even have a name picked out."

"Let's hear it," she said enthusiastically.

"Alotto Gelato."

"Oh, that's awful." She laughed. "But I see the potential."

They smiled at each other, and he instinctively reached up to tuck one of her loose curls behind her ear.

She let his hand linger, enjoying the moment.

As they walked back, she felt lighter in spirit than she had in months.

IN THE KITCHEN, Dot stirred the creamed spinach while Grace mashed the potatoes with a mixer. They chatted about life in Cedar Falls.

"How long has the farm been in the family?" Dot asked while she set the table using dishes and silverware from an antique sideboard.

"About a hundred and forty years, believe it or not," Grace said. "Joe's the sixth generation. It's a tough way to make a living, but we wouldn't have it any other way."

She looked out the kitchen window where Joe was feeding the dogs in the fading sunshine. A car with its headlights on pulled into the drive.

"Are we expecting one more?" Dot asked, counting the number of plates and people again.

"Oh, that'll be Danny. Remember him from the bookstore? He comes every Sunday."

"Ah, yes. Of course. Great." Dot tried to sound casual about it despite the flutter in her heart. Straightening her back and smoothing her hair, she wondered if he'd remembered her.

Because, despite her pledge to focus on her career for the year before looking to date again, the sad-eyed boy from the bookstore had been on Dot's mind.

Chapter 25

Let's pray." Joe Taylor offered a palm to Harper who sat next to him, and after a beat, she caught on and held his hand. Everyone around the table joined the chain. Joe said grace.

"Amen."

The table was filled with wholesome, nutritious food. Grace had plated a fresh green salad with mustard vinaigrette and a fresh roll with salted butter at each setting.

To Mary's relief, the main dish was pot roast, not chicken.

Jake caught her eye and winked. "Gotcha," he said.

She rolled her eyes in reaction. Though after seeing the axe, she didn't want to think about how the beef got to the table either.

Dot sat across from Danny, who was quiet but laughed at the banter. The twins teased him a lot, and he seemed to like it. They told stories of how he used to fall asleep in the living room when they played video games and how Grace would call Danny's mom and say she'd take him to school in the morning.

"All my best childhood memories are in this house," he said.

"And he was always the best behaved." Grace put a hand on Danny's back.

Dot liked hearing about his childhood—she was fascinated by his story and curious about, well, him. She tried to put the brakes on her feelings, but someone, maybe Danny, had cut the lines.

AFTER DINNER, DESSERT was a platter of Scotcheroos.

"What are these?" Mary asked.

"You don't have Scotcheroos in New York?" Jake teased. "You haven't lived."

"They're a Wisconsin special," Grace said. "A mix of peanut butter Rice

Krispy treats with chocolate on top. Always served with homemade vanilla ice cream."

"Courtesy of Bessie," Tommy said to Harper.

"Every grandmother in Wisconsin knows how to make these," Joe said.

While they enjoyed dessert, Dot asked Joe to tell her more about what rural Wisconsinites were feeling about the election.

"Oh no! Mom's got a rule. No politics on Sundays," Tommy said.

"It's all right." Grace nodded for Joe to go ahead. "They're here to learn, not to argue."

Joe said things had really changed since he was a young man. "Growing up, everyone I knew was a Democrat," he said. "Now just about everyone outside of town votes Republican."

"Why do you think that is?" Dot asked.

"It's hard to say exactly. The politics here evolved over time. Certainly, economic issues like trade and energy have affected us a lot. We need more customers to buy our products, but when the cost of fuel gets too high, we can't make a profit."

Dot nodded along.

"And then you've got Washington thinking it knows how to take care of this land better than we do. I say, this farm's been in my family since the eighteen hundreds. You think we don't know how to care for it?" Joe said, stopping to take a sip of iced tea. "But also, to be honest, there's been a lot of the cultural issues that drove people to the right."

"I agree," Grace said. "It feels like politicians took all of us for granted all those years and just went for the city vote instead."

Dot took it all in, making mental notes. She didn't offer a defense of the Democrats, feeling it wouldn't be polite. And that she didn't know enough to be persuasive anyway. They were making some good points.

"But there's pressure coming from all sides against us farmers now," Joe said. "You see, when these boys were growing up, and that includes Danny here, Grace took them to the Future Farmers of America and the 4-H clubs. That helped build character. And for youngsters to learn some skills. And now, I think about the kids in those clubs today and don't know if they'd have anywhere *to* farm in the future."

"Why?" Mary asked, leaning in.

"I'll give you an example. You see, our farm here is large by Wisconsin standards. Just over twelve hundred acres."

"How big is that?" Harper had no idea how big an acre was.

"I'd guess it's about the dimension of Central Park. So, a good size. Not the largest, by any means. But for this area, it's a fair size."

Joe gave them the short story of his great-grandfather emigrating from England to start the farm with his brothers and their wives.

"It's a great all-American story," Harper said. "Almost like *Little House on the Prairie*."

"It was a bit like that in the beginning, that's for sure. Over time, the farm grew and matured. We have good soil, too. And yet, we're dangerously close to losing it all." His words caught The Crew by surprise.

"Wait. How?" Dot asked.

"Well, right now we're in a dispute with the governor's office and the president. Don't get me wrong, I agree with them on creating more jobs and fulfilling campaign promises to get the economy going again—heck, I'm a Republican, too. But they want to build some big manufacturing factory here, and they've determined that our farm, and two neighboring properties, are the best place for it."

"Why your place?" Dot asked, listening closely. "Seems like there's a lot of farmland out here."

"Well, we're just outside of town, so the utilities would be easy to hook up. They wouldn't have to put new electric lines in. Plus, they're claiming this so-called public-private partnership will bring three hundred manufacturing jobs to the area and the nearest housing is in Cedar Falls. They want us to sell, and they say they're offering a fair price. And if we don't take their offer, they're willing to shut us down and make us move. It's happened before. My high school buddy lost his farm in the same type of thing. Now he's selling RVs over in Appleton."

"But isn't there any way to fight back?" Dot asked.

"Well, I could sue, and I've got a lawyer looking things over. But I'd like to solve this without having to resort to court. I've been in touch with the Secretary of Agriculture—I've known the guy for ages, and he loves farming. And farmers. At least I thought he did. Heck, he grew up on a farm. But every time I manage to get him on the phone, it seems like his hands are tied."

Joe looked through the big picture window out toward the barn. "And once they make that determination, it's hard to beat it back."

"But will they up their price and make it worth it to you?" Harper asked.

"They can try. In fact, they came in a few months ago with what they think is a good deal. It's supposedly 'fair market value' but they don't consider that a lot of the value in this place is the history of it. My ancestors built all of this from scratch. They even held on during the Great Depression. I'll be damned if I lose it to the government for what could be a boondoggle.

"Bunch of guys south of Milwaukee got burned by this same argument about a decade ago. They lost their farms to eminent domain when a foreign company said they'd start making some big TV screens. Those jobs pay well—in theory. But around when Covid struck, the company was already in decline, and they used the pandemic as an excuse to walk away. Not a single manufacturing job was ever created. It makes me so mad." He pounded the table once to make his point. Dot flinched.

"It's hard to believe that they didn't learn the lesson that time," Grace said, placing a hand on her husband's forearm to calm him, even though she shared his anger. "Those farms would still be in business today if they hadn't been pressured to sell."

"So, what can you do about it?" Dot asked.

"Well, sometimes you can't do anything. You see, both Republicans and Democrats fall for these big plans. Then they use the government power to try to buy your farm. And if you don't want to sell, well sometimes they just take it."

"How can they do that? This is your land!" Harper said.

"Yes, I learned about this in law school," Mary said. "These disputes come up from time to time and get a lot of attention. It's like David versus Goliath, and America loves to root for the underdog. But they also like new highways and sports stadiums. As I recall, the lawsuits can drag on for years and even end up at the Supreme Court."

"Yep, that's right. But that's what I'm trying to avoid. I'd like to get them to back down based on the fact that we run a productive, historic farm. And I don't want to look out onto my fields and see some big, ugly factory spewing Lord knows what into the air. I don't want to fight with them, but I will if I have to."

"We're with you, Dad," Tommy said.

"So, do you think you can get the government to back down?" Mary cut to the chase.

"Great question. It depends on who has better lawyers," Joe said.

"Who do you think has better lawyers?" she asked.

"Well, *that* remains to be seen. There's a hearing in a few weeks. Our guys better be ready."

Everyone around the table let that sink in.

"And it's unclear who the real investor is. I've got my suspicions," Joe said.

"And what are those?" Mary asked.

"I think there's some foreign entity behind it. Probably China. They've been trying to do this for years. Started with farms near military bases. And now it's all about energy."

The mood in the room had taken a dive with the thought of the Taylor farm being lost.

"Okay, enough of this. Let's change the subject!" Grace sent the twins in to do the dishes, and the rest of the guests moved into the family room for coffee.

WITH THE DISHES done, everyone gathered in the sitting room around the large television. The Big Ten basketball tournament played on the big screen.

Danny caught Dot's eye.

"How do you like Cedar Falls?" he asked, making a side conversation for just the two of them.

"Oh, it's very charming." Why did she suddenly feel so formal, like she was in nineteenth-century England?

"It is." He nodded, a man of seemingly few words.

"I just want it to warm up so that I can get out and run like I used to in the city," she said.

"Come on, it's not that cold. I run all the time."

"You do? It's freezing!"

"I love to run in the cold. Clears my head," he said. He was quiet a moment.

Dot didn't fill the silence.

Finally, he broke it.

"Tell you what, when it warms up a bit, I'll show you my favorite route. Goes up by the covered bridge."

"I'd like that." Dot had tired of running on the treadmill at their rental. And running with Danny would make her stick to good form.

Danny served her a coffee.

"How do you take it?"

"No sugar and a dash of almond milk, if they have it."

"Almond milk? You know that's not milk, right?"

"It's milk. It says so on the carton."

"Milk comes from mammals, not nuts."

"Then why do they call it milk?"

"To fool you into buying it," Danny said, looking around. "Don't tell Joe you call it milk. He has thoughts on that."

"I bet he does. Okay—let me change my order," she said, catching herself flirting. "No sugar. Dash of *real* milk."

"That's more like it." He poured her a cup and handed it to her. They clinked their mugs, nodded to each other. They each took a sip while maintaining eye contact.

Dot was the first to break the gaze. "By the way, I really love the bookstore in town," she said. "The Jankowskis are so nice. Harper's going to start reading for them during the Wednesday children's hour."

"They've always been very good to me," he said. "I really want to try to help them figure out what they're going to do with the store."

"Do you think they're going to have to sell it?"

"I hope not. But if they do, I'm afraid it won't stay a bookstore."

"That would be a shame."

"Well, maybe they'll think of something." Danny's knee moved and touched the side of Dot's leg.

A spark shot through her, sharp and undeniable.

"I've been mulling over an idea for them," Dot said, looking away, getting ahold of herself. "And it's something I think you'd be perfect for. It's a way to fix up the store and make it a little more . . . contemporary."

"I'm all ears," he said.

Feeling bold and excited about her idea, she decided to throw caution out the window. "Should we get together for a coffee and I can run it by you?"

He pulled out his phone and handed it to her. "Absolutely. Okay for me to have your number?"

Dot's heart skipped a beat as she typed her number into his phone. She handed it back to him with a smile.

Grace and Joe noticed and made eye contact over Dot's and Danny's heads.

Joe waggled his eyebrows. Grace nodded. Another successful Sunday supper in the books.

Chapter 26

March turned to April. As the days got longer, the ice melted into mud season, and The Crew started to venture out a little more.

"I am starting to feel my fingers again." Mary had never gotten used to the cold.

To take advantage of the warmer weather, Dot mapped out walking routes and used Manhattan landmarks as a guide to explain how far each was.

"Imagine going from the High Line at The Standard up to the Javits Center and back. Or, if you want something longer, we could do one that's like going from Columbus Circle, up and around the Great Lawn, and over to The Plaza."

"And then we have brunch?" Harper asked.

"Yes. With endless mimosas," Dot replied.

"Then I'll do either one. Mary, you choose."

"The Plaza. I had to take the bar exam at the Javits. Awful."

AROUND THEIR NEIGHBORHOOD, yellow daffodils and orange tulips sprung from the ground, and the pink cherry blossoms, dogwoods, and redbud trees punched through with bursts of color.

Gradually, then suddenly, there were more people outside their homes, getting their spring and summer landscaping in place. Cedar Fallers took great pride in their yards.

Everyone waved at them as they passed by.

"Nice weather, eh?"

"Beautiful day!"

"Have a good walk!"

The Crew wasn't used to this much friendliness, but after dropping their initial suspicions, they enjoyed it, waved back, and even hollered return compliments.

"Gorgeous flowers!"

"Pretty tree!"

"Love the porch swing!"

As much as she welcomed the warmer weather, Harper's allergies acted up terribly. She carried tissues everywhere she went.

"Bless you!" Dot and Mary called out to her throughout the day.

"Thank you," she said. "It's nothing." She refused to complain about allergies when there were so many other problems in the world. She avoided allergy medicine, because it made her sleepy and wired at the same time, and she wanted to stay sharp to write.

While Dot was busy from morning to night with the election, and with Mary working remotely for the law firm, Harper had to figure out how to keep busy. She'd never had so much free time and sometimes—well, most of the time—she didn't feel motivated to write. She'd read in his book *On Writing* that Stephen King wrote every day, no matter what and even when he didn't feel like it.

So, needing a kick in the rear, she took his advice to heart and found a routine that worked well for her. She got up around 7 a.m., poured herself a coffee that Dot or Mary had brewed, and read the *Daily Skimm* and Apple News on her phone. After that, she put her phone in the closet to avoid distractions and took her laptop up to a loft area in the house where she wrote for a few hours without interruption.

On some days the words flowed out of her imagination and onto the page. On others, she would stare at the blinking cursor for a while hoping that an idea would come to her. All in all, she was making some progress. But she still didn't feel confident enough to share her pages with anyone.

At noon, Harper would stop writing and go for a walk. She'd take her laptop in her backpack and headed to Curds and Whey for a Cedar Falls Classic smoothie—banana, cacao nibs, peanut butter, and vanilla protein powder—or a superfood bowl with beets, crisp chickpeas, and blackberries.

After lunch, she'd often pop into the Democratic offices where the For the Win team was parked until the election to chat up Dot, Fletcher, and Rose. Then she'd stroll down Main Street and stop at the bridge to watch the creek flow by for a few moments, before she made her way to the Sin Bin. Once there, she'd set up in the back corner to write for a couple more hours.

She liked the afternoon hum of the place. It helped to have something going on around her. She still wasn't used to the small town quiet.

And, if she was being honest with herself, she enjoyed seeing Tommy Taylor. She'd steal glances of him over her laptop screen when she was sure he wasn't looking. And while he gave her space to write at his bar, he'd occasionally catch her eye and stop to talk. She liked chatting with him. He was easy company, and so different from Kai the surfer who had been charming but, looking back on it, way too self-absorbed.

Tommy made her feel . . . happy. And she found herself spending more time at the Sin Bin. She'd met a few of the regulars and they'd call out to her, "Hey, Harper—how's the great American novel coming along?" She'd blush and wave them away but felt the early excitement of making new friends.

On Wednesdays, Harper took over the children's reading hour at Reader Falls Bookshop. The Jankowskis loved having her around, and the number of parents and children coming to the store noticeably grew. So did sales. Harper chose books that she loved as a child, including *Charlie and the Octopus*, *The Pigeon Wants a Puppy!*, *The Adventures of Pippi Longstocking*, *Eloise*, and all the Beverly Cleary books about Ramona and Beezus. Kids begged their parents to buy copies of these books so they could take them home, and the parents preferred buying books over candy or video games. Anything to get them off their screens.

In the evenings, Harper made dinner with Mary and Dot, or they chose a new local place to try. Her favorite was a new farm-to-table place called the Butter Half. She loved the roasted chicken with baked apples, cauliflower puree, and the raspberry crumble. And ever since she tried milk at the farm, she'd been letting herself have cream in her coffee and the occasional scoop of butter pecan. It turned out that Tommy was right—she *wasn't* lactose intolerant. She was glad to shed that label and limitation. She was feeling comfortable in her own skin. That was new for her.

Life in Cedar Falls was being good to Harper Lee Adler.

ONE WEDNESDAY, TOMMY texted her.

"Hey! Will you be at the Sin Bin tomorrow?"

"I was planning on it. What's up?"

"I have something to show you."

"Can't wait!"

Harper tried to write the next morning but kept thinking about Tommy. What could he possibly want to show her?

She got to her perch at the bar around two in the afternoon, her usual time. She kept looking up at the door every time it opened, expecting to see Tommy. The suspense was killing her.

Finally, around three, Tommy arrived, carrying a medium-size cardboard box from one of the bar's vegetable deliveries.

"Hey, Harper," he called to her.

"Hi, howdy, hello."

"Would you mind coming back to the office? I need to set this down back there."

"Sure." She shut her laptop and decided she could leave everything at her high top. She'd never risk that in the city, but Cedar Falls was a different kind of place.

She walked past the bathrooms toward the Sin Bin's back offices. Paperwork was strewn everywhere. Tommy certainly didn't ascribe to Dot's clean desk policy.

On the wall across from his desk chair was a bulletin board pinned with order forms and schedules. A Packers' calendar hung on the wall next to his computer. She took a glance and saw "Harper" written in blue and underlined twice on that day's date. Her eyes widened and her heart skipped a beat. But she pretended not to have noticed.

"What's going on? You sounded so mysterious on the phone," she said.

He set the box on top of the papers on his desk. "Before you say anything, let me explain."

She nodded and ran her closed index finger and thumb across her lips to zip them shut.

"Last night, after closing the bar, I was in a hurry to get home. When I was backing out of the parking lot, I almost hit a small dog."

Harper's eyes widened. "Oh no!"

"It jumped out and almost went under my tires. Poor little thing was very skinny, and her fur was matted. Looked like she'd been homeless on the streets for a while."

"Is she okay?"

"I took her to the emergency vet. They say she needs medicine and someone to take better care of her. They think she's around two years old. Some sort of tiny doodle mix. She wasn't wearing a collar and there's no chip to tell us who she belongs to. I've put up some flyers around town and posted on Facebook to see if anyone lost her, but so far no one has come forward."

"Oh goodness." Harper pointed to the box. "Is she . . . in there?"

"She is. And this is where I need your help."

"Sure, what can I do?"

"Well, you've seen how crazy it can get in here. And with my hours, I can't take proper care of her. So, I wanted to ask . . . just until we can find her a permanent home . . . do you think you'd be able to look after her?"

Harper's hands went to her chest. "Me? Oh wow. I mean, yes, of course." She immediately wondered if Dot and Mary would be okay with this. But she could deal with them later. "Can I see her?"

Tommy carefully lifted the lid of one of his supplier's ventilated cardboard boxes that he was constantly breaking down for recycling.

Inside the container was a very small, freshly bathed dog, curled up on a soft teal fleece blanket. She had short cream-colored fur that looked like she'd been knitted by Harper's grandmother back in Brooklyn. The dog opened one black eye, seemed to smile at Harper out of the side of her mouth, and then snuggled back into her bed.

"Oh, she's the cutest!" Harper couldn't get over it. Her heart melted. She put her hand on the dog, who was so warm and cozy in her makeshift bed. She felt the gentle push of the dog's rib cage as she breathed.

"Isn't she? I just can't take her to the shelter. I'm afraid of what may happen to her there." He picked the dog up and held her to his chest. "I'd take her out to the farm, but you saw my mom's Labs. Ray and Floyd play so rough."

"How long do you think it'll take to find her owners?"

"Hopefully not long. And if no one steps forward, I'll think of a plan B."

He didn't have to ask her twice. "I'll do it," she said.

"Thanks, Harper. I'll make it up to you."

"Oh, it's no problem at all." Harper rubbed her nose with the hand that had been petting the dog.

"I wish I knew her name. I've just been calling her 'the dog.'"

"I think that works for now." Harper sneezed. And sneezed again.

"Bless you." He handed her a bag from It's a Dog's World pet store. "Here's some food for her. And I got two small bowls, one for water and one for food, and a leash. Packers swag, of course. And a stuffed lamb chop toy, but she didn't seem interested in it."

"She's probably just out of sorts." Harper took the supplies. "I'll take her back to the house with me now." She barely got the sentence out before she sneezed again.

"Bless you. Are you okay?"

"I'm fine! It's just allergies, nothing to worry about."

But inside she knew that she'd be sneezing on the hour if she took care of this dog. She decided it was worth it. For the dog. And for Tommy.

She reached down and picked the dog up and held her paws cradled to her chest. The dog blinked a couple of times, but then stretched and settled down.

"Thank you, Harper."

"Ah-choo!"

"And bless you."

"Thank you," she said, laying the dog back in her box and pulling a tissue from her pocket to blow her nose.

The dog was still sleeping, and Harper thought it was best to let her. The box was too big for her to carry several blocks. And she didn't want to ask Tommy for a ride since he was already serving customers.

She considered her options while she carried the dog back into the bar and to her table where she'd left her laptop and backpack. She pulled out a cloth tote that she always carried in case she needed an extra bag for her shopping. Then she placed the pup's rear at the bottom of the bag, with her little face sticking out of the top, eyes wide open now.

"I think we're set," she said to Tommy.

"Hold on, I gotta take a photo of this." Tommy grabbed his phone and took a few different angles. "You two are adorable."

Harper latched on to that compliment and said goodbye to Tommy. They agreed to catch up later so she could say how everything was going when she got home.

Then Harper left the Sin Bin and carried her new charge down the street toward Maple Avenue, the bag gently hitting her hip with each step.

"What am I supposed to call you, little one?" Harper asked. She only got a blink in reply.

"We'll have to come up with something better than that." Harper sneezed, patted the dog's head, and started for home.

Chapter 27

In the weeks following their dinner on the farm, Mary kept thinking about Joe Taylor and the pressures he and other farmers were under to sell their farms to the government. After she'd finished filing a brief one day, she called her partner who focused on property law. She knew Patricia Parker from a mentoring match breakfast the firm had held the year before. Since day one at the firm, she'd kept in touch with all the mentors through handwritten thank-you notes and the occasional friendly yet purposeful email to stay on their radar.

Patricia's expertise was more in coastal cities and shore access than in farm country, but the general principles were the same. Mary prepared for the call with specific questions so as not to waste the partner's time. She was especially interested in the precedents where the property owner had prevailed over the government.

"It's not *impossible* to beat city hall, but it's really tough." Patricia told her what she'd look for in the case. "My advice is: Follow the money. You might find something at the end of that trail. Look for any discrepancies. If there's anything that suggests the project isn't on the up and up, like they're hiding something, that can often be enough to make the threat of eminent domain go away."

Mary made a note on her pad, "Follow the money," and underlined it three times.

"And, Mary, you could always think about getting the media on the story. They tend to love these kinds of controversies, and I bet local news will be more sympathetic to the farmer than to the government. It's worth a shot."

"That's an interesting idea. But Mr. Taylor is so private, it's like he doesn't want anyone to know what's happening. I'll talk to him about that, though. It's a good idea." She had what she needed to take the next step. "Thanks so much, Patricia. You've been a great help."

"Call me if you get stuck. These fights can escalate quickly."

MARY CONTINUED TO poke around looking for clues as to whether there was anything fishy about the government plan to force the Taylors into selling the farm.

She searched for "Taylor Farm" to see what she could find. There were a lot of links to crop sales and records, and some articles in trade magazines like the *Wisconsin Agriculture Journal.*

> Joe Taylor takes farming seriously, but he laughs easily. The Taylor Farm has grown by five hundred acres under his care. They've added more crops and a few more dairy cows as well. The farm is a bit of a throwback and one that Joe intends to keep in his family. He's been a county commissioner and the chairman of the Colby County Fair. His three boys all played football . . .

There was a link to a photograph of Mike, Jake, and Tommy. She clicked on it. They were in their high school football uniforms, their helmets under their right arms, hair mussed, and squinty faces in the bright sun. All-American kids.

She kept scrolling and found a link for "Sergeant Jake Taylor." She clicked. There was a group shot of several Marines all gathered around an armored vehicle, posing for a photograph. "Al-Anbar—Iraq." She zoomed in and picked him out right away. She knew he'd been in the military though he rarely mentioned his service and she hadn't pressed.

Jake was smiling, looking right into the camera, with his head shaved. Sunglasses rested on his forehead. The dimple in his cheek clearly visible. He held his arms folded over his chest, his biceps bulged, and his legs were crossed at the ankle as he leaned on the tank's door. He looked like a man who was right where he wanted to be. Even if it was in a war zone.

Mary had never been attracted to a military man before, but she had to admit, Jake Taylor was hot. And solid—in more ways than one.

Shaking off her daydreams, she searched for Wisconsin cases of farm takeovers. She sent herself several links to review in her spare time.

But before she logged off, she clicked again on Jake's photo. Then she sent it to herself and saved it in her camera roll. "Research," she told herself.

Chapter 28

Dot laced up her sneakers and put on a slim puffy vest in hot pink over her white long sleeve running shirt. She grabbed a royal-blue For the Win baseball cap and pulled her blond ponytail through the back opening. After patting down her pockets to make sure she had her lip balm, phone, credit card, and an emergency twenty-dollar bill, she looked in the hallway mirror and thought, "Feet, don't fail me now." She was due to meet Danny Dawson at Reader Falls in twenty minutes.

She hadn't been running as much as she had in New York. Her schedule at the FTW offices plus the weather had kept her from getting out. And running on the treadmill at the house wasn't the same. She hoped she could keep up with Danny and not die on the first hill.

When Dot arrived, Danny was already inside the bookshop chatting with the Jankowskis. She observed them from outside the door for a moment. Danny towered over Ted and Jeanie. Jeanie held her husband's hand and had her other hand on Danny's forearm. He wore medium-length running shorts and a white T-shirt under a red University of Wisconsin hoodie. On his head he wore a green "Dawson Construction" cap, and his black hair curled up under it. "Wow, he's so cute," she thought.

"There she is," Ted said when the bell rang, announcing her arrival.

"Don't you look darling, Dot!" Jeanie said. "Isn't she darling, Danny?"

His cheeks reddened at his older friend's obvious attempt to push him toward his running date.

"Right as always, Jeanie." He smiled shyly at Dot, knowing full well what was up.

"Love your shoes," Dot said, pointing to his New Balance 9060s, feeling awkward with the heavy-handed hints by Jeanie.

"It seems we both have good taste," he said, pointing to her sneakers. They wore the same brand.

"Great minds think alike." She smiled and casually leaned toward the "New Release" table to rest her hip against it but misjudged the distance and nearly fell over. Danny reached out and caught her.

Embarrassed, she looked up at him through her top lashes and said, "Thanks. I promise I run better than I walk."

His hands were strong and warm, and he held her a few seconds longer than necessary to ensure she was secure on her own two feet.

"I'll be there in case you need me," he said. "Besides, it's good to test my reflexes."

"Looks like you've not lost a beat," she said.

"Oh, you've still got it, Danny," Ted said. "I'm the one that's losing my grip! I can barely unscrew the pickle jar anymore."

Danny casually put an arm around Ted's shoulders and turned to Dot.

"So, just before you arrived, these two were telling me about a polka competition they're going to in a few weeks down in Monroe," he said.

"Polka competition? That will be amazing. Next stop, *Dancing with the Stars*!"

"More like dancing to the oldies," Jeanie said, laughing. "The only thing is that we can't close the store during tourist season."

Dot didn't hesitate. "I could cover for you. I'm sure Harper would pitch in as well. You wouldn't have to worry about anything—we'd just need to learn how to ring up the sales."

"We couldn't ask a young woman like you to do that. You have a life to live. And parties to go to," Ted said.

"You overestimate my social life, Ted. I love this store. It reminds me of my grandmother. Plus, I could meet more people in the area, which would be good for me and For the Win. Please just say yes."

"I think you should take her up on it," Danny said.

Jeanie ran a hand over her hair to smooth it. "Well, Ted. What do you say? One more polka before they put us out to pasture?"

"It's very kind of you, Dot. I'm inclined to say yes," Ted said.

"Great! I'll stop by this week after Harper's reading hour and go over the details. I'm excited. This will be so fun." She hugged the Jankowskis with enthusiasm.

"All right, you kids go get some exercise. Run an extra quarter mile for me, okay? It's about all I could ever manage." Jeanie ushered them to the door.

Out on the sidewalk, Dot adjusted her hat and pulled her ponytail tighter. She stretched her quads but tried not to make a big show of it. She was trying to be super casual and wasn't sure she was pulling it off.

"I THOUGHT WE'D go this way, up to the covered bridge. It's one of the last left around here and has a historic designation," Danny said. "It'll be around a four-mile loop."

"Perfect. Lead the way."

"Let me carry that for you," he said, reaching for her water bottle. She almost refused but let him have it. Their fingers brushed each other. And a shiver of electricity bolted up her arm.

They set out running. Danny kept the pace slow, and Dot pushed a little in front, showing him that it was okay to go faster.

Danny's route took them to the opposite side of Main Street and onto a trail that followed the river. Along the way, he pointed out the elementary school he and the Taylor boys had attended.

"I bet you three were so cute together."

"I'm not sure about that. We caused Mrs. Taylor a lot of headaches and she ended up doing more than her fair share of laundry. But I'm also not sure what my mom and I would have done without them. With my mom's hours as a nurse at the hospital, I ended up at their place a lot."

"Grace told me she loved it and that you were never a burden."

"She's an amazing woman," he said. "She's been like a second mom to me."

They jogged past the original wool mill, next to the firehouse, and down from there to the beautiful City Hall, which had just been refurbished. Small businesses of all kinds were tucked alongside the historic stone buildings—sewing shops, chocolatiers, and clothing boutiques.

Lavender, deep purple, and royal-blue wildflowers covered the riverbank.

As they settled into a rhythm together, Dot asked him about his construction business. He mainly helped families remodeling their historic homes.

"I like helping people stay in town instead of seeing them move to one of those cookie-cutter subdivisions nearer Milwaukee. Cedar Falls is such a unique place. I want to keep it that way."

"It's so nice to know where you want to be." She pumped her arms to keep up while they talked. "Have you ever been to New York?"

"Never had the chance. Maybe one day I'll get there. The news makes it sound pretty rough."

"Certain areas are. But I'd love to show you the good parts. It's *such* a great city. I think you'd love running in Central Park."

"Running from what exactly?" he teased.

"Ha! It's not as bad as that." She waited a few paces. "Usually."

They ran in silence for a while.

"How often do you run?" she asked.

"Enough to clear my head. So, most days I put in a few miles. Helps keep me sane."

"Same for me. If I don't run, I don't know how to burn off my nervous energy."

"You don't seem like a nervous person to me."

"Looks can be deceiving. I'm like a duck gliding across the pond."

"You have webbed feet?"

"No, you just can't see me furiously paddling below."

"You're a pretty cute duckling, though," he said.

She smiled at the surprising flirtation. He thought she was cute. She felt she could run a few more miles after that.

They turned right toward the river.

"That's the bridge ahead," Danny said. "It was built in the late eighteen hundreds. When I was a kid, you could still drive on it. Now it's only for pedestrians." They slowed to a walk as they came to the historic site.

"It's gorgeous," she said. "Like out of *The Notebook*." The stream ran into a lake and all the trees were budding with new spring leaves in light green. A few families with young children were there with fishing poles and picnic baskets.

"Here, let me take your picture for you," Danny offered. "Something you can send to your friends back home."

"Oh, okay. Sure." Dot stood in front of the bridge, hands on her hips, feeling a little awkward.

Danny snapped a few photos from different angles, like he knew how to be a good Instagram boyfriend.

"All for the 'gram," Dot joked, taking back her phone and texting the shot to the family chat.

"I wouldn't know. I don't have any social media."

"You don't?" she asked, surprised and impressed.

"Nah. I tried it for a while. I just never got anything out of it. And I just really don't like comparing myself to others. I've got enough pressure without trying to keep up."

Dot took that in. She thought about what Jeanie told her. How Danny had suffered such heartbreak when his fiancé and unborn baby girl were killed in that accident.

"You're right. That's the awful part. 'Compare and despair,' my grandmother would say. But I use it for work a lot. And I send my sister tons of funny dog videos."

"I've seen some of those. If there was only dog content on the Internet, we'd all be better off."

"Agree." They smiled at each other and held each other's gaze, lingering past the point of casual.

"Thanks for bringing me here. It's beautiful," Dot said, forcing her eyes to look around.

"You bet. I figured if you're only going to be here a short while, you should see the sights."

Dot did the math quickly in her head. She only had six months left in Cedar Falls. Suddenly, that didn't feel like enough time.

Chapter 29

In late May, Dot and Fletcher headed to Milwaukee for the annual Wisconsin Democrats state convention. As the election neared, it was clear that Wisconsin was the must-win state for both sides. Its ten electoral votes could literally be the difference maker for the presidency. There was a lot on the line, and Kitty Bell wanted For the Win to be up front and center at this meeting.

Since the convention started early on the Saturday morning, Fletcher suggested they go the Friday night before and visit one of the restaurants his parents had told him about. Dot had never spent time in Milwaukee, so she agreed. In an instant, she envisioned them together at their table sharing a bottle of wine, her head thrown back in laughter, him looking sharp in open collar and blazer. "Snap out of it!" she told herself. This is a work dinner, not a date dinner. But still, the image stuck in her mind.

"You're going to spend the night with *Fletcher* in *Milwaukee*?" Mary teased. "You should do something I would do . . . have some fun. He's gorgeous!"

"I'm not spending the *night* with him, Mary. We're going to a work function and leaving the night before because it starts early. That's all," she said.

"Oh, okay. Keep telling yourself that." She threw a piece of popcorn Dot's way.

Exasperated and blushing, Dot took her beige Madewell trench out of the closet.

"Tell her she's crazy, Pippi," Dot said to the dog sitting in Harper's lap. No owner had ever come forward to claim the little dog, so Harper had kept her. She named her after her favorite character from her childhood bookshelf.

"Pippi," she said, whenever a passerby asked her name. "As in Longstocking." Harper had become very attached to the little dog, despite being allergic. She told Mary and Dot that she was getting used to it, but she'd succumbed to taking a heavy dose of Zyrtec every day.

"Mary's definitely crazy, Dot. How can you leave me here alone with her for two days? We'll probably end up in jail."

"That's the spirit, Harper. It's about time you got into trouble," Mary said, raising her Stanley to toast the moment.

"Well, Mary wants to get into trouble so she can have a reason to call Hot Cop Jake," Dot said.

"Sometimes you have to break the law," Mary said, looking out the big kitchen window and thinking about it.

A horn honked outside.

"That'll be Fletcher. Okay, be good girls. See you Sunday." Dot hugged them both, grabbed her wheelie bag, her backpack, and her light blue Tory Burch tote and headed for the door.

Next stop, Milwaukee.

IN THE CAR, Fletcher and Dot talked shop for a little about how the contest was coming down to the governor of Kentucky versus the young state senator from Georgia.

"Those are two very different visions for the party," he said.

"Which one do you prefer?" she asked.

"I just want to win."

Fair enough. So did she. They turned on the Al Franken podcast and listened to the episode about how the Democrats needed to communicate better with younger people.

"How old is Al Franken?" Fletcher said, hitting pause.

Dot searched on her phone for the answer. "Wow, he was on *Saturday Night Live* when Bill Clinton was president."

"Exactly. It's time for some new blood. The older folks need to clear out," he said.

"I know. Though it seems to be happening more and more. A lot of our candidates are younger this cycle. At least that's what Kitty said about the House and Senate races this year."

"Did you see the new Pew poll? Twice as many posts from influencers are still for the Republicans. We've got problems." He started the podcast again without waiting to hear Dot's opinion.

Dot tried not to be put off by Fletcher's know-it-all tendencies. The

Democrats did need to kick their communications into higher gear, but she believed slow and steady would win the race. She decided to put it out of her mind and just listen as she watched the scenery.

Al Franken kept talking, but Dot's mind kept drifting to someone else. Danny Dawson.

Chapter 30

The traffic into Milwaukee was heavier than they expected. Fletcher suggested they go straight to the restaurant before checking into the hotel.

"The reservations are hard to get. I don't want to be late, or my mom would be mad."

Dot was fine with that, and even thought it was nice that he was close with his parents. And that they could get them reservations to nice places and go to Europe for two-week vacations. It certainly wasn't the way she grew up. They were more of a "Let's go to our local place for clam chowder" type of family.

Fletcher's parents were lawyers and had met during the early days of Facebook. As some of Zuck's first employees, they had made a lot of money and then invested it well. In his college days, his dad had played basketball for Cal Berkeley, and Fletcher had inherited his dad's height. His mom was the daughter of Mexican immigrants who'd worked the fields in the San Fernando Valley. He'd inherited her slight build, dark eyes, and high cheekbones.

As Mary said, "He definitely won the genetic lottery."

At seven, they pulled into DanDan, an award-winning Chinese American restaurant on Erie Street. One of the owners had been on *Top Chef*.

"Perfect timing," he said, flashing Dot a smile.

They checked in with the maître d', and as they sat down, their waiter came over.

"What a beautiful couple," he said.

"Oh, we're not . . ." Dot started to say. But Fletcher put his hand on her knee.

"Thank you! She'll have a Community Effort, and I'll try the Freddie's on Fire." He returned the cocktail menu to the waiter and then turned back to Dot. "I studied the menu last night, so I'd be ready to go."

She was surprised he ordered for her rather than asking her what she wanted. But it turns out that *is* what she would have ordered. So, who was she to complain?

"Right away, sir."

Fletcher looked sheepishly at Dot.

"Don't worry, I know we're not a couple. But we'll get better service if they *think* we are."

"Oh, sure. Ha. Okay." Dot thought it was a little weird and controlling, but she was also hungry.

Over the course of the meal, they ate several small dishes. The smashed cucumber dim sum was Dot's favorite appetizer, and Fletcher's was the chicken and dill dumplings. They ordered two entrees: salt and pepper shrimp and kung pao chicken. For dessert, they shared the mango crème brûlée.

Throughout dinner, Fletcher made her laugh with stories from his childhood, and she found him very entertaining and charming. He was smart and well-read.

They had a very similar vibe on political issues. After her cocktail, she wondered if they could be a couple after all.

"Believe it or not, I was an awkward child," he said. He'd switched to nonalcoholic beer since he had the keys.

"I find that hard to believe."

"I was. I grew tall so quickly that everyone thought I was a lot older than I was. So it was kind of hard to be a little kid. I had to grow up kind of fast."

"You consider yourself grown up now?" she teased.

"Ouch! But I'll allow it," he said. "What were you like as a young girl? I bet you were cute."

"Oh, I was a big troublemaker and was always in detention and had to go to juvie for a bit."

"No way!"

"Totally not," she said. "I don't know, I was . . . normal. Had a lot of good friends from different groups. I was in theater and worked on the yearbook. That kind of thing."

"Did you ever think you'd be here today?"

"At a gourmet restaurant with a guy working to get Democrats elected in Wisconsin? Definitely not."

"Same. But I'm glad we're here."

She raised her glass to his. "Me too." They finished the last sips of their drinks.

"I'm so full. I won't need to eat at all tomorrow," she said.

"That might be a good thing. Can you imagine how bad the food will be at this?"

"Don't be a snob, Fletch! I know you love cheese curds as much as I do."

"Admittedly, they're delicious."

"Hey, let's quickly go over what we want to show them tomorrow about the FTW efforts so far in Cedar Falls. I was thinking I could point out the new social media post ideas they could copy across the state. Our engagement for get-out-the-vote was solid last week."

"I like that. And I can show them how I'm using AI prompts to get better results from the contact spreadsheet. I've literally got it down to a science."

"Perfect. I'll send Kitty a note in the morning detailing our plan. Have you noticed she's been irritable lately?"

"A little. But she's just under her own pressure. She's got the five-hundred-grand win bonus and the cover of *Washingtonian* on her mind. Ignore her when she gets snappy. You're doing an awesome job."

"You think so?" Dot asked, seeking reassurance.

"I know so. I see it every day. We have great new volunteers who only signed up because of you. And the office is cheerful and productive. Can't ask for more than that."

"Thanks, Fletcher. I needed a boost of confidence."

"You're the most confident person I know, Dot."

"If you only knew."

"Come on, let's end this night on a high note. Shots?"

"Absolutely not!"

"I was kidding. I'm driving, remember?"

They walked out of the restaurant together and went to their respective doors of Fletcher's car. Before getting in, he said, "Hey, who said you can't mix business with pleasure? This was fun."

And she had to admit, he was right. It had been a fun dinner . . . and date?

Chapter 31

After dinner, they made their way to the Pfister Hotel.

"Hi. Checking in. One room for Dorothy Clark. And another room for Fletcher Abbott."

"Dorothy. Ha! That's such a grandma name." Fletcher covered his face trying not to laugh.

Being a good sport, she chuckled, too.

"I'm sorry, I only see one room for Mr. Abbott. I don't have a reservation for Dorothy Clark."

"There must be some mistake. Can you check under Dot Clark?"

The clerk typed into the computer.

"No, ma'am. There's no reservation for you. Only one for a one-night stay for Mr. Abbott."

"Well, can I get another room?"

"I'm afraid we're fully booked. The state Dem convention is in town. Good luck with *that*." He laughed. The desk attendant was *definitely* not voting blue this year. Dot let the dig at the Dems go as she was more worried about what she'd do about getting a room.

Her heart sank. This was terrible. Where was she supposed to sleep?

Fletcher stepped up.

"Tell you what. Is there a couch in the room?"

"There is. We have you booked in a junior suite, sir, so there's a small living room separate from the bedroom. But the couch isn't a pullout. I could see if we have a rollaway mattress for you, if you'd like?"

"No need. I'll sleep on the couch. Dot, you can have the bed."

"Oh, no. You can't sleep on the couch. Maybe I can just find another hotel."

"It's late and we have an early start. Please. Just say yes. And then we'll find an additional room tomorrow. I'll be a gentleman. I promise." He held his hands up to show his innocence.

She wasn't worried about him taking advantage of her, but this felt highly inappropriate. But what choice did she have? Taking a deep breath and sighing it out, she said, "Okay. One night."

"Very good. Here's your room key." The employee slid the card across the desk to Fletcher.

"Could we have two keys, please?" Dot wanted to make sure everything was clear to Fletcher. And to the hotel clerk.

THEY ENTERED THE sixth-floor room and surveyed the small couch. There was no way that a man over six feet tall was going to be comfortable on that overnight.

Seeing her face, Fletcher said, "Don't worry. My dorm room bed was too short for me, too. I've got all sorts of hacks for sleeping. I'll be fine."

Dot felt terrible but what could she do. "Okay for me to use the bathroom first?"

"Knock yourself out. And after that, I'll be super quick and leave you to get your beauty sleep."

She changed into her pink-and-white-striped hemp pajamas, pulled her hair into a bun with a scrunchie, washed her face, lathered on her serum and moisturizer, and brushed her teeth. She put everything back into her toiletry bag to save room on the small counter.

"All yours," she said. Then she sat on her bed, cross-legged, pulling her novel out of her bag.

He entered the bedroom, and she noticed he'd changed into men's joggers and a gray fitted T-shirt.

"Good book?" he asked.

"It's okay. Everyone is reading it, so I thought I'd find out what the hype was," she said, closing it to look at the cover. Her face reddened when she realized he'd seen the title: *All Fours*. "I mean, it's fine. Not my typical read."

"Noted," he said. Then he closed the bathroom door behind him, and she heard him brushing his teeth. He was humming a Morgan Wallen song they'd heard on the radio just before arriving at the hotel. They'd sung along as Fletcher drove through downtown Milwaukee.

After just a few minutes, Fletcher opened the door to go back to his couch.

He stopped and leaned against the doorjamb.

"I like you without any makeup," he said. "Dot Clark. All-American girl."

"I was worried you were going to start calling me Dorothy." She blushed, despite herself.

They looked at each other, the air charged with the possibilities provided by a hotel room in a new city, neither of them having an attachment now.

"So, I . . . I guess I'll be in there." He pointed to the TV room. "If you want me . . . I mean, if you need me, for anything."

"I'll keep it firmly in mind." She tapped her temple with her forefinger.

"Yeah. Okay. I'll just . . ." He ran his right hand over his hair and pointed to the couch.

"Yep . . . you just . . ."

A silence hung suspended. They stared into each other's eyes for a moment longer than normal. But neither made the next move.

"Right. Good night, Dot."

"Good night, Fletcher."

He gently closed the door behind him.

After the latch clicked, Dot got up from the bed and went to the door. She leaned her head against it, wondering what would happen if she turned the knob. On the other side, Fletcher rested his head against the door, too, hoping she would turn the handle and make the first move. Several moments passed.

Ultimately, Dot decided it was more responsible to go to bed. She tried to read but after going over the same paragraph five times, she decided to call it a night. She turned out the light and could hear Fletcher already snoring in the other room.

Chapter 32

Fletcher had been true to his word and slept without complaint on a couch way too short for his long frame. He cranked his neck to the left and right to loosen it after being cramped on the sofa.

"I'm sorry about that," Dot said, pointing to his neck as they got ready to leave for the convention the next morning.

"Hey, it's nothing. Easy," he said. "A cup of coffee and twelve Advil, and I'll be good to go."

Dot was aware that they'd likely be seen leaving the hotel room together by someone going to the meeting. She braced herself for the questions and the judgment.

But to her surprise, no one was in the hallway. Still, she felt guilty about . . . something.

LATER THAT DAY another room opened in the hotel, and Fletcher moved into that one for the second night.

The convention went smoothly, and the Democrats were feeling good about where they stood at that point in the cycle. Fundraising was near record-breaking, and For the Win got several shout-outs on panels and breakouts for its creativity and organizational skills. In addition to their content and plans, the state director specifically asked Dot and Fletcher to explain their new system to track voter interest. And then, trusting her instincts, Dot raised her hand and was called up to the microphone on the makeshift stage in the large ballroom.

"Hi, it's me again, I promise this is the last you'll see of me." She tried a little self-deprecation and mustered her strong voice to make another pitch to the group.

"I just wanted to take this opportunity to underscore that while we have been a little better and creative in targeting younger audiences, we can't forget Wisconsin's rural voters, especially the farmers." She relayed the story Joe and Grace Taylor had told her about their votes being taken for granted over the years.

"So, in the end, if we want to win the state decisively, we need the farmers' votes. We shouldn't write them off and think they'll never vote with us again. They're open-minded, though we can't just say we want their votes—we must explain to them why we intend to *earn* their votes."

She got a generous round of applause, led supportively by Fletcher. She noticed he liked to be the first one to clap for others, and that was a nice quality in a person.

Throughout the day, Dot took detailed notes on her phone and sent the file to Kitty.

"You two keep at it. Great point about the farmers—they might tip the balance, at least the ones we have talked to in Colby County," Kitty texted, adding several exclamation marks. "It's the key to the entire map."

"Agree," Dot responded, and then before hitting send, she added two exclamation points to make sure it was clear to Kitty that she shared her enthusiasm.

Over lunch, a buffet in the hallway outside of the hotel's big meeting room, Fletcher suggested they head over to the Milwaukee Art Museum before they went home.

"Some culture! Great idea," Dot said.

They put their suitcases in the car and drove over to the waterfront where the museum stood. The white building was stunning against the blue sky and the even deeper blue Lake Michigan, its fringed top looking like the wings of a giant seagull.

"It reminds me of the Oculus," Dot said, thinking of the transit hub near the 9/11 Memorial.

The sun was bright in the sky and the temperature was warm. A light breeze came off the lake.

They chose three collections to see: American, Contemporary, and Photography and Media Arts.

"This place will give any big-city art museum a run for its money," Fletcher said.

"It is as good as the Whitney."

"High praise, Dot!" She was impressed he knew what the Whitney was. Or that he was intuitive enough to fake it.

After bouncing through a few rooms of modern art, Dot persuaded Fletcher to go see the antique furniture too. The early twentieth century reminded her of her grandmother's apartment.

"The lines are so clean," she said.

"Look, a fainting couch for the ladies," Fletcher said, pretending to be interested. She playfully punched him in the arm. He caught her hand and then held it. She didn't move to let go, letting herself be caught up in the moment.

After wandering through the collection, they stepped outside onto a deck to take in the lake view.

"It's as big as an ocean," Dot said, admiring the deep blue water. "I had no idea."

"I went to school with a kid who grew up on Lake Michigan. We went to his house one summer. It was such a scene. Great parties," Fletcher said. "The Sleeping Bear Dunes National Park. It's massive. I'd love to take you some day."

He put his arm around her. She leaned in. He smelled good.

For the briefest moment, she allowed herself to imagine a future with him.

"I'd like that," she said.

"It's a deal."

The breeze picked up, and a bumblebee came near them.

Fletcher screamed. "Ack! ACK!"

Granted it was a big bee, but he started running around, his long slender arms swirling like a windmill as he tried to get away. He screamed again.

"Fletcher, it's just a bee! It's more likely to hurt you if you run like that."

"Ack! It just brushed my arm," he yelled.

"Just stand still, it's not going to sting you!" How could she be calmer about a bee than he was?

"I *hate* bees!" He yelped again as it came near him and rushed inside, leaving Dot out on the deck. He sounded like . . . a girl.

She was mortified on his behalf. And just like that, any thoughts of Dot's future with Fletcher disappeared.

She took another look at the beautiful lake and calmed down before following him back into the museum.

"Ick," she said.

Chapter 33

Back in Cedar Falls, Dot set her suitcase by the staircase.

"Hi! I'm back," she called.

"We're in the family room. Come. Tell us everything," Mary hollered from the back of the house.

Dot grabbed an Orange Cream Poppi from the fridge and joined Mary and Harper in the family room.

Harper paused the latest episode of *Love Island* and patted the cushion next to her and Pippi.

"Sit."

Dot sat down and patted her lap. Pippi hopped into it. She'd become a part of The Crew.

"So, how was it?" Mary asked, tucking her legs underneath her, settling in for a good story.

"It was great. Lots of energy in the room. We got some credit for being super-organized. Met some nice people. Wisconsin is going to be tough but GOTV and . . ."

"No. Not the meeting. The weekend away with *Fletcher*!"

"Oh, *that*." Dot looked to the ceiling, as if the answer was written on it. "Well . . . it was fine."

"Fine?"

"I mean, it was good. He's very nice. Charming. And handsome. Plus, we agree on just about everything."

"So, what's not to like?" Harper asked.

"Well, um, right before we left Milwaukee to come home . . . I got the ick."

"Oh, no! What did he do?" Mary said. "Wait. Let me guess."

"Okay, you can try, but I don't think you'll ever get it. It was . . . Something I've never seen."

"Did he try to use a coupon?" That was Mary's opening bid. "Or does he play air guitar when talking about songs?"

Harper joined in and she and Mary ping-ponged Dot with questions. The Crew had a long list of icks.

"Analyze the bill for too long at the restaurant? I hate that," Harper said.

"Did he check himself out in the mirror too much?" Mary hated that.

"Oh, I know. He was mean to the waiter!" Harper threw in one more guess.

"No, no, no. It was none of those things. It was worse," Dot said. First, she explained what had happened with them having to share a hotel room. "He was a perfect gentleman . . . which surprised me and, to be honest, kind of disappointed me at one point. I was *almost* ready for more, but we stayed apart that night, which was probably for the best."

"So, if *that* didn't happen, what did?" Harper asked.

"Well, we went to this great art museum. You can't believe it's in Milwaukee—it's amazing. Before we left, we popped outside for a view over Lake Michigan, which is gorgeous. Anyway, when we were outside, he . . . he ran away from a bee. Like a girl."

"A *bee*?" Mary blinked wide and threw her head forward, making sure she'd heard that right. "Like a wasp?"

"No, it was a bumblebee."

"Oh ick," Harper said, pulling a face of secondhand embarrassment for Fletcher.

"Yeah. That's what I said." Dot started laughing, covering her eyes and shaking her head to get the image out of her mind.

Mary was doubled over laughing. "Is he allergic?" she asked.

"I don't know, but that ick's gonna stick," Dot said.

Poor Fletcher. He had no idea he'd been icked.

"I need to get some exercise," Dot said. She wanted to stretch her legs after the long weekend and to get the feel of the Milwaukee trip off her.

Though, if she were being honest with herself, what she was really hoping was that if she took the trail up to the covered bridge, she'd run into Danny Dawson.

Chapter 34

Dot was up and out early the Saturday of Memorial Day weekend. This was For the Win's big summer kickoff at the county farmer's market to help register more Democrats and increase yard signage, post support on social media, and get out the vote.

It was still chilly that spring morning as Rose, Fletcher, and Dot all arrived at their booth before 8 a.m. They wore their FTW vests over long sleeve T-shirts. Dot snapped a photo for their story then texted it to her sister in Colorado.

"It's cold here, too—we're expecting a foot of snow this weekend. Late spring snow. So great!"

Her sister had a weird idea of what great weather was.

At their booth, Dot and her team worked together to hang up their banner and set out their supplies while chatting with their farmer's market neighbors. One was a young mom who made the town's favorite flavored popcorn, and the other was a farmer and his wife who sold pickles in lots of flavors like classic, spicy, cherry dill, and German mustard.

"Garlic parmesan or beer cheese popcorn?" the lady from Pop It Like It's Hot offered the FTW team while tossing a handful of it into her mouth.

"Wow. How nice." Dot didn't want to be rude but it was a little early for that combo meal.

"Oh, I just ate but thank you. I'll buy some to take home, that's for sure." She gave her a bright smile along with that little white lie.

Mimi from Flour Power came by with a box of hot coffee and some pastries that FTW would hand out to anyone who stopped by.

"Oh nice. You're my new best friend, Mimi," Fletcher flirted. He winked at her, and Mimi smiled shyly. Dot thought they'd make a cute couple. She had cooled on Fletcher since the bumblebee incident. Maybe Mimi would be good for him instead.

The sun started to warm up the temperature, and the early birds out walking their dogs and babies came through the middle of the pedestrianized street. Everyone had their groceries, with heads of light green lettuce, big bags of cucumbers, boxes of tomatoes, and bundles of radishes. There were strawberries, blueberries, and cherries, plus hunks of cheese—Colby, muenster, and Dot's favorite, buttermilk blue. Big bouquets of fresh flowers spilled out of carts, and everyone carried a hot drink of some kind from one of the carts selling cappuccinos, matcha, chai lattes, and hot chocolate. A local musician tested his sound system, getting ready for a few hours of entertainment.

"A girl could get used to this, Rose," Dot said, elbowing her friend.

"The farmer's market is one of the reasons I've never left Cedar Falls. Been coming here since I was a little girl."

Having Rose with them was key to getting people to stop by their booth. She knew so many people, and would ask about their children and grandchildren, which made them linger a little longer. After a while, Rose would ask them to make sure they were signed up with For the Win.

"Remember, democracy's a participatory sport," she'd say. "You have to suit up and play." Her spunk was infectious and inspired Dot and Fletcher. By late morning, they had gone through their pastries and signed up dozens of people, many of them first-time voters.

"I'll go get some more goodies from Mimi," Fletcher said. "Think that's okay? Or do you need me to stay?"

"Good idea," Dot said. "Take your time. Rose and I can manage for a while."

She watched him walk away. He was incredibly good looking. But the bee thing stung.

AROUND NOON, DOT kept an eye out for Mary and Harper, who had volunteered to pass out FTW flyers for the get-out-the-vote campaign. They were due to help at the booth for the last couple of hours the market was open. After, they planned to get lunch at Brew and Chew, a local brewery and sandwich joint that had live music every Saturday and Sunday. They could sit outside with Pippi on their laps or in her tote bag. Dot had a feeling they'd be spending a lot of time on that patio over the summer.

Fletcher came back just as they were wrapping things up.

"Sorry I didn't get back sooner with some doughnuts. Mimi was crushing it—there were so many people there. I got behind the counter and tried to help."

"That's so nice of you. I'm sure she appreciated it," Dot said. "We had plenty of customers—even without doughnuts. It was a decent first effort."

"Cool. I'm going to head back to the bakery after we put all this away."

He's moving fast on Mimi, Dot thought. Good for him. And her.

"Hey there, For the Win, everybody!" Mary's Staten Island accent was unmistakable. And her outfit was unforgettable. She wore dark gray leggings, tall beige leather boots, a white button-down, a tight red sweater, and a faded jean jacket with the sleeves rolled up. She had a navy NYPD baseball cap on, and her dark hair tumbled down her back.

"Hi, guys! We're almost done here." Dot was so glad to see them. She was ready to kick back for the afternoon with her girlfriends.

"We ran out of flyers," Mary said, showing her empty hands.

"Yeah, all the guys wanted to chat up Mary," Harper said.

"Well thank goodness for that," Rose said. "We'll have to keep you two around!"

"Sorry we're running a little late," Harper said. She had on a long cotton printed dress with a rope belt, white sneakers, and Pippi in a cloth Reader Falls Bookshop tote bag. "We stopped and got some doggie macaroons and venison jerky." She held up her bag of goodies for the dog.

"We've had a great day so far. Here," Dot said. "Can you put this spicy buffalo popcorn in your bag? I bought it from the lady next door."

"Sounds delicious," Mary said. "Give me some of that now." She opened the bag and took a handful.

The Crew and the For the Win team finished cleaning up their booth, formed a line, and carried everything back to the offices.

"See you Monday!" Dot said to Fletcher and Rose. "We have a call with Kitty at nine. I think she'll like our update. And soon we'll have an actual nominee."

"Whether it's Governor Stone or Senator Lopez, I'm ready—let's effin' go," Rose said.

"Rose!" Dot laughed, a little shocked by Rose's profanity. It wasn't like her.

"Sorry, I got that from my grandson," she said. "Hey, you kids work hard. Thanks for letting this old lady be a part of it."

"You're our secret weapon, Rose. We couldn't do it without you," Fletcher said.

Dot agreed and gave her a hug goodbye.

Then she hooked her elbows through Mary and Harper's arms and said, "I'm starving. Feed me."

"We've got you, girl." Mary led the way.

ON THEIR WAY to lunch, Dot stopped on the sidewalk.

"Mary, I think Hot Cop Jake is over there."

Mary's head shot up.

They looked over at the Bethesda Lutheran Church stall selling fruit, vegetables, nuts, cheese, baked goods, and fresh flowers. Jake and Tommy were hauling boxes into the back of a large pickup truck bed.

"Oh, Tommy's there, too." Harper waved. "Hey, Tommy!"

Tommy shielded his eyes from the sun and looked for the source of the voice calling for him.

"Oh, hi, Harper! Dot, Mary. And Pippi, how's my girl?" Tommy walked over and patted the dog's head. "Cute dress, Harper."

"Oh thanks," Harper said. She wasn't used to getting compliments. "It has pockets."

"New York, New York," Jake sang as he walked over to join them. "Why are you loitering out here? Up to something, huh?"

"Still deciding," Mary said. "I like to strike when it's least expected."

"What are you all doing today?" Tommy asked, as he wiped his hands on a cloth.

"Just heading to lunch at Brew and Chew. Want to join us?" Harper said.

"We would," Jake said. "But we're helping our parents with their stall at the market."

"Hey Mom, Dad, look who we ran into," Tommy said as Grace and Joe Taylor came around the corner. They gave The Crew hugs.

"So nice to see you girls," Joe said.

"Oh, thanks. We talk about our fantastic night out on the farm all the time," Dot said.

"Well, you gotta come back out. It's real nice out now with all the fields planted."

"Mr. Taylor—I've been wanting to come talk to you about the farm," Mary said. "I've got a little information that might be worth sharing."

Jake looked at her, grateful that she cared about his parents' worries about holding on to the farm.

"I'd love to get your thoughts," Joe said. "There's a big hearing come up on it in a few weeks, and our lawyers aren't optimistic. Duncan's Doughnuts and Diner on Tuesday? It's just off Washington Street. I have a fairground meeting at ten a.m. that day. I could meet you before."

"I love a breakfast date," she said. "My favorite kind."

"Heck, if it's a date, maybe I'll come along," Jake said.

"Hey now, I asked her first!" Joe playfully elbowed his son in the ribs.

"You know, I was thinking," Grace said. "You boys should take these girls out to a traditional Wisconsin supper club. They can't go back to New York until they've gone at least once."

"That's a great idea." Tommy nodded, "Maybe I can get somebody to cover for me at the Sin Bin one night. We can recruit Danny to come along."

Dot's ears perked up on hearing that idea.

"A supper club? Sounds fancy," Harper said.

"Oh yeah, it's really sophisticated. Wait until you see it," Jake said, rolling his eyes a bit in jest.

"I'll make a reservation for next Saturday night for the six of you. How about seven o'clock at the Cedar Falls Inn?"

Mary thought Grace was hilarious as she played matchmaker for her sons. And she didn't mind one bit. "You bet. Will be there with bells on," she said directly to Jake.

"Great. You'll love it. The supper club is Wisconsin at its finest," Grace said.

THE CREW TURNED to head to lunch, the sun warming their backs.

"Well, Mary, Hot Cop Jake is *definitely* into you. Wisconsin's finest indeed," Dot said, throwing an arm around Mary and hip checking her.

"Oh, stop!" Mary said. But she had to admit it. Dot wasn't wrong. And the feeling might be mutual.

Chapter 35

The week was flying by.

On Tuesday, Mary met Joe Taylor for breakfast and impressed him with her order—steak and eggs and a side of silver dollar pancakes.

"A girl's gotta eat," he said, when the waitress asked Mary where in the world she put it all.

Mary smiled at Joe and sipped her black coffee. She liked Duncan's Doughnuts and Diner—though she worried when and if the owners would be sued by the big corporation for trademark infringement. Better not to call attention to that idea.

It was an old-fashioned diner, with big high-backed upholstered booths and a counter where you could eat alone in peace or have a chat with the server. The noise from the kitchen was fun to listen to—lots of energy as orders were called out, the cook heckling the waitstaff part of the entertainment. Looking around at the characters in the diner that morning, she could tell a lot of Cedar Falls business got done here.

"So, Joe, I called one of the partners at my firm in New York. She does a lot of work in this area. Just not the kind that would be on your side of things."

"Big-shot lawyers. Always tough."

"She gave me some tips and I did a little digging."

"Find anything? It's the damnedest thing—there's very little about who's behind this push. We know it's a foreign company and that they want to put some sort of high-tech whatchamacallit factory there. But no one has any details—not the state or our congressman. Not even the local Chamber of Commerce. At least none they're willing to give us. Hell, even the governor won't return my calls, and we went to high school together."

"Well, she told me to follow the money. So I started down a trail. And I came up with a company I'd never heard of."

She handed him a folder with her notes.

"Ever hear of these guys? Intermedium? Seems like they are based out of Washington, D.C."

Joe took out his reading glasses and gave the papers a once-over.

"That doesn't surprise me. I've had a suspicion that this wasn't on the up and up. It seems like there's a push and pull from inside *and* outside of our country."

"It seemed a little odd, I agree. But I couldn't find a direct paper trail that would tell us what actual company is trying to buy up all these farms."

"Mind if I keep this? Could come in handy with our team of lawyers."

"Absolutely. And if I find anything else out, I'll send it to you."

"That's really kind of you, Mary. I'm sure you have lots of other things to do instead of helping an old farmer."

"It was a pleasure. It's been sweet getting to know you and your family." She did not specifically mention his son who had typed his number into her phone at the end of the night when they'd had dinner at the Taylor farm. She had laughed when Dot changed his name to "Hot Cop Jake" in her contacts after she'd left her phone unlocked on the kitchen counter.

Joe signaled for the check and handed a fifty-dollar bill to the waitress.

"Keep the change, Peg."

"Thanks, Joe. Give Grace my best."

"You bet."

They got up to leave and Joe held the door for her. On the sidewalk they enjoyed a few more moments together in the sunshine.

"Another beautiful day in paradise," Mary said.

"When we start the corn harvest, we'll have you all back up to the house for a party."

"I'd love that," she said, and leaned in to kiss his cheek goodbye. She started to walk away when she turned back and called out to him.

"Mr. Taylor? One question—what would I wear to a corn harvest?"

Joe looked at her. She was wearing a navy pencil skirt, a white silk blouse, a red scarf, and nude heels. "Something casual. So I'd say . . . not that."

"Got it." Mary nodded.

They both laughed and went their separate ways, her billing hours, and him tilling fields.

Chapter 36

That week, Dot hosted a Democratic get-together at the Cedar Falls Community Center to watch the results come in from the Virginia primary. The race was still coming down to two candidates—Governor Ramsey Stone of Kentucky and State Senator Lucia "Lucy" Lopez of Georgia.

Kitty Bell had predicted this back in February at the Democratic debate in Madison. Stone was widely considered the more traditional and, thereby, safe choice, while Lopez was seen as more exciting, but riskier.

Governor Cal Ashby of California had flamed out in April, failing to win enough delegates to keep going. His fundraising dried up, and so did his ideas. He'd finally thrown in the towel and announced he'd be pursuing a career in acting.

"That sounds like an excellent decision," Lopez had said at the time. "I wish him well." She knew how to needle her opponents.

After Virginia, only New York was left on the primary schedule.

"All right, time to put your cards on the table," Fletcher said to Dot. "Who do you want to win?"

"I'm torn. I think both have strengths. Stone's got experience and credibility. But Lopez has passion and energy."

"If only we could meld them into one candidate, it'd be a lock."

"All I'm worried about is who can beat the Republicans. The country will be in huge trouble if we don't win this time," Dot said, echoing what most Democrats were saying across the country. Then, turning to her own concerns, she added, "Not to mention what *I'm* going to do after the election. I still have no plans."

"You worry too much," Fletch said.

"Story of my life." Dot knew it was true. She just didn't know how to turn off the worry spigot.

"I don't think you need to worry," Fletch said, scanning his phone for the latest polling numbers. "We can win. People are tired of the current administration. They want something new."

Dot wasn't so sure Fletcher was correct. She read the polls, too, and yes, a majority people said they were ready to turn the page. But when it came down to the electoral college, did enough of *those* people live in the states where they needed the votes? What she and Fletcher agreed on, however, was that the key to an electoral win—and Kitty Bell's half-a-million dollar win bonus—was Wisconsin.

"Things would be easier for us here if the Democrats on the coasts weren't having total meltdowns," she said. "What consultant told them it was a good idea to ban cows because they're bad for the environment? Policy ideas like that makes us look unserious and out of touch."

"I know what you mean. And our senior leadership is still, well . . . senior. They won't retire."

"Oh, I know. Half our senators are over seventy-five." Dot shook her head.

"Yeah. Explains why AARP is more powerful than the oil and gas lobby now."

Fletcher had a way of making her laugh. The workday flew by when they were side by side. Sometimes when she looked at him, the image of him running away from the bee in Milwaukee came into her mind and she'd try to erase it. While she'd settled on not being into him romantically, she was two thumbs up on working with him. They made a good team and he kept things light around the office with his quick wit and cheerful moods.

Her phone buzzed and she glanced down at a text from Danny Dawson. They'd been going back and forth with flirty but harmless texts for a few weeks. She knew he liked her but seemed skittish.

"Give me a call?" he said.

"Be right back," Dot said to Fletcher, pointing to her phone then gesturing she needed to go outside.

"Hi, it's Dot. Everything okay?"

"Hi. Yes, sorry. Everything's fine. I just don't like to text that much. Phone calls are easier."

"For sure. What's up?" she asked, curious what was on his mind.

"Remember that idea you had for fixing up Reader Falls?"

"Yes. I think it would help the store so much. It's a little rusty."

"Well, I couldn't sleep the other night and came up with some plans for a surprise for Ted and Jeanie when they go out of town in for the polka competition. You're still up for watching the store that weekend, right?"

"I am. What do you have in mind?"

"I'd love to show you. Can you meet me at the Sin Bin tomorrow for lunch? If you're not too busy saving American democracy, that is."

She vibed with his light tone. Suddenly, she didn't care what was happening election-wise.

"I think the republic will stand while we have lunch. Let me check my calendar, hold on." She pretended to look at her schedule. "I think I can move some things around. What time?"

"Noon? I could stop by your office, and we can walk down together."

"How about I meet you there at twelve?"

"Great. See you then."

Dot smiled and thought about what she'd wear the following day. She might have to raid Mary's closet.

After she hung up with Danny, Dot headed back to the primary party. The results were starting to come in. It looked like Lopez was going to prevail. Dot stood next to Fletcher trying to concentrate on the Virginia vote tally, but she was daydreaming about lunch with Danny.

When the deejay played "Georgia on My Mind" they knew it was a lock. Lucy Lopez had won. The Democrats were really going to roll the dice on this one. A young, single Latina as their nominee? It was equal parts exciting and terrifying.

Dot's phone buzzed again. Kitty Bell was texting her Wisconsin FTW team.

"Got insider info that Stone's backing out before New York primary. Lopez will be nominee."

"Oh my gosh—that's amazing. Think she can win in Nov?" Dot responded.

"Huge challenge, but she's a winner. I can feel it. Talk in an hour?" Kitty was raring to go.

Fletcher and Dot looked up from their phones and waved Rose over to them.

"We better get going," Fletcher said, noting they had information that no one else in the community center had.

"Yes, let's head out," Dot said, feeling invigorated by the news. She was drawn to Lopez and wanted to help her win the White House. "We have more history to make."

Chapter 37

The Crew called an Uber and arrived at the Cedar Falls Inn just as Jake, Tommy, and Danny were walking in from the parking lot. Wisconsin was experiencing an "oh crap what happened to spring" heat wave and all of them were anxious to get inside the supper club's cool air.

Jake held the door for them and shook his head.

"New York. You are trouble with a capital T."

"What makes you say that?" Mary asked, walking right past him in her red strapless short summer dress and five-inch-tall black sandals. She carried a white cotton cardigan in case she got cold or there was a need for a touch of modesty.

They walked to the hostess stand and were greeted by the owner and her son.

"Well, well, well," Melinda Meier said when she saw Danny and the Taylors. "If you all haven't grown up into the pride of Cedar Falls!" Melinda was in her eighties and had known the boys their entire lives.

"Hi, Mrs. Meier. Mom and Dad said to give you their best." Jake kissed her cheek.

"Well tell them to come in. It's been an age."

"They insisted we bring our new friends to meet you and have a traditional Wisconsin experience for them to remember," Tommy said.

"Yes, this is Dot, Mary, and Harper," Jake said, gesturing to The Crew. "They're living in town for a year. They're from Manhattan—New York, not Kansas."

"All the way from New York! Well, welcome to the Cedar Falls Inn." Melinda shook each of their hands with both of her own. "You're all so pretty. And dressed up! Customers used to dress to the nines when they came to the supper club. But things change." She sighed, remembering the good old days. "Anyway. I hope you're hungry."

"I'm always hungry," Mary said. "What's your specialty?"

"Prime rib. But the walleye is fresh tonight, too, if you want fish. Oh, and we have Jack Czarnecki performing tonight. He can sing just like Frank Sinatra. Close your eyes and you'll think it's Frank, who actually sang here when my grandfather opened this place."

"Sinatra! I never thought I'd get to see him live." Dot was charmed by the proprietress.

"We'll make sure you have a nice night," Melinda said, putting an arm around Mary's waist. "My goodness aren't you just the tiniest thing. We need to feed you."

"Oh, don't worry. I'll eat," Mary said.

Melinda excused herself as another family she knew entered the restaurant.

"Okay, let's get a drink and order. Follow me," Jake said. He took their cocktail orders, got himself a non-alcoholic beer, and picked up menus from the bartender.

Mary commented on his beer choice. "My dad loves Athletic. Said he always wanted a non-alcoholic version that actually tasted like beer."

"Well, I'm driving tonight. Dad loaned us the Suburban so that everyone can fit."

"Our hero," Tommy said, and slapped his brother on the back good-naturedly.

The Crew consulted each other on what they'd order for dinner.

"Everything's good. Can't go wrong. And everyone gets the salad bar, too." Jake had transformed into a cruise director for the supper club.

After placing their orders with the bartender, Tommy and Harper fell immediately into an easy conversation about Pippi. The Crew's neighbors had offered to keep her for the night.

"They said it's easier to babysit a dog than to cave to their kids' pleas for one," Harper said. She wore a light blue midi dress trimmed in red and ivory espadrille wedges that tied at the ankle.

"That's for sure. Every kid needs a dog, and every dog needs a kid."

"I wish I'd thought of that line to use on my parents when I was young," Harper lamented. "I was never able to convince them to get us any pets."

"Have you told your family about Pippi yet?" he asked.

"Oh yes. My brother is so jealous. My parents think I'm just a temporary guardian—and that this dog is too much responsibility for me at this point. But it's not like I have a real job or a place to live back home. I told them that you're still looking for the owner."

"Far and wide. The search party is out."

"But if you find them, don't tell them where she is. I couldn't possibly part with her now."

"You got it," Tommy said, sealing the deal by clinking Harper's glass.

Jake went over to the wall and put a coin into a dispenser, then came back and handed a small card, about the size of a baseball card, to Mary.

"Here, another ticket for you, Miss Russo," he said, fully smiling, dimple and all.

"What's this?" Mary turned the card and examined it.

"It's one of our traditions. Just peel back these tabs, and you could win up to two hundred and fifty bucks. It's like a paper slot machine."

"Well, let me try my luck!" She pulled back the tabs. Not a winner. "Bummer," she said. "I'll keep it as a souvenir. Or maybe it's my get out of jail free card in the future."

"Smart. I'm sure you'll need it someday."

"I don't plan on causing any trouble. At least not any that I can't get out of."

"You're kind of a smooth criminal, New York."

Meanwhile, Danny and Dot talked about their plans for a major remodeling surprise of the Reader Falls Bookshop.

"How did it go when you talked to the Jankowskis?" Dot asked. When they'd met for lunch at the Sin Bin, Danny had showed her his plan for remodeling the shop in a three-day sprint. He had it all organized with the construction workers he employed and several volunteers in town.

"I didn't give them any details—didn't want them to have an excuse to say no. I just asked them, 'Do you trust me?' And Jeanie said of course they do. Then I said, leave it with Dot and me."

"I can already see the new shelves, a fresh coat of paint, clean rugs. It's going to be great."

"Yep. It's a go. Hope you don't have any other plans next weekend. It's going to take the full seventy-two hours they're gone for us to get it done."

"No other plans. I told Fletcher and Rose, and they're going to cover for me Friday. I can check my phone regularly and respond to anything, especially if Kitty rings any fire alarms. And then they said they'd come help after they close the office that evening. And Harper and Mary are in, too."

"So are Jake, Tommy, and the guys who work for me during the week," Danny said. "They're gathering materials this weekend so that everything will be ready."

He smiled and didn't look as sad as when she first met him. She felt a gentle pull toward him.

As if sensing her observation, he added, "It's nice to have something to look forward to."

"Always," Dot said, and raised her glass to him. "Cheers."

"Cheers." He winked at her and she melted a little despite the cool air-conditioning.

Chapter 38

When their seats were ready, the six of them took their drinks and sat in front of the stage at a table that held a relish tray filled with gherkins, radishes, and carrots. They'd already placed their dinner orders before taking their seats. Young servers made their salads as customers pointed out what they wanted.

"Extra sunflower seeds, if you don't mind," Jake said.

"You are so extra," Mary said. She was having fun aggressively flirting.

When they sat back down, the girls took a moment to admire their surroundings. The room was painted a deep hunter green and was decorated with paintings of fishing and hunting in Wisconsin. Several mounted animal heads served as decoration.

Tommy pointed all of them out to Harper. "That was a big buck. Whoo-wee. And look at that elk. Must have been huge."

Harper hated the ideas of hunting or taxidermy. She pretended to look at the stuffed animal but fixed her eyes to a spot just below his head.

The guys started reminiscing about making their first deer, and she became desperate to change the subject. Suddenly, Harper pointed to a wall lined with signed headshots of famous past performers.

"Look at that!" Harper pointed to the wall behind the stage. "Glenn Miller, Louis Armstrong, Doris Day, and, just as she said, there's Frank Sinatra!"

"My Nonna would love it here," Mary said, craning her neck to see the picture more clearly. "She knew Ol' Blue Eyes. I think she may have dated him."

"Wow, you are *so* New York," Jake teased her.

"He was actually from Jersey," she said.

"Remind me to take you to my next old crooner trivia night," he said.

"If you want to win, I'm your gal." Mary winked.

"This place is so cozy," Dot said. "I almost feel like I've been here before."

Tommy agreed. "I know what you mean. We love this place. When we were kids, our dad wouldn't eat the entire day because he knew we'd be coming here for supper. Then he'd put away a whole lake of fish."

"And they'd let me tag along," Danny said. "I always got the fish fingers and a baked potato. I'd put so much butter and sour cream on it that Grace would say, 'Danny, you don't even know you're eating a vegetable!' And then she let me order an extra meal for my mom for when she got off her hospital shift."

"Yep. Lots of great memories," Jake said, looking around the room. Several people came by to say hi to the Taylors and to thank Jake for his service. He was kind to all of them and showed a humility that Mary hadn't seen before. And he was very polite to all the older folks who stopped by for a word.

"So, what do you think the three best things about living in Wisconsin are?" Dot asked the table to get a discussion going after their entrees were served. She was still trying to understand more about this midwestern state and why it swung from one party to the other every four years.

"Well, that's a good question," Jake said, sitting back to let his rib eye digest. "For me, the best thing is that we have this collection of friendly small towns that are all unique and combine to make up one state. I don't think there's anywhere else like that in the States."

"It still has traditions," Danny said. "Take this place. The supper clubs live on because people still want a place to get together that isn't a chain restaurant in a strip mall."

"Though you gotta admit that the Cheesecake Factory is great," Mary said.

"Fair point," Tommy said. "That menu is killer."

"What about you, Tommy?" Harper wanted to know what he thought. "What do you think the best thing is about Wisconsin?"

"Believe it or not, we used to get a day off school on the first day of deer season. I mean, if that's not a great reason to miss school, I don't know what is."

Harper tried to erase the image in her mind of Tommy dragging a deer carcass through the forest, but he saw her face.

"I can't imagine you ever killing an innocent animal," she said.

"Hey, don't shoot," he said, trying to get her to laugh. When she didn't, he said, "Look, I promise I never shot at Bambi," he said. "Besides, all the best conservationists will tell you, it's good to hunt—it helps manage the population of the deer. And we ate everything we killed. It taught us a lot about responsibility."

"I'm going to take your word for it, but I'll just keep pretending that food magically appears on my plate," Harper said.

"May I ask if it's strange to live in such a purple state when it comes to politics? Where so many people disagree and every four years each side tries to rip each other apart here?" Dot asked.

"It's worse than it was when we were growing up. Lots of animosity—but that's not really how it is in Cedar Falls. Folks mostly get along—even if they don't agree. Heck, I'm friends with a lot of Democrats," Jake said.

"Does that mean you're a Republican?"

"That's how I vote. Same as these two." Jake gestured to Tommy and Danny. Dot took that in, confirming her suspicions.

"Does it bother you that we're Democrats?" Dot asked.

"It should bother *you* that you're Democrats," Tommy joked.

Harper nudged him with her elbow. "Watch it!"

"I'm kidding. I don't give a rat's behind how you vote. That's how we were raised. Our mom and dad taught us to be good to everyone," he said. "If we felt like we couldn't work or be neighbors with people who had different political views, well it'd be hard to run a business."

"Or be a cop."

"Or build them a house," Danny said, jumping into the conversation.

"But do you ever think the Republicans are . . . well, that they go too far on some things?" Dot pressed the point.

"Sure—just about as much as the Democrats do," Danny said. "Here's my take—there are extremes on both sides. I tune that out. I go about my business. I don't let politics get in the way of a good time."

"Speaking of a good time," Mary said, veering toward a conversational off-ramp.

A platter of desserts arrived, and the Sinatra impersonator took the stage. They applauded as he broke into "Summer Wind." Mary hummed along, loving the vibe, her bare, narrow shoulders swaying to the beat.

"What's all this?" Dot asked, looking at the dessert selection. "This could feed a small army."

"I ordered us a variety. Wasn't sure what everyone would want. But I know I'm having a bite of that Snickers pie." Jake used the large serving spoon and heaped some onto his plate. Then he passed spoons around to everyone before taking a bite.

He'd ordered an ultimate sundae, a cherry cheesecake, a vanilla bean custard crème brûlée, a Schaum Torte, which was a mix of whipped cream and fruit in a meringue shell, and the Snickers pie.

Everyone commented on their favorite.

"It's the cheesecake for me," Dot said. "Better than Junior's."

"I'm with you there." Danny took another bite as the singer softly sang "Strangers in the Night."

"But the crème brûlée is hitting," Mary said as she took another scoop.

"I liked the cheesecake," Harper said.

"Told ya that you weren't lactose intolerant," Tommy said.

"I have to rethink my whole dessert game!"

"What about you guys? What's so great about living in New York?" Danny asked.

"Oh, I love this question. Give me a second. Let me think of the best thing," Dot said as she licked her spoon one last time and imagined her walk to work in the morning. "Okay. I love Central Park. I used to walk through the park to get to work and back. In the mornings, all the dogs are there running off the leash, having the best time. It really is the greatest park in the world. And then I'd run there in the evenings and on the weekends. There are people from all over the world there. And you always see something interesting. Or crazy."

Harper chimed in. "I love that you have all these interactions with people through your day—like the woman next to you on the subway making her way to work at a hospital, or the barista making your coffee. And there's the hustle of figuring out how all these people are going to live together on this little island. It's a huge city, but in your neighborhood, you can feel like it's a small town. Kind of like Main Street here, but with a lot more bagels and neurotic people."

They looked at Mary. "What do you think?" Dot asked her. As if on cue, the impersonator struck up Sinatra's "New York New York."

"It's interesting to think about. Because I grew up there and never wanted to live anywhere else. My family is a big part of that. But it's also inspiring to see all these people doing *something*—creating, building, dreaming. It's not a place to sit still. It's a place to do things. Anything."

"Well, I'd love to visit one day. I really want to see Times Square," Tommy said.

"Oh my gosh, Tommy. Anything but Times Square!" Harper said and The Crew laughed.

No one went to Times Square.

Chapter 39

Outside the Cedar Falls Inn, the evening sky was still light, but the temperature had come down a little bit. Mary struggled to put on her cardigan and Jake stepped in to help.

"Well, that was really great," Dot said. "Thanks for taking us."

"The night is young," Tommy said. "What do you guys think about taking them over to the White Horse Saloon? They've got karaoke to-night."

"We have a White Horse bar in the Village, too," Mary said.

"Do you think it's the same white horse?" Jake asked.

"Better than your high horse, Officer," she teased back.

"Mary can sing!" Harper shouted. Mary shot her a look.

"All right, New York. You're full of surprises," Jake said. "I say we do it."

"Fine. One round. One song. That's it," Mary said, climbing into the front seat of the Suburban. Harper and Dot scrambled into the far back telling Danny and Tommy they were happy to sit back there.

About fifteen minutes later, they pulled up to the bar. It was in the middle of nowhere, surrounded by huge pine trees, and there were several pickups and SUVs in the parking lot.

"Oh yeah. This is my kind of place," Jake said, pulling into an open parking spot.

Inside, the bar was hopping. It was a casual spot, with men dressed in jeans and T-shirts, and women in light summer dresses or shorts and T-shirts. The Crew stood out.

A large man in a plaid shirt and jean shorts came over. "By golly, it's the Taylor boys. It's good to see you. You too, Danny!"

"Ladies, this here is Big Keith," Tommy said. "We went to school with his daughter. Keith, this is Mary, Harper, and Dot. They're from the Big Apple. Thought we'd bring them to a *real* bar."

"Welcome," Big Keith said in his booming voice. "Ladies, you're doing me a favor. This joint could use a little classing up. First round's on me."

The walls of the place were wood paneled in rough planks, and a long bar stretched across the entire length of it. Stools that swiveled lined the bar, and several bartenders stood ready to serve. They poured beer from the tap or mixed vodka and sodas into plastic cups. Whole peanuts were given away for free, and customers were free to throw the shells onto the floor. Long tables with benches filled the rest of the bar, and a makeshift stage took up one of the short ends of the building. At the other end, a few guys played darts. They definitely weren't in the Big Apple anymore.

Danny snagged a table and Jake took their drink order up to the bar. Tommy wrangled them some peanuts and shelled a few for the girls.

A group of women in their forties were having a birthday party there. And one of them was up singing "Before He Cheats," by Carrie Underwood.

"I imagine there's a story behind that choice," Tommy said.

"Oh, definitely." Harper winced, thinking of being humiliated by Kai in Africa. Why did that still sting so much? Here she was, with her friends, a good-looking guy that she liked. She didn't know why she tended to self-sabotage any possible good opportunities. She vowed to just let herself have fun for the rest of the night.

"Who's getting up there?" Jake asked. "Danny? Should I put your name in?"

"No, no, I'll just watch," he said, trying to get out of it.

"Not allowed. But I won't make you go first." He looked around. "Okay, Tommy. It's you and me."

Jake put their names on the list, and they waited through a seventy-year-old man singing "Free Bird" and a young woman who gave Taylor Swift's "Shake It Off" a try.

"Yikes," Mary said.

"What, you don't think they'd make it on *American Idol*?" Jake asked her.

"I mean, you've got to have standards."

Finally, the twins were called. The Crew and Danny cheered them on and while they did their best with "Don't Stop Believin'" by Journey.

"Crushed it," Danny said to Jake when they'd returned. "If this cop thing doesn't work out, maybe Tommy will let you sing at the bar."

"I could work for tips," Jake said.

"You'd starve. No one is paying to hear you sing." Tommy loved to tease his brother.

The night was going well, but Dot thought of a way to spice things up. "I have an idea," she said.

"You always have an idea," Mary said. "No one can keep up."

"Ignore her, Dot. Tell us." Harper elbowed Mary.

"Let's try this. Karaoke roulette," Dot said. "We split into two teams. We'll pick three songs, and you three pick three songs, then we'll take our chances for who has to sing what."

"I'm down," Tommy said.

"Sounds like it's boys against the girls," Jake said.

"I love it," Harper said.

"Well, I'm not very competitive," Mary chimed in. "But we *will* win."

"Well, let's see what you've got, New York." Jake couldn't wait to hear her sing.

Dot found a napkin and borrowed a pen to divvy up the challenges.

They were on another round of drinks and Jake also brought a big pitcher of ice water for the table. "Everyone needs to hydrate," he instructed. Mary admired how he took charge. She downed a glass of water.

They turned in their picks and the deejay got a kick out of this game. He got to choose the song *and* who would sing it.

Up first was Harper. They gave her "Since U Been Gone." "Seriously, you guys? Kelly Clarkson, please forgive me for what's about to happen." She covered her face with her hands. Mary shed her sweater and she and Dot got up to sing backup to help Harper out.

"You were wonderful," Tommy said, hugging Harper. She felt embarrassed but let herself be squeezed tight.

Tommy was chosen to sing "Sweet Caroline," which was what the entire bar wanted to hear. And then Jake went for it with the "Folsom Prison Blues." Then the three guys were challenged by The Crew with "No Sleep Till Brooklyn."

"How am I supposed to sing about a place I've never been?" Danny laughed, having more fun than he'd had in ages. Dot cheered him from her seat. When they finished, they clasped hands and Dot praised him.

"You were so good!" She showered him with praise.

"You're crazy," Danny said as he leaned in to kiss her cheek. She felt his lips on her skin long after he'd pulled away and took his seat.

Next was Mary. "Song choice is everything," Jake called. She went up and found out what they'd chosen.

"You have to be kidding me." But she knew she couldn't get out of it. She looked to the ceiling to gather herself. Then she belted out Tina Turner's "Proud Mary." Everyone in the White Horse Saloon was on their feet, dancing and singing.

"Rollin' on the river!" Mary finished, threw her arms in the air, and curtsied twice before handing back the mic.

In a surprise move, the deejay called up Danny and Dot.

"'Shallow'? Oh my gosh," Dot said, instantly realizing what this was. A setup. She wondered if Danny would be okay with this, while she shot the group a look, wondering which of them had dared to do this.

At first, they didn't look at each other while they sang. But then, Danny reached for Dot's hand, and she lifted her eyes to meet his. The crowd roared their approval and gave them more confidence to keep going. Dot knew she was no Lady Gaga, but she also knew that Danny gave Bradley Cooper a run for his money in the looks department.

They made a striking couple. Mary leaned over to Harper. "We're far from the shallow now, that's for sure." Harper raised her eyebrows and nodded.

Danny and Dot's chemistry was undeniable. They finished and smiled at the crowd, put their arms around one another, and took a bow.

"That was . . . Well, that wasn't terrible," Danny said when they'd sat down again.

"No. Not at all," Dot said, reaching for a glass of water to cool down.

The last song of the night was one for the entire bar to sing. "Friends in Low Places" brought the house down, and everyone settled up with Big Keith.

Suddenly, it was two in the morning.

"I haven't been out this late in ages," Harper said.

"Who needs the city that never sleeps when you can have Cedar Falls?" Tommy asked.

Jake, sober all night long, drove The Crew home. Everyone got out of the Suburban and gave each other hugs goodbye. Dot and Harper started toward the house and Danny and Tommy got back into the vehicle.

Jake and Mary stood alone on the sidewalk. She'd taken off her heels and carried them in one hand, her clutch under her arm, and her sweater tied around her neck. He reached for her free hand.

"Can I see you tomorrow after my shift, New York?"

"You won't leave me hanging?"

"Save room for dessert. I'll pick you up at eight."

Mary counted down the time. Eighteen hours until she'd see Hot Cop Jake again. This was so impractical, she thought, knowing their stay in Cedar Falls was only temporary. But still, she could hardly wait.

Chapter 40

Danny had everything ready for his big bookshop refurb. Dot met him there early in the morning and together they saw the Jankowskis off for their weekend polka competition.

"Have a great time," Danny said. "Don't worry about a thing."

"And break a leg!" Dot said, then wondered if that was a bad suggestion for people in their eighties. "I mean, knock 'em dead!" Oh gosh, was she making it worse? She settled on, "Show 'em how it's done!"

"There's life in the old girl yet, Dot," Jeanie called from the passenger seat. "Let's see if we can come back with a trophy for the mantel."

"And thanks, kids. We appreciate you so much," Ted said. Grateful, silly tears welled in his light blue eyes.

"Come on now, Ted. Let's get going before the traffic builds up." Jeanie still had her British stiff upper lip, but she looked at them tenderly as Ted rolled up his window and pulled away.

Danny and Dot stood on the sidewalk waving as the Jankowskis headed off to polka glory.

Danny looked at Dot. "Thanks for being here."

"No place I'd rather be."

"Even if you could be back in New York?"

"Well, you can't beat a bacon egg and cheese for breakfast, but this weekend is all about Cedar Falls and redoing the shop for Jeanie and Ted."

"Then let's do this!" He whistled and gathered his construction workers, who were milling around their trucks in the parking lot. He hopped into the bed of his truck as the team gathered around it. He reached for Dot's hand and helped her up.

"Welcome, everyone. Thanks for coming," Danny said. "This is Dot Clark. She's a friend of mine and the Jankowskis. Her friends, Harper and

Mary, are going to be helping us out, along with some volunteers we've recruited.

"Fellas, we have seventy-two hours to remodel a bookstore that opened in the 1960s. It's going to be a huge challenge, but I've planned for that. And heck, if they can do it on TV, we can do it in Cedar Falls."

"Heck yeah," one of the guys yelled.

"First, we need to pull everything out of the store. Then we'll sand the floors and restain. We'll let that dry overnight. See the guy in the orange cap over there? That's Preston. He's my second-in-command—any questions, just ask one of us."

That was Dot's cue to weigh in. "And as we move everything out back, we have a big dumpster it can go in," she said. "I'll be there with Harper to note anything we need to keep, and we'll put those items into the empty storefront next door. The landlord said we could use it."

"All right. Let's go!" Danny said. His team sprang into action. They were up for the challenge.

While the guys started moving everything out, Mary, Harper, and Grace Taylor chose books to sell that weekend outside of the shop.

"It's the annual Cedar Falls sidewalk sale this weekend, so it's perfect timing," Grace said. They selected a variety of books to display outside: new releases, Wisconsin history, cookbooks, young adult series, and children's books, plus Reader Falls Bookshop totes and T-shirts.

Harper, with Pippi in her tote bag to tag along, made a sign that the weekend's children's hour would be at the pavilion in Liberty Park. She drew her best picture of a dog and wrote "Pippi will be there!" Harper knew her small dog was a big draw.

Those tasks completed, the girls started pulling books off the shelves and putting them in boxes. Grace Taylor labeled the cartons so that they'd know what went where when the new shelving was up. It was Dot-level organized.

Meanwhile, Joe Taylor and his sons pulled out the rugs and furniture. Dot considered the piles and decided what was staying and what was going. Grace took the rugs to the cleaners where they were prepared for the rush job. Dot decided which sofas and chairs were staying and going.

"It's hard to let these plush couches go, but they're really past their prime," Dot said.

"When in doubt, throw it out." Grace patted the back of one of the sofas.

With that advice, and realizing they needed to move more quickly, Dot got more decisive.

"Out," she said, pointing to an old leather sofa that was missing a foot and several of its buttons. She had to be ruthless. There was no time for sentimentality.

"I'll take that one for my office at the bar," Tommy said, pointing to one of the deep leather chairs with a matching ottoman. "It's perfect for all the deep thinking I do back there."

"Sold!" Dot said, pretending to wield a gavel.

A while later, Fletcher and Rose came by after For the Win's offices closed.

"Wow. You weren't kidding when you said there was going to be a transformation!" Fletcher surveyed the debris coming out of the shop.

"Ted and Jeanie would have heart attacks if they saw this," Rose said.

"Let's just hope we finish before they get back on Sunday at six!" Dot said. Then she asked Rose to help Harper with the outside display for the weekend and assigned Fletcher to help the guys who were taking down the plaster off the side walls. Danny had a feeling they'd find beautiful blond bricks that matched the historical facades of the buildings on Main Street. Sure enough, they were in perfect condition.

"You called it," Dot said, and Danny gave her a high five.

At eight o'clock, several pizzas arrived from Slice of Life. According to Danny, it was the best Italian pie in town. Mary and Rose teamed up to set up a buffet line with paper plates and rolls of Bounty for napkins. Mimi arrived with cupcakes she'd made that afternoon. They were decorated with the Reader Falls Bookshop logo.

"Sweet," Dot said, handing a cupcake to Danny. When he took a bite, she bopped his hand, and green frosting covered his nose. His eyes widened in surprise.

"Okay, so we're doing this, huh? Better watch out, Miss Clark."

"I'll take my chances." She was in an open flirt with him now. "I'm sorry, I just got you so good on that."

The team worked until about ten that night then called it a day for everyone except the guys there to sand, level, and stain the floors. The plan was to let the floors dry overnight and then everyone could gather again at noon the next day and keep going.

Danny dropped off The Crew at their house. "Get some sleep. We're going to need it," he said.

"It's been so fun. I can't wait to see how it turns out," Dot said, feeling happy and glad to have the election off her mind for a day. She reached up and kissed his cheek and he ran his hand down her neck to her collarbone. She shivered from the sensation.

As she tucked herself into bed just before midnight, Dot meditated on Danny's command of the project and how he'd caught her eye in the middle of the controlled chaos and smiled just for her. She rewound the scene over and over in her mind.

And as she was falling asleep, she realized she was also falling for Danny.

Chapter 41

Over the next two days, Dot and Danny's team painted, put up the bookshelves, relaid the carpets, brought in the new furniture, and restocked the books.

Mary and Jake took on painting the frames for the front two bay windows.

"I'll tape, you roll," Jake said.

"Deal." Mary had on short denim overalls, a hot pink cropped tank, and white canvas sneakers, and had her hair in a high ponytail.

At one point, Jake ran a white paintbrush up one of Mary's legs.

"Watch it, Jake Taylor!" she said, fully putting on her Staten Island accent. "I have three older brothers, you know."

"Yeah, but one's a priest."

"That's no use to you. He'll only pray for you after kicking your butt." She tried to dot his dimple with her paintbrush, but he caught her hand, and they wrestled for leverage.

BY SUNDAY MORNING, everything looked a mess.

"I don't know how we'll possibly finish by six tonight. This place is a wreck," Dot fretted as she looked at the piles of books to be shelved. "We haven't even hung the paintings up yet. And the children's section is under a pile of scrap."

Danny caught her shoulders and said, "We've got this." Then he pulled a list from his back pocket and took a pencil from behind his ear. "Look. I've got it all planned out. You don't have to worry. Let me run point here and I give you my word, it'll be done."

She realized she'd been trying to control everything. Maybe he was right. She should trust him and follow his lead.

"I just want it to be perfect," she said.

"It'll be perfect, I promise." Danny held her gaze for a beat longer than normal. Then he pulled her into a hug and kissed her forehead. While she was distracted, he brought his hand around and poured a small cup of water over her head.

"Ack! What in the world?" She shivered and shook her head. Droplets flew around her.

"That's for the cupcake." He backed away before she could playfully swat him.

"Hey, you two." Tommy walked in with coffees from the Roasted Rooster coffee shop. "Black coffee for Danny and a vanilla latte for Dot." He handed a cup to her. She was glad for the interruption.

Dot admonished herself, "Get your head in the game." This was no time time to get sidetracked.

OVER THE NEXT few hours, Dot could see that Danny was right about it coming together.

After just three days of work, the floors gleamed with a new oak stain and the rugs perked up in color after their cleaning. New shelves filled the store and were straightened, polished, and packed neatly with books. The children's section now had colorful plush cushions, cozy chairs, and a small table for crafts. They'd painted the walls a creamy ivory and added sconces to bring in more light. Slimmer yet comfortable seating was placed strategically to get people to sit and stay awhile. And one of the best features was a table Danny had made himself that was perfect for displaying new releases, which would help draw customers to check out the latest stock.

While it was shiny and more modern, Readers Falls still felt warm and inviting. It smelled fresh, like new paint and sunshine.

"I love it when a plan comes together," Danny said, as he gathered everyone outside. He'd had a new awning made for the store, and it was time to mount it before the Jankowskis got back.

"I just want to say, on behalf of Dot and myself, that it really means a lot to us that you'd give us one of your summer weekends to do this for Ted and Jeanie. They're special people. And this community really needs this bookstore." The team clapped their hands at that.

"I love how it turned out. And I . . . well, I love you all. Thank you for being here." Danny blushed and looked away. He wasn't used to giving speeches.

Jake saved him from showing any more emotion. "Let's go, Reader Falls!"

Everyone cheered as Tommy and Fletcher, the two tallest men there, hoisted and affixed the new sign to the front of the store.

"Is it centered?" Fletcher yelled to Harper, who was on point to make sure it was placed correctly above the door.

"A little to the right. Now a little to the left. Down a bit. Okay. There! It's perfect." Harper gave a thumbs-up from across the street.

After Tommy and Fletcher came down off the ladder, Dot climbed up a few rungs to say a few words.

"Well, everyone. We did it. Look at this." She gestured to the sign above, and toward the shop. "It's even better than I imagined."

Dot looked around at all these new friends, in this temporary home she'd only been in for a few months, and she really couldn't believe her good fortune. The work with For the Win had been rewarding, challenging, and fun. But the people she'd met in Cedar Falls—well, she hadn't realized she was building a community, too.

"Let's give Danny a round of applause. His design, donations, and ability to manage a major project made it all possible."

Calls and hoots for Danny rose up from the crowd.

"And in just fifteen minutes, the Jankowskis will be here. So, are we ready?"

"Yes!" the crowd answered.

Tommy and Jake popped bottles of champagne, and Mary and Grace passed around plastic flute glasses for when Ted and Jeanie pulled up.

A few minutes later, they saw the Jankowskis' royal-blue Ford Escape turn onto Main Street.

"Here they come!" Danny called out. Then to Dot, more quietly, he said, "Pray that they like it."

"They'll love it. How could they not!" She elbowed him in the ribs, and they went to meet the older couple in the parking lot at the corner.

"Welcome home! How was the competition?" Dot asked as soon as Jeanie opened her door.

"We came in second overall. Look!" Jeanie held up a big red ribbon. "I'm over the moon about it. Ted danced like he was twenty years old again!"

"We had a great time. I've never seen Jeanie look prettier." Ted put an arm around her shoulders. "But we rushed back. We can't wait to see what you've done!"

"Well . . . Ted and Jeanie, if you'll allow us . . . we have some blindfolds," Dot said, handing one of the blindfolds to Danny. They started to put them on the older couple, who were giggling at the fuss. "We'll guide you over."

They walked down the block and Dot signaled to the small crowd of helpers to get ready.

They stopped across the street from the shop.

"This is how Ted first surprised me when he bought the bookstore," Jeanie said.

"We know. Ted told us all about it. We wanted it to remind you of that day and all you've done with this place since then," Danny said.

Jeanie reached for their hands and squeezed.

"Ready?" Dot looked at Danny. "On three. One. Two. Three!"

They pulled off the blindfolds and Jeanie's hands flew to her mouth. The workers and volunteers cheered.

"Oh my gosh! I can't believe it," Jeanie said.

Ted hugged Danny. "My boy. Look what you've done!" Dot could tell it meant so much to them both, the man who'd never had a son and the son who'd never known his father.

Grace handed Ted and Jeanie a flute of champagne.

"Come see!"

The crowd applauded and flanked either side of them as they went into the store.

Ted and Jeanie were amazed.

Jeanie's hand again covered her mouth. "I almost don't recognize the place and yet it still seems like our store, just . . ."

"Better!" Ted finished Jeanie's sentence.

Harper and Grace showed them the refashioned children's section, and Ted tried out the new couch.

"Wow. Comfortable!" he said, pleased as he could be.

Danny caught up with Dot over by new releases.

"Well. Mission accomplished. I couldn't have done it without you."

"We make a good team."

"We do." He winked at Dot, and she rewarded him with a joyful smile.

Then they sat down on the new sofa, put their feet up on the long ottoman, and basked in the afterglow of accomplishment and the feeling of new beginnings.

AT THE FRONT of the store, Mary sipped her champagne and checked her phone. There were three texts from her mother and several from her brothers.

"Call me, sweetheart. It's your grandmother." Mary kept scrolling through the messages trying to get a read of what was happening.

Oh, no, not Nonna.

Jake saw her face fall. "What's wrong?" he asked, gently touching her shoulder.

"It's my Nonna. She's in the hospital. She may have had a stroke." Mary scrolled through the messages from her mother. "I need to go home. My mom says there's an eight-fifty flight tonight."

"Let's go get you packed. I'll take you to the airport. We can get you to New York tonight."

"I don't think we'll make it in time."

He looked at her like she didn't realize who he was and who he worked for.

"We will."

And so, she let him drive her to their house in his police cruiser so that they could push the speed limit. At home, she threw a few things in her carry-on and then they sped off to the airport.

JAKE AND MARY arrived at Milwaukee Mitchell International Airport with half an hour to spare. He got out of the car and grabbed her suitcase from the trunk, pulling out the handle so she could roll it easily into the terminal.

"Thank you." She stood on her tiptoes and lifted her face up to Jake. Her lips found his and she felt a pull of longing to stay and a dread to go home in case Nonna didn't make it.

"Go on now, New York."

"I'm not sure when I'll be back," she said.

"I'll be here. Whenever that is."

And she knew she could trust him. And she realized that *trust* in a man was a different feeling for her. She turned to go into the terminal then stopped to look back.

He was waiting until she was safely past security.

He nodded.

She nodded.

"See you soon," Mary whispered and waved.

Chapter 42

Two weeks flew by before Mary returned to Wisconsin. Her grandmother had recovered relatively quickly from what proved to be a minor stroke and miraculously hadn't lost any movement or language.

"We were lucky," Mary's mom said as they gathered around the makeshift sofa bed in their living room. "You have to slow down and rest, Ma." She smoothed her mother's hair back from her forehead.

Nonna blew that off. "You won't be rid of me for a while yet," she said. "Besides, I'm going to be around for Mary's wedding. And to hold the grandbabies she's going to give me."

She gauged Mary's reaction, but Mary just smiled and quickly looked away. She couldn't stop thinking about Jake but hadn't told anyone she'd met someone. In *Wisconsin*, of all places—she didn't want the third degree about any of that.

To change the subject, Mary went into the kitchen and shoved her head into her parents' refrigerator. "Is there anything to eat around here?"

Of course there was.

Mary took out containers of meatballs and red sauce, and her mom started boiling water for pasta. It was good to be home, but she missed The Crew. They'd grown closer in the last few months by spending so much time together. And instead of tiring of each other's company, they'd bonded more than ever.

While in New York, Mary checked in at the firm's office and made the rounds with her associates and the partners. All of them said they missed her but admired her work even from afar. She hadn't missed a beat and had even troubleshot a major problem in a brief that saved their client hundreds of thousands of dollars.

"Thank goodness for your sharp eye," Sofia Garcia said when she stopped by to see her. "And I'm glad it's all worked out. You proved my point that you could be trusted to work remotely."

"Thank you. I've missed being in the office, but it's been a great experience so far. Interesting to be in another part of the country, especially during an election year."

"Tell me—what's the word on the campaign trail? I've maxed out my Democratic contributions to the House and Senate candidates, and I keep refreshing RealClearPolitics to stare at the polling averages. It's still so close."

Mary gave her the take as best she understood it from Dot, Fletcher, and Rose.

"So, you're saying there's a chance?" Maria asked, tilting her head.

"Definitely!" Mary wanted to leave on an optimistic note. "Thanks for making time for me today."

"You were the bright spot in my afternoon." She stood to shake Mary's hand. "Keep me posted on the election. And we look forward to your return."

It felt good to be missed.

Before she left the office, she popped down a floor to also see Patricia Parker, the eminent domain expert. She told her she'd been trying to follow the money to find who was behind the effort to push the Taylors to sell their farm.

"Keep digging. Sometimes the best clue is hiding in plain sight," Patricia advised.

Mary made a mental note to look through all the paperwork again.

Once she was sure that everything was settled at home and that her Nonna was okay, Mary decided it was time to go back to finish out her year in Wisconsin. It was midsummer, and she had just five months left in Cedar Falls.

Chapter 43

Mary's flight landed late afternoon on a Sunday. As the plane taxied to the gate, she opened her phone and sent a message to Dot and Harper.

"You won't believe what I saw on the flight."

"Tell me." Dot was the first to write back.

"This good-looking guy, tall, Dallas Cowboys hat, jeans, and a gray T-shirt, is in the row ahead of me. I checked him out before takeoff, natch. But then you wouldn't believe the movie he watched on the flight."

"What was it? *Braveheart*?" Dot took a wild guess. Ryan and his friends had loved that flick. They always quoted from it.

"No. Worse. *Frozen*. A cartoon!"

"Oh, ick!"

"Exactly! Add it to the ick list."

"Added! See you at dinner?" Dot asked. They planned to get Ubers and meet up after she landed and was on her way to Cedar Falls.

"Yes. Where should I tell the driver to drop me?"

"New spot," Harper wrote. "Buddha Bootie. Asian fusion. On Washington Street. I'll send a link."

"What's on the menu?" Dot asked.

"Wonton tacos and burrito pho—phorittos. Sound good?" Harper had checked it all out.

"Pho sure," Mary responded and added a chopsticks emoji. "See you soon!" She tucked her phone into her white belt bag and got off the plane.

The terminal was quiet as she wheeled her duffel bag on top of her carry-on to the exit.

She wore a long cream-colored linen halter dress, a blue jean jacket, and wedge sandals that tied around her slim ankles. Her hair was thrown up in a high bun and she wore large gold hoops.

When she took a left into the baggage claim area to exit the building, there was only one other person there.

Jake.

He had caught the sun, and his blue eyes looked even bluer against his suntan. He wore sneakers, khaki shorts, a white T-shirt, and a light blue long sleeve cotton button-down with the sleeves rolled up.

He held a posterboard sign that said, in big block letters, NEW YORK.

She shook her head at him and walked to where he was standing. She pushed up onto her toes to find his lips. And he put his arms around her and she snuggled into his chest. They stood there for several moments.

"I can't believe you're doing the airport pickup," she said.

"I couldn't leave you to fend for yourself in Milwaukee. Besides, I missed you."

"You did?"

"Yeah, crime is way down in Cedar Falls. I kept wondering what sort of trouble you were getting up to back home."

"So, you were fantasizing about me?" She cocked her head and winked at him.

"Troublemaker."

He took her suitcase and duffel bag and started toward the exit.

"So, what do you want to do?" he asked.

She was quiet for a moment. She'd been thinking about the answer to this question on the entire flight from New York as she looked out over the small towns, rivers, lakes, and fields on her way to Wisconsin. She had rested her forehead on the window and daydreamed about the future.

On the one hand, she pictured herself in a corner office at the firm, having made partner by the age of thirty. She'd have a gorgeous apartment in a high-rise with a great view, beautifully decorated by a hotshot designer, and a closet full of modish clothes. She'd throw dinner parties, donate to the Met, and still make it to Sunday supper at her parents' house. In this scenario, she wouldn't have any financial worries and she'd be the best aunt to all her nieces and nephews.

And on the other hand, since she'd watched her brothers and their wives and children doing all the family things these past two weeks—going to Little League games, throwing birthday parties, chastising the kids for not finishing their homework and leaving their bikes scattered on her parents' lawn—she realized she wanted that in her life, too.

What she couldn't do was merge the two pictures. She just didn't see how she could have both the career she wanted and the family she dreamed about. The two paths seemed incompatible to her.

And she wasn't sure what she was going to do about Jake. She knew herself well enough to recognize that she was falling for him. It had gone from harmless flirtation to something approaching serious.

But it was never far from her thoughts that he lived in Wisconsin. She couldn't see staying in there—her life was in New York. But her heart . . . was her heart with Jake?

It was impossible to sort it out in her head. Not to mention that a committed relationship with Jake was not in the cards. Nowhere in her life's plan was there a vision of not going back to New York. If there was one thing that she was sure about, it was that.

"I'm not sure I'm ready for a relationship," she blurted quickly.

"Okay. . . . I'm not sure where that came from." He turned toward her and said, "Let me try again. What do you want to do *right now*. I could take you home. To dinner. To confession?"

"Oh. Ha," she said, a little embarrassed at her presumption. Having no good idea, she said, "Um, how about you just drive? Take me somewhere you love."

"I can do that."

They walked to where his car was parked, and he put her suitcase in the trunk while she texted Dot and Harper.

"Hey—sorry. Change of plans. Go without me. Jake picked me up. I'll be home later. Xoxo."

"An airport pickup. Unheard of," Harper said to Dot. "Even my parents make me get a cab."

"This is getting interesting!" Dot said to Harper while she texted back to Mary, "No problem. We'll leave a light on for you."

She snapped a selfie with Harper and Pippi, her face sticking out of her tote bag, and sent it to Mary.

MARY KICKED OFF her sandals as they drove back past Cedar Falls. When Jake turned into the Taylor farm, she said, "So, this is a place you love. I could have guessed."

"More than anywhere else. I want to show you the best place on earth to watch the sun set."

He pulled up next to a pond, way out of sight of his folks' farmhouse. There were a few big oaks that grew along the edges of the pond. Several giant weeping willows lined the shore, their branches laden with leaves that stretched down to the water.

An old wooden picnic table was placed in the shade of the largest oak. They got out of the car and Mary didn't bother putting her shoes back on. Jake pulled a picnic basket and a blanket out of the trunk.

"Do you always have that ready to go . . . just in case you pick someone up at the airport?" she asked.

"Well, you never know who you're going to find wandering around baggage claim." He kissed her and then said, "Come on. Let's set this up. We have twenty minutes before we get one of the best shows on earth."

She followed him to the benches and helped him unpack a loaf of homemade sourdough, a hunk of cheese, slices of prosciutto, and a bottle of red wine from the basket.

"I'm starving," Mary said, pulling a piece of bread from the loaf and popping it into her mouth.

"I've learned that's a constant with you. I never want to see you hangry."

"It's not a pretty sight."

"Oh, I'm sure it's pretty. Pretty dangerous."

They snacked for a while as the sky turned a deeper shade of pink. The sun was making its way down.

"Come over here. This is the best view." He took her hand and walked to a double tree swing. "My grandfather put this up for my grandmother when they got married. They used to bring us out here and we'd fish, skip rocks, and eat the cookies Grandma made for us. They loved to watch the sunset."

He sat down on the seat and patted the spot next to him. There was enough room, but Mary decided to sit on his lap instead.

"I'll sit here." She reached up to grab the ropes in each hand.

"Oh, okay. I'll allow it." He put one arm around her waist. "Hold on tight." He got the swing started and together they kept it moving, pumping their legs in and out.

The sky turned light pink, then orange, then a deep red, and finally, an unreal shade of violet. After a while, they stopped the swing. Then Mary turned her torso around, reached her hands around Jake's neck, and he pulled her in for a kiss. He held her with one arm, and with his other hand he reached for her hair and undid her updo. By the time they came up for air, the stars were out.

Mary texted The Crew. "Don't wait up. Catch up tomorrow? Dinner at the Sin Bin. On me."

She added a kiss emoji and two hearts and pressed send. Then she silenced her phone. She wouldn't be needing it for the rest of the night.

Chapter 44

"Hey, Shakespeare, any plans this afternoon?" Tommy texted Harper one sizzling summer Monday in late June.

Harper had been stuck on a scene in her book when she felt her phone buzz. She perked up when she saw it was from Tommy.

"No plans. Trying not to melt. What's up?" she asked. Play it cool, she told herself. Don't be too eager.

"The Sin Bin is super quiet. Hamilton said he'd watch the bar for me. Good day for fishing. Want to come?"

She was thinking through her reply when she saw his three dots flashing.

"You don't have any ethical concerns about fishing, right?"

"Fishing's fine. Not as cute as Bambi."

"Tastes better than venison, too. Cool. Pick you up in thirty. Bring Pippi. Mom made us some snacks. She said she'll grill up anything we catch."

Harper sent a thumbs-up, saved her document one more time, and closed her laptop.

"Well, looks like we're going fishing." Pippi's ears perked up at the word "going," and she hopped onto the tote bag that Harper used to carry her. "Yes, that's right. You get to go, too." Pippi's separation anxiety was surpassed only by Harper's. They'd become so close, and Harper hated leaving her home.

Harper smiled at the unexpected chance to get outside, to try something new, and to do it all with Tommy.

She realized she thought about him quite a bit and often wondered if they'd ever be more than friends. He was great to hang out with. He was well-read, kind, and funny. He was a responsible adult, not living off a dream or a trust fund. He wasn't trying to be an influencer—he even had his own business and had told her about opening another on the family farm.

She just didn't know if this was friend zone or . . . more. And what was the point, really, if in a few months she was going back to New York anyway?

When she'd told Mary and Dot how she was feeling, Mary told her to snap out of it.

"Not everything has to be so deep, Harper! Let yourself have some fun for a change. You're a gorgeous, talented, whip-smart young woman and he *likes* you. So, let him!"

Harper pulled on khaki shorts, a royal-blue V-neck tank, and her baby blue canvas sneakers.

Her legs were pale as she sunburned easily and stayed out of the sun. And she hated the smell of self-tanner, so she never used it. Plus, the time she'd tried applying it in college, she'd ended up with orange hands for a week.

"You're supposed to use latex gloves to protect your hands, Harp!" Dot had tried to help but even bleach couldn't remove the stains.

"Rookie mistake. Next time call a pro." Mary had showed off her perfectly bronze legs to make her point. For a week, Harper had kept her hands in her pockets any time she went out in public.

Harper stood in front of the entryway mirror, posed with her pale legs, and took a selfie. She sent it to Mary and Dot.

"Does this say 'Yes, I'll go fishing with you but don't get any ideas'?"

"Why wouldn't you want him to have ideas?" Mary responded immediately.

"I don't want to come off as too interested."

"But you are interested!" Dot said.

"Just tell me—should I look more sophisticated?"

"To go fishing? No. If anything, wear shorter shorts and just a sports bra." Mary wasn't helping.

"I think your outfit is perfect. You don't want to be too dressed up. Just go have fun!" Dot was trying to build Harper's confidence.

"And don't do anything I wouldn't do," Mary said.

"Don't worry. It's not like that."

Dot jumped in. "He's taking an afternoon off to bring you along for his favorite thing."

"Hopefully fishing isn't his favorite thing." Mary added a winking emoji.

"You two are so helpful. What would I do without you?" Harper's sarcasm showed through their screens.

"Have fun and tell us everything later!" Dot said. Mary sent her signature xoxo.

In the end, Harper decided she'd stick with the outfit she'd already put on. Her anxiety was already off the charts and changing again might put her over the edge and have her cancel on the entire afternoon.

Looking around the bench with Mary and Dot's summer gear, she threw sunscreen and bug spray into her backpack. Her hair frizzed terribly in the humidity and it was hard to get all the stragglers into a red silk scrunchie. She pulled a floppy sun hat with a string to hold it in place down over her head.

She looked at herself in the mirror one last time. She turned from side to side to get a sense of how she looked.

"Not so bad, eh, Pip?" she said, grabbing her sunglasses.

A horn honked and she raised onto her tiptoes to peek out the window. Tommy arrived in his old, black F-150 pickup that pulled a fourteen-foot Lund with an outboard motor. "If my brother could see me now," she thought, "he'd make me pay for some carbon offsets for riding in such a gas guzzler or forever be labeled a hypocrite."

Tommy popped out of his side and came around to open her door. She didn't recall any guy ever doing that for her. Though, to be fair, most of the guys she dated didn't drive. They were city kids who charged rides to their parents' Uber accounts.

Her stomach did a little flip, a feeling she'd not had since her breakup.

"Hello!" she called, waving to Tommy. She climbed into the pickup, settled Pippi on her lap, and buckled her seatbelt. Tommy made sure she was fully in her seat before he gently closed her door.

"You look great!" Tommy said through the open window, and for a moment, Harper believed him.

ONCE THEY WERE on the water and Tommy had found a spot he liked to drop anchor, he grabbed the tackle box and handed Harper a fishing pole.

"So, how do I do this?"

"Well, first you need some bait."

"Please don't tell me you actually use . . ."

"Some of these." He pulled out a small bowl and took the lid off.

"Tommy! That's so gross!" she said as she spied night crawlers writhing around in some muck.

"Might be gross to you, but it's lunch for them." He pointed to the fish below the surface of the pond.

She tried not to gag.

"I'll do it for you, don't worry." He took her line and starting baiting the hook.

She turned her head around and tried not to look.

After the worm was on the hook, Tommy wiped his hands with a cloth and then came behind her on the boat.

"Now let's get these little suckers in the water," he said, putting his hands over hers and showing her how to cast a line. She was glad when the squiggling night crawler was out of her sight.

He repeated the routine for himself, and they both sat down and looked around the lake. The water was clear that day, the sun a bright blue with some puffy white clouds for decoration, and the treelined shore hugged the narrow sandy beaches.

"This is like being in a postcard," Harper said, grateful for the breeze that cooled her skin.

"One of my favorite spots," Tommy said. He reached into the cooler and brought out some flavored seltzers.

"A cocktail, madame?" he asked, faking a British accent.

"Don't mind if I do." She tried to mirror his attempt. "Have you thought of everything, Mr. Darcy?" She surprised herself with a flirtatious tone.

"Hope so, Miss Bennet. Because it's a long way back to the truck," he said.

That he was well-versed in Jane Austen made her smile. She thought of Kai and how he only looked at hot chicks on Snapchat or surfers catching double overheads.

They sat for a while in comfortable silence until Harper wondered what was next. Pippi was fast asleep on her back, all four paws in the air, not a care in the world.

"So, now what do we do?" she asked Tommy.

"Now we wait."

"For how long?"

"Until they bite."

"How long until they bite?"

"Until they're hungry."

"Oh."

"Yep. So now we just wait . . ."

"But . . ."

"Quietly."

Oh.

"But when will we . . ."

"The fish decide."

Double oh.

Harper had no choice but to sit and wait. There was never a nibble on her line. After a while, she fell into a quiet meditation and came up with a few ideas for her plotline. Pippi curled up on the seat between them, alternating between looking around and snoozing.

At one point Harper also felt sleepy, but then she realized that she wasn't tired. She was just relaxed. She wasn't used to this feeling of being chill and carefree. In New York, she always felt like she needed to move. There was so much to do and see. And so many people to keep up with and compete against. There was constant movement, and she loved that racy feeling. Fishing was so boring, but maybe slowing down was good for her.

She pictured herself taking a rod down to the East River where the old-timers fished on weekends, just hanging with them, listening to their stories, and then bringing back her catch to gut and clean her fish with a big, sharp knife and cook in her tiny kitchen, her roommates gagging at the smell.

Except so far on this first voyage into the world of fishing, there was one little problem. They'd not had even a nibble on either of their lines.

The sun started to make its way to the exit, and Tommy said he was sorry they hadn't caught anything.

"Ready to go?" he asked.

"No. I'd rather wait."

"For what?"

"Until they're hungry."

"But now I'm hungry."

"How can we leave without a fish?"

"That's the best part about fishing. There's always tomorrow," he said, as he packed up.

"So that's it—we just leave?"

"We live to fish another day."

"Whatever happened to beginner's luck?" she asked. "I was looking forward to, like, a filet o' something . . ."

"How about I make it up to you and take you to the Ugly Walleye for dinner?"

"That sounds . . . horrible."

"The uglier the walleye, the better the taste. I promise—it's good." Tommy put their poles away, started up the engine, and got them back to shore.

AT DINNER, THEY sat outside on the patio. A local jazz trio entertained the diners, and Tommy and Harper ate their fill of walleye, lemon mashed potatoes, and corn on the cob. They hand-fed Pippi little bites off their plates as they chatted easily about growing up.

"Name your favorite board game," he said.

"Great question. I loved Clue, but my brother always wanted to play Monopoly. You?"

"We had an old game of Life at my grandparents' house, and they loved to play that with us. That was probably my favorite. I kind of liked Operation, too."

"Oh, that one gave me a lot of anxiety. My hands are shaking just thinking about those tweezers." She shook her head at the memory.

"You're cute even when you're anxious," he said.

"You really think so?" She blinked.

"I do."

As the sun started to set, Tommy went inside to pay the bill, and Harper decided to check her phone. She opened Instagram and did a double take. Two-timing Kai had liked the selfie she'd posted of herself and Pippi at the lake. She hadn't had any communication with him in months.

"The nerve!" she said. But she was curious why he'd like that photo. Why now? Was he lonely after getting dumped again? Or was he just bored? Or did he miss her?

She thought about DM'ing to ask how he was, and why he'd liked her picture. But a different feeling came over her. She realized he'd probably liked it because she looked happy. And she *felt* happy.

Kai did not make her feel happy. But Tommy did.

So, instead of responding to the like, Harper clicked on his name. Her finger hovered over the mute button. "Mute stories and posts?" She hesitated. Then she did the right thing and hit "unfollow." And just like that, she was free of Kai. She looked over the water and imagined him receding until he was almost out of sight.

"Bye!" she said.

"Who are you talking to?" Tommy had just returned.

"Oh, no one. Absolutely no one."

"Ready to go?"

"Ready."

Harper picked up Pippi and they made their way to Tommy's truck.

Before opening her door, he looked her in the eyes and said, "You're one of a kind, Harper Lee Adler."

"Is that a good thing?" She thought that's what he meant, but still she searched his eyes for interest.

"It's a very good thing." He reached out and gently bopped her nose, then brought his lips to hers. A gentle warmth flooded her body. Feeling brave, she put one arm around him and held onto Pippi's leash with the other. He put his hand in her hair.

"My hair is so . . ." she said, through the kiss, embarrassed by the frizz.

"Beautiful," he said. "Your hair is beautiful." They kissed for several moments, enough that Pippi finally barked at them, as if to say, "What about me?"

Tommy pulled back reluctantly and said, "Let's get you home."

As Harper buckled in and looked back at the lake, the stars coming out in the sky, the band's music still reaching them in the still night, she had a strange feeling.

For the first time in her life, somewhere besides the city felt like home.

In fact, for Harper, on that warm summer night, Manhattan had never felt so far away.

Chapter 45

Dot took her red Sharpie and crossed through another day on her New York picture calendar. July first brought a new photo of people strewn across Central Park's Sheep Meadow in the summertime. She felt a twinge of homesickness and did a quick count on her fingers.

"July to August, August to September, September to October, October to November."

She glanced behind her where Fletcher was working on a voter contact spreadsheet.

"Yikes, Fletch. There are only four months to November."

"One hundred twenty-nine days to Election Day. It's going to fly by."

"Do you think we have enough time to get her in position to win?" Dot was hyperaware of the pressure they were under to help Lucy Lopez win Wisconsin. Kitty Bell was relentless, asking them for detailed updates every day, as if the only thing standing between her and a White House job—and a win bonus—was Cedar Falls in Colby County, USA.

"Right now, Wisconsin could go either way. But with Stone on the ticket, Kentucky could go blue, so that gives us a little cushion," Fletcher said.

"I love that she picked Governor Stone, and not just for the eight electoral votes and how it scrambles the GOP's map," Dot said. "He really seems to truly support her. And their onstage chemistry is great."

"No doubt. They seem to genuinely get along. Plus, if she can deliver Georgia and add sixteen more votes, our ten could put them over the top." Fletcher kept a board with all the states that could flip red or blue, depending on how the polls were that week. The first week of July, the GOP was ahead by more than thirty votes. "In some ways more time might not help us," he said. "The longer this goes on, the tougher it could get."

"Well, when she's here, we'll have to make the most of it," Dot said. They were preparing for the candidate's event in Cedar Falls.

"What are you thinking we should have her do while she's in town?" Fletch bounced a foam basketball off the wall as they talked.

"Well, she's hitting her marks with younger voters, especially since even she had a tough time buying her first house," Dot said. "So, I think we need to get her with the swing voters we're targeting, as well as the farmers. I don't see her moving too many rural voters yet."

"Yeah. That's a gap we need to fill."

"Maybe we diner tour her through small towns between Milwaukee and Minneapolis? Or maybe out to one of dairies. Have her milk a cow?" Dot was just spitballing.

"Do you think that's a good idea? If it went badly, the videos could crush her."

"Good point. Maybe she could help can vegetables?"

"Is that too obvious? Like that meme of Hillary Clinton baking in the nineties. That one kills me." Fletcher was king of memes.

"Yeah, you're right. I just need something that gets her out of the 'I'm a hot young Latina with great style and charisma' vibe. Don't you think?"

"Maybe a visit to a rural schoolhouse?" he asked.

"I like that. But it would probably be better once school starts up in the fall."

"Good point. You're always thinking, Dot." He tapped his finger on the side of his head.

They laughed as she grabbed the ball out of the air and tried to sink a basket. "Air ball!" he said.

Dot really enjoyed working with Fletch, who was a cheerful colleague who pulled his weight, and they pushed through the next few hours of the workday.

After seven o'clock, Dot logged off her computer.

"Hey, Fletch, I'm going to get out of here. You okay locking up?" Over her arm, she threw the white cotton cardigan with the embroidered red roses on the trim that she'd paired with her sleeveless navy blue shift dress. She didn't mention she was meeting up with Danny Dawson. He'd asked her to dinner to celebrate Reader Falls Bookshop's amazing month since the remodel.

"No problem. Want to meet up for a drink later?" he asked.

Dot hesitated long enough that he jumped in before she could answer to fill the space.

"There's a bunch of us going to the Sin Bin to watch Yankees-Brewers," he explained. "Mimi is going to go over after she gets the bakery set for her early morning."

"Is that baseball?" she bantered, relieved he wasn't asking her for a date and seemed to be spending more time with Mimi.

"Soccer, actually," he teased.

"I'll pass. But let me know how many touchdowns they make."

"It's baskets," Fletcher teased back. "Three-point homers from half-court."

"Good to know. I'll file that away for trivia night."

She waved goodbye and searched in her bag for her light pink lip gloss. The humidity hit her fully in the face.

"I won't be needing this," she said, swinging her sweater over her shoulder.

The sun was still warming the air, and blooms were spilling out of the flower baskets that decorated the shops and restaurants on Main. Summer looked good on Cedar Falls, and the walk helped her transition from the workday to her evening, as it had in Central Park.

All the polling, voter preferences, and the demands of Kitty moved to the back burner for a few hours.

It was Danny time.

Chapter 46

Want to share a dessert?" Danny looked over the Barley and Bone menu. The upscale farm-to-table restaurant had a long list of homemade treats.

"Sure. What are you thinking?" Dot leaned in to look at their options. Her meal of wood-roasted cod, field greens, and fresh green beans had been delicious. She'd left room for the sweet course, having checked out their website earlier in the week in anticipation of their date.

"I'm torn between the citrus olive oil cake or the chocolate espresso tart," Danny said.

"Wow. Tough choice."

Dot took her time deciding. It was cherry season, and she narrowed her choices down to three: the chocolate pot de crème with cherry compote, the Door County cherry cheesecake with a gingersnap crust, and the cherry Danish kringle, which had to be good.

"I'd usually go for chocolate," she said.

"Noted for the future."

"There's a future?"

"If you play your cards right with this decision."

"Then I'll place my bets on . . . the cherry cheesecake this time around," she said.

"And we have a winner." Danny signaled to their server and ordered.

"Excellent choice. I'll bring two forks." The waiter took the dessert menus with him as he turned on his heel, gracefully balancing a tray of cocktails for another table.

"I love getting complimented by a waiter." Dot refolded her napkin over her lap.

"I like learning these things about you," he said.

"You do?"

"I do. Tell me more."

"Oh. Okay." She thought for a minute. What was worth telling him? "Well. I mentioned I have a younger sister. Anne. She's in Colorado working as a hiking and skiing guide. She's incredibly good at skiing and prefers powder to ice. She couldn't wait to get out of New England. Anne's the family favorite, and I'm not even mad about it."

"She sounds great. I'd love to meet her one day. What else?"

"Well, I think you know I like to read. Fiction, mostly. I consume so much news during the day for work that I like an escape at night."

"My mom was a reader. She loved historical fiction."

"That's one of my favorite genres. I love reading about Tudor England."

"Who's he?" he said. "Kidding. I know the time frame. Henry the Eighth. Had a lot of wives. Unfortunate end for most of them."

She liked how he made her laugh so easily.

"I should read more," he said. "It's just that after the long days working on houses, I keep falling asleep when I read at night. Without fail, I'll read the paragraph I left off on the night before, a new paragraph, and start another before I find my eyes closing. Then the next night I do it again. It takes me ages to get through a book."

"Ever tried listening to a book? I love it. It's like story time."

"I should give that a shot."

"I'll set up an account for you." She made a mental note and already had a couple of books she could put on his list.

"Okay, I've got another very important question." Danny looked very serious as he held a forkful of dessert near his mouth.

Dot braced herself. "Sure. Ask me anything."

"Dog or cat?" he asked, taking a full bite of cake.

"Dog." She didn't hesitate.

"Good answer."

"Is this a girlfriend screening?" she thought. Not that she minded.

They bantered a bit more, and when they got down to the last bite, Danny put his fork down.

"It's all yours," he said.

"Oh, I couldn't. You have it."

"I insist. Around the Taylors' farm, we called the last bite on a plate 'The Shame,' and we usually fought over it. But someone's gotta eat it."

She realized he wasn't going to budge, so she bent down and made a show of having the last bite. She closed her eyes, swallowed the cake, and raised her fork in triumph.

"Oh, the shame. Delicious!" she said. "I have to say, the food in Wisconsin has been a wonderful surprise," she said.

"Glad to hear it. What else surprised you?"

"That's a good question. I've been so busy with For the Win that I haven't explored as much as I'd like. But my biggest takeaway is that no matter who you meet, people act like they're already your friend."

"Wisconsin nice is a real thing," he said.

"Yes! You get instant connections here. A lot of people in New York have an edge—they kind of have to. It's a game of survival. But here, people you meet for the first time invite you to dinner before you say goodbye. That's how I felt about the Jankowskis and the Taylors."

"The Jankowskis adore you. They've started to think of you as the daughter they never had," Danny said.

"That's really sweet. It's too bad they don't have anyone to pass the store to once they retire," Dot said. "The community has really rallied around the shop since the remodel."

"It's true. Cedar Falls really is a great place to grow up. And it's a great place to raise a . . . family." He winced in pain and Dot caught it immediately. She was sensitive to his past heartbreaks, and she let the silence hang for a respectful moment. Danny was miles away in an instant, the sorrow she'd first noticed in his eyes back in a flash.

She let a few moments pass, not sure how to fill the silence. Finally, she decided to ease back into the conversation. "Are you okay?" she asked gently, reaching out to let her fingertips touch his forearm.

He was slow to look at her, his eyes deep and dark and sad in the moment. "I know Grace told you all about what happened to me and my . . . fiancée. And our daughter." He took a breath and caught himself before tearing up. "It's been a few years, but even so it's not easy. I admit that it's still sometimes hard to close my eyes. I'm afraid of what I might see."

She focused intently on him, letting him talk.

"That's why I work a lot. And I often go over to the Taylors or to the Jankowskis for dinner or just to help them with whatever they need doing around the house. It's easier than going home."

"I can understand that." She placed her hand, palm up, on the table. He rested his on top of hers. She squeezed gently. He squeezed back and held on tightly.

"For a while I just wanted to be left alone. But lately, I've been wanting to get out a bit more."

Dot felt a shot of hope that she had something to do with that.

"You know that weekend when we fixed up the store—well, I think that might be the first time I really felt . . . alive since Sadie and the baby . . . since they . . . since the accident."

She could tell how hard it was for him to say the words. She decided to go ahead and ask the question that had been on her mind.

"Earlier, when you said that Cedar Falls is a great place to grow up. When you think about your own future, do you still want to do that? To raise a family one day?" The question was a bit forward, but she wanted to know.

Danny took a beat before answering. "It was always my dream. I knew I was never going to go pro, but playing football helped me get a degree. And I knew if I had that, then I could be the dad I didn't have. I always dreamed about a house filled with love and traditions. For the mother of my children not to have to worry about working double shifts to make ends meet to feed a hungry kid. I wanted a chance to do better as a man. To be more like Joe Taylor, to be honest."

"Joe and Grace Taylor would make anyone want to be better people. They're a lovely couple."

"I owe them a lot," he said. Catching himself letting the dinner date slip into melancholy, he shook himself and sat up straight. "But hey, enough about all that."

He took the credit card receipt out of the small holder and Dot noticed he was a generous tipper.

"It's getting late." He checked his watch. "And I know we both have work tomorrow. Shall we get you home?"

"Of course! I'm all yours." Then catching herself, she said, "I mean, I'm all here. I'm all fine. I'm . . . oh, let's just go."

Danny laughed and reached for her hand.

Chapter 47

As Dot and Danny were leaving the restaurant, a group of four women studying the menu suddenly looked up.

"Danny! Hi!" A young woman, around thirty with skin like porcelain, looked surprised to see him. Her light brown hair was cut into a French bob, and she wore a flowered linen sundress and a delicate gold chain around her neck.

Danny let go of Dot's hand.

"Oh hey, Maddy. How are you?" Danny seemed uncomfortable and stiff after being so at ease over dinner. "Hi, Lauren, Zoe, Marissa. This is Dot."

They all nodded hello with what Dot thought was a friendly-enough greeting.

"She's a friend from NYC working here for a year," he explained.

"Oh, where do you work?" the one he'd called Lauren asked.

"I'm just here for the election." Dot braced herself. This could go either way in a state like this, but most young women she met were Democrats.

"The election? Which side?"

"Oh, ummm . . . for the Democrats." Dot tried to soft-pedal it.

Zoe wrinkled her nose. "Are you the one sending all the texts for donations? Because it's annoying and I'm never giving them a dime."

Dot winced.

"Zoe! Let's not ruin our night with politics," Maddy said. Dot assumed she was the ringleader of the group. "Where are our manners? Let's start over. Welcome to Wisconsin. I see you've met a good friend of ours." She nodded to Danny.

"Yes, I've been fortunate to meet a lot of great people. And it's a pleasure to meet you, too." Dot poured on a little extra charm. "I love your outfits."

"That's kind of you to say," Maddy said, glancing down at her dress. "Of course, we don't have Saks Fifth Avenue. We're more like Kohl's, right?" There was a hint of sarcasm in her tone.

"Oh, I love Kohl's. Marshalls too . . ." Dot cheerfully said, trying to salvage the moment. Where was the Wisconsin nice?

Danny stepped in. "Well, we better get going." He put his hand on the small of Dot's back and pushed her toward the door. "See you around."

"Bye, Danny. I'll call you." Maddy staked her claim right there in front of Dot.

Dot felt him tense. Did those two have a history?

"Sorry about that," he said as they walked outside into the warm summer night.

"No need to be sorry. They seem . . . great."

"We all grew up together around here. Just about everyone stayed around this area. They can be a little territorial."

She felt uneasy after meeting his friends, like she didn't belong there at all.

He opened her door to let her into the passenger seat of his pickup. She glanced up into the night and tried to put the restaurant encounter behind them.

"I love that you can see so many stars here."

"Well, they're the same stars you'd see in New York, right?"

"Nah, so much light pollution. To be honest, I don't think I've ever seen stars in the city." She settled into the seat and reached for the seatbelt.

"Well," he said, "maybe I can help make up for that while you're here," he said. Then he waited a beat before gently closing her door.

DANNY PULLED UP to The Crew's house to drop Dot off. He shut off the engine and neither of them moved for a moment.

Mary and Harper were on the porch with Pippi enjoying the cool night air—their air-conditioning was on the fritz, and the repairman said he couldn't come fix it for another couple of days. They couldn't quite see the street, so they strained their necks to make out what was going on.

"Do you think they're going to hook up?" Harper asked quietly.

"What, is this some sort of rom-com?" Mary whispered.

In the car, Danny said, "I had a wonderful time, Dot," and turned to look at her.

"So did I," she said.

He leaned in toward Dot, and she thought he was going to kiss her. But he pulled back at the last minute. Maybe he's just not that into me, she thought, a bit disappointed.

"Let me walk you up," he said, opening his door. He came around to open her side of the truck and helped her down.

They walked slowly up the steps. Mary and Harper sank back down. Harper placed a hand over Pippi's head to keep her from giving away their location.

Dot stood on the first step and leaned against the column holding up the porch. They were more evenly matched in height now that she had the elevation advantage.

"Well, thank you for a great evening," she said, sounding a bit too corporate, as if they'd just had a business meeting rather than a fun, romantic dinner.

"Thank you for joining me." He matched her off tone. "Would you . . . I mean, could I . . . well, heck, let me just ask. Do you mind if I kiss you good night?"

Dot was surprised by his shyness and chivalry. Guys in the city usually just assumed they'd be coming upstairs after buying one meal.

"Yes, please," she said, smiling with a little giggle.

Mary and Harper grabbed each other's hands and squeezed.

Danny brushed a lock of blond hair away from her forehead and leaned over to kiss her. His lips were firm and soft, and his touch was light. Dot's knees wobbled.

Danny pulled back and looked at her, a pleased smile on his face. "Thank you," he said.

"You're welcome," she replied.

"Hey, the fireworks show is Saturday—we're going to watch from the roof of the Sin Bin. It's got the best view. You all want to come?"

"I'm sure we will." She was pleased to see him already making future plans, even if it was for a group hangout.

"Sounds good."

"Good."

"So, I guess this is . . . Well, good night, Dot," he said as he started heading backward down the walkway.

Nearby, a car alarm blared. That spooked Pippi and she wiggled out of Harper's arms and jumped down, barking loudly at the offending noise.

"Pippi!" Dot bent down to scoop her up. She glanced over her shoulder and saw the shadows of Harper and Mary in the dark. "You guys! Were you there the entire time?"

"Sorry! We were trying to be discreet," Harper said.

"We didn't want to spoil the moment," Mary said, then she called to Danny, "Don't leave on our account!"

"Ha, thanks—maybe next time. I gotta work early in the morning." He waved to the girls on the porch. The car alarm went silent.

"Okay. We'll hold you to it," Mary said.

Dot turned back to the street, still holding Pippi, as Danny opened his truck door.

"Good night," Dot said as he waved and took off.

She turned back to the house. "I can't believe you eavesdropped on that entire goodbye," she said.

"We didn't want to interrupt," Harper said, taking a bag of frozen peas and placing it on the back of her neck.

"Scoot over," Dot said, working her way in between Harper and Mary and resting her head back. Pippi wriggled out of Dot's arms and onto Harper's lap.

"Here, take one of these." Harper reached down and got another bag of frozen peas from a cooler. "Cool yourself down."

"I'm not *that* hot and bothered," Dot said, closing her eyes and reliving her kiss with Danny.

"Could have fooled us!" Mary sat up and tucked her legs under her on the love seat slider. "That looked . . . like more than a 'thank you for helping me remodel the bookstore' dinner."

"And he's already asked you out again," Harper said.

"I'm not sure exactly what it was," Dot said. "But falling for Danny Dawson of Cedar Falls was *not* part of my plan."

"Tell us about it. We came for an adventure, to keep you company on your election gap year, and now we've fallen for guys we never would have met in the city," Mary said, thinking of Jake and the night on the swing. "*And* they're Republicans!"

"This wasn't on our bingo card," Dot said. "I was supposed to focus on my career not a guy. Let alone one that won't vote for a Democrat."

"Tell me about it. Once, I was giving Jake a hard time about supporting the other side, and he asked me if it really mattered to me how he voted. My initial thought was that yes, it did, but instead I said, 'Just kiss me,' and that was the end of that."

"So that's the trick—your sexual attraction has to be bigger than someone's politics?" Dot asked.

"Well, it's working so far," Mary said.

"So, what are we going to do now?" Harper asked.

"To be honest, Harp. I don't know," Dot said. "And maybe, it's okay not to know. At least not right now?"

"Maybe."

"Yeah. Maybe."

In turn, The Crew laid back on the love seat, frozen vegetables pressed to their foreheads. Dot used one foot to push the glider for them, rocking them gently while they each thought of the Wisconsin boys who'd rocked their worlds.

Chapter 48

Mary paced the baggage claim area waiting for her parents, Tony and Christine, to arrive at Milwaukee's airport. She was excited for their visit, though as she forewarned, and Dot and Harper knew full well from their college days, "They're a lot."

It was Mary's birthday weekend, and her mother hadn't missed one of her birthdays in twenty-five years, and she wasn't going to let distance keep her from celebrating her daughter's twenty-sixth. So, once they were sure that Nonna was okay and would be looked after by one of Mary's brothers and his wife, they bought plane tickets and planned a three-night visit.

She was eager to see them and show them around historic Cedar Falls. She knew her mom would love all of the boutiques, and her dad would be interested in the old mill that helped establish the town in the mid-1800s. He loved his dad history.

Dot and Harper had helped plan the entire weekend, which included a visit to the Taylor farm for a barbecue one day and then back to the Cedar Falls Inn supper club the next for her birthday.

Mary was also determined to demonstrate that she hadn't completely lost her mind when she'd decided to come with Dot for a year to the middle of the nowhere, though she was already bracing herself for the lectures from her mother about finding a man and settling down. When she was back home for those couple of weeks in June, her mom couldn't help herself one night at dinner.

"Soon you'll be on the other side of twenty-five. You're going to be left behind," Christine Russo had said.

"Ma. That's a little extreme."

"No, it's true. You remember Veronica Conti? She just married Vinnie

Gallo last winter, and they're having twins any day now. They bought a house over in Silver Lake and they're redoing the basement, so they have a mother-in-law's suite." She looked at her sons to telegraph she thought this was a very good idea and that they should think of doing the same.

"And then there's Erica Moretti," she continued. "Remember she dated your brother in high school? She's having her third baby this fall and they got a second house down at LBI. Can you imagine? They already have a second house—and it's at the shore."

"The traffic to LBI is horrendous. They'll spend years of their lives on the Parkway." Mary wasn't biting.

"Come on, Mary. It's happening all around you. And it's not good to wait too long. You must think about getting married as if it's part of your job."

"But I have a job, Ma. Besides, you're doing the work for me."

"Don't get me wrong. We're so proud of you. But you don't want to be an older mother, trying to catch up to everyone else."

"Yep, Ma. You don't have to worry. I've always got my eyes and ears open," she said, smiling and acting like she was taking it all on board. She raised her eyebrows at her favorite older brother, Father Gabe, to get him to change the subject.

As the conversation turned to what in the world her cousin Gina was thinking having a destination wedding, "In Mexico of all places!" her Nonna said, Mary let her mind churn on the question of her personal life.

First, she couldn't bear her mother's obsession with her future. It wasn't that she didn't think about it. She just didn't fixate on it. And second, she hadn't told them about Jake. She wasn't even sure what she'd tell them about him. That he was a hot cop who was fun to be around? And that he was intelligent, generous, responsible, and funny? Or that she was falling for him—the way he made her knees buckle when he walked in a room and how he matched her game of wits and made her feel more alive and understood than she'd ever felt in her life?

She wasn't ready to answer her parents' one thousand and one questions about him. So, she'd said nothing. Besides, she kind of liked having this secret. Her brothers couldn't tease her about it, and her parents couldn't interrogate and talk her out of it. For now, Jake was all hers.

But they'd find out soon enough. Their plane had just landed, and they'd soon be at the Taylor farm.

"Ma! Dad!" Mary called loudly as they came out of the terminal. She hadn't anticipated how excited she'd be to see them.

The Russos were a good-looking couple, and they stood out in the Midwest. Her mom was of medium height, and thin like Mary, with the same thick black curly hair. She wore a tan sleeveless top with a plunging neckline and black linen shorts with spotless white platform sneakers. Huge sunglasses were pushed up on top of her head. She carried a black and white leather Prada bag and sported a large tennis bracelet and matching earrings.

Her dad had on his weekend uniform: khaki shorts, a white fitted T-shirt, and his Magnanni loafers. He was still fairly fit at fifty-five years old. He'd been a boxer in his youth. Lately his waist had thickened a bit, and he looked a little more like a taller Danny DeVito than an Al Pacino. When his friends from the neighborhood chided him about gaining a little weight, he'd pat his belly and say, "My Chrissy's cooking is *almost* as good as my mother's!" *That* was high praise for Mrs. Russo.

Mary did a little jog to jump into her dad's arms. He picked her up easily and twirled her around.

"There's my girl," he said, and his Staten Island accent sounded like home. He set her down to give his wife a chance to hug the daughter they'd always adored.

"You came inside? I don't think that's happened for us since before 9/11," Christine Russo said. "What a nice surprise—we thought you'd text us from the curb."

"Tell me about it. But I found parking and, guess what? It's free for the first thirty minutes! Come, let's get your bags and get this weekend started." She linked her arms through theirs.

Two large suitcases covered in tight plastic came down the shoot.

"What, did you pack for three days or three months, Ma?"

"She brought all of her shoes, for one thing," Tony said.

"Well, I wasn't sure what I'd need!" Christine defended herself. "And there's a bunch of goodies in there that Nonna insisted we bring for your birthday."

"Yum! I hope there are some pizzelles in there."

"I thought we'd take some to the farm. I can't show up empty-handed," Christine said.

"They'll appreciate it. And there won't be any leftovers, that's for sure." Mary imagined Jake eating some of her Nonna's amaretti and pignoli cookies then snapped out of her food fantasy and guided her parents to the parking garage.

AS MARY TURNED off the highway and into Cedar Falls, her mother remarked on the flowers spilling out of planters from the residences and business, and her dad admired the clipped grass and solid construction.

"They take good care of things around here," he said, nodding approvingly.

"Everything is so . . . Americana! It's very cute." Her mother was charmed. "And they have so much storage with these two-car garages. We could have an entire extra refrigerator and freezer with space like this. Their Costcos must be gigantic. Can you imagine that, Tony?"

"Yeah, hon." Mary's father agreed with his wife no matter what.

Mary parked the Jeep outside the house and helped her dad get the bags out of the back of the compact SUV.

"Who lives here? Ted Kennedy?" her dad said, rolling his eyes at the Lopez-Stone signs in the yard as he carried the suitcases up the sidewalk.

"Don't start, Dad."

"What! I didn't say anything!" he said.

"Yes, you did. Not another word," Christine said. His wife wasn't going to let politics get their weekend off to a bad start. Mary always suspected her mom was a little more liberal than she let on.

"Fine. But don't come crying to me when everything goes to hell if they win. I was watching *The Five* and Greg Gutfeld was saying . . ."

"Dad!"

"Sorry, sweetie. I'll stop."

"Thank you."

"But I'm right."

"Tony!" Mary playfully pushed him down the hallway. "Come on. Your room is this way."

Tony and Christine complimented the place and noted their daughter had thoughtfully put water bottles and a little chocolate piece on the bedside tables. Their little girl was growing up.

"I'm so glad you came." Mary had her hand on the doorknob before giving them a moment to unpack and freshen up. "We're going to have the best time."

Mary prayed that would be true.

Chapter 49

First time in Wisconsin, Tony?" Joe Taylor asked while he manned the grill in the front yard of the farmhouse. The smell and sizzle of hamburgers and hot dogs filled the air.

"Yep. With my construction business, I haven't traveled much. But me and Christine—we've been to Chicago. Now that's my kind of town, if you know what I mean."

"I know what you mean. We love Chicago, too," Joe said. He'd already taken a liking to Tony.

"Well then we're going to get along just fine," Tony said, and clinked his beer bottle with Joe's and they both took a sip to mark their new friendship. The sun was shining, and the humidity was low for late July. "Beautiful place. Been in your family for a long time?"

"Oh yes. My ancestors got this farm around 1850. They were some of the founders of Cedar Falls," Joe said. He gave Tony a bit of the farm's history.

"Well, you've done a great job," Tony said, gesturing around the place. "I'm sure your folks are looking down on you with a lot of pride."

"I hope so, Tony. But I worry, especially for my boys." Joe motioned toward his sons. "Things are changing a little too fast for my comfort."

"How so?"

"Well, for one thing, we're under pressure to sell for some big corporate development plan. Some sort of AI energy thing, I guess. That's how the state and federal government are trying to sell it to the public. Been holding them off but it's getting tougher. The government is now threatening us—that if we don't sell, they could take it over for what they call the 'common good.' As if a farm that produces food for everyone isn't a part of the common good. It's all a bit of a mess."

"Sounds like it," Tony said.

"But I have to tell you, Mary's been very helpful to us. She even talked to one of the partners back in New York on the legal front," Joe said. "She's a real firecracker. We've enjoyed getting to know her."

Tony looked over to where Mary and Christine had joined Grace to set up the side dishes on the buffet table.

"I'm glad to hear that. She's a good girl. The smartest of my kids," he said. "And I think I understand what you're saying. I took over my pop's construction business, and I work with my sons now. Our eldest became a priest, so I hope to pass the business to the other two. But it gets harder to see how they'll manage with costs going up so much. And the pain of complying with so many regulations. Not to mention the government taxing us to death. And then after death, too."

"Damn right. Death taxes—the worst idea. We may come from different worlds, but we speak the same language, Tony." Joe gestured to Grace it was time to ring the bell. "Come on, let's eat."

"OH, COULD I ring the bell?" Harper asked Grace, having heard Joe from across the yard. "I've always wanted to. It's like a scene from *Little House on the Prairie*."

"Go for it, Harper," Grace said. "Give it a good tug and we'll get everyone fed before the 4-H kids arrive to practice for the fair."

"What are 4-H kids?" Harper asked.

"You don't know about 4-H? It's been going for over a hundred years," Tommy said.

"Think of it like the Scouts—you have the Scouts out your way, don't you?" Joe asked.

"Yes. I don't know a lot about it, but there's this dating app that lets you filter for Eagle Scouts."

Tommy laughed. "Well, I don't know about Boy Scout Tinder, but I think it's fair to say that 4-H is like Scouts in rural America."

"But do you have Scouts, too?" she asked.

"We do. And all my sons are Eagle Scouts." Joe leaned in closer to Harper's ear. "In case that's of interest." Harper's face reddened.

With everyone wanting to eat, Harper handed Tommy her phone and asked him to take a video for her Instagram. Then she went over and pulled down on the bell five times.

"Come and get it!" she yelled enthusiastically.

"Oh my gosh, does she think this is the Wild West?" Mary asked Dot as they sat and watched their friend pretend that she was out on the Plains. She yelled, "Harp, this is Wisconsin, not Dodge City!"

"Hey. Don't look now, but your parents just sat with Jake and Tommy," Dot said.

Mary whipped her head around.

"Do they know anything about you two?"

"What's there to know?" Mary asked, feigning innocence. "Let me see if I can handle this . . . delicately."

"Good luck with that!" Dot said, grabbing a plate to go through the line. Danny met up with her, brushing her hand with his, in a subtle way of reconfirming his interest. They'd been spending as much time together as possible given their busy schedules. Dot lit up whenever he was around, and even Grace had said she thought Danny was looking more like his old self.

"I love to see him happy," Grace had told her in private that afternoon.

Dot kept stopping herself from letting her mind wander too far into the future—she wasn't sure what would happen when she went back to New York in a few months. She decided to push those worries to the side and live in the moment (or so she told herself every five minutes).

"IT'S A PLEASURE to meet you, Mrs. Russo. But wow, you could be Mary's sister," Jake said to Mary's mother, his dimple deepening and blue eyes twinkling. He could pour on the charm.

"Oh stop!" Christine blushed, cherishing the compliment.

"So, Jake, your dad says you're a police officer?" Tony said. "And he told us about your military service, too. Thank you for that." He stood and put out his hand and Jake shook it firmly.

"It was my honor. Learned a lot. Made good friends. Saw a bit of the world—parts I don't ever need to see again," he said.

"That's right. One and done." Tony was warm toward him.

"And I always wanted to be a policeman. Now I'm living the dream. I can be near to my mom and dad, help them when they need it, and serve the community. Plus, my mom insists we be here for Sunday supper."

"I insist on Sunday supper, too!" Christine said. "So did my parents and their parents. I expect all my children and grandchildren to be there. Mary was given a one-year pass while she's here, and then I need her back on gravy duty."

Jake and Mary met eyes quickly. Her mom, who missed nothing, clocked the something that passed between her and Jake.

"Sunday is my favorite day of the week," Tony said. "It can be a bit chaotic with all the grandkids now. Our family isn't known for being quiet."

"That's the truth. One time, Mary brought home a boyfriend from college. What was his name? Aston or something like that."

"Colin," Mary said. She looked at Jake. "It didn't last."

"Ha! It lasted exactly one night!" Tony said.

"I'll never forget it," Christine said. "So, this kid, Colin, he'd never been to Staten Island, or even to an Italian American house. He came all dressed up. Even wore a tie! Poor kid was so uptight, too. But polite. Very polite. Anyway, our family likes to talk, and we talk loudly. He thought we were all fighting and got so upset that he locked himself in the guest bathroom! My mother had to go coax him out of there."

The Russos laughed at the memory. "We never saw that kid again," Tony said.

"My family can be brutal on anyone I bring home." Mary remembered feeling sorry for Colin. They had mutually ghosted each other after that night.

"I bet I could handle it," Jake said, nudging Mary's knee under the table.

She pressed her leg firmly back against his and held it there, grateful for his support under her mother's scrutiny.

"I think you'd be a good match for my brothers. They could use a challenge." She smiled at him then took a not-so-dainty bite of the steamed corn she'd scooped onto her plate.

Tony and Christine nudged each other under the table, too. They looked at each other, a wordless question asked between them: Is she seeing him?

"You'd be welcome anytime. It's a shame you live so far away, we'd love to have you over," Christine said.

"Thank you. I'd be honored to visit. Maybe one day I'll get over there to see the Big Apple for myself." Jake pressed his leg harder against Mary's.

"Do you plan on staying here forever?" Christine tried to sound casual, but Mary knew that her mother was digging for clues on whether they were a serious item. Mary listened to his answer, because she wasn't so sure either.

"Oh yes, ma'am. There's no place I'd want to raise a family other than right here in Cedar Falls. To me, it's the best place to grow up. It's safe. Good schools. Family still matters a lot. And I love my work, fishing and hunting, and, most of all, the Packers. I can't imagine ever leaving."

"Well, I'm happy for you that you know what you want in life," Christine said, looking at her daughter and nodding. Her eyes said, "Yes, he's gorgeous and wonderful, but you're not leaving your family so don't get any bright ideas." Mary smiled back tightly.

"Packers will be good again this year," Tony said, jumping at the chance to get Christine off the young man's case. He could tell his daughter liked Jake, and he didn't want to upset her. He'd have to talk his wife down later. "Are you one of the shareholders? I've always said that it was cool how the fans get to own the team. Can't imagine that'd ever work for the Jets. The fans would declare bankruptcy after one season. There's always this massive buildup and then they're a complete letdown. I mean, they even tried to make Aaron Rodgers a thing. Ashamed to say I bought into it at first."

"Yeah, he was a hero of mine for many years, but no longer. He's kind of dead to us. But I don't have any shares. My chief does, though," Jake said. "Since he was a kid. Offers us his seats from time to time. Did you see we have this great new defensive lineman that's come on this year? Kid out of Alabama."

As the guys started talking about sports, Mary said, "Ma, let me show you the chickens."

"I can see the chickens from here."

"But let's see them close up, Ma." Mary took her mother's elbow and steered her away from the table. She wanted a word.

Chapter 50

Why did you jump on Jake like that?" Mary steered her mom away from the guests and over toward the chicken coop.

"Carissima, I didn't jump on him. But tell me what's really going on. Are you *dating* him?" She plowed on, knowing the answer. "Whatever it is, I can tell you're not just friends. Why didn't you tell us?"

"You *did* jump on him. And I *didn't* hide anything . . . I just didn't tell you."

"So, what . . . are you in love with him?"

"Ma! No! I mean, I don't think so. I don't know. Maybe?" Mary was uncharacteristically flustered. "I guess I haven't let myself think about it too much. Why can't you just let me be young and free before I have to make so many big decisions?"

Christine put an arm around her daughter.

"Maria Theresa, your father and I want what's best for you. We were happy you had this little adventure with Dot and Harper. But we know you. You're going to want to raise your children near your family, and making everything more complicated doesn't make sense." Christine sighed heavily, breathing out the worry she always had for her kids. "Look, Mary, I know he's good looking, charming, fun, strong . . . I mean, believe me I get it. The guy's hot."

"Ma!"

"I have *eyes*, Mary. And he has a lovely family. But you heard him. He said he's *never leaving here*. And would you want to leave us, to move here, to be a . . . farmer's wife?"

"Ma, you're getting carried away. First, he's not a farmer, he's a police officer. Second, we haven't ever talked about 'whatever this is' as you say. And third, you always undermine my decisions, and I need you to trust me. And to be there for me whatever I decide. Please, Ma, enough already."

She leaned her head on her mother's shoulder.

Christine turned and kissed the top of Mary's head. "Okay. Okay. Don't be upset. I trust you. You're the most brilliant girl I've ever known. You're beautiful. A successful young woman. You have a very bright future." She put an arm firmly around her daughter. "But do me a favor. Don't waste time. Life goes by fast, Mary. I don't want you to look back and wish you'd taken my advice. I'd hate to have you say, 'You were right, Ma.'"

"Ha! There's nothing you'd like more than for me to say that!" Mary laughed, wiping a tear away and lifting her head to look at her mom's face.

"Not on this one, kid. Not on this one." They both put their arms around each other and hugged tightly.

When she pulled back, Mary said, "The thing is, I really like him. From the moment we first met. I feel like myself when I'm around him" She had tears in her big dark brown eyes. "But I know it's complicated."

"All right. We can't have him see you upset."

Mary blotted her eyes. "Okay. I'll pull myself together."

"That's my girl. Now let's step away from all this chicken crap," Christine said, lightening the mood but seeing what was plain to everyone willing to admit it.

Her daughter was in love.

AFTER EVERYONE ATE, the 4-H kids arrived on a small school bus, and it was time for them to practice their presentations for the upcoming livestock show at the fair. The Taylors did this every year since their boys were young. Grace had run the 4-H club, and anyone under her tutelage always swept up a lot of ribbons.

Joe doled out assignments to the adults—Mary and Jake were given the sheep, Dot and Danny the cows, and Harper and Tommy the rabbits. He and Grace took the pigs.

The Crew had dressed more appropriately for this visit to the farm: old sneakers, cutoff jeans and tank tops.

"This is not a pretty business," Mary said to Jake, as he helped a young girl set her lamb in the right position for when the judges saw her the following weekend. She wiped her cheek, and the mud transferred from her hand to her cheek. At least she hoped it was mud.

"I don't think I've ever seen you prettier," he said. She looked up at him and smiled.

Christine and Tony saw the exchange.

"Oh boy," Tony said, reaching for his wife's hand.

"She looks happy," Christine said. "In fact, Tony, they all do. It's like getting out of New York for a few months reset their circuits. Must be all this fresh air. Dot doesn't seem as stressed-out by having to be perfect. And Harper isn't depressed about that surfer boy anymore."

"Well, let's see what it can do for us then," Tony said, pulling his wife over to Harper and Tommy with the rabbits. Harper was sneezing like crazy because she'd forgotten to take her Zyrtec that morning.

"Bless you!" the kids yelled out after another one of her attacks.

Christine handed Harper a new tissue and gave her a hug. "It's good to see you, Harper. You seem happy."

"Thank you, Mrs. Russo." Harper beamed. "I really am." She sneezed again.

"Come on now, show us how you're going to win this thing next week," Tony said to a young boy feeding a carrot to his rabbit.

Tommy explained to everyone what the judges would be looking for. "So, the judges look at the rabbit's eyes—they need to be bright and clear. They need to be the correct weight and can't have any sores or injuries. Healthy fur matters a lot," he said.

"And what about our little camper?" Tony asked. "Does she get judged, too?"

"Yes, that's a big part of it." He gestured for the young girl to get ready to handle her rabbit. "What are some of the things you need to show, Josie? And use your big girl voice, okay?"

The young girl squared her shoulders then confidently said, "I need to be able to handle my rabbit well and to know all of his parts, like the loin and dewlap." She pointed to the bunny's parts correctly.

"What else?" Tommy asked.

"I also need to explain how I feed and house him. And keep him safe from disease."

"Good girl. That's it!" Tommy was proud of her. He told her she was free to put away her rabbit. After Josie had him inside, Harper helped her secure the cage.

"She'll do well, but the rabbit competition is tough." Tommy wiped his hands and turned back to Tony and Christine.

"First place blue ribbon. I can feel it," Tony said.

"Can you say that again?" Josie asked.

Tony said it again then asked, "Could you not hear me?"

"Oh, Mister, I could hear you just fine, I just wanted to hear you say it again," Josie said. "You talk funny!"

"You little rascal," Tony said, pretending to chase her. Josie ran off to play with the other kids.

As the demonstration practice ended, Joe Taylor found Tony.

"Hey, before you head out—want to give my new John Deere a spin? Mary told me you love to drive." It was a new row crop to replace one he'd had for years, since the boys were still in high school. "We're getting ready to break it in at harvesttime."

"Now we're talking, Joe! You think I can handle it?" Tony joked and he gave the big green farm vehicle a once over.

"No doubt about it."

"Hey, Christine. Get over here! Let's take this thing for a ride!"

Christine had been holding one of the steers with a leather rope and chatting with some of the parents who were loading up the livestock to take back to their homes.

"If you'll excuse me," she said gently. Then in her typical voice, she yelled, "Don't you dare leave without me, Tony Russo." She jogged over to the tractor and shimmied her way up onto his lap. "Yee-haw, let's go." She pretended to swing a lasso as Tony started down the road.

The Taylors watched them go, and Mary had her hands over her eyes. "I can't watch," she said. "Please don't hit the barn."

Jake laughed and put his arm around her, and suddenly Mary didn't worry anymore if her parents knew that she had fallen for him.

AFTER THE 4-H rehearsal, the Taylors called everyone over for homemade ice cream. They had a choice of vanilla bean, strawberry cheesecake, and maple bacon.

"All three for me," Tony said, having the time of his life. Christine playfully swatted his belly but talked herself into a scoop of vanilla bean.

Joe Taylor ducked into the house for a moment and came back with an envelope.

"Mary, do you have a minute?"

Mary finished her ice cream cone and wiped her hands on a napkin.

"Sure thing. What's up?"

"I got this in the mail yesterday. Grace and I wondered if you'd look at it. Some big law firm from Washington, D.C., we've not heard of before sent it—it's an increased offer. It's a serious number, but we still aren't selling. Our neighbors got one too, too, and I'm not sure how strongly they're committed to holding out."

"You bet." Mary glanced at the letter and took her phone out of her back pocket. She snapped a photograph of the letter. "I'll take a look at it later and send you a note."

"Thank you, Mary."

"Happy to."

"Hey, your parents are a real kick in the pants."

"They're something else, that's for sure. Thanks for having us."

"Thanks for brightening up the day. We like having you around, Mary." He glanced over at Jake. "And so does our son."

Mary smiled and tried to hide her blush.

Chapter 51

The countdown was on. For the Win had worked for several days on the upcoming candidate visit. The Lopez-Stone ticket was making a stop in Cedar Falls, and Dot, Fletcher, and Rose had been working around-the-clock to help with stage, crowd, and message management.

They'd split up the duties—Rose on ticketing for interested visitors and Fletcher on logistics with the candidates' advance teams.

Meanwhile, Dot was working with a local reporter on a large profile of Lucy Lopez with the *Milwaukee Journal Sentinel* that would run the morning of her visit. She'd also set up a panel of Wisconsin-based influencers so that they'd get as much as possible out of the hours Lopez would be there.

In the lead-up to the big day, the three of them took a midday shift at the Democrats' fair booth.

"I wonder if she's giving them a piece of her mind," Dot said to Fletcher as they observed Rose talking to a group of local Republicans who had their booth across and down from their section.

"Hope she's picking up some good intel. She comes off as so innocent, but she's stealthy. Could've been a CIA agent," Fletcher said.

"Think we should go over and extract her like I have to do with Mary when guys won't leave her alone?"

"Well, if one of those guys hits on Rose, I'll allow it." Fletcher stole glances at Rose and tried not to make it obvious he was keeping tabs on her.

The fair was hopping that Saturday afternoon in mid-August, and they'd been lucky with the weather. There wasn't a cloud in the sky, and a gentle breeze had picked up. It was welcome after a couple of weeks of extreme heat. Kids rode on their dad's shoulders or ran this way and that, safe under the watchful eyes of the adults. Teens moved in packs, sharing their inside jokes and flirting out of sight from their teachers, coaches, and parents. It was the culmination of summer—the crops were coming in nicely, and everyone in Cedar Falls seemed to be in a good mood.

Later that afternoon, The Crew was meeting up with the Taylor boys and Danny at the midway, and Dot was getting anxious to see them. Well, specifically, to see Danny. The pair had been dating for several weeks—mostly casual dinners, runs out to the covered bridge and back, and a few late nights talking and making out on the porch. Danny was running through her mind on a loop, and it had become her favorite daydream.

Dot jolted out of her daydream and turned to a young woman carrying a small boy who had reached toward the treats on their table. Rose had nailed it—they literally needed eye candy to lure people over so they could get them to talk. Mimi had made individualized Flour Power cream puffs, packaged in cellophane and tied with blue and white ribbons.

"Hi! What a beautiful boy. Are you registered to vote?" Dot asked.

"Oh, um, no. I'm not into politics," the woman said, a bit shy about her son wanting the cream puff anyway.

"I can understand that," Dot said as she handed her the treat. She'd heard this reply often at their get-out-the-vote events. "Though with your little guy there, I'm sure you're taking more of an interest. And if you're a Wisconsin resident, your vote matters more than ever this cycle."

"Why is that?" She set her toddler down then opened the bag and tore off some bites for him.

Dot explained Wisconsin's unique value in that year's electoral college map. Then she encouraged her to come back the following day to hear Lopez give a speech at the fairgrounds.

"Oh, I've seen some of her videos pop up in my feed," the woman said. "What do you think of her?"

"She's amazing, and I think she's got what it takes," Dot said. "She's a state senator from Georgia, not a Washington insider. And she's different compared to the party's more recent candidates—young, smart, beautiful, and funny. Her passion is education, women's rights, and making life fairer and more affordable for working people. I think you'd like her."

"Maybe I'll try to make it tomorrow. I just have so much going on." She wiped her child's hands and mouth with one of the wet wipes and took a flyer from Dot. Then she scooped up her son and set him on her hip.

"He's a cutie," Dot said.

The woman smiled warmly, appreciating the compliment. "Thanks. He's also a handful."

"I know you want the best for him. Come tomorrow if you can. Her speech is at two—just before the championship steer round. Wouldn't want to miss that either!" She hoped her fair barn pitch would be the closing argument.

"I'll give it a shot," she said as she got her son to say thank you for the treat and wave goodbye.

When the woman and child had walked away, Fletcher said, "Nice job, Dot. Light touch, focus on the future," he said. "Who could say no?"

"We'll see if she comes back. I know it's not easy to make time for politics when they're just trying to get through the day. And babysitters are so expensive," Dot said. "But we need these moms to vote for Lopez. Otherwise, we have no hope of winning in November. Or any time after that, the way things are trending."

The state of the race had Dot nervous. That week a new poll from a reliable outlet showed the Republicans had pulled ahead nationally *and* in Wisconsin. Kitty was in meltdown mode and crushing Dot and Fletcher.

On their video call that week, Kitty had been a minute late. Dot immediately sensed something was up.

"What are we all doing to get these numbers back up?" Kitty implored. "I'm counting on you to make this work."

Fletcher had jumped in to calm her down. "Hey, that poll could be an outlier. There's no logical reason that they're ahead by that much." He made a good point. It was the only poll that had them down that much.

Then Dot had used her PR climb-down tactics with Kitty.

"We hear you," Dot had said. "The good news is, the fair's a big deal, and we've got a plan. Plus, there's a feature on Lopez coming soon in the *Milwaukee Journal Sentinel*. The reporter seems completely charmed by her. Once it's out, we'll get that up on all the socials. I promise, we're pulling out all the stops for the candidate's time in state."

That seemed to calm Kitty down for a moment. But then Dot knew things were dire when Kitty made them an unexpected offer.

"Look, we all know that Wisconsin matters the most, even if these whiz kids at the DNC think they know better," she said, taking the edge out of her tone. "I've got an incentive for you. If Lopez wins Wisconsin, I'll give you and Fletcher twenty percent of the win bonus to split."

Dot did some quick math in her head. If Kitty was to get $500,000, that meant she and Fletcher would split $100,000. An unexpected fifty grand? That would be amazing—especially since she didn't have a job lined up for after the election.

"You know we're not in it for the money," Fletcher said. "We're in it for the country."

While Dot agreed, she also thought she could be in it for the money as well. "It's an incredibly generous offer. You've got a deal."

"Great," Kitty said. "Keep me posted."

The gravity of their situation wasn't lost on Dot. For Kitty to offer to give them part of her win bonus must mean she knew that Lopez's chances of victory were dwindling.

Back at the fair, Fletcher pointed to where Rose was still laughing with the Republicans over at their booth. "She's sure having a good time."

"She's got friends everywhere, doesn't she. People who are too online wouldn't believe that people from opposite sides of the aisle got along that well here in the real world."

"Yeah, I know what you mean, and I'm all for civility," Fletcher said. "But I still want to kick their ass on Election Day."

"Same," Dot said, nodding sharply. "It's going to be so close."

"Yep. Too close for comfort."

Rose walked back to them smiling.

"Get any dirt on what the Republicans are up to, Rose?" Fletcher asked.

"Ha! From Charlie Cooper? Heck no. We're just friends from way back. He and my late husband used to play tennis over at the club. I haven't seen him in a dog's age. It was good to catch up."

"How are they feeling about their chances in November?" Fletcher asked.

"I don't know. I didn't ask."

"You didn't?" Dot asked, incredulous.

"No, I didn't. I vowed long ago never to let politics get in the way of a friendship."

Dot and Fletcher looked confused.

"You two see me every day, and you know that I'm a true-blue Democrat. I've never voted for a Republican. Politics is what I do, but it's not who I am," she said. "And some of my best friends are Republicans. Charlie and the other guys over there, well they didn't ask me how we're doing either We just live our lives respecting each other. It's always been that way around here, at least for the folks our age."

"Sort of like the Jankowskis at Reader Falls," Dot said. She'd long admired how their mixed political marriage had worked out perfectly for them. She couldn't help but think of Danny then. She knew Danny voted Republican, but he rarely brought it up. And even if he was conservative, he'd never held her politics against her. He was the most supportive guy she'd ever dated who understood her passion for politics and didn't give her a hard time for working evenings and weekends. More important, she realized to her surprise that her attraction to him and how she'd come to care about him meant that she didn't really care how he voted—she just loved being around him. It made her realize she didn't really like Ryan all that much after all.

And then her mind flashed to how he'd held her the night before when they had slow danced to one of Dierks Bentley's latest tracks in front of the headlights of his truck.

"Snap out of it!" she told herself. She had too much work to do to daydream about Danny.

"Rose, I have a lot to learn from you," Dot said, bringing herself back to the here and now.

"Oh, stop." Rose brushed off the compliment. "Senator Lopez's visit tomorrow is going to be critical. The stakes are as high as the corn. We need to have a good turnout."

"Yep. That's on our minds, too." Dot tapped her fingers on the desk.

"We're on it," Fletcher said. "We've got a bunch of folks already signed up, and I just hit social media one more time. Plus, Kitty increased our budget to provide food for everyone who shows up. We're offering free soda and brats. Gotta feed this crowd to keep them happy in their seats."

"All right. Let's get to it," Dot said. "Rose, you might not feel competitive with those guys, but we do."

Rose winked at her. "Oh hey, listen. The local GOP knows I fight to win. And they don't underestimate me."

"Well, maybe everyone in politics is smarter than I thought!" Dot said.

Rose laughed. "Don't count on it."

Dot's phone vibrated in her back pocket and she pulled it out and saw a message from Kitty.

"Oh no, guys. We've got trouble," she said.

"What's wrong?" Fletcher craned his neck to read Dot's phone.

"They're canceling Lopez's visit tomorrow and sending her to Texas to be a part of that education protest."

"But that's crazy!" Fletcher was exasperated. "We're not going to win Texas! It's redder than Mars. We've actually got a shot here."

Rose folded her arms across her chest. "Typical. This is what the D.C. whiz kids did to us last time, too. They chase all the wrong rabbits. Then they wonder why we lose."

Dot went quiet. This was a huge problem. They'd built up this visit so much that breaking the news that Lopez wasn't coming was going to cost them the momentum they'd gained over the weekend.

"I'm heading back to the office," Dot said. "I need to figure out how we're going to fix this mess."

Her first call was going to be to the one person who needed to weigh in more heavily—Kitty Bell.

Chapter 52

Dot spotted Harper and Mary before they saw her. Mary was wearing a short, hot pink and white gingham dress with skinny shoulder straps, white wedge sneakers, and a light pink crossbody bag.

"You look like brunette Barbie," Harper had said when Mary came downstairs. "In a good way."

Mary tossed back her hair, put her hand under her chin, and flashed a smile. "Thanks!"

Harper wore jean cutoffs, a white button-down with its sleeves rolled up, and the red cowgirl boots her parents had sent for her birthday in May.

"Those are hot!" Mary had said when Harper opened the gift.

"Yeah, these don't seem like me." She wondered if her parents had been drunk when they bought them. But she'd put the boots on and checked herself out in the full-length entryway mirror.

"Which is exactly why I'm going to make you wear them one day. Gotta get you out of your comfort zone, Harp!" The fair was just the place.

"Hey, girls!" Dot called to them, feeling drab in her royal-blue FTW T-shirt, white shorts, and dusty sneakers. She wished she'd brought a change of clothes. "You look great. I should have upped my game."

"Come here. Let me fix it," Mary said. She pulled Dot's T-shirt out of her waistband and knotted it, exposing some of Dot's stomach.

"That's a little much, don't you think?" Dot asked, feeling a little self-conscious.

"She *never* thinks it's too much," Harper said.

"Look, this might be the only fair we ever go to, and I aim to make it a memorable night." Mary fussed with Dot's hair and then added some lip gloss. "There, that's better. It's giving more Sexy Dem than political volunteer."

There was no mirror for Dot to check herself out in. "I guess I'll have to trust you."

"When has *that* ever steered you wrong?" Harper asked.

"I have no idea what you mean." Mary looked at them innocently. "Come on. I want to find the guys and see if any of them can win us a prize."

"WHAC-A-MOLE IS MY specialty," Dot said, challenging them all to a round.

"I like the confidence," Danny said. "But I've been playing since I was a kid. I don't lose."

"It's on!" Jake said, handing over cash to buy a game.

"Go! Go! Go!" Each of the girls and guys banged their mallets frantically down on the moles. No one held back.

"Wow, competitive group," the carney said. "And the winner is . . . this young lady right here."

Harper looked shocked. "Me?"

"You! Pick your prize."

"Oh, wow. Ummm . . . I'll get that little panda. For Pippi."

"I'm not sure that's a dog toy," Tommy said.

"Yeah, he just wants you to give it to him. He still sleeps with his stuffed animals," Jake said, and Tommy play-tackled him.

"Let's try another game," Danny said. "Dot, you choose."

"Okay," she said, looking around. "How about that one?" She pointed to a football game where you had to throw a spiral into a small hole. "You three compete."

"Great call. Boys, you up for it?" Danny handed over the money and he, Tommy, and Jake grabbed a football each.

"Okay, play nice!" The carney started the clock.

The guys talked smack to each other as they tried to show they still had it.

"Come on, Danny, didn't you used to be on scholarship for this?" Jake jeered.

"Jake, you're embarrassing yourself!" his twin said.

"Shut up, Tommy, you throw like a girl . . . No offense, ladies!"

"None taken!" Mary shouted, cheering him on.

In the end, Danny won by a point. The carney asked them if they wanted to go one more time to try to win a bigger prize. Challenge accepted.

Danny blew them away this time, and Dot was impressed. She felt like she was in high school and dating the quarterback.

"Which one of these beauties do you want?" the carney asked.

"I'll take that one," Danny said, pointing to a black and white stuffed cow with big blue eyes. He gallantly passed it to Dot.

"My hero!" she said, hugging the cow and acting like it was best gift she'd ever received. She shot up on her tiptoes and kissed him. It was a little surprising to publicly display their affection, but they'd gradually become much more open about their feelings for each other.

Mary and Jake looked at each other in a way that said, "This is getting interesting."

"Let's eat!" Tommy said, pointing toward the food court. Jake led the way.

Tommy bought them a bunch of things to try. Deep-fried mashed potatoes on a stick, enormous barbecued turkey legs, glazed donut ham sandwiches, cheese curd tacos, and flash-fried lemon bites. The guys washed it down with Solo cups of Spotted Cow beer, and the girls had margaritas.

"I'm throwing in the towel," Dot said. "I've going to need a juice cleanse from this fair."

"Don't give up on us now. The night is still young," Danny said. Their chemistry was so obvious it practically radiated, impossible for anyone to miss.

"Hey, I want to go on the Ferris wheel," Mary said.

"Ferris wheels are for girls, Mary," Jake said.

"Perfect. Send the three of us up and you can wait for us on land."

"Deal." Jake stood in line for their tickets, and then they climbed on, sitting three across.

Dot held her stuffed cow on her lap in between Harper and Mary. The ride operator checked they were securely in; Danny snapped a picture and sent it to Dot for her Instagram. She posted it right away. "Three Gotham girlies making the world go 'round in Wisconsin!"

The operator turned up the country music and away they went to "American Kids" by Kenny Chesney, climbing high over the midway. The sun had gone down and the lights of the fairgrounds came on in the most magical way. The wind gusted up and blew their hair around.

"I ate so much crap," Harper said, putting her head in her hands. "I don't feel well."

"Come on, Harp. This is a very gentle ride. We're barely moving," Mary said. "You'll be okay." She gave Dot a sideways glance, rolling her eyes at the latest gastro drama.

"Oh, guys, I'm not so sure. I think I'm going to be sick," Harper said.

"Well make sure to puke over the side, not on us!" Mary was still joking, but Harper wasn't.

Then Dot realized. "Wait, Harper. Did you take an allergy pill before we left the house?"

"Yes. I had to with all the animals and dust out here."

"But then we had those margaritas. And they were strong," Dot said, reality becoming clear.

"Oh my gosh," Harper groaned. "You're right. No *wonder* I feel sick."

"Take some deep breaths," Mary said. "Focus on one thing in front of you. There—in the distance—see the lights at the fair entrance? Just look there, not all around."

"We'll get you some water as soon as the ride stops," Dot promised.

They were still going around and around. Each time they passed ground level, Jake, Tommy, and Danny waved to them. Mary waved back, while Dot held tight to her cow, and Harper held on for dear life.

At one point the ride stopped while they were on top. Dot assumed it was because the operator was letting some people off and bringing others on for their turn. "It's almost over, Harp." The poor girl's face was nearly green.

After a bit, when they hadn't moved, Mary started wondering if something was wrong.

"We should be moving by now, right?"

"I'm sure we'll get going any minute," Dot said. Harper moaned in discomfort.

Suddenly, the wind picked up and a siren blared. Then the lights of the fair all went dark at once.

"What's happening?" Harper asked, panic rising in her voice.

"Hold on." Mary fumbled in her pocket to get her phone. She texted Jake.

"What's going on?"

Three dots danced on Mary's screen waiting for Jake's reply.

"Seems like the power might be out. They're working on it. Just hold tight."

"What's the siren mean?" she typed.

"Tornado warning. Doesn't mean a tornado's coming—it's just a warning." Jake was getting updates from emergency management on his work phone. His texts to her were calm, but her adrenaline was racing.

The wind picked up, lightning flashed, and the thunder roared.

Dot was holding her stuffed cow tight with one hand and held Harper's hand with the other. They could hear cries for help from others on the ride. They saw people on the ground running for shelter.

"You guys. I'm scared," Harper said. She was taking big gobs of breath. Her head hurt and she felt like she was falling.

"It'll be okay," Dot said, trying to convince herself as much as Harper.

"I love you guys. You mean so much to me." Now Harper was crying.

"Hey, hey—please, we're not going out on a Ferris wheel, Harp," Dot said.

Mary reached over and grabbed Harper's knee. "Hang on. We're fine." But she wasn't sure she believed that. The wind howled and dirt flew in their eyes. Dot tried to shield them behind the big stuffed cow.

Then as suddenly as the wind started, it stopped. The sirens still wailed and then gradually tapered off. The Crew picked their heads up to look around. The fair was still dark save for some of the emergency lights. The Ferris wheel hadn't moved to bring them down.

Mary looked down trying to see Jake.

"Oh my gosh—they're bringing a huge ladder over to us. Holy smokes," Mary said, envisioning how they'd have to get down from the top of the ride. Dot and Harper craned their necks to see.

A few moments later, they heard Jake's voice. He was nearly to the top of the ladder.

"Fancy meeting you here," he said, trying to lighten the mood. Then more seriously, "Are you all okay?" He placed a hand on Mary's shoulder.

"A little freaked. What happened?"

"A tornado touched down about three miles from here. We got lucky."

"Why wasn't there any warning? This is crazy!" Dot said.

"It can happen. But let's get you unstuck. Do you think you can climb down the ladder to the ground? You just hold on tight, always having one foot and one hand on the rung to steady yourself."

"I can do it," Mary said. "But Harper is sick. I don't know how we're going to get her down."

"Let's try this. You go first, then Dot. I'll bring Harper down with me."

"Okay. Ummm . . . what about him?" Dot pointed to her cow, only kind of joking. She wanted it as the prize Danny won for her the night they almost died in a tornado in Wisconsin.

"Give it to me." Jake took the cow and called to Danny. "Heads up!" He let the cow fall, and Danny leapt to his right and caught it with one hand.

"Show-off," Jake said, as he unlocked the bar that held the girls' in place.

"Okay, Mary. You're up. Just don't look down. Keep your eyes on me and then look straight ahead. Got it?"

She nodded. Bravely, she turned and made eye contact with Jake and slowly made her way down the ladder. About halfway down, she looked straight ahead and then she was on the ground, wrapped in a hug by Tommy.

Next was Dot. She did the same, looking at Jake until he was out of sight. Danny was ready for her as she reached the ground. He put his arms around her.

"You're shaking," he said.

"I'm okay, I'm okay." She let herself collapse into him and looked up to see Jake below Harper, his hand guiding her, as they slowly made their way down.

"You've got this, Harper!" Dot called.

"You're so brave!" Mary shouted.

Finally, Harper was on solid ground and Tommy put his arm around her to help hold her up.

"I need to lie down," she said. "I need to go home."

"You got it. We'll get you in bed ASAP," Tommy said.

Dot and Mary made eye contact. They didn't think Harper was saying she wanted to go to their house in Cedar Falls.

In that moment, they knew that Harper really wanted to go home—to New York.

Chapter 53

As they walked to the exit, the lights for the fairgrounds all came back on. Danny was carrying Dot's stuffed cow, and Tommy was helping Harper to walk. She was unsteady on her legs. Jake and Mary were holding hands when they heard women trying to get the guys' attention.

"Danny! Jake! Tommy!"

They stopped and searched for who was calling them.

"Oh boy," Tommy said. "Here we go."

"Hey, Maddy, how's it going?" Jake said, taking the lead. It was the same group of women that Dot and Danny had run into at dinner earlier that summer.

"We're great. Are you going to introduce us to your friends?" Maddy asked.

"Sure, yes. Well, you remember meeting Dot," Danny said. "And these are her friends, Mary and Harper." Turning to The Crew, he said, "And these are longtime friends of ours. We grew up together. The queens of Cedar Falls." He meant it as a compliment, but Maddy was shooting daggers at him.

"Oh yes, how could I forget? A bunch of Carrie Bradshaws from New York City, right?" Her tone was light but had an edge. Marissa, Lauren, and Zoe stood behind Maddy, backing her up as if this was a showdown.

Mary decided to step up to cut the tension. "Hi, I'm Mary. Pleasure to meet you." She stuck out her hand, seeing if Maddy would take it. After a beat, she did, a fake smile on her face.

"So nice to meet you, too," she said.

"And this is Harper," Dot said. "She's feeling a little unwell, so we were just headed out."

Harper was dizzy but moved forward to be polite. "Hi, I'm Harp—" and she vomited her drinks, allergy medicine, and fried fair food all over Maddy.

No one said a word for a moment, stunned into silence.

"Oh my god, oh my god, oh my god." Maddy started to panic, her hands flapping at her sides.

Jake stifled a laugh, and Mary fought back a giggle.

"I'm sorry . . . I'm so sorry," Harper said between retches. Maddy's friends dug in their belt bags for anything to help clean up the mess. "I've been unwell. It was the allergy medicine and then the Ferris wheel and then . . ."

Tommy put an arm around Harper and said, "We were just leaving to get her home."

"Let's go get you cleaned up," Marissa said to Maddy. She took the lead, and the Cedar Falls girls scurried away.

"I'm so embarrassed," Harper said, drinking the water Dot handed to her as they walked to their vehicles. "I haven't been sick like this since college."

"Well, Harper, it could have been worse," Mary said.

"How so?"

"It could have been me." And everyone laughed, despite themselves.

"I think the fair has done us in," Dot said, realizing that her night with Danny was not happening.

She looked longingly at him, and he returned her gaze with a steely intensity.

"I'll call you tomorrow," he said.

THE NEXT MORNING, Harper didn't rise until ten.

"Hello, sleepyhead," Dot said, bringing her some electrolytes in a large Stanley cup and a mug of coffee. Behind her, Mary held a tall glass of lemon water and two aspirin. They were going to make her drink all of it.

"How are you feeling?" Mary asked.

"Like I was put in a tumble dryer," Harper said. Pippi was curled up next to her on the bed.

"You basically were. Here, drink this. Then take a shower, and I'm taking us to the Brady Brunch for breakfast," Dot said as Mary laid out clothes for her. She chose a white tank, a pair of navy joggers, Harper's favorite NYU hoodie, and her Birkenstocks. The perfect cozy Sunday outfit.

"Come on, Pippi, lazy girl. You need to go outside," Dot said, picking up the dog who grumbled but then settled her head on Dot's shoulder. "We'll leave at eleven."

At brunch, Harper held Pippi on her lap in the tote bag and fed her bits of waffle. She'd recently asked a favor from a cousin who worked as a psychologist in Brooklyn to have Pippi designated as a companion dog. That way she could take her anywhere. It was just a harmless little lie, she'd told herself, hoping the negative karma wouldn't be too harsh when it came.

"We're lucky to be alive," Mary said. "Jake said that sudden weather like that can happen this time of year."

"I'll never forget being up there and feeling so helpless." Dot held her coffee mug with both hands. "Especially when all the lights went out. It was so eerie."

"And I will never mix allergy medicine and margaritas again, that's for sure. It's like I roofied myself." The color was slowly coming back to Harper's face.

"That's a good lesson for all of us, Harp," Dot said.

The Crew continued to rehash the night, and by the end of breakfast, they were finally laughing about what happened.

After paying the check, Dot said, "Oh no. No, no, no, no, no."

"What?" Mary asked, then looked in the direction Dot was facing, and there were the Cedar Falls queens having breakfast. They had no choice but to walk by their table on their way out.

"Oh gosh. I'm going to have to apologize again," Harper said. She stood up and pushed her chair back under the table then walked to the other table.

"Hi, Maddy, right?" Harper said smiling shyly.

Maddy jumped as if Harper was going to throw up on her again.

"I'm terribly sorry about last night. I will happily pay for the dry cleaning of your outfit."

"Are you kidding me? I threw it away. It was ruined."

"I'll reimburse you. I can Venmo." Dot and Mary arrived to stand just a step behind Harper.

"Why don't we just pretend it never happened. Disgusting."

Harper felt like she'd been slapped in the face. She'd not gotten sick on purpose. And she felt terrible about what happened. Sensing tension, Pippi started to scramble out of her tote bag. Harper gently pushed her down so that only her head was showing out of the top.

"Oh, okay." She was at a loss for words.

"By the way, dogs aren't allowed in here," Marissa said, raising her eyebrows at Pippi.

"Oh, she's a companion dog," Harper said a little defensively. "I even have a certificate."

"Not surprised you need a companion—perhaps you should get someone who can prevent you from getting plastered," Maddy said.

"Let's go, Harp. Again, we're very sorry. It wasn't intentional," Dot said. She tried to think of something else to say but was too stunned by their rudeness. It was so unlike anything she'd experienced in Cedar Falls.

Maddy wasn't done. "It figures. City girl can't hold her corn dog, and won't be able to hold her new man either. Tommy isn't a long-term prospect. Take it from Marissa." Marissa scowled at the memory of being dumped in high school by one of the cutest boys in town.

Dot steeled herself. "We're leaving." She grabbed Harper's hand and led her to the door.

Mary followed them but before exiting, turned on her heel, and then marched back over to Maddy's table.

"Hey, Maddy," Mary said, a bite in her voice.

"What?"

"I was just thinking. Your name suits you."

"Oh . . . thanks?"

"Let me ask, are you seeing anyone?"

"Um, no. Why?"

"Well maybe you should start. Therapy can really help." She smiled and knocked her knuckles on their table. "Okay. Have a great day, girls."

Then Mary walked out, leaving the town girls in her wake.

Chapter 54

After the Lopez campaign scuttled the candidate's visit to Cedar Falls, For the Win kept making the case that it needed to be rescheduled. Lopez and Stone were crisscrossing the upper Midwest, but mainly hitting the bigger cities with the larger media markets. Dot was convinced that Cedar Falls was key. She saw it in Fletcher's spreadsheets and felt it in her gut. If Lopez didn't come to town, she might fall short in the county's vote tally—and then not only would Kitty, Fletcher, and herself not share in a win bonus, but also Lopez wouldn't be in the Oval Office come Inauguration Day. Dot kept plugging along, mission-focused and not panicking. Not yet.

August flew by, and suddenly, summer was ending. Cedar Falls was in back-to-school mode.

"Remember these?" Dot turned to Mary and Harper, holding up a box of Crayola 64 Crayons with the sharpener in the back. She set it back and continued pushing their shopping cart down the office supply aisle at Target. They'd come to get basic cleaning supplies but as usual ended up getting sucked into browsing.

"Check these out—washable Sharpies," Harper said. "I wonder if they work. My mom would have appreciated them, especially when Ernest drew a mustache on my Harry Styles concert T-shirt. I cried for hours. I swore I'd never talk to him again." She shook her head at the memory.

"My mom was furious with my brothers when they painted my pigtails with a new glue stick," Mary said. "She made them eat the rest of it."

"That sounds *exactly* like Christine," Harper said, watching a mother and her daughter going through their supply list. "I love that 'back-to-school' feeling. Even as a teacher. Though I don't have a school to return to." Her tone was wistful.

"That wasn't your fault," Dot said.

"Yeah, that was the creepy headmaster. You didn't do anything wrong," Mary said. She maintained Harper should have sued him.

"I'll say one thing, though—it's all very expensive." Dot scanned the prices up and down the aisle. "We were just talking about this on a call with Kitty. Polling shows people are still unhappy about high prices, and they usually take it out on the party in power. It's the biggest election issue by far, especially when it comes to back-to-school costs. Rose said her kids are overwhelmed by the cost of her grandkids' fees, too, for sports and activities."

"Is Senator Lopez pushing that?" Mary asked.

"Trying. We had her make a quick video for social last week, straight to the camera, making her big push for a major education tax credit. It got decent play on the mom sites." Kitty had been impressed when it went viral and acknowledged Dot's idea was a good one. "But the president hit her for not having 'lived experience' because she doesn't have children."

"That's rich coming from the guy who made so much money in the stock market, he never had to worry about the cost of raising his kids," Harper said.

"Exactly. We're trying to show that she gets it, but there's always more we could do." Dot picked up a colorful spiral notebook and put it in their cart.

Harper took it right back out and returned it to the shelf. "You have five of these lying around. Let's keep going before we accidentally spend another hundred dollars on stuff we don't need."

"Like this Mediterranean Fig candle?" Mary said, taunting Harper by pulling it out of the cart.

"I actually need that." Harper laughed and grabbed it out of Mary's hands and returned it to the cart.

Dot's phone buzzed and she looked down to find a text from Kitty Bell to her and Fletcher.

"Uh-oh."

"What's wrong?" Harper always worried something bad was going to happen.

"It's from Kitty." Dot read the message out loud. "Emergency. Hit job coming. Conference call at eight tonight."

"Whoa. Hit job! Any idea what it's about?" Harper's imagination ran wild to the worst scenario.

"Not sure. Must be bad, though," Dot said, feeling her pulse race a bit.

"Let's go then," Mary said. "We can check out and be home just in time." She took over the cart and headed to the register. "I'll pour you a glass of wine in a Yeti, and you can pretend it's water."

"Love that plan. Make it the one with a straw," Dot said. Then she replied to Kitty that she'd be on the call.

AT TWO MINUTES before eight, Dot pulled her hair into a ponytail and logged on to the videoconference. She thought better when her hair was off her face.

Darn it, Kitty was already there.

"Hi," Dot said, waving to the screen and noting Kitty's light makeup and hair in a topknot . Kitty wore a sleeveless navy blue top and small diamond earrings. "This must be her Sunday casual look," Dot thought. "Did this woman ever just throw on a T-shirt?"

Kitty was in her office, a bookshelf behind her where everything had been arranged by a decorator who never intended for the shelves to hold books useful in an office. *Dior in Bloom* wasn't exactly something you'd need for reference in political communication. But she had to admit, the aesthetic was on point.

"Hi, there. Thanks for getting on. Where's Fletcher?"

"He just texted me. Should be on any second." Dot prayed that was true, hoping his tardiness wasn't a reflection on her.

And right on cue, Fletcher beamed in, unaware that *early* is on time.

"Hi, there! This must be good, Kitty. Or bad."

"Well, it's not great. The DNC got word about a story that's going to hit soon. Super-negative about Lucy's personal life," Kitty said. Dot clocked the first name reference. The two women must have grown quite close.

"What did they find?" Dot asked, cringing at how bad this was going to be.

"They have oppo research about a disgruntled former boyfriend of hers from years ago, and apparently he's willing to talk. That's what got *The New York Times* to bite."

"Does the DNC know which reporter is on the story?" Dot ran through a mental list of political reporters on the election beat wondering who it could be.

"Not yet—working on it. Chances are I'll have crossed paths with them—especially if they're D.C.-based.

"What do they get out of digging up an old boyfriend from years ago?" Fletcher asked. "What's their angle?"

"I imagine it's that she's single, unreliable, unable or unwilling to commit. A frenzied mess. Apparently, they'll plant seeds of doubt about her because she's never been married. They couch it as 'just asking questions,' but we all know that's code for a childless woman who can't hold on to a man; and someone who doesn't have the right temperament to be commander-in-chief."

"They're going to throw it all against the personal wall," Dot said.

"So, we have to make sure it doesn't stick." Fletcher tapped his index finger on his chin in thought.

"That's the play. Any ideas?" Kitty asked.

"Can we go back a second?" Dot asked, needing more information. "Going after her for being a single, independent woman . . . that's not going to help them with the youth vote they need."

"In theory, yes," Kitty said. "But the youth vote is somewhat fickle, and we've been shedding young people's support for a few cycles now. But the GOP also wants to drive up their numbers with older women. Heck, *any* women. If they can win more of their vote, they don't have to worry as much about the other groups."

"And if they do that enough times, in enough states, they'll take the electoral college again," Fletcher finished Kitty's thought.

"Okay, let's say this attack strikes," Dot posed. "How do you think she'll react? It'll be good to be ready for whatever her response is going to be."

"Good question. I can't say for sure, but I've been around her enough to believe we'll get a decent mix of gracious and sharp. She's cool under pressure, which is reassuring about how she'd react in a crisis. But there's a fine line between resolute and overreacting, especially for women. If she can ignore it or manage it with a smile and a spark, that'd be the best outcome."

"This is why I'll never run for office," Fletcher said. "I'd get so mad."

"Well, we can get mad on her behalf," Kitty said.

"And we can also get even," Dot said.

"I like where you're going with that, Dot. Make no mistake, the story will be brutal. Jilted lover stories will draw headlines and clicks. I think that's why she's always been very protective of her private life—she wants to focus on the issues, while social media just lasers in on her personal life."

"So, there's a danger in under-responding, too," Dot said. "If she decides not to dignify it with a response, all the accusations go unanswered."

"Exactly. And those impressions are hard to erase," Kitty said.

Fletcher clapped his hands together. "So, where do we come in?"

"We have about forty-eight hours before this story is supposed to hit. I was hoping you two can put your heads together and see if we can offer something to break through the DNC's brick wall of running scared responses. It takes forever and a day to get them to approve anything. So many of them are canned and just don't work. I want to go around them."

"Do you have any suggestions?" Dot asked. "Or do we have a blank slate?"

"Blank slate. Brainstorm some ideas but do it fast. Send me something by noon tomorrow?"

"You got it." Fletcher said that he'd side-text Dot.

"We're on it," Dot said, the gears of her mind already turning.

They ended the videoconference and immediately Dot's phone rang. It was Fletcher.

"Okay, here's what I'm thinking," he said. "What about a video of all the scandalous headlines from Republicans in the last twenty years. Try to make this look like no big deal compared to their haul of junk."

Dot didn't like that approach. It was too obvious a response, and the DNC would do that anyway. That was their go-to move. They needed to be more creative and to think of something that would get people's attention.

"Let me think. I may have an idea," she said, which was Dot's polite way of saying "Your idea is not going to work."

She hung up and put the kettle on.

It was going to be a long night.

AROUND MIDNIGHT, MARY came down to the kitchen to find Dot still there in the dark, the only light coming from her laptop.

"Can't sleep?" Dot asked.

"I was doing some proofreading for this brief the firm has to file tomorrow in Manhattan. The partners are still up working, so I thought I'd stay up with them."

"They're so lucky to have you," Dot said.

"I'm just a first-year associate. Nothing special." Mary waved away the flattery. "How's the brainstorming going?"

"I finally told Fletcher to call it a night. His ideas were too bro for me."

"What's your gut telling you?"

"Okay. Good question."

Dot put two hands around her big ceramic mug and took a sip of hot peppermint tea.

"Well, here's what I really think. Since she's a state senator and only recently in national politics, there's a sense that no one really *knows* her. She's overly protective of her privacy. I mean, I get it. But it's too much. I think it's held her back. People want to get to know her. The *real* her."

"You mean she needs to show a little more leg?"

"Something like that. But no, not like *that*." Dot imagined their candidate wowing everyone with her beauty and nice figure. That wasn't exactly what they were going for here. "We might need to save that move for the weekend before the election though." She laughed a little at the thought.

"It might make my dad take a second look at her."

"Yeah, but he still wouldn't vote for her."

"True. Okay, go on."

"I think she needs to let her guard down, let people hear from her in her own words what she's like beyond what they see on the screen. They know she's tough and beautiful and intelligent, even funny. They know her dad was in the military. They like her two dogs. And Democrats know her platform—that she's for bringing back jobs, helping regular folks afford to live the American dream, and making sure kids are learning to read and write so they can have a fighting chance in an increasingly competitive world job market."

Mary leaned in for more.

"But if we're thinking of independent voters, like some of our neighbors here, they barely know her name. And if the GOP is going to flood the airwaves with a bunch of lies about her personal life and make it sound like she's weird or a . . . a . . . a slut or whatever—well, that's going to stick in their minds. And in their algorithms."

"I'm with you so far," Mary said. "So, what can you do?"

"I have an idea, but I don't know if anyone will go for it."

"I'm listening."

"Okay. Here goes: What if she created a dating profile that revealed all sorts of interesting details about her—not for her to get a date for the weekend, but something that shows she wants to have a committed relationship with the *country*."

"Sort of like, 'She's just like us.' I like it. Go on."

"We could have her be vulnerable, open. Someone with big dreams and desires. Someone you'd want to get to know—to have as your friend, your neighbor—or even your president."

"Looking for a long-term relationship?"

"Right. And because a candidate has never done this before—created a dating profile as a campaign push—she'd get a bunch of stories written about her. It could go viral. Well, that would be the goal, but you never know what's actually going to work."

"It's clever." Mary sat a moment, her lips pressed together as she mused on the idea. "I love that no one has ever done this before. It's fun and creative. Think she'll go for it?"

Dot looked out the big picture window toward their backyard, the oak tree lit by the moon, its branches swaying slightly in the wind.

"It's a risk—but we need to swing for the fences here."

"Nice baseball reference."

"Oh, that's about baseball? I thought it was hockey," Dot joked, and Mary rolled her eyes.

"Enough. Let's call it a night." Mary led the way up to their bedrooms.

As Dot drifted off to sleep, she imagined what she'd write for the candidate the next day.

"This better work," she thought. "We need a win."

THE NEXT DAY, Dot sat back on the bar stool at the kitchen counter and twirled a long strand of her hair. She scrolled back through her draft dating profile once more before sending it to Kitty and Fletcher for reaction:

> Hi—Reporters at *The New York Times* think they know something about my personal life that make voters think I don't have what it takes to be President of the United States. Let me assure you, they don't.
>
> Instead of responding in the press, I wanted to speak directly to you.
>
> So, here's my first ever dating app profile—let me know what you think:

Name: Lucy Lopez, 44
Location: Georgia

The first thing you should know about me is . . .

I love America. I always have. I'm the oldest of three daughters. (Firstborns, represent!) For the last six years, I've served as a state senator in Georgia. My legislative track record is all about good-paying jobs, excellent educational opportunities for children, and making sure the American Dream is achievable and affordable for all. I have found my purpose and fulfillment in public service—it suits me perfectly.

A few things about my background . . .

I grew up in a military and immigrant family. My dad fled Cuba when he was a teen and lived with his aunt and uncle in Atlanta. He never saw his parents again—they were executed by the government after participating in a protest.

My dad joined the Marines at eighteen and retired from the military after serving this country for nearly forty years. My mom's parents came to America from Puerto Rico when she was a small girl. They didn't have a lot of money, but they had a lot of love.

My mom graduated from high school and then worked as a hotel housekeeper for years. She was a wonderful mother. Each of her children still thinks they're her favorite.

My parents' love story taught me . . .

My parents met on a blind date when my dad was stationed at Camp Pendleton in California. Neither of them wanted to go on that date, but it was love at first sight. They married three months later, and then my dad deployed. I was born while he was away. My favorite photograph is of him holding me on the tarmac when he was home on leave—the first time he met me.

My parents have a great love story. Unfortunately, I have not found my soul mate yet. But I keep my heart open in the belief that one day I, too, will find the love of my life. Just like they did.

While that search continues, I am open to a strong commitment—one with this country. I want a long-term relationship based on mutual trust, respect, patriotism, faith, and joy. I want to fully dedicate myself to America for the next four years.

What makes me different . . .

I am not a creature of Washington, D.C. I have experience that mirrors that of most of our country, and I believe we live in an exceptional nation. America is bold, free, strong, and a beacon of light in this world. I believe that we all deserve a leader who is fully committed to our great country. One who isn't beholden to the richest of our country. One who fully understands the dire situation at our nation's schools and is determined to make tough changes to policies and to surge resources so that every child can read and write at grade level.

If you like what you're reading . . .

If chosen to lead this great nation, I promise you my full and undivided attention. And if you're looking for that kind of relationship, too, double tap to like this profile—and I'll see you soon.

Pet personality test . . .

P.S. I love dogs (but if you need me to like cats to get your vote, I'll get a cat). Here's a picture of my two best buddies, Javier and Jaime. Don't you think they'd make great White House pets?)

After the last read, Dot added the line about the pets. The candidate's dogs had been popular on social, so why not use them to get a little attention? And maybe garner some sympathy after this *Times* hit piece came out.

She took a deep breath and sent the email to Kitty and copied Fletcher. Pippi had been sitting on her lap while she typed.

"I hope they like it," Dot said to the small dog, and then she sat and waited for their reaction.

A few minutes later, Dot's phone rang. It was Kitty video calling her. Dot considered her casual dress and no-makeup look and wished she'd at least thought to brush her hair and throw on some under-eye concealer that morning. Pippi hopped off her lap at the interruption and went to find a quieter spot.

"Hi, Kitty." Dot was nervous to get feedback. She didn't need to be.

"Dot! This is *genius*. Did you come up with this?" There was a hint of disbelief in Kitty's tone. Dot decided to dismiss it and take the rare paise.

"Yes, it was my idea last night."

"It's so good."

"Thank you! I just felt like voters don't know the real her and this might be a way for her to break through."

"Well, I love it. Love it! It talks past the story without reacting to her ex-boyfriend. And it really could go viral."

Dot felt the rush of creative satisfaction that had led her into communications in the first place.

"Okay, hang tight," Kitty said. "I'm going to run it by her."

Dot gave a thumbs-up. "I'll be here. And"—she looked down at her old T-shirt—"dressed."

Kitty laughed lightly and ended the call before Dot could say goodbye.

Chapter 55

While Dot waited to hear back from Kitty's call with the candidate, she poked her head into the living room, where Mary and Harper were watching the *Kardashians* and scrolling through TikTok. Pippi had moved to Harper's lap during Dot's call with Kitty.

"Hey, you two." She grabbed a seat on the couch and tucked her legs under her. "Danny said when he picks us up for dinner that we need to make a quick stop by the bookshop before we go. Cool?"

"Yep, sounds good. I'll head upstairs to get ready." Harper gently got out from under Pippi and slid off the couch.

"What are you wearing?" Mary asked. "Are we Wisconsin nice or Manhattan naughty tonight?"

"When have you ever dressed as Wisconsin nice?" Dot asked.

"Yeah, you're right," Mary said.

"Whatever you wear, I bet Jake tries to take it off later," Harper said, jetting up the stairs with Pippi close behind.

"A girl can dream," Mary said, tilting back the last of her sparkling lemon water.

THAT NIGHT, DOT took extra care getting ready. With her project for the day behind her, she was excited to see Danny.

She brushed her hair and then added two gold clip barrettes in a half-up, half-down look for the evening. She chose a hot pink midi column dress with a light pink suede leather jacket and gold slingbacks with kitten heels she'd ordered on Amazon. She added a pair of sparkly drop earrings and a spritz of the Delina perfume her parents had sent for her birthday. She turned left and right in front of the bathroom mirror then took a selfie and sent it to her sister in Colorado.

"Fancy," Anne texted back with a dancing girl emoji. Then she sent her sister a photo of herself in light colored jeans, a plaid flannel shirt, a trucker's cap, and her hiking boots. "My evening attire."

"Do you even own a pair of heels?" Dot loved to tease her little sister, but she was happy she'd landed right where she wanted to be.

Dot slipped her phone into her small gold handbag that went with everything and called for The Crew to get ready to load up. Danny would be there any minute. The thought of seeing him gave her a warm shiver down her spine.

Downstairs, Harper was settling Pippi in for the night on the couch with a chew toy, a blanket, and a promise that she'd be home soon.

"I always come back," Harper said. Pippi gave her a pitiful "How could you leave me all alone here?" look but curled up in her bed and sighed loudly, resigned to her fate.

"She breaks my heart," Harper said, kissing the dog's head.

She had on white straight-leg pants, tan high-heeled clogs, and a Bohemian top in a deep copper that went well with her coloring. She'd left her hair loose and curly.

"They've evolved to make us feel guilty. It works! Anyway, don't you look fresh!" Dot complimented her outfit.

"I don't know. Are you sure?" Harper said, twisting this way and that, second-guessing her choice.

"It's great!" Dot reassured her then called upstairs, "Mary! Danny's almost here."

"Coming!" A few seconds later, Mary came down the stairs in a black mini-halter tiered dress and silver spiky heels. She wore chandelier earrings and a stack of silver bangles on her wrist. She carried a black leather jacket over her arm and swung a new sleek black bag with a chain over her shoulder.

"Are you trying to give Jake a heart attack?" Harper asked.

"Yes," Mary said simply as she applied one more coat of Tay Tay's favorite Pat McGrath red lip gloss. She play-kissed the mirror, and Dot ushered them out and closed the door behind them.

They walked onto their porch and Dot waved to Danny as he pulled up in his four-door pickup. As they were getting into the truck, Dot felt her phone buzz in her handbag. She pulled it out and saw the message from Kitty she'd been waiting for about the dating profile.

"She loves it. No edits. Post anytime then send me the link," Kitty said and added a star emoji.

"Oh wow," Dot said.

"What's up?" Danny asked as he pulled his truck onto the street to head to the bookstore.

"Long story—just a work thing. I've got one more thing I need to do tonight."

"Need to stop at the office?" he asked.

"Nope! I can do it right here." Dot waggled her phone at him. She read her Lopez dating profile one more time just to make sure there were no typos. "Okay, here we go." Her finger hovered over the send button. This was so risky. But it was also exhilarating.

She hit "post" and said a silent prayer that it would work.

Chapter 56

Danny pulled up outside of Reader Falls and parked.

"Are you okay to stop in for a few minutes before we meet Jake and Tommy for dinner?" Danny asked. "The Jankowskis said it should be quick."

"Sure, I love them!" Dot said. They all climbed out of the truck.

"I could pick up a new novel, too," Harper said.

"Another one already?" Mary said.

"It's my one indulgence!" Harper defended herself.

"Give me the one you just finished. I've been dying to read it," Dot said.

"You two need to watch more TV!" Mary couldn't keep up with Dot and Harper's insatiable reading habits.

Danny got to the front door of the bookshop first and held it open for the girls to walk through.

The lights were off, and Dot asked, "Is anybody here?"

"Surprise!" The lights came on and The Crew was shocked.

The entire bookstore was decorated for a party, and all their Cedar Falls friends were there. Grace and Joe Taylor, Ted and Jeanie Jankowski, Mimi from Flour Power, Fletcher, Rose, the florists from the farmer's market, and a few of the guys who worked at the Sin Bin. There were little white fairy lights hanging from the ceiling and a big "WE LOVE NEW YORK" banner hung over the register.

"What in the world is this?" Dot asked, hugging Ted and Jeanie.

"We wanted to do something nice for you. You've been such a joy to have around, and the bookstore has done so well this summer after the remodel thanks to you all, we thought it was time to have a party," Ted said.

"And even though you've become honorary Wisconsinites, we thought you might like a little taste of home," Jeanie said, gesturing around the store. "So, we roped the boys in to help us create this night in Manhattan just for you."

"I can't believe it!" Harper said. She found Tommy and hugged him.

Tommy took her hand and twirled her around. "Welcome to New York, Harper!"

"This is amazing!" Mary spotted Jake at a makeshift bar.

"Manhattan?" he said, holding a plastic martini glass for her.

"Don't mind if I do," she said, kissing him fully on the lips.

Grace elbowed Joe. "Oh boy. They're an item, aren't they?" she whispered to her husband, out of earshot of Jake and Mary.

"We'll see!" he said, putting an arm around her. Joe was glad to have a night to get away from his worries about keeping the farm. The pressure was mounting as another one of his neighbors had just agreed to sell. He was nearly the lone holdout.

"We put Tommy in charge of food. We even got you some New York–style pizza," Ted said to The Crew. "I've never liked thin crust over deep dish, but for tonight, I'll enjoy it on your behalf."

"And your mom pitched in with something special, Mary," Grace said.

"She did?" Mary wondered what it could be.

"How about some of her Sunday sauce?" Joe said.

"You're kidding me!" Mary went over to the buffet line and breathed in the gorgeous aroma of roasted tomatoes, garlic, and her mom's special touch. "It smells just like home."

"It was Jake's idea," Grace said, as if she needed to help her son pursue this young woman.

Mary thought her mom must have been impressed with Jake for the ask.

"And I got you a banana pudding and cupcakes from Magnolia," Danny said, holding the special desserts in his hands.

"There's one right by my apartment!" Dot said. "I can't wait to take you all when you visit." She smiled widely, though every time she thought of leaving Cedar Falls, she felt a pang of regret. The fact that their time in Wisconsin was coming to an end was at the periphery of their minds.

Still, the party was humming, and everyone was having a great time.

After enjoying a plate of food, Dot sought out the Jankowskis. "Wow, you two." Dot took their hands. "You didn't have to do this, but we're so glad you did." Then she turned to Danny. "You're pretty good at keeping a secret, aren't you?"

"Indeed," he said, leaning down to kiss her. She took his hand and led him to the cocktail bar.

Ted pressed play on his Bluetooth speaker and started the playlist that he'd had the boys put together. All the songs had to have a New York connection. There was T-Swift, Billy Joel, Alicia Keys, JLo, and many more.

In a fitting tribute to the season, Ella Fitzgerald and Louis Armstrong kicked it off with "Autumn in New York." Seeing Mary sway to the music, Ted asked her for a dance. She accepted. He took her hand and started a foxtrot in the children's reading area. She was graceful even in spiked heels.

"My, my. You can dance, too!" Ted said.

"My Nonna taught me when I was young. Said it was a tradition that couldn't be lost to the generations."

"Your Nonna is a wise woman!"

"You'd love her." And Mary wished she could bring her entire family here to experience the warmth of the people she had befriended in Cedar Falls.

When the music turned to the Beastie Boys, Mary and Ted took a break and the twins started rapping along to Jay-Z's "Brooklyn's Finest." Harper danced in the middle of their circle.

"What's Brooklyn like?" Danny asked Dot.

"When you're in the city, Brooklyn feels far away. Like you need a passport to go there. People who live there love it. That's where Harper grew up."

"I went to Brooklyn once. I visited a friend from England who had moved there to work at a publishing house in Manhattan," Jeanie said. "They have the cutest bookstores."

"I should go check them out," Dot said. "When I was young, I always thought about owning a bookstore one day. A place where I knew everyone that came in and could help them find the perfect book. I even wrote that down in my third-grade career day workbook."

"You never told me that," Danny said. "I thought you'd have grown up wanting to work in the White House."

"If only the White House were in New York," she said.

"Dot only wants to work for Democrats, but maybe we'll talk some sense into her in the next couple of months." Jeanie winked.

Ted poked Jeanie in the ribs. "Don't think you can get a tiger to change its stripes. The girl's got a big mind and an even bigger heart."

"Hey now. No politics at this party!" Dot said. "That's the new rule. Let's have dessert instead!" She led the way back to the buffet.

The Jankowskis had invited Fletcher and Rose from the FTW office, and of course Mimi from the bakery. They were already in line, ladling Christine Russo's Sunday sauce onto bowls of rigatoni that Grace had cooked.

"I saw you posted the dating profile," Fletcher said. "I have a bunch of texts from friends saying it's awesome."

"Thanks. Let's hope it works. Or that it doesn't flop," Dot said, nervous about how it was playing. She was dying to check her phone in the back where it wouldn't look rude to their hosts.

Harper walked up to the table. She leaned into Dot and whispered, "Did you have the pizza? I mean . . . it was sweet of them to try."

"Oh yeah, it's not Joe's. Let's just pretend to love it," Dot said quietly. She looked for Mary and said more loudly, so that Ted and Jeanie would hear her, "Mary, your mom's sauce is unreal. And we *love* the pizza, too, right?"

Catching on, Mary said with a wink, "Oh, so good. I had two pieces!" She had not had two pieces. Mary could play poker against seasoned professionals.

Frank Sinatra was playing through the speaker, and Ted and Jeanie started dancing again.

"Hey, we should all meet up in New York after we go back!" Harper said, thinking that sounded like great fun.

"Let's not talk about going back to New York," Tommy said. "I mean, I know you're going, but we'll miss you. I'll miss you."

Harper blushed and leaned into him. "You're right. Forget I said anything."

"It's a good idea, Harper," Mary said. "But we're here for a couple more months and we're going to make the most of it, aren't we?"

Jake put a protective arm around Mary, Danny looked away, worry crossing his already sad eyes, and Tommy scrunched up his mouth thinking of something to say to change the subject.

"Let's not think about goodbyes," Grace said. "Come, let's have some cheesecake. I picked one up today from Piggly Wiggly." She wielded the knife expertly and placed narrow slices on small paper plates for everyone.

Harper took a bite. "This slaps."

"Remember when you were lactose intolerant?" Tommy laughed, and she playfully punched him in the arm. "Think of what you were missing."

Dot smiled, but she took Tommy's sentence and put it in the future tense.

"Think of what we will miss," she said to herself.

Chapter 57

After a couple of hours at the bookstore's Manhattan-themed party, Dot found a moment to excuse herself. She headed to the Jankowskis' back office with her phone. She held her breath and logged onto the dating app to see how it was landing.

"Oh my gosh," she said. The profile was on fire with tens of thousands of likes and comments. And it had only been a couple of hours. Dot refreshed the screen, and a thousand more likes appeared.

A text from Kitty was in her inbox. "Dot—it's absolutely blowing up. And it's almost *all* positive! The Republicans will be spitting mad. We beat them to the punch!" She followed up with another message, "Call me tomorrow—we'll debrief. And thank you. This is incredible!" For a woman who rarely used exclamation points, it was clear to Dot that Kitty was excited and pleased.

Dot scrolled down and quickly scanned messages sent to Lopez's new dating profile:

I love this!
You're amazing.
You've got my vote!
You're hot.
It's a date, Madame President!
You're my role model!
I have a Havanese, too.
Let's do this, Democrats!

The positive reactions went on and on.

"Fletcher!" Dot called out toward the main room. He came running.

"What's up? Is something wrong?" He looked worried.

"It worked!" She handed him her phone. His face changed as he realized what he was looking at.

"Dot. It's totally going viral. You did it!" He hugged her and they did a little tap dance of excitement.

Dot blinked back tears. She felt so much relief that her idea hadn't backfired. "It's so great! I can't wait to see what happens next." Fletcher put an arm around her shoulders and squeezed. She threw and arm around his waist and beamed up at him.

Just then she turned to see Danny walking through the door, a surprised look on his face.

"Oh, I was just looking for you, Dot. Sorry to interrupt," he said, starting to backpedal as if he'd caught her and Fletcher in some awkward moment.

Dot rushed over and hugged him. "It's okay! Remember the work thing I did in the car? My idea worked. I'm so happy!"

"Oh, that's great," Danny said, lacking enthusiasm. Dot caught the tension in his answer. She wasn't sure if the downshift in his mood was because he really didn't want the Democratic party to win the election, or if he thought there was something between her and Fletcher that went beyond a work friendship.

Fletcher didn't pick up on the vibe. "Yeah, Dot just amped up the Lopez campaign. Big-time."

Thinking fast to save the evening, Dot realized she had to counteract what Danny thought he'd seen when she and Fletcher were celebrating. She transitioned into a more work-like posture to prevent Danny from thinking she had any attraction to Fletcher. She'd never told him about the bee incident. Maybe she should have.

"Thanks, Fletcher—I'll catch up with you at the office." She nodded at him and then cocked her head a little toward the door. It was subtle, but both Danny and Fletcher got the message.

"Yeah, uh, yep. I'll just be going now. See you tomorrow, Dot." Fletcher saw himself out.

"Come. I want to share this moment with you!" Dot reached for Danny's hand and lifted her chin for a kiss. Danny couldn't help but meet her lips. But after a moment, he pulled back.

"What's wrong?" she asked.

Danny hesitated a beat. "Dot, you know I really like you, right?"

"Yes, I think so. Why?"

"Anything ever happen between you and Fletcher? You two seem awfully close."

"Oh, no. I swear."

"You're sure? I'd understand. . . . I just need to know because . . ." Danny didn't finish his sentence.

"I'm sure," Dot said, looking him straight in the eye. "I promise."

She wrapped her arms around his neck and got as close as she could to him. She felt the tension release from his shoulders.

"All right. May I ask you to come back to my house tonight?" He leaned down and whispered to her, deciding it was finally time to fully jump into this relationship.

A wave of warmth rippled through her at the thought of going home with him.

Danny lifted her up and she wrapped her legs around him. "It sounds like another great idea."

And that was the permission he needed. He gently set her down, took her hand, and they snuck out through the back door without saying goodbye.

IN THE MORNING, the sun's first rays of the day fell across Dot's eyes. Her blond hair was strewn across Danny's pillow. She opened her eyes and stretched like a cat. Danny was lying on his side, the covers pulled up to his waist, watching her.

"Good morning," he said.

"Good morning."

"I have an important question."

"Wow, already? What time is it?" She tried to make light of the moment but dreaded what was coming. His dark eyes looked so serious. She took a deep breath. "Okay. Ask me anything."

"How do you take your coffee in the morning?"

Relief flooded her brain. She smiled with her full face.

"A bit of milk—real milk." She didn't want to trigger his almond "milk" sermon.

"No sugar, right?" he asked and she nodded.

"Right."

"Be right back." Danny scooted off the bed to go get the coffee.

Dot sat up and pulled his white T-shirt over her head. It smelled like him: a mix of Old Spice and Ivory soap. She put the collar of the shirt up to her nose and breathed deeply.

Danny was back a couple of minutes later.

"Here you go," he said, handing her a steaming mug of coffee. Then he opened the blinds of the large window and twisted the handle to open it, letting in the fresh morning air. Birds were singing and she could hear a leaf blower in the distance. There were no sirens or honking horns. It sounded like suburbia. And Dot realized she kind of liked it.

She sat up and leaned against the headboard.

He climbed back into bed and said, "Cheers" and clinked his mug against hers.

"So . . ." Dot said.

"So . . ." He returned her serve.

"That was . . . lovely."

"It was." He ran his fingers over her forearm.

"What do you have on your schedule today?" she asked.

"Nothing." She actually had a thousand things to do for the campaign. They needed to keep the momentum going with the dating profile. But she shoved those thoughts to the back of her mind, determined to focus on Danny instead of work for at least another hour.

"Nothing?"

"Nothing," he said, and then he raised his eyebrows at her. "Unless there was something you wanted to do."

"Hmmmm. Let me think."

"I think that you should stop thinking so much." He set his mug down on his nightstand and gently took hers and put it next to his.

"You're probably right," she said.

"Excuse me?"

"You're right."

"Oh, I heard you," Danny said. "I just wanted to hear you say it again."

That made her laugh, and they laughed as they greeted the day with their unexpected plans.

A couple of hours later, Dot started to make a move to head home. She picked up her phone.

"Wait. You can't go before the second cup," he said, grabbing her hand.

"Why?"

"The second cup is when all the good stuff happens. Where you learn all the secrets. At least, that's what my mom always said."

"Well then, let's have a second cup." She set her phone down. This was the longest she'd gone without looking at her phone in ages.

She realized that she really didn't miss it.

Chapter 58

The next couple of weeks flashed by. Ever since their night together, Dot found she was crushing big-time on Danny. She thought about him constantly and found it hard to concentrate at work or to sleep when she wasn't with him. She couldn't even read the books Harper passed on to her. Every page, every paragraph became a blur.

At the same time, the campaign was in full force and the race was back to being tied in Wisconsin 48–48, with four percent undecided.

"Who, at this point, hasn't decided?" she asked Fletcher and Rose, exasperated.

"No idea. Just about everyone I know is voting early," Rose said. "They're sick of the ads and the arguing. They just want to vote and be done with it."

"I hear that. It's relentless. But I can tell from the data, she's got more rizz than the president," Fletcher said. "Polling shows people are ready for someone new."

"What's 'rizz'?" Rose asked.

"Charisma! You know, that special something every candidate needs."

"Then why don't you just say 'charisma'?"

"Too many syllables." Fletcher loved to tease Rose.

"Can rizz get us what we need in a month's time?" Dot asked Fletcher.

"We have just about eight weeks to get those four percent, or at least more than half of that four percent. I hope the DNC is paying attention to what's happening here," he said, obsessing over his get-out-the-vote spreadsheets. Wisconsin allowed early voting for fourteen days before the election, so every scrap of information they could capture about who was likely to cast a ballot mattered. That way, they could target every possible voter—even the reluctant ones.

"We really need that Lopez visit," Rose said.

"We're pressing. I almost want to drive to D.C. and confront those campaign pros in person," Fletcher said.

"I don't think Kitty gives them a moment's rest," Dot said. "But she's one of those people you want on your side. It's not good to have that kind of energy working against you."

She had to admire Kitty's diligence. She'd even arranged a surprise for Dot after the dating profile was a huge hit.

The FaceTime had come one day when Dot was in the office. She didn't recognize the number, but she answered the call anyway. Immediately upon saying hello, Dot realized who it was—Lucy Lopez herself.

Dot sprinted into the conference room and shut the door behind her for some privacy.

"Dot, hi! I called to thank you." Lopez had her long, dark hair pulled over one shoulder. She was wearing a cap-sleeved white T-shirt with her campaign logo and her red lips were on point. Her warm smile made her look even prettier.

Dot was shocked but pulled herself together immediately. "Oh! Hi! Senator Lopez, it's so nice to get a call from you. I know you're extremely busy."

"Well, you really turned things around for us with that dating profile. It was great to get the drop on *The New York Times*. I knew it was a great idea, but who knew that so many people could relate to it?"

"Well, you're a pleasure to work for, ma'am," Dot said sincerely.

"I know you're working hard up there. How do you think it's looking? Be brutally honest."

"I truly think you've got a great shot of winning here. Our get-out-the-vote is strong. And we're slightly ahead of the Republicans in new voter registration. In addition to that, it *feels* good out there. We have more energy than the president's team."

"No doubt thanks in part to your efforts," Lopez said.

Dot felt bold enough to make her pitch. "I do believe we need you to visit Cedar Falls though, ma'am. The voters here need your personal touch before they'll commit. When your campaign canceled in August, it blunted our momentum."

"Got it. I agree. That was an unfortunate outcome. And that trip to Texas was likely a waste of time. Thanks for being clear. I like that in a teammate. I'll talk to my scheduler to see what we can do." Dot watched her write down a note. "So, what are your plans after the election, Dot?"

"Oh, me?" Dot didn't have a ready answer. "Actually, I'm not sure. I mean, I'm going back to New York. That's where I live. But I don't have a job to go back to yet."

"Well, let's keep in touch on that. You never know how things are going to turn out."

"Wow, okay, thanks. Yes, I'd be glad to let you know what happens. And, before you go, I just want to say that I believe you're going to win. And that you'll make for an amazing president."

"Well, thank you. I'm realistic. That keeps me motivated. I know it's *really* tight. But we're hitting all our numbers. And we need a bit of luck, too. These next few weeks will be brutal, but I'm with you—I also have a good feeling about the grind."

"We'll keep at it," Dot said. Then she got the courage to ask her something that had been on her mind. "Senator, may I ask you something kind of personal? Off the record, of course. It's just something I've been wondering."

"Of course. Shoot."

"Well, when I was writing the profile, I wondered . . . Have you *ever* been in love?"

"Wow. That *is* a very personal question," Lopez said.

Dot cringed, worried she'd overstepped.

"But I don't mind at all." Lopez looked away for a moment then turned back to the camera. "Yes. I was in love once. I dated a wonderful man for several years. He adored me. We were very happy."

"What happened?"

"Well, it kind of sounds ridiculous now. But we were on very different career paths. He was an international businessman, a successful architect. Our lifestyles weren't compatible. And after a while of trying a long-distance relationship, we finally called it quits. He got married about a year later and has two children now."

"Oh. That must have been hard."

"It was. It is." Lopez went quiet for a few moments. "And the thing is, it didn't have to be that way."

"What do you mean?"

"I mean that we could have worked it out. I realized now that I could have made a different choice. Choosing to be with him didn't have to be a career-limiting decision. It just might have been a different career. But he'd have been with me. And I wouldn't be facing this alone."

They let that sit there for a moment.

"I appreciate that, thank you," Dot said. And then, out of respect for the candidate's time, decided it was time to wrap it up. "Is there anything else I can do for you?"

"Just help us win, Dot. Keep up the good work. Oh, and, if you happen to have a chance to be loved—don't pass it up."

Dot tucked that advice into her pocket. "Thank you, ma'am. We're pulling out all the stops for you in Wisconsin. Don't worry!"

"I'm not worried." She winked, flexed like Rosie the Riveter, and waved goodbye.

Dot sat for a while thinking about what she'd said. And while Lopez's advice made her feel a little smarter, it left her with more questions than answers.

Could she and Danny stay together and have a long-distance relationship? Would he move to the city? How could he? His entire life was here. His business was here. And she didn't even have a job in Wisconsin. Not to mention she couldn't imagine living anywhere but New York.

Plus, was she falling in *love* with Danny? What would her friends think if she didn't go back to New York? How could she stay here without a job? How could she ever choose . . . and what if she didn't have a choice?

Her mind was jumbled, and she leapt from thought to thought. She felt her next set of decisions were big ones—it would matter. She needed to figure out what she would like to do, who she was, and most important, who she wanted to be.

Chapter 59

After Labor Day, Dot worked from early in the morning to late at night every day, even weekends.

When she could get away, she and Danny ate dinner together, met at Cocoa and Cabernet for dessert, or went for a run up to the covered bridge and back. She appreciated that he was supportive of her work and didn't complain or tell her she was working too much.

"I run my own business—I get it," he reassured her that he understood.

Dot spent the night at his house on weekends, enjoying the privacy they could share together there. Mary and Harper continued their romances with Jake and Tommy, so no one was left home alone. But their time in Cedar Falls was running out.

One morning, when all the kids were back in school and the air was a bit cooler, Dot was tying the belt to her trusty Manhattan trench coat before she left for the office. She opened the door and there was Danny on the sidewalk, holding two cups of coffee from Flour Power.

"Good morning," he said, freshly shaved and wearing his Carhartt jacket and blue jeans. "Stopped by Mimi's for these."

"What a nice surprise," she said. "I didn't expect to see you this morning."

"I thought I'd walk you to work before going to my site today." Danny was remodeling another house on the outskirts of town. "I parked by the bookshop and will head out after I drop you off."

She reached for the coffee and kissed him good morning. "Well, you already made my day and it's not even eight yet!"

"I'm glad you think so." He tapped her nose. "I love seeing your face in the morning." He had a way of making her feel special. And he got over his shyness when he was around her. "I missed you last night."

"Same. I couldn't sleep."

"Well, maybe we can fix that tonight."

"I'm not sure that will entail sleep."

"Good point." He kissed her, and they held hands as they walked to Main Street together, sipping their hot coffees, the early autumn air fresh and chilly. The leaves on the trees were turning from green to bright red, orange, and yellow. How was it already fall? The months had flown by.

"Are you still able to go to the Packers' game this weekend?" He knew her schedule was tough heading into the last month before the election.

"I wouldn't miss it. Mary's already planning her outfit," she said.

"The tailgate is going to be a blast. Our seats are great."

"I can't wait. My dad is filled with envy. He's always wanted to go to Lambeau Field, even though he's a big Patriots fan."

As they arrived at the Democratic offices, Dot stopped short of the door. "Oh no!"

The large front window of the offices had been smashed, a huge hole in the center of the glass.

"Why don't you call Jake—see if he can come over right away. And I'll go in first to see if anyone's in there," Danny said. Dot hurriedly unlocked the door, and Danny pushed it open to take a quick look around.

"This is terrible," she said, surveying the damage.

"All clear," Danny yelled from inside. He stepped over shards of broken glass as he returned.

"I guess I shouldn't be surprised. Someone sabotaged all the GOP signs in the neighborhood last week. Some guy came over and accused Fletcher of doing it. They almost got in a fight."

Danny picked up the red brick and turned it over. Spray-painted in black, it said, "RIP Democrats." He showed it to Dot. She shivered.

He went to the back and grabbed a push broom. "Let me clean this up." He started pushing the shattered glass into one pile.

"Oh, I can do it," Dot said. "You need to get to work."

"I'm not leaving you to do this. I'll stay until Jake can come over and investigate. He'll want to see the security camera footage."

"Good idea," she said, pulling out her phone. She took several photos of the broken window, the damage to one of the computers, and the brick and sent them to Jake. Then she texted Fletcher, Rose, and Kitty with the news.

"All right. I'm almost done here," he said. "I'll send one of my guys over to replace the window today, or at least board it up immediately. It's too chilly outside to leave it like that."

"Thanks. I hope this doesn't get any worse. We have five weeks to go. Everyone is too amped."

"Agree. I had to turn off the news last night." He leaned on the broom with one arm. "The nation needs a circuit breaker. Too many angry people," he added.

"I'm so glad you never get angry." Dot went over and put her arms around his waist.

"It's a choice. I don't get too worked up about politics," he said. A year ago, that comment might have irritated her. Now, she found herself appreciating his approach. "We all agree on most of the big things. What we need is a little common sense."

"I think Lopez has great common sense," she said. "Maybe I'll get you to vote for her after all."

"No chance of that," he said, but his tone was light.

"All right. It was worth a try. A kiss before our day gets taken away from us?" He obliged.

A few moments later, Jake pulled up out front. "Political violence and you two are making out?"

Danny scoffed, and she took the broom from him.

"Hope you can find out who did this," he said. "Things are a little too hot around here."

"Looks like it." Jake laughed and smacked Danny's back.

"I'm out of here," Danny said, a smile on his face. "I'll call you later, Dot."

She waved and started from the beginning as Jake took down the details for his report.

Chapter 60

The Crew was up early that Sunday morning in early October. Jake was on his way with Tommy and Danny in the Taylors' Suburban to pick the girls up for the Packers game that afternoon. The guys were excited to show them a good time.

"Where in the world did you get those?" Dot was in the kitchen drinking tea when Mary came in wearing green sparkly spandex leggings. Her legs looked impossibly long.

"Amazon," she said. "I'll probably only wear them once, but totally worth it, don't you think?"

She twirled and Dot had to admit, "Absolutely worth it."

Dot's dad had sent each of them a Packers' sweatshirt through the team's page, so they were coordinated in green and gold, ready for this Wisconsin rite of passage.

"Let's take a pic for my dad," Dot said. She gathered Harper and Mary on the stairs. Harper held up Pippi in her own little Packers' sweater.

"Cheeseheads!" Dot snapped the photo and texted it to her family group chat, "#GoPackGo."

Harper jogged over to their neighbor's house to drop off Pippi for the day. "Bye, Pip. Be right back. Like five minutes," she whispered in Pippi's ear. She hated to leave her but knew she might not be able to sneak her into the stadium.

Jake honked and they piled into the SUV. He faked having a heart attack when he saw Mary's long, thin green legs and her Packers merch. "You're killing me," he said.

Mary winked and buckled into the front seat for the two-hour drive up to Green Bay.

Harper and Tommy took the next row, and she immediately showed him some funny memes she'd seen the night before. Danny and Dot sat in the way back, holding hands.

"All right, let's go!" Jake said, turning on the Fox Sports pregame show. "We've got a couple hours in the car to get there. Think you can behave?" he asked more to Mary than anyone else.

"We'll see," she said.

An hour into the ride, Jake turned down the volume on the radio.

"Okay, we need to talk about some rules. So that you won't embarrass us." He smirked at Mary.

"Rules?" She looked at him over her sunglasses.

"First up, so you know, the Packers are playing the Detroit Lions. Biggest game of the year."

"You mean the team Vince Lombardi coached, right?" Only Mary could make playing dumb sound so smart.

The guys laughed. "Whoa, Mary, how did you know that?" Tommy asked.

"Just a lucky guess. All right. Lay it on us. What are your rules, Jake?" she asked.

"First, no talking about fashion. Uniforms aren't *adorable*."

"I agree. Yellow and green is a terrible combo," Harper said.

"How dare you!" Tommy pretended to be offended.

"Anything else?" Dot asked.

"Yeah, let's not hear anything about cute butts. This is serious business today," Jake said.

"So, we can't talk about the tight end?" Dot joked.

"Jake, here's a rule we need you to follow—eyes on the road, hands at ten and two!" Mary turned the pregame back up and reached over to lay her hand on his knee.

"EVERYONE IS SO *nice*," Dot said.

"You're always saying that." Danny put his arm around her as they walked through the residential neighborhood in Green Bay where they'd paid a friend of a friend to park for the day.

"Because it's true!"

"Anyone want a brat?" an older woman decked out in green and gold gear called out to them.

"I'll take one!" Mary said. "How much?"

"All yours, darling! Just cheer on the Pack for me, okay?" Mary gave her a quick hug and accepted the sausage roll, added some mustard, and took a big bite.

"Delicious!" She offered a bite to Jake.

Tommy led the way through the crowd, high-fiving guys as he walked.

"Do you know them?" Harper asked.

"Nope. I mean, not really. But we all kind of know each other on game day."

"It's like in the Village back home. We don't necessarily know each other, but New Yorkers share a thing," Harper said.

"Except the people are different," Dot said. "A different kind of nice, though."

"As in, *not* nice!" Mary said. "Just like in the movies."

Tommy bought a round of burgers for everyone, including Mary.

"Where do you put it all?" Harper asked.

"I can't help it. I'm hungry!" Mary said, caught up in the fanfare.

"I'm glad it isn't going to be too cold today," Dot said. "I feel like all I've ever heard about is the frozen tundra of Lambeau Field."

"I love it when it's snowing and blowing. There's nothing like a football game in a snowstorm," Tommy said. "Gives us an advantage, too."

"Except for our recruits out of the SEC," Jake said. "Give me Big Ten linemen all day. They know how to play in this."

"True." Tommy nodded.

"I'm glad we got such a nice day though," Harper said. The sun was shining, and the sky was a bright blue. A light breeze blew off the lake. Everyone had left their work and worries behind for the day, and it all felt perfect.

"Let's take them over to Kroll's before we go into the stadium," Danny said. "That way they'll get the full experience."

"What's Kroll's?" Harper asked.

"It's this great place. Kind of a dive. It's been in business since the mid-1930s. It's a must-see place for anyone visiting Green Bay."

They arrived and the diner was already packed with the Pack.

Jake led the way and muscled his way up to the bar. The others crowded in behind him. They had to yell to hear each other. "Spotted Cows for everyone, okay?" he asked.

Dot didn't like beer too much but nodded. "When in Green Bay . . ."

Jake passed the pints from the bartender to the group. "Cheers!" They clinked their glasses together and took a pregame sip.

"Go Pack Go!" a chant started in the bar. They joined in.

Dot looked at Mary and Harper. "Would you ever have imagined this a year ago?"

"You mean when I tried to hit on a gay guy and Harper was chased around the Oyster Bar by her boss? No." Mary shook her head, laughing.

"Despite that night at the fair, this has been one of the best years of my life," Harper said.

"Mine, too," Mary said.

"Mine, three," Dot completed their circle.

"WHAT ARE WE doing?!" Harper yelled at the Packers. It was just the first quarter, but she and Tommy were going to lose their voices. Green Bay was down by a touchdown and had just fumbled going for it on fourth down.

"Wow, she's really into it," Dot said to Danny, leaning toward him.

"Tommy's created a monster." He kissed Dot's cheek, and she scooted closer to him, her thigh pressing hard into his.

The Packers rallied on the next drive and were up by two points going into the second quarter.

"The uniforms are so old-school—they're like off a vintage postcard," Harper said, deliberately breaking a rule.

"And I was just noticing the cute butts!" Dot added, and Mary whistled toward the field.

"Focus, ladies." Jake was biting his lip watching the Lions drive down the field.

"Well, if the defense would stop blitzing then maybe they could stop the run," Mary said, matter-of-factly.

Jake, Tommy, and Danny stared at her.

"Just who in the world are you?" Jake asked.

Mary shrugged and started heckling the Lions' bench.

ALL THROUGH THE game, Dot felt guilty about not working. Rose and Fletcher were running the door-knocking volunteers that day. They'd encouraged her to go to the game, and she said she'd handle all the late nights that week, but still—she felt that mix of flaking out and FOMO.

To get a moment to check in with the office, she thought she'd run to the ladies' room to respond to any messages before halftime instead of working on her phone in the stands.

"Excuse me, I'll be right back," she said.

"You want me to come with you?" Danny asked.

"No. You stay. I'll just be a couple of minutes." She squeezed past the other fans, apologizing along the way.

Near the concession area, Dot pulled out her phone from her crossbody bag. There were several messages from Fletcher and Rose to her and Kitty. A quick scan told her everything was going well in Milwaukee.

"We locked down a couple hundred people today. I'll update the spreadsheet and send it around tonight," Fletcher's text said.

Dot sent back a thumbs-up. Then she heard a huge eruption from the crowd. She looked up to the screens above the concession stand. The Pack had scored again. The fans around her were pumping their fists and yelling.

She was swept up in their enthusiasm and wanted to rush back to Danny, but she checked her phone one more time and noticed an email from someone she didn't know—Bailey Bickle. Who was that? She opened the message.

"Hi, Dot—we haven't met, but I'd love to change that. My name is Bailey, and I work for the American Progress Center—we're a Super PAC like FTW. I'm friends with Kitty. You come highly recommended by her and Sen Lopez's campaign. We want to talk to you about coming to work for us after the election. The position is director of comms. Based in D.C. Let me know ASAP if you're interested."

Dot was shocked. She read the email again. D.C.? As in *Washington*, D.C.?

Her stomach roiled with a mix of emotions. She'd never considered going to Washington after Cedar Falls. She was a New Yorker, through and through. She was flattered that they'd recommended her. She also *really* needed a job after the election. And she'd loved working on politics instead of corporate PR. This could be a dream come true.

So, why did it feel like a letdown? Instead of being energized by the opportunity, she felt . . . flat. First, the job wasn't in New York, but Washington. She didn't want to live in Washington, even though she'd realized that's where national politics happens. Like finance was to New York and country music was to Nashville. You had to *be* there to make it there.

And more than the communications job not being in New York—it also wasn't where she was standing right now. In Wisconsin.

Bailey Bickle's email had come at a terrible time. Dot was having a great day and had even successfully pushed the future out of her mind for a couple of hours. But the email had yanked her back to her running tab of worries. She needed to confront the issue of what she and Danny were going to do, if anything, about their relationship. Where was this going? And how soon could she figure it out? She was running out of time.

Dot took a breath and put her phone away and headed back to Danny. She found him alone at their seats. He stood for her, always the gentleman, while she sat down.

"Jake took Mary on a tour, and Tommy and Harper went to get some snacks," he said. "Everything okay?"

"Totally. Everything's fine."

"Fine? So, not good?" Danny had learned the universal lesson all men eventually understood.

"Sorry. I'm good. Great." She decided to put on a brave face. Why ruin the day? She took Danny's hand, and he lifted both of their hands up and kissed the back of hers. Then they turned their attention back to the game.

RIGHT BEFORE HALFTIME, Jake said to Mary, "I have a surprise for you." He led her down toward the field. There, they met up with a stadium worker.

"Hey, Jake. Good to see you, man!"

"You too, Ridge. How's it going? Hey, this is Mary Russo."

Jack Ridgely took his cap off and shook Mary's hand.

"Well Jake certainly has reeled in a beauty! It's nice to meet you."

Mary was charmed. "It's nice to meet you." She still didn't know what the surprise was.

"Ridge and I were in the same unit in Afghanistan. One of the best poker players I consistently beat."

"Then why do you still owe me fifty bucks?" Ridge asked.

"You know I'm good for it!" Jake said.

"You two ready?" Ridge asked, leading the way onto the field.

Mary knew this was a big deal. Her brother Frankie was mad about sports and had texted her to explain just how cool it was to go to Lambeau Field. The crowd was cheering, the Cheeseheads were going crazy.

And that's when Mary decided to go for her big reveal. She slipped her hand from Jake's grasp and whipped off her Packers sweatshirt to reveal an old Packers' Aaron Rodgers jersey.

The atmosphere changed immediately. People on the field backed away from her, and the crowd started booing.

"Mary! What in the hell are you doing?" Jake cried.

"What? I thought you all love him!" she cried.

"Loved! Past tense! We hate him now."

"But he won you a Super Bowl."

"It's a long story. But he's dead to us."

"I had no idea!" Mary scrambled to put her sweatshirt back on, feeling terrible about ruining the moment for Jake. The boos from the Cheeseheads continued to rain down.

Jake caught Ridge's attention and led Mary back to safety.

"I'm so sorry. I thought it would be fun. Or at least funny!" she said.

"It was actually the funniest thing I've seen in a long time." Jake and Ridge were laughing, and she was coming down off the embarrassment.

"Come here." Jake wrapped Mary in a hug. "I know you know a lot about football. But you have some things to learn about Green Bay!"

"Maybe you can teach me more about it," she suggested.

"Next time, you'll know everything you need to know."

She liked the sound of that—next time.

MEANWHILE, TOMMY AND Harper returned from a halftime run up to the concession stand. They'd brought back bags of cheddar popcorn for everyone.

Tommy tore one open and offered some to Harper. She grabbed his hand and kissed him.

"Get a room!" someone behind them yelled. "We're trying to watch the game here!"

Harper's face reddened as she pulled back from Tommy. He held up a hand in apology, and they sat down to watch the rest of the game.

IN THE END, the Packers beat the Lions, and eighty thousand fans were in a great mood.

"What happens when they lose?" Harper asked.

"You don't want to know," Tommy said.

Before they left their seats, Dot asked a fan behind her to take a group shot of them. Then she posted it to her story and tagged Harper and Mary. #Packers #WisconsinLife #FriendsForever

"This was a great day," she said to Danny as they got in the car for the drive home.

It was over an hour on the drive back before her wheels started to turn and she remembered the job offer.

Did that mean she didn't want it?

Chapter 61

A few days after the Packers game, Dot came home from the office to find a small package waiting for her on the kitchen island.

"What's this?" she asked Mary, picking up the box. It hardly weighed anything.

"I'm not sure. That cute UPS driver dropped it off around noon."

"The UPS driver is cute?"

"Oh yes. Super-cute," Harper said, sitting at the breakfast bar with her laptop. "Great legs."

"Yeah, he's really into cycling. Training for the Olympics." Mary sat in the family room in the deep cushioned chair, her long legs crossed with her feet resting on the ottoman, computer on her lap.

"He grew up in Green Bay but moved here to be closer to his coach," Harper said. "*And* he's single."

"How do you know so much about this cute single bicycle guy?" Dot asked.

"Research," Harper said.

"Aha—is that what your book is about—hot delivery cyclists?"

"Nice try."

"Come on, Harp, when are you going to share this book? We're dying to read it."

"I'm superstitious. I'm afraid that if I let you in on it, it'll fall apart."

"Whatever it is, *definitely* work in the hot cyclist somehow," Mary said. "You know, like, 'the UPS driver with a *very special delivery*.'"

"She's right. That would sell," Dot weighed in, thinking she needed to see this cyclist for herself.

"I'm not writing a soft porn." Harper rolled her eyes playfully and grabbed her laptop. "I'm heading up to the loft so I can think straight. Come on, Pip." Pippi leapt out of her bed and scrambled after Harper.

Dot picked up the package and noticed the postmark was from Vail, Colorado. It was from her sister Anne. She used a knife to slice through the tape and discarded the box in the proper recycling bin.

Inside the small pink box was a gold bangle, and on the inside, it had been engraved with one word: *Breathe*.

Dot put the bracelet on and sent Anne a text right away. "Wow, thanks for the bracelet. I love it. And I needed that reminder. It's been a whirlwind."

"I knew it. You always hold your breath when you're stressed. Like when you almost passed out in high school during the school play."

"Don't remind me. Still embarrassed by that." She snapped a pic of her wrist and added it to their exchange. "Thanks, sis. I'm already wearing it."

"Maybe you can visit after the campaign and ski for a few days? We already got a good snow."

"I'd love that." She added suitcase and skis emojis and then she put her phone down.

Just *thinking* about what would come after the campaign was making Dot feel anxious.

Plus, she didn't have time to concentrate on what was next, because with just a month to Election Day, the race was back to 49–49 in Wisconsin, about 51–48 nationwide. The Republicans had a slight edge. The Democrats hadn't been able to break out with a lead for more than a day or two at a time. And even when they got a small lead in the battleground states, it evaporated quickly.

The pressure at For the Win was mounting. Kitty was serious about that half-a-million-dollar win bonus she'd be set to get and was still dangling the 20 percent share with her and Fletcher if Lopez won. Not to mention if there was no Democratic win, there'd be no White House job for Kitty. Dot and Fletcher did what they could to keep their D.C. boss supplied with data.

"I'm going to bury her with numbers for a few hours," Fletcher said on a day when Kitty just wouldn't let up.

"Good. We need some breathing room," Dot said, taking a minute to pull herself together.

Early that week, Dot had interviewed with the American Progress PAC. She'd approached the meeting with a mix of curiosity and seriousness, determined to ask them as many questions as they asked her. She tried to tone down her New York attitude, not wanting to make it seem like she was one of those Manhattan snobs who looked down on Washington. She wore a white button-down and a gray blazer to show how professional she was. It'd been ages since she'd interviewed for a job.

Bailey Bickle, the one who'd sent her the original email, was on the video call, along with two other staffers—one in comms and one in operations—to see if they'd be a match. At the end of a good exchange, they seemed eager to have Dot join them in Washington. Soon after, they sent signals that they were likely to offer her the job. And while it was enticing and paid well, she just couldn't see moving to D.C. instead of returning to Manhattan. She was a New York girl. She'd never pictured herself working in the capital city. That was more for the Kitty Bells of the world—the navy suit and pearl earring types. At least she'd come to that conclusion during her time in Wisconsin. Knowing that she didn't necessarily want to live inside the Beltway was worthwhile, she guessed.

But if she didn't have any work in New York, would it be better if she just moved to D.C. to check it out? It didn't have to be forever. Besides, if she was going to work in politics, didn't she *have* to live in D.C.?

The biggest complication—and the one she had no idea how to handle—was knowing in her heart that she was in love with Danny Dawson.

And, at his invitation, for the nights she slept over, she'd kept a toothbrush, face oil, and sunscreen in his bathroom. He loved to make her coffee in the mornings, and she'd sit up in bed reading the headlines until he brought her a coffee, and they'd talk about the next time they'd see each other.

She always stayed for the second cup. He'd been right. That was when the good stuff came out in their conversations.

Still, they hadn't yet had a talk about their feelings. And while she believed he might feel the same way about her, they both held back. Neither of them brought up the future and both just tried to ignore that the clock to Election Day and her departure was ticking down.

Because there was one thing she knew for sure—come mid-November, Danny was not going to be in Washington, D.C., *or* New York City. He would be in Cedar Falls. She had to come to terms with that.

And so, Dot held her breath. Her mind was on a loop.

In the kitchen that night, she twisted Anne's bracelet on her wrist and sighed, ready to mentally move on with her evening.

"Wine?" Dot asked Mary, getting two glasses out of the cupboard.

"Thought you'd never ask."

Dot poured them each a glass of Sauvignon Blanc. They clinked glasses and turned their backs to the kitchen island to look out the big window to the backyard, where the autumn leaves were turning from yellow to gold and orange to copper. They were beautiful, but they also signaled the end of their season in that house.

"So, counselor, what are we going to do?" Dot asked, leaning her head against Mary's.

"That's a good question. I don't know. We'll figure it out." Though even Mary didn't sound as confident as usual. And Dot had her doubts as well.

Chapter 62

That week, Dot bumped into Jeanie Jankowski outside of Flour Power after running an errand to FedEx for the campaign.

"Oh, Dot. Hello! Say, I was hoping to run into you. Do you have a few minutes to sit?"

Dot did not have a few minutes, but she couldn't say no to Jeanie.

"Of course. Want to pop into Mimi's?"

"Perfect. It's nearly teatime anyway." Jeanie was fully a Wisconsinite, but she held true to some of her favorite British customs.

Dot opened the door to Flour Power and ushered Jeanie inside. "I'll get us a table." Dot shot a text to Fletcher and Rose that she'd be a few minutes late.

She waved to Mimi and led Jeanie to a seat by the window. It was chilly outside but cozy in the bakery. Jeanie unwrapped her burgundy shawl from around her shoulders and Dot peeled off her bright blue puffy jacket. It was that time of year when you left the house with an extra layer but then accidentally left it behind because the temperatures rose higher than expected.

Mimi called over to them. "English breakfast?"

Dot nodded enthusiastically and turned to Jeanie. "It's so good to see you. How are you and Ted?"

"Oh, we're great. We have our aches and pains, but we can't complain," she said. "And the shop is doing very well. Ever since you and Danny redid the store, we have so many customers that we can't keep up. Books are flying off the shelves. After a few lean years, that's been a welcome development."

"I love to hear it," Dot said, pausing a moment before asking what was on her mind. "Have you thought any more about what you might do . . . you know . . . in the future?" She didn't want to use the word "retirement" because Jeanie had said that she believed the best way to stay healthy was to keep working.

"Not really. Mostly we just avoid the subject, though we will have to figure all that out soon. We either sell it or close it at some point. Ted wants to have things organized for when . . ." Jeanie didn't finish the sentence. Instead, she changed the subject. "Anyway, he's at the diner with his men's group this afternoon. They sit around and try to put the world to rights. He took Danny with him today. They're trying to get younger people to join them to carry on the tradition."

"Danny mentioned that. He was looking forward to it."

Mimi brought them each a hot cup of tea and freshly baked shortbread cookies. "Those are on me. New recipe—I added some pumpkin spice. Let me know what you think," she said as she set down the small plates.

They each dipped one of the cookies into their coffee to soften them up and took a bite.

"Mimi! These are great. I'll take a dozen back to the store," Jeanie said.

Dot agreed. "Mind if I help promote these for Mimi?" she asked Jeanie before picking up her phone.

"Go for it," Jeanie said. "You're very thoughtful, Dot. I've always liked that about you."

Dot arranged their tea and cookies and took an artsy photo. She immediately posted it to her story, "New shortbread recipe at Flour Power—pumpkin lovers RUN DON'T WALK to get yours today!" She noticed two unread messages from Fletcher, but she put her phone in her pocket so she wouldn't be tempted to look at it while she caught up with her friend.

"So, how are you and Danny?" Jeanie asked. "I haven't seen him this happy since . . . well, since Sadie was in his life, if I'm being honest."

Dot took that in. She and Danny hadn't talked about his late fiancée much. They took the long way around conversations to avoid the subject.

"I hope I didn't overstep by saying that," Jeanie said.

"Oh no, that's okay. I'm glad to hear that you think he seems happy. I'm very much . . . well, I'm very attracted to him. And I care about him. A lot. Plus, we have so much fun together."

"I hear a 'but' . . ." Jeanie sensed Dot's hesitation.

"It's just that I'm not sure where it's going. I need to be honest about things. I'm going back to the city in a month. And it just feels like Danny and Dot could be a dead end."

"It doesn't have to be."

"It doesn't?"

"Absolutely not."

"But I am going back to New York. And I don't even have a job for after the election. Heck, I don't even know who is going to win at this point. And besides that, I don't know what I even want to do." Dot reminded herself to breathe.

"That's a lot of uncertainty."

"I feel like so much is up in the air." Dot put her head in her hands for a moment to gather herself.

"So, may I ask—what *are* you certain of?" Jeanie sipped her coffee and looked at Dot over the rim of her cup.

"That's the problem. I'm not sure."

Jeanie set her cup down and took Dot's hands in hers.

"Listen. I remember when I fell in love with Ted. He swept me off my feet. And never in my life did I think I would marry an American. And then to make a life in *Wisconsin*! No less, with a bookshop of my own. It was unimaginable."

Dot listened. "So, how did you decide to leave England and move to America?"

"Well, at some point, I got so tired of the indecision and of second-guessing myself, that I decided the only decision that mattered was trusting my heart."

"But you and Ted knew you were in love. Danny and I haven't . . . well, we haven't said that."

"Do you love him?" Jeanie was direct.

Dot looked at Jeanie and then broke away and looked out the window. She paused for a long while and thought about what to say. Jeanie didn't try to fill the silence.

"I think I love him. But I don't know if he's open to loving me after what happened to Sadie and the baby. And I don't think he'd want to move to New York. So, I just . . . I don't know." She looked back at Jeanie who was stirring a sugar packet into her second cup of tea.

"Here's what I think," she said, setting her spoon onto the saucer. "Sometimes, you have to go for what you want, even if that means you won't necessarily get it."

Dot nodded. "Go on."

"Look, I've known that young man his entire life. I've seen him grow from a shy kid—who'd been dealt a tough hand because his father was never in the picture—into a handsome and responsible adult. And yes, he went through a terrible ordeal. But his heart has healed over time. And, Dot, you've been a big part of that. So, maybe you should tell him how you feel."

"And how do you think *he* feels?" Dot asked.

"I think he's head over heels," she said. "But I think he needs a little push."

Dot's stomach fluttered at the thought.

Chapter 63

With Jeanie's encouragement, Dot thought about the little push she might give Danny to see if they were going to take this to the next level or . . . Well, she didn't want to think about the "or" just now.

Danny was planning to have her over for dinner at his house on Friday night. He was going to cook for her. She was already thinking of what she'd wear and wanted to stop into the Couture Closet to see if there was anything new that she'd like to get for that evening. If everything went well, it *could* be the night that decided the rest of her life. She started to allow herself to imagine Danny moving to New York, remodeling the expensive town houses on the Upper West Side.

In her mind, she could picture their runs in the park, dinner at Joanne's during open mic night, weekends in the Hudson Valley at cozy bed and breakfasts. Letting her mind wander to these possibilities put a pep in her step.

After wrapping up at the office, she walked a couple of blocks down Main Street and ducked into the shop. She immediately took in the scent of fallen leaves and crisp air. She noticed a Yankee Candle next to the register: Autumn Daydream. "Nailed it," she thought.

A rack of cashmere wrap dresses in dark gray, hunter green, navy, and black caught her eye, and she started looking through them.

"Dot? Is that you?"

Dot didn't recognize the voice. She turned and saw Maddy, Zoe, Lauren, and Marissa. Ugh. The Cedar Falls townies. And she was outnumbered without The Crew or Danny with her.

"Oh, hi. How are you?" Dot asked, summoning up some enthusiasm to sound sincere.

"Fine, thanks," Maddy said, her friends standing behind her like backup singers. "Hey, I've been wanting to have a word. Do you have a second?"

"Sure. Go ahead," Dot said, feeling on guard.

"You're dating Danny, right?"

"Well, yes. We've been seeing each other for a few months now."

"Is it exclusive?"

"Why?"

"Because Sadie was my best friend. I was going to be the maid of honor at their wedding," Maddy said. "And, as you know, they never got married because she and her daughter were killed in the accident."

"Yes, I know. I'm so sorry."

"And here's the thing. You're a New Yorker, right? You don't seem the type that would ever want to *live* in Cedar Falls. It's way too small for a city girl like yourself, isn't it?"

Dot stared at her.

"If you care about him, why would you risk breaking his heart again, if you don't plan to stay? *That* will hurt him. It will set him back. I think it's cruel, if you ask me." Maddy crossed her arms over her chest.

"Well, I, I . . ." Dot was at a loss for words. She just wanted to bolt out of the shop and go home.

"Look, if you think New York is so great, *Dorothy*," Marissa chimed in with a mouth full of snark. "Why don't you just click your heels three times?" Maddy and the other townies laughed. "There's no place like *home*, right?"

Dot's cheeks stung with the hurt and embarrassment. She couldn't think of anything to say and didn't want to cry in front of them. This was like a scene out of *Mean Girls*.

"Excuse me," she said quietly, holding her head as high as she could while moving to the door.

"He won't leave Cedar Falls, you know," Maddy said to Dot's back.

Dot let the door close behind her. She reached for the bracelet her sister had sent, took a deep breath, and quickly started walking home, fighting back tears.

Along her walk, she saw the warm glow of the Cocoa and Cabernet restaurant's candlelit tables. She slowed down to take in the scene. When she tilted her head to look inside, what she saw made her catch her breath in shock.

At a table with a single tall candle sat Danny and a very pretty brunette. She was a woman around his age, and each had half-drunk glasses of wine in front of them. They looked easy in each other's company. Danny was laughing and she had a hand on his forearm. She was obviously telling him a great story or joke, and he looked comfortable and relaxed.

Dot felt her heart slice in two. She backed away from the restaurant and scrambled for her phone. She texted Harper and Mary.

"Crew up? Meet me on Main."

Three dots appeared immediately.

"Yes. Where?" Harper said.

"Ummm . . . I'm near"—she turned around and frantically looked for a place to pop into. Then she saw the place from which they often got delivery—"Thai-tanic." She winced. The restaurant's name fit the moment a little too well.

"Order the tom yum. We're on our way," Mary said. She added a siren emoji.

Outside of the restaurant, Dot wrapped her arms around herself. There was a chill in the air that matched the one she felt in her heart.

Chapter 64

Dot grabbed a booth in the back of the restaurant.

"You said there will be three of you dining with us tonight?" The waiter started to fill the water glasses.

Dot nodded, still in shock at what she'd seen a few doors down at the wine bar. While it was true she and Danny had not talked about being exclusive, it was obviously exclusive. Wasn't it? Didn't it go without saying?

And then there were those townie girls. Dot sat thinking of all the things she *should* have said. But she'd choked when she had the chance, and now she was kicking herself.

She looked up as the door to the restaurant burst open.

"Where's our girl?" Mary said, dressed in black leather pants, heels, a dark gray sweater, and a red puffy vest. Her hair was down and wild.

Dot waved from the booth. She gave Mary a double take.

"Oh no, did I screw up your plans? You look like you were going out."

"What? In this? No. I was just hanging at the house," Mary said.

"I thought the same thing," Harper said. "But Jake's on duty tonight." Harper was wearing much more sensible clothing for an emergency meetup on a weeknight at the local Thai restaurant. Jeans, navy suede ballet flats, and her ubiquitous NYU hoodie.

The waiter came by and asked if anyone wanted a drink.

"Yes!" they said in unison.

Mary picked up the plastic drink tent from the table and quickly studied it. "How about a round of Basil Mojitos?"

"Excellent choice," he said and rushed to get their cocktails.

"Okay. Spill. What happened? Who do we need to murder?" Harper was ready for the drama.

"Yes, tell us everything." Mary leaned in, her elbows on the table. Dot had their full attention.

They patiently listened to the entire story stopping only to order tom yum soup, green papaya salad, pad Thai with shrimp, mango sticky rice—all to share.

"Okay, first, we take out the townies. They're horrible," Harper said.

"I mean, it *is* self-defense," Mary said. "We'd probably only be sentenced to twelve years. We'd be paroled in six with good behavior."

"So, you'd do the full twelve?" Harper asked.

"Yeah, probably." Mary scooped another helping of the shrimp entrée onto her plate. "But how do you know that Danny was on a date? Couldn't he just have been catching up with a friend?"

"It didn't look that way to me. They were so into each other. She had her hand on his arm. He couldn't take his eyes off her. I know what I saw." The longer Dot thought about seeing Danny at that candlelit table with the wine flowing, the more convinced she was that it was *definitely* a romantic dinner.

"Why don't you text him to see if he responds?" Harper asked.

"I don't want to seem desperate. Or that I'm checking in on him."

"But aren't you desperate to know?"

"Yes. But also no." Dot put her chopsticks down. "I don't know. I've been thinking about what Maddy said. And while she's an awful person, maybe she had a point. Maybe she was trying to protect him. I know that Danny has been through hell. And I absolutely have fallen for him. But we've never talked about being exclusive. It's not like he's said that he loves me."

She took a sip of her drink and set it down. And immediately picked it back up again. "And we go back to New York in a month. Then what? It isn't fair for me to string him along and then leave, is it?"

Mary considered this. "Do you love him?"

"Oh gosh, I don't know. I mean. Yes. Maybe. But it's so complicated."

"Why is it complicated?" Harper asked gently.

"Because my life is in New York. I left a good paying job—that I hated, I know—to try this. I dragged you here with me on a whim and now . . . now I just . . . ugh. I don't know."

Mary signaled to the waiter that they'd have another round. "I know that you have so much on your mind," she said. "We all do. But before we get carried away, let's just pause for a moment."

"Yeah. My mom always tells me not to think too far ahead," Harper said.

"How's that going for us?" Dot asked, with more bite than she intended. "Wait. I'm sorry. I'm a wreck. You're right. I know. I should just take a minute and think things through."

Mary considered her from across the table. "You love him. I can tell."

Dot blushed and lifted her eyebrows. "You've always known me better than I know myself."

"But you're hiding something. What else is going on? Tell us," Harper pushed.

Dot still hadn't told them about the Super PAC job opportunity in Washington, D.C.

"Okay. There's one other thing."

"Oh, here we go." Mary sat back, bracing herself for whatever it was. "You slept with Fletcher in Milwaukee. I knew it."

"No! I have a job possibility. Working for a Super PAC doing strategic communications. A more senior role. Good pay."

"That sounds amazing," Harper said.

"There's just one little thing though. Well, it's a big thing."

Harper motioned for Dot to keep talking.

"It's in Washington."

"D.C.?"

"Yes."

"But you live in New York," Mary said.

"Exactly."

"Do you want the job?" Harper asked.

"I want that job, but I want it to be in New York."

"Is that an option?" Mary asked.

"No. It's an in-office job. No remote work."

"So, you'd move to Washington?" Harper asked.

"I don't know," Dot replied.

"So, this is more complicated than just what you and Danny will do?" Mary hit the nail on the head.

"Yes."

"Perhaps you're making it more complicated than it needs to be," Mary said as she signaled the waiter for the bill.

"Well, things get easier, especially if Danny is dating other women," Dot said.

"You don't know that he's dating other women," Harper interjected.

"I saw what I saw."

"Maybe you're telling yourself that's what you saw without even asking him about it," Mary said. "Like you're trying to talk yourself out of being in love with him and looking for an easy way out."

"Ouch." Dot felt hurt.

Mary reached over and took Dot's hand. "You don't have to have everything planned out, you know."

"But I must have some sort of plan. I need a job. I have bills to pay. I need to get my life going." Dot was spiraling.

"Shall we go home and get some sleep. See how things look in the morning?" Mary started to put on her coat and the waiter came over to help her into it.

"Thank you, you're such a gentleman." She bestowed a smile on him and rested her hand gently on his shoulder, making his day.

Harper pushed them toward the door. "Let's get out of here before he asks for your number."

As they left, Dot glanced down the street at Cocoa and Cabernet, where she'd seen Danny and his date. The restaurant was closed for the night. The lights were off, and it was dark.

Like her mood.

Chapter 65

Mary woke sleepily and slowly stretched her arms high over her head in the big four-poster bed with its high thread count linens. She was reluctant to open her eyes, savoring the dream she'd gotten to live in her first weekend away with Jake.

Just minutes before, she'd heard him leave their room in the Sunny Side Inn in Egg Harbor that Jake had heard about from a colleague. Rolling over to place a hand on his pillow, her palm landed on a piece of paper. She picked it up and read, "Coffee run. Don't move." She rolled back over, holding the note to her chest.

"Keeping this one," she said. She wore Jake's white T-shirt from the night before, and she pulled the collar up over her nose and breathed in his scent.

The night before, Mary and Jake had arrived for a weekend away. He had taken the weekend off from work, which was a rarity. But he had to be on duty later that month for the annual apple harvest and festival in town and wanted to take Mary up to Door County to show her another part of Wisconsin before she returned to New York.

"Trust me, it's one of America's best-kept secrets."

"That's setting the bar pretty high," she said.

"High bars keep things interesting."

"Do you think I'm interesting?" She teased him constantly, flirting with one raised brow.

"Let's say you've held my attention longer than most. Think you can keep that up?"

"I love a challenge," she said.

At the end of their two-hour drive from Cedar Falls, he had already cleared the bar. The Sunny Side Inn was like autumn bottled into a jar—

gold and red leaves framed sailboats drifting on blue water, and the sun warmed gently while the air cooled, scents of pine, pumpkin, and cinnamon in the mix. Charming red barns dotted the landscape on their drive up, and glimpses of the shimmering Lake Michigan caught her attention for the entire ride.

After checking into the Inn, they'd dined early at Al Johnson's Swedish Restaurant & Butik. They shared the pickled herring, cheese curds, Lake Michigan perch, and the Schaum Torte with lingonberries. After their meal, they fed the goats that roamed the property. They tried to coax the ones that had gone up onto the roof to come down and get some treats, but they didn't have any takers.

"They must be stuffed," Jake said.

"So am I." Mary rubbed her stomach.

"Well, then. Mission finally accomplished!" he said, reaching to tickle her. She jumped back and playfully jogged to his car.

When they'd returned to the bed-and-breakfast, the owners had left them two bottles of wine from a local winery, Door 44, and a big bar of locally made dark chocolate.

"It's like they read my mind," Mary said, charmed at the touches.

They took a bottle and two glasses and headed out to the backyard, where a large fire was going in a stone firepit.

They settled into an Adirondack-style loveseat, covered up with the big heavy blankets provided by the Inn, and sat watching the fire, talking about everything and nothing, and occasionally making out. When another couple came to sit by the fire, that was their cue to take their party of two upstairs.

And had they ever.

As Mary stretched off her long sleep, she felt completely happy. This was just what she needed after a long week of billing hours for the firm.

She took her long black hair and tied it in a knot on top of her head. Jake came in with two cups of coffee and set them on the nightstand. He had on jeans, a black long-sleeve T-shirt, and a red and black checkered flannel shirt.

"There's my lumberjack. You were gone too long."

"I love it when you put your hair up like that."

"But you love taking it down more."

"Exactly," he said, kicking his shoes off and reaching for her.

"First, coffee!" She playfully pushed him away. "And then we'll see."

"You're killing me," he said. "Here's yours." He handed her the cup and said, "Hey, my dad sent me a note early this morning. He said they got a notice that the final offer is coming this week, and that if he doesn't take it, the government will exercise its right to take the farm."

Mary reached for his phone. "Can I see?" He opened the message and gave it to her. She scanned it quickly and emailed it to herself and Patricia Parker in New York with the message, "Mind taking a quick look?"

"Tell him I'm going to do another pass on it. Maybe we've missed something. And tell him not to worry."

"That's exactly what I said." Jake let her have one more sip of coffee, then took her cup and placed it on the table.

Then he gently rolled her back onto the bed and started to undo her bun.

"What about breakfast?" she asked. "That bacon has been calling my name since seven this morning."

"They serve breakfast for another two hours."

"You've thought of everything, haven't you?"

"I have."

"Show me." She lifted her lips to his.

Challenge accepted, Jake proved to his Staten Island girlfriend that he had indeed thought of everything.

Chapter 66

At breakfast, Jake was amused by how much Mary ate.

"What? I worked up an appetite."

"I'm glad to hear it. Can't wait to see what you have for lunch. It could be a great afternoon."

He signaled the waiter for another round of freshly squeezed orange juice, hot black coffee, and crispy bacon.

"Hey, do you know why Dot's not answering Danny's texts?"

Mary knew. But Dot had sworn her to secrecy.

"She's not answering his texts?" Mary asked innocently.

"No. He said he knows she's really busy, but that it isn't like her to not respond. He said he's worried that she's ghosting him."

Mary hated the thought of Danny being upset or worried. But she knew that Dot was devastated by what she'd seen in the window when he was with that other woman. She decided to test the question.

"Do you know if Danny is seeing other people while he's dating Dot?" Mary asked.

"Danny? Dating? Hell no," Jake said. "Who would he be dating? He's got his eyes fully on Dot. Why?"

"Well, what if Dot might have seen him with another woman?"

"When? Where?" Jake asked, moving into investigative mode.

"Oh, Jake. Dot made me promise not to say anything. But she called us in a total panic a few nights ago," Mary said, knowing she was revealing one of Dot's secrets. "That mean girl Maddy had just confronted her in a store about Danny and when she was walking home, she saw him through the window with another woman at Cocoa and Cabernet. She was devastated."

"Wait. This isn't right. Something else is going on here. Danny's not dating anyone else. And that girl, Mad—she's been a pain since junior high.

She was friends with Sadie, but she has no business getting in between Danny and Dot. This is crazy. I have to tell him. He has a right to know. There's got to be a mix-up."

"No! You can't. At least not yet," Mary said, trying to slow Jake down. "Let's think about it. Maybe there's been a huge mistake. Or maybe he's like most guys and plays the field."

"What do you mean like most guys? Are you including me in that?"

"No, I . . ."

"Why do you think that all guys are the same?" His face turned red. "Look, Mary, I don't know what men are like in New York, but I sure as heck know that what you're describing about Danny and what you're insinuating about me is not accurate."

"I know that. I'm sorry," she said.

Jake set his napkin down over his plate. He'd not finished his meal. "I'm done."

"Okay, let's go," she said, pushing her chair back.

"I mean, I'm done right now. I need a minute," Jake said.

"Jake, I said I'm sorry. I didn't mean it."

"But Mary, maybe it's time we talked about this."

Oh no, she thought. Was this the big talk she'd been dreading?

It was. He read her reticence and plowed ahead anyway.

"Mary, we need to talk," Jake said. "We can't keep avoiding it."

She nodded. "Okay. Let's do it. You first."

Jake took a breath and squared his shoulders, then looked directly into Mary's eyes.

"All right. What do *you* want out of this? Am I just a guy you hooked up with while on your great Midwest adventure with your cool girlfriends from the big city? Or do you actually care about me?" Then, in a softer voice, he said, "I thought we had something special here."

"We do. I know. But I don't know. I mean, you live here. Your entire life is here. Mine is in New York."

"So, you'd not consider being here with me—even if I asked? And don't worry, I'm not asking . . . yet."

"Well, when you put it that way, I have to say that I don't see myself being *here*. But I see myself being with *you*."

"I can't leave here though, Mary. My family is here. I'm a cop in Cedar Falls. Coming back from the service that was my plan."

"And mine was to be a lawyer in New York," she said, pounding the table a little too hard and making the dishes jump.

She caught herself before her frustration got the best of her. She sat back in her chair and sighed loudly. She brought both hands to her face and wiped the moment away.

"I didn't even have a chance to celebrate," she said.

"Celebrate what?"

She looked away. "I got a letter from the firm. They're making me a senior associate when I get back and putting me on the partner track. It's a big promotion. About two years ahead of my plan. It tells me they think I have promise."

"Mary, that's amazing," Jake said, grabbing her hands. "You *do* have promise. This is very well deserved. Congratulations!"

"You really think so?" She felt a small surge of pride and hope.

"Yes! You're a kick-ass lawyer. You amaze me. You know exactly what you want and go out and get it. It's so great. And really hot."

She rolled her eyes at that.

"You know that the job is in New York, right?" She bit her lip and said, "I'm going to have to go back home."

Jake pulled her onto his lap. "Yeah, I know." They were silent for a few moments. He drew one of her hands up and kissed it then said, "I guess I've known all along that my dream of you being here with me was just that. It's not reality."

"I hate reality right now." She laughed, feeling exasperated with the difficulty of deciding what to do with Jake. Then, getting more serious, she looked at him directly and said, "I don't want this to be over."

They kissed deeply and the other B&B guests at breakfast pretended to ignore them. She put both arms around his neck and nuzzled her face against his.

"It doesn't have to be over," he said into her hair.

"But what are we going to do?" she asked.

Jake let the question hang there for a couple of seconds. "I don't know. But I also know what my dad's always said. Sometimes deciding *not* to decide is the best decision at the time. So, let's just not think about it right now."

He felt her ribs move up and down as her breathing matched his.

"Your dad's a wise man."

"Well, we are related."

"What would your dad suggest we do now?" she asked.

"I think he'd say take that woman outside and show her how beautiful Door County is and maybe then she'll never want to leave."

She kissed his lips and then put her forehead to his. Jake smiled and looked around. Their PDA had cleared the breakfast nook.

"Let's get our coats, New York."

Her smile was bittersweet at the nickname she'd come to love.

Chapter 67

Harper walked Pippi down to the Sin Bin one Monday afternoon in October. Tommy closed the bar on Mondays so that he'd have one day off a week, but had asked her to come down to help him get ready for the Cedar Falls Apple Festival that was taking place that weekend. It was one of the biggest community events of the year, and Tommy had agreed to cochair the refreshments committee. He needed some help organizing the registration, and Harper had readily agreed.

"Believe it or not, I'm great with a spreadsheet," she'd said.

She pushed open the door to the bar and called out, "Hello! Tommy, we're here." She let Pippi off her leash and the dog went running to find her other favorite human. Harper was sure it had to do with the little bits of bacon he'd save for her from the kitchen.

"In the back!" Tommy called.

Harper made her way to his offices. There were papers everywhere and Tommy looked ragged.

"Wow, it's like a tornado came through here." Harper assessed the situation. "How can you work like this?"

"I know. It's awful. I really need to get more organized." He got up to give her a hug and they kissed lightly on the lips.

"Okay, we can clean up later. What's up?" she asked.

"I'm so glad you're here. I'm lost. There are too many moving parts to this festival. And I'm already dealing with complaints about booth locations. I'm afraid the Hungry Hens are going to peck Porker's Provisions to death before this is over. He took his baseball cap off and smoothed back his hair before putting it on again. "I'll think twice before I offer to do this next year."

"As my mom used to beg me, 'Stop me before I volunteer again.'" She looked for a place to sit.

Tommy cleared a space on a chair for her on the other side of his desk. "Here, take this spot, and let me try to make some sense of these piles." He kissed her cheek, and she smiled warmly at him. Pippi stood on two legs looking for his attention. He picked her up and tucked her into his chest.

"Would you mind grabbing my laptop?" Harper asked. "I left it on the bar when we came in. I made a sample spreadsheet we can use."

"Sure, be right back." Tommy retrieved the laptop and returned to his office. He handed it to Harper, and she showed him what she'd already accomplished. The chaos was being tamed right in front of his eyes.

After a couple of hours, Harper got up to stretch. "I'm going to run to the ladies' room. If you want to keep going, you can input these vendors and their booth numbers."

Tommy came around to see what she was pointing to, and she showed him the two columns she wanted him to continue filling out.

"I see. Got it."

"Shall I make us a couple of sandwiches?" she said. "I know where everything is in the kitchen."

"That would be great. Though I should be making sandwiches for you. You're saving me here." He gestured around his chaotic office.

"Next time." She left the office then came back right away and put her head around the doorframe. "Turkey, Swiss, mayo, no mustard, salt, pepper, dash of tabasco, lettuce and tomato? Side of chips?"

"Perfect."

Harper liked knowing his order—it felt intimate yet easy. With Tommy there was no pretending, no drama. That wasn't something she'd felt with previous guys she'd dated. With Kai, she always felt on edge, wondering if she was pretty or interesting enough to be with him. But around Tommy, she lost her self-consciousness and could just be herself.

It wasn't lost on her that she'd met the first guy who ever made her feel comfortable in her own skin and that she was about to go back to Manhattan where the dating scene was horrendous.

Sometimes, she'd let her imagination go to places where she and Tommy stayed together right there in Cedar Falls, with her writing novels and teaching, and him growing his business and maybe even opening that ice cream shop on the farm that he dreamed about.

After a few minutes of these daydreams, she'd shake herself back to reality. She didn't believe that staying in Wisconsin was an option for her.

Harper made the sandwiches in the bar's big kitchen, placed them on two sturdy paper plates, and added pickles that she found in the fridge. She managed to pick everything up in one go thanks to a waitressing job she'd held for a couple of summers and headed back to the office.

As she walked in, she saw Tommy staring at the computer with his eyes wide, his face red, and one hand covering his mouth. He moved quickly to shut the laptop.

"What's wrong?" she asked, concerned the entire file may have been lost and they'd have to start again.

Tommy was speechless. "I . . . uh . . . I . . . wow . . . Harper, I didn't know . . . and I'm like . . . wow."

"Tommy, what is it? What are you talking about?" she asked, her brow creased.

"Well, I . . . I wanted to look up something about the festival, so I minimized the spreadsheet to get to the internet, and then I suddenly was reading these paragraphs about . . . well, about . . . a god and a goddess in a death match on the ice in the heavens and then they . . . they . . ."

Harper's heart went cold. Embarrassment and dread flooded her system. "Oh my God, Tommy. You were reading my book? How could you!"

"I'm sorry, I didn't mean to. I swear. It was an accident. Please believe me," he begged. "It was just there, and it caught my eye and . . . and it was very good." He was trying to salvage the situation but failing.

She put down the plates and reached for her laptop. "I gotta go. I can't believe this. I trusted you of all people not to betray me."

Tommy put a hand on her arm, and she jerked it back. "Harper."

"Don't touch me!" She had held back tears but now they were flowing over her cheeks. "Pippi, let's go." The dog's ears were flattened back on her head. She'd never seen her owner that upset and had started to shiver. Harper motioned for Pippi to hop in the tote bag and threw that over her shoulder. Then she stormed out of the bar in a huff.

She got two steps outside and realized she'd left her forest-green puffy coat in the Sin Bin. It had been warm when she arrived, but a cold front was coming in that could even bring snow that evening. She hated to go back in to get it, but it was a long walk home and one of her favorite coats she had in Wisconsin. She turned around and pushed open the door.

"Oh good, you came back." Tommy had been coming after her. "Harper, I . . ."

She put up her hand to stop him talking.

"I just need my coat." She grabbed her jacket off a stool at the bar and wiggled her way into it. "And I am *not* coming back."

"At least let me drive you. It's cold, Harper."

"You're cold, Tommy!" It was the only insulting thing she could think of in the moment. She knew she sounded childish, but she was so mad that her emotions got the most of her.

Tommy decided it was better to back off than to push her. He held the door for her to leave.

"Harper, I know you're mad at me. But it was an accident. And, honestly, I was very impressed with what you wrote. I was just a little surprised. You've never told me what it was about."

"Don't, Tommy. Just don't." She didn't look back as she took a left and headed to Maple Avenue.

"I should have known it would never work," Harper said to Pippi, who bounced along her hip. She wiped away her tears and felt regret heavy on her shoulders.

As the door closed behind her for the second time, she felt the finality of another breakup. She stormed off, walking as fast as she could back to their house.

At least she knew how that felt—it was a feeling with which she was way too accustomed.

HARPER CAREENED INTO the house and the door slammed behind her.

Mary's head popped out of the kitchen.

"Hey. Are you okay?" she asked Harper, who was still visibly upset.

"I'm fine. I just need a minute." She took Pippi out of her bag and handed her to Mary. "Mind feeding her?"

"Sure, but do you want to talk about it?" Mary asked.

"Not yet."

Mary knew not to push. Harper went upstairs to her loft, while Mary gave Pippi something to eat and fresh water.

"What happened out there, Pip?"

The dog tilted its head, trying to understand.

Chapter 68

Dot came home that night around 9 p.m. She'd been working very long days at the office on the campaign. It was crunch time. There were just two weeks until Election Day.

"Drink?" Mary asked.

"Just one. But be generous." Dot shrugged out of her long, pastel pink, faux fur coat and hung it in the closet.

"So, how are things looking?" Mary was following the campaign closely. "Get any new numbers?" She got out a bottle of Sancerre and poured them each a glass and handed one to Dot.

"Oh gosh, it's so close. Too close to call. And we just found out the Republican ticket is coming back to Wisconsin twice more this week. So now we need to get Lopez and Stone back here, too, but they also have to hit stops in Arizona and Nevada. The travel for them is brutal. But Wisconsin is ground zero. We're just waiting for confirmation that one of the stops she makes is Cedar Falls. If she wins here, she likely wins the entire thing."

"And makes history," Mary said.

"That's the goal. I feel like everything will be a blur from now until then."

"Have you heard from Danny?" Mary asked.

"Not since a couple of days ago."

"Did you ever respond?"

"I didn't."

"Dot!"

"I know! I don't know what to say," Dot said.

"Jake said that there's no way he was with another woman. At least you could get back to him and just ask him what happened that night?" Mary was relieved when Dot had quickly gotten over her anger when she'd revealed that she'd told Jake what was up during their weekend getaway. Mary knew all of this was killing Dot *and* Danny.

"It's excruciating," Dot confessed. "I think about him all the time, but now I worry that not only has so much time passed that he probably doesn't even think about me anymore, but what's the point if we're leaving right after the election?"

"That's not true. He's *obviously* thinking of you. If he didn't care about you, he wouldn't have asked Jake to help him figure out why you'd ghosted him. You're just telling yourself that because you're afraid of the truth," Mary said.

"What truth?" Harper resurfaced from the loft and entered the chat. She wore her matching pajama set in a plaid print and had her hair in a scrunchy on top of her head. Her eyes were red from crying. She carried her laptop under her arm.

Dot and Mary did a double take at their friend's appearance.

"What happened to you?" Dot asked.

"Gee, thanks," Harper said, taking a glass of wine from Mary and getting some frozen cookie-dough bites out of the fridge.

Mary caught Dot's eye and mouthed, "Yikes."

"Come on, Harp. You've been upset since you came in earlier. What happened?" Mary asked.

Harper munched, and Mary and Dot both reached for some cookie dough. Mood eating went better with others.

"So, it was Tommy," Dot said, making an educated guess.

"Sweet Tommy? What could he have done to make you cry? I'll kill him!" Mary tried to lighten the moment.

Harper was finally ready to spill the beans. "I was over there helping him get ready for the apple festival. He's in charge of all the food vendors, and I put together a spreadsheet for him to help get it organized."

"So far, so good," Dot said, patiently waiting for Harper to get to the point.

"Well, I went to make us sandwiches while he plugged in data, and when I came back, he was reading my novel."

"He was? The novel that even *we* have never seen?" Mary couldn't believe it.

"Yes. And he was . . . he was red in the face, and I got so mad. I don't want anyone to read it until it's done. I'm afraid it's terrible. And I'm superstitious that if anyone reads it before I write 'The End' that it will never be a real book."

"First of all, that's crazy. Second, why was his face red?" Dot asked.

"Oh gosh, I can't tell you!" Harper's face was now turning pink.

"And did he go looking for it on purpose—to read the novel while you were out of the room?" Mary was dubious.

"He said it was an accident. That he went to do a Google search, and that the novel was on the screen."

"That sounds plausible, don't you think?" Mary asked.

"But still!" Harper said.

"But still what? Aren't you overreacting? He didn't mean to," Mary said.

"I still want to know why he was red in the face—what did you write that would make him embarrassed?" Dot asked.

"I don't think he was embarrassed." Harper's hands covered her face.

"So, what was it then?" Dot pressed.

"I think he was . . . aroused."

"Aroused? What are you writing? You must show us now. What's the harm?" Mary asked.

"Yeah. Your writing is already cursed, so . . ." Dot said.

In a quick move, Mary reached for the laptop. Harper held on to it, too. They tussled for a moment, but Mary won. She opened it.

"Password!" Mary demanded.

"Ugh, you guys!" Harper said, but she spun the laptop around and used her finger to open the screen.

Dot came behind Mary and they both started reading. Harper covered her eyes with her hands, feeling extraordinarily uncomfortable, not sure how her friends were going to react.

Mary scrolled down as they read quickly together, and Dot's eyebrows popped in surprise. Within a couple of pages, it was clear.

"Hot damn, girl!" Mary said. "You *wrote* this! It's amazing." She got up to hug Harper from the side. Harper kept her hands over her eyes, filled with embarrassment.

Dot kept scrolling, and then read out loud, "Lit by starlight, the rink shimmered in the clouds, a slick of ice set in the heavens. Gods and Goddesses darted across, their blades sparking trails of fire, frost, and lightning. Every strike of the puck sent shock waves through the skies—and to the young Goddess of Light. She gripped her stick tighter, breathless as the

God of Storms cut across her path. They locked eyes, and her pulse stuttered, but she refused to falter. This was not just a game. It was war dressed as sport—and desire disguised as rivalry."

Dot smacked the counter. "This is *incredible*!" She was truly impressed. "Holy smokes, Harper. *Romantasy*! Everyone loves this stuff. It flies off the shelves—just ask Jeanie Jankowski. You're going to have an instant bestseller!"

Harper opened her fingers to look at them. "You think so?"

"No doubt!" Dot raised her glass, and they clinked glasses. "Look at this." Then she showed them how on TikTok the romantasy hashtag had a gazillion views. "You hit the *jackpot*."

"What I want to know is—who gave you such romantic ideas, huh?" Mary teased her. "No wonder Tommy was red-faced. He was like, wow, my girlfriend is sexy! Wait . . . is this about you and him on an . . . ice rink?"

Harper giggled and said, "Maybe."

"Come on, Harper. Text him. Tell him you forgive him. He didn't mean to ruin your surprise. He's the nicest guy. Don't torture him," Mary said.

Harper bit her lip and thought about it for a moment. "You're probably right. I'm just so embarrassed."

"Then get over it and send him a note." Mary handed Harper her phone and urged her to start typing.

"I think I'll take this upstairs." She grabbed her laptop and the wine and popped one more cookie-dough bite into her mouth before heading to her room. Halfway up the stairs she turned back. "Thanks. . . . You really like it?"

"It's hot, Harps. It's going to be a bestseller! I can feel it," Dot said, gathering the wine glasses and turning on the hot water to wash them in the sink. "Plus, I'll do your publicity."

"And I'll do your contract," Mary said. "And remember—you promised I'd be a character in the book. I'm counting on that."

Feeling inspired, Harper thanked them again and bounded up the stairs, a new pep in her step.

"That goes for you, too, missy." Mary swatted Dot with a kitchen towel.

"What?"

"You should text Danny. You're letting your worries about getting hurt get in the way of what you know you should do. I get it—you're afraid that if you fully open your heart that you'll get hurt. But that's not fair to him and I think deep down you know that."

Dot sighed heavily. "Maybe you're right."

"Of course I'm right," Mary said. "Plus, I know he's reached out to you several times. Jake told me. At least you could respond. Give him a chance to explain who he was with that night. And even if the answer is that he's seeing someone else, at least then you'll know."

Dot set the glasses on the drying rack. She knew Mary was right. And that her pride was getting the best of her.

"What's the worst that can happen if you text him?" Mary asked. "You're always advising us to consider the worst-case scenario. Have you done the same? You're being overly cautious, and it's hurting someone else."

"You have a point." Dot gave Mary a hug. "I'll sleep on it." Then she headed upstairs to answer more emails about the campaign.

Mary wrapped up the cookie dough and put it back in the freezer.

"When did I become the responsible one around here?" she asked.

Chapter 69

The apple festival pulled together all the good parts of autumn into one weekend. The leaves that had already fallen to the ground crunched under boots that had been put away for the summer. The sun was warm, but the air was crisp, and people stood chatting around the stalls, wearing puffy vests and holding steaming mugs of apple cider and munching on bratwurst piled high with sauerkraut.

Kids with sticky fingers lined up for the apple pie eating contest where the prize was even more apple pie but with a side of pride. Guys had their arms around their girls but one eye on the University of Wisconsin football game score that they pulled up on their phones. And their wives and girlfriends caught up on the latest town gossip and traded ideas for weekend getaways once the football season was behind them.

A local band strummed fiddles, guitars, and banjos on a makeshift stage. Their music got toes tapping, and a few couples, like Ted and Jeanie Jankowski, made a little space in the crowd so they could dance together, feeling light on their feet. For those too shy to dance, a sway or two got them into the spirit of the festival.

For a few hours that weekend, the outside world was far away, and Cedar Falls felt like the center of the apple universe.

Joe and Grace Taylor arrived after the festivities were underway.

"The weather cooperated today," Grace said as Joe parked their Suburban in the town lot.

"Yep." He was clearly distracted.

"Joe, is anything wrong?" Grace put her hand over his before they got out of the vehicle.

"There's a lot wrong, Grace," he said, grimacing. "I'm afraid we're nearing the end of the road. We may not have enough time to save the farm. It's not looking good."

"Have you heard anything more from the lawyers?"

"Nothing. They said they're being stonewalled by the governor's office. At first it was excuses, polite delays. Now it seems like they're being ignored so the government can run out the clock."

"Well, let's pray the good Lord is listening, since apparently the governor has no ears."

"Well, let's also pray He has a heart," Joe said. "He may be our only hope of holding on to our place." Then, not wanting to worry her any more than he already had, Joe put a smile on his face and said, "Come on. You love the apple festival. Let's go have a good time."

Knowing when not to push, Grace readily agreed with the plan. They'd go have fun even if the concern about losing the farm was like a stone in their shoes—impossible to ignore.

"You got it," she said, opening her door to get out of the vehicle.

Joe came around to shut her door for her. She stopped him from just moving on. He turned to her, and she wrapped her arms around his neck and kissed him more deeply than over forty years of marriage usually provides. She felt him give in to her and his arms pulled her strongly into his chest. They let the kiss linger awhile.

When they finally pulled apart, Joe asked, "What did I do to deserve that?"

"You're a good man, Joe. I believe in you." She knew what he needed to hear, and what she needed to say.

"I don't deserve you, Grace," he said, then he gently took her hand and they walked to the festival with smiles on their faces to mask their worries.

WITH JAKE ON duty for the apple festival and Dot working on the campaign, Mary and Harper walked with Tommy down the middle of Main Street. Cars were banned from downtown for the day, and citizens spilled into the streets, taking in the sights, sounds, and smells.

Mary wore dark brown suede pants tucked into tall brown leather boots, and a navy, green, and light pink plaid coat. Harper stepped out in her black leggings, her well-worn cordovan ankle boots, and her green puffy jacket.

A big sign above them stretched across the street that said, "Cedar Falls Applefest 2028—Life Is Sweeter Here." Pippi rode along in her tote bag, and Tommy carried it for Harper.

"Can't that dog walk?" Mary asked him.

"Why walk when you can ride, right, Pip?" Tommy asked, patting the dog's head. Pippi licked his hand in return.

Harper and Tommy had made up after the book reveal. For all her fears, she had no idea that her book wouldn't be an embarrassment; rather, it turned into quite the turn-on.

"I wasn't embarrassed. I was impressed . . . my foxy friend," Tommy had said when Harper had bypassed a cold text and had opted to call to apologize instead. He'd been relieved that she'd forgiven him, and they'd been inseparable ever since. They held hands as they walked through the crowd. Harper noticed several locals catching their affection for each other. "There goes another eligible bachelor," she imagined them saying.

The three of them stopped to listen to a local singer-songwriter who'd grown up in the area but made it big in Nashville. He had a hit song on the radio, recorded by a big-named artist. Still, the success hadn't gone to his head.

"I love coming home," the singer said, before launching into the hit that helped him and his wife buy their first home. Their three young children sat in the front row, cheering on their dad.

"The festival is a huge hit, Tommy. Look at all these happy, smiling people. They have no idea how much work goes into it," Harper said to Tommy as she looked around at the booths.

"Well, I learned a lot, that's for sure. I'm just glad we kept the two gourmet jam booths separated," he said. "They might have come to blows."

"And the food is so good," Mary said, tossing some apple-popcorn into the air and expertly catching it with her mouth.

Joe and Grace met up with them at the bandstand, and the group made their way to the finish line of the Applefest 5K. They'd volunteered to hand out snacks and waters.

"Hurry. Some of these folks run fast and could finish the race before we even get there." Tommy led the way through the crowd.

Joe, Grace, Mary, Harper, and Tommy found their table and started grabbing mini waters to hand out, along with bananas and, of course, apples.

A familiar face came through early on: Danny Dawson, with his big dark eyes and floppy hair. He'd barely broken a sweat on his run.

"Hey, guys," he said, taking a water from Harper.

"Hey, Danny," she said.

"How've you been, Danny?" Mary asked, fearing the answer was "not well" given that Dot had been slow to send him a note, and they'd not even seen each other in weeks. She knew Dot was miserable—did Danny feel the same?

"I've been better," he said. He motioned Mary to step out of the way of the other runners. "Is Dot here?" He sounded hopeful.

Mary shook her head. "I'm afraid not. Senator Lopez is finally coming to town tomorrow for a big rally here at the fairgrounds, so she had to work. She's literally not done anything but work with the election so close now."

"I see." He looked away. "Do you think she'll ever come around? I . . . miss her."

"I'll see what I can do, Danny. I promise." She gave him a hug, noting she'd made a lot of promises that afternoon.

"Sorry, I'm probably sweaty from the run," he said.

"You look like you walked two blocks instead of running three miles."

"Three point one. Don't forget the point one. Hardest part of the race."

She gave him another big hug and spotted Jake, in uniform, working the fair shift for the police department, making his way to them.

"Come on, let's make Jake a little jealous."

They both laughed as Jake came over.

"Hey, hands off my girl!" Jake said.

"She's all yours, bro." Danny laughed, but his sad eyes came back. "You're a lucky man, Jake."

"Don't I know it." He put an arm around Mary and pulled her close. She looked up at him and smiled. She loved him in his uniform.

Just then she felt her phone buzz. She'd just received another email from Patricia Parker in New York. "I found another something regarding the Taylor farm." Mary jumped. "Jake, can you run me home?"

"Right now? I thought you wanted to stay and eat some more Wisconsin delicacies." He loved her big appetite.

"I just need to get going. It's . . . about work." She didn't want to say she had a possible lifeline to save the farm until she was sure it was solid.

"All right, sure. My shift ends in five minutes. We can go. I'll just radio the guys." He spoke into his shoulder mic, and they waved goodbye to everyone.

"What's this about?" Jake asked as they pulled out of the parking lot in his cruiser.

"It's actually not about my work. It's about the farm. I have a lead," she said.

Upon hearing that, he stepped on the gas.

Chapter 70

At home, Mary pulled out a folder.

"What's in there?" Jake asked.

"It's our lease agreement for this house. When For the Win rented it for us, Kitty Bell had her fiancé's law firm draw up the contract." She rifled through the papers. "Here it is."

Then she got her phone and went to the email from Patricia Parker.

"Bingo," she said.

"What did you find?"

"Patricia said that the law firm representing the manufacturer that wants to take over the farmland also represents a lot of Chinese defense companies. And the name of the law firm rang a bell with me. I was right. It's the same firm."

"So, how would that help my dad save the farm?"

"Well, it could be a big no-no. Any law firm that represents the interest of a foreign country or business must register with the government. It's called FARA, or the Foreign Agents Registration Act. With China's history, any time there's a connection, it triggers this requirement."

"Why?"

"Because all businesses in China are ultimately owned by the Chinese government."

"Ah, okay. I get it. But what are the consequences for lying about that?" Jake reached into the fridge and got two seltzers for them. He opened them both, then handed her one. "Aren't lobbyists and lawyers always lying?"

"If I'm right, the joint manufacturing partnership—between the federal and state governments, along with this private company—would require a national security review. So, any of these so-called investments must go through this committee for approval. I won't bore you, but it's called the Committee on Foreign Investment in the United States. I've not seen anything in your dad's paperwork where this proposed deal has gone through any review. And so, if they've hidden it, or were playing loose with the facts, then the whole thing can come to a screeching halt."

"Because it could be a matter of national security?" He was catching on.

"Exactly. But we need proof."

"How do we get that?"

"Well. I need a little bit of time and to run this by one of the law partners in the city," she said, taking a sip of the cool sparkling water. "Mind if I do a little work instead of going back to the festival? I'm meeting up with your dad in the morning."

"Tell you what. You go to work, and I'll go get a couple of steaks to grill. We can stay in tonight. I'll light the fire."

"It's a gas fireplace, all you do is flip a switch."

"That isn't the fire I was talking about."

She caught on. "Oh, I see."

She leaned over to kiss him. He pulled her in close, but she pushed him away. "I'll work fast."

Chapter 71

The night before Lucy Lopez was finally due to visit Cedar Falls at the apple festival, Kitty Bell came to town and brought a couple of For the Win's donors with her. She'd organized a dinner off Main Street and invited Dot, Fletcher, and Rose to attend. They knew they weren't just invited for a meal. They were to sing for their supper by showcasing how FTW's work was going to flip Wisconsin from red to blue. Kitty needed those contribution checks to keep coming.

Even though Dot and Fletcher pled their case with the D.C.-based campaign for a rally in Cedar Falls, the politicos at Lopez-Stone headquarters kept making excuses for why it couldn't happen. This was despite the candidate herself saying she needed to go—she'd been pushing her team for it ever since she got the request directly from Dot. Her campaign kept blaming the schedule, though Dot and Fletcher knew it was because they didn't think it was worth it.

"They think we're stupid," Fletcher had said. "If they'd get out of Washington and touch some grass, they'd see we're right about this."

"And this is one instance when I don't want to say 'I told you so'—we have to get them to change their minds and get this on the schedule. Soon. We are this close." Dot held her index finger and thumb a millimeter apart.

Kitty had been helpful in aggressively pushing for the Lopez visit, and the candidate herself had put her foot down. She was going to the apple festival. Her campaign relented.

"It's on," Kitty had texted the thread.

"LFG!" Fletcher wrote back.

Dot sent a thumbs-up and immediately felt stressed. Now that they'd gotten their way, the pressure was real.

So that night, on the way to dinner at the Golden Grate, Dot, Fletcher, and Rose brainstormed their best points to prove that the FTW money was being spent wisely. By the time they arrived, each knew their part—Dot was on messaging and media, Fletcher on turnout and social, and Rose on volunteers. It was go time.

When they walked in, Kitty was already there. Of *course* she was. She air-kissed each of them and then turned to introduce them to her guests, a young tech-rich couple named Michael and Iris Vale.

Dot did a double take. The wealthy donor was someone she knew. And someone she'd hoped never to see again. It was her horrible client, Stanford Michael, who'd berated her when she was at the firm because she'd not been able to book him for a cable news hit. He of "who's the boss of you" fame.

"*Dot Clark*?" he asked, incredulous. "What the hell are *you* doing here?"

"Wait. You two know each other?" Kitty was confused.

Dot felt herself shrink. Why did this man sap her confidence?

"Hi, Michael," she managed, while weakly shaking hands with him and his wife. Then to Kitty she said, "We used to work together. When I was in New York. He was a client at the PR firm."

"So, you didn't go on to some great job, I see," he said. "You left New York for *this*?" He gestured around dismissively at Cedar Falls. "I can't believe you're working on the most important campaign in our lifetime. I thought For the Win was a serious outfit, Kitty."

Kitty flinched. Fletcher stepped in. "Whoa, buddy. We haven't met. I'm Fletcher Abbott. It's good to meet you. Listen, I'm not sure where you got that impression of Dot. I've never known anyone with instincts as good as hers—and she can execute a plan like no one else."

Dot was grateful for the defense. She stood a little taller.

"I doubt that," Stanford Michael scoffed.

His wife placed a hand on his forearm. "Honey, maybe this is a waste of time."

"We're already here, Iris. Might as well eat, even if this place is a little too *Midwest* for my taste." He had an annoying habit of emphasizing words to drive home insults.

"Well, Kitty, I hope you know what you're doing," he said. "I'm not in the habit of wasting money."

Dot smirked. All the guy did was waste money on ego-driven publicity stunts. And now he was trying to get involved in politics, too. The party had too many of these rich people mucking things up.

Kitty suggested they move to their table, her face frozen in an icy smile. Rose picked up the conversation and asked the Vales about their trip from California and told them about the local weather forecast. Safe topics.

Fletcher held back and tapped Dot on the shoulder. "Are you okay? That guy's a jerk."

"I'll tell you the whole story tomorrow. Looking back, it's silly. But basically, he's the reason I decided to leave the PR firm."

"I know his type. They're crawling all over the Bay Area. They think they're so tough, but they're just insecure asses."

She laughed. "Well, thanks for sticking up for me. You didn't have to do that."

"It was easy. Because it's true. You're the best at this, by far." He looked at her tenderly.

And all of a sudden, she saw Fletcher again for the first time. This gorgeous lanky boy with the cheerful nature, full of ambition and wit. And now, as she'd witnessed, a total gentleman. She loved a man who stuck up for others. For a moment, Dot wondered if she'd been too quick to dismiss the idea of her and Fletcher. She even imagined she could forget all about the bee incident. Could chivalry erase an ick? It felt possible in the moment. Maybe Fletcher was someone she should consider giving a second chance.

But before she could think about that more, Fletcher was pulling out her seat for her and she sat down. Stanford Michael and his wife were at the other end of the table. She locked eyes with Rose, silently thanking her for the quick thinking on the seating arrangement.

"So, what is everyone in the mood for?" Kitty said, hiding her face behind the menu. Dot could only imagine what she was thinking—but it was probably that her Georgetown parties were much better than this.

ON THE MORNING of Senator Lopez's visit to Cedar Falls, Mary heard Dot leave the house before dawn. She reached for her phone and texted her friend, "Good luck!"

"Thanks—it's make or break," Dot replied.

Mary felt the same way about the Taylor farm's fight against the government. She was due at Duncan's Doughnuts that morning to meet Mr. Taylor, so she rose early and re-read everything she thought she'd discovered after Patricia had sent the email from New York. Remembering her first call with Patricia, she kept repeating to herself, "Follow the money."

She triple-checked her work and decided the lead was solid. In fact, the law firm in D.C. hadn't registered under the Foreign Agents Registration Act. That was more than a technicality. That was fraud.

She suited up in a long flowered dress patterned in orange poppies, a dark blue denim jacket, and ankle boots she'd recently bought at Vintage Vibes off Main Street. Joe Taylor was walking into the diner when she arrived, and he held the door for her.

"You're as pretty as a picture this morning, Mary," he said. She wore the compliment well and flashed him a smile.

They took a booth and ordered coffee, water, and doughnuts. Mary jumped right in.

She pulled a manila folder out of her suede tote and laid out several pages for Mr. Taylor. She'd highlighted the names of the law firms and noted the discrepancies.

"As far as I can see, based on the documents you've shown me, this D.C.-based firm pops up only in this filing. But if you look over here"—she pointed to another page—"they represent several Chinese companies. And one of those companies has listed Cedar Falls as one of its main targets for land acquisition."

"And you think the dots are connected?" he asked.

"I think it would be a heck of a coincidence if they weren't. And if they are, you have a good shot of backing them off of your property." She sat back, satisfied that she'd made a good case.

"By gosh, Mary, this might be it. I don't know what we'd have done without you."

"Well, let's not count any chickens before they hatch."

"Wow, Jake's been teaching you some farming lingo," Joe teased.

"Our cultures have collided. Why don't you take this back to your lawyers, and we'll see how it goes?"

"I've got a hopeful feeling about this, Mary. More than I've had in a long time."

"Me too," she said.

They stuck around for one more cup of coffee before they headed back to the apple festival. It was going to be a big day.

MEANWHILE, OVER AT the festival, politics entered the chat. The town was practically buzzing in anticipation of the Democratic campaign rally. By midafternoon, the air was thick with the scent of bright red candy apples, fresh and squeaky cheese curds, and the earthy richness of roasted corn. Folks washed it all down with mulled cider, local craft beers, and apple-infused water for those determined to stay hydrated. Everyone seemed to be in a good mood—the sugar highs from the apple treats were hitting at just the right time.

Dot bounced lightly on her toes, unable to stand still. Lucy Lopez was due to arrive any minute, and Dot assessed the crowd at the fairgrounds arena with Rose and Fletcher. For the Win had done all they could to help the Lopez advance team set up the visit. The stage was decorated with hay bales, giant pumpkins, and huge baskets overflowing with apples. It had a midwestern, homey vibe, which was the perfect setting for their candidate. They'd expected her vice-presidential pick to join her—but at the last minute, the Lopez-Stone campaign decided to split the ticket up and had sent Stone to Nevada to rally with the gaming union.

"At least it's not for another event in Texas. Nevada is at least another purple state," Dot said upon learning the news. "I'd say it's worth a gamble."

"Clever girl," Rose said as she appreciated the corny joke. "Now get moving." They'd worked hard to make sure the turnout was impressive. They needed the visuals for the press and for their own social media push.

"Not bad," Fletcher said, taking a video of the crowd. "Room is full. How does it compare to previous rallies, Rose?"

"I'd say this is a great turnout. The venue can hold about three thousand people, and we've got standing room only. And there's still a line outside."

"I'll go make sure we've got all of them signed up in the voting list," he said, working his way out to where the volunteers were set with iPads to capture everyone's contact info. They'd use that to confirm that their contacts had voted. Then they'd send all that to the campaign and the DNC so that they could get a rough count of how things were likely to go, even before the polls closed on Election Day.

"Hey, Rose—look over there. I think that's that young woman I met when we were last here. She had a baby with her that day," Dot said.

"You've got a good memory. You may have a voter there, Dot."

"She looks like she's by herself. I'll be right back. I'm going to chat with her."

"I'll stay put. I don't want to give up my spot." Rose had made sure to stake a location offstage where they could see both the candidate and the crowd's reaction.

Dot approached the young woman. "Hi. We met before. You're the one with the cute baby."

"Wow, you remember that? I'm impressed," she said.

"I'm Dot Clark, by the way."

"Emery Brewer." They shook hands.

"Where's your son today?" Dot asked.

"My mom has him. I told her I wanted to come check this out. You were right—I really like Senator Lopez. She seems very real."

"She is."

"I like what she has to say about the economy. It's not easy being a single mom—the cost of everything is so high, especially day care. I have my mom to help, but she's still working, too. She cleans rooms at one of the hotels near Milwaukee."

"Well, you're not alone. The cost of living is high on everyone's minds—all of our polls show that. You'll hear her talk about that today," Dot said. "And she has a proposal to keep day cares safe but to let up on some of the regulations that have pushed providers out of the business. She wants that done within her first one hundred days. If she wins."

"I hope she wins," Emery said. "I feel like the only way I can make my life work is if there are two of me."

Dot felt her phone buzz. She reached into her back pocket for it. There was a text from Sen. Lopez.

"Hi. Pulling up soon. Meet me for a chat right before I go on? I'd love a briefing on the crowd."

Dot shot back, "Will be there." Then to Emery, she said, "Can I give you my number in case you need anything?"

"Sure. And could I get a picture with you?" Emery asked.

"With me?" Dot was surprised.

"Yes, with you." Emery took a selfie of them. "I'll send it to you."

"Thanks!"

"And Dot? Please let Senator Lopez know we're counting on her."

"You bet. I will." Dot waved goodbye and felt a swell of pride and of nerves. The stakes were so high in this election, and now she had to pull herself together to brief the candidate.

SENATOR LOPEZ HAD the crowd on their feet for forty minutes. She nailed her stump speech, and had the crowd laughing, crying, and then laughing again.

"Laugh, cry, laugh—the perfect formula," Dot said to Fletcher on the sidelines with Rose where they cheered along with the rally-goers.

At the end of her speech, Lopez worked the rope line, and Dot asked a volunteer to bring Emery to the end of it. She watched Emery's surprise at being spoken to at all, and then she made eye contact with Dot and understood what was happening. Dot met her in the line.

"Senator Lopez, this is Emery. She's a single mom, and this is her first-ever rally. You've really inspired her."

"Emery, what a beautiful name," Lopez said, fully focusing on the young woman as if she didn't have one thousand other things on her mind. "Thanks for coming. Can I count on your vote?"

"Yes, ma'am. And my mom's, too."

Lopez reached for Emery's hands and lifted them high. "Let's do this!" She was the kind of candidate that got more energized with a rally, rather than fatigued from the effort. Her energy was contagious.

Turning to Dot, Lopez said, "Great job. Thank you. Are you happy with the turnout?"

"Absolutely. We'll pull some clips for social, and the local media will be strong. The president's team isn't coming back before Election Day, so we may edge them out here in this county," Dot said. "We're banking a lot of early votes."

"That's good to hear. We have to win Wisconsin. I don't see another path without it." Lopez kept smiling and waving as she and Dot talked. "Ride with me to the airport?"

Dot was thrilled to be asked. "I'd be honored." She took one last look around the venue and felt a jolt of excitement and purpose. And then she stopped in her tracks.

At the back of the room was Danny Dawson. He was standing there with his tan Carhartt jacket and baseball cap, watching her intently. Their eyes met, and the impact tore through her—the world came roaring back to life in color and sound.

Her heart wanted her feet to run to him, but duty rooted her in place. Lopez's security detail was trying to usher her out, and Dot had to follow her. She kept Danny's gaze and put a hand to her heart. She knew that he'd come for her, not for the Democrats' election rally.

Dot hadn't seen Danny or returned any of his messages since she saw him with that other woman at Cocoa and Cabernet nearly a month before, though she'd missed him so much. Her stubbornness wasn't charming—it was pulling her under. And seeing Danny, his dark, sad eyes penetrating her thoughts, crushed her. Her heart had regrown a protective barrier as her brain kept reminding her that soon she'd be back in Manhattan. What was the point of trying to repair her relationship with Danny when she'd just have to say goodbye in a few weeks? Wasn't it better for both if they just cut their losses now?

Knowing she had to get into the limo with Lopez, she took a deep breath, pulled her eyes from his, and scurried to the awaiting motorcade.

In the car, Dot and Lopez relived some of the highlights from the rally.

"The crowd was great, Dot. Think we'll get them to the ballot box?"

"I think we've got a chance, yes." Dot was all business, sharp and alert despite seeing Danny at the rally. "We'll know a lot more in a week. We have a great tracking system for early voting. That way we can focus on the ones who wait to vote until Election Day. The numbers here are pretty good. But don't worry—we're not taking anything for granted."

"That's a good motto to live by no matter what," Lopez said. "When it comes to women in politics, well, my experience is that we have to work harder. You can't rest for even a moment."

"You seem to have endless energy. What's your secret?" Dot asked lightly, though she actually was curious.

Lopez looked out the window and waved to some folks walking to their cars, having had their fill of the fair. "Remember when you asked me if I'd ever been in love."

Dot nodded. "I hope that wasn't too personal."

"Not at all." She turned her gaze back to Dot. "As I said then, I did want to marry. In fact, I'm open to it even now. But one thing I've learned is that you shouldn't measure yourself against anyone else's choices. I've been thinking about you."

Dot couldn't believe that Lopez had time to think about her.

"If your dream is to go back to New York, Dot, then do that. But think about whether that's just the safe choice. All of us need to be willing to take risks. Don't scurry back to Manhattan if there might be a great chance for you to work in Washington. Follow the option that makes your heart beat a little faster."

Dot took that in. "You make me feel like maybe I could do it, too. Meaning follow my passion and that everything will work out."

"Not maybe. You can."

"How can I thank you?" Dot asked, grateful to have been given such specific guidance for her next steps.

"All I ask is that one day you pass it on to the next generation," Lopez said, gathering her things to exit the vehicle as they pulled up to the private plane waiting to take her to Detroit for another campaign stop. "Keep the mentoring chain going."

They got out of the car and Lopez gave Dot a quick hug before turning and bounding up the steps to the awaiting jet. Dot stood on the tarmac and watched Lopez ascend the stairs. Before going inside, she turned back to wave at Dot. "See you soon. Let's win this!"

Dot gave her a thumbs-up. When the plane's doors closed, her mind was ping-ponging with thoughts of what her options were after the campaign. Maybe she should more seriously consider going to Washington. What was the worst that could happen?

But try as she might to focus on her career and keep her head in the election game, Dot was distracted. She kept replaying one part of the rally over and over. It was nothing Lopez had said in her speech.

It was when she'd spotted Danny watching her, his eyes on her every move.

Chapter 72

Suddenly, it was the week before Election Day.

"Hi, Mr. Russo!" Dot and Harper got behind Mary to wave hello into her phone. Tony Russo had called to check on his daughter. He was anxious for her return to New York.

"There's my girls," he said. "Hey, I just sent some money to Mary for you to buy some Halloween candy for those kids. Don't get any of those small ones. Go full-size. Give them what they really want."

"That's so nice of you, Mr. Russo. I'm not sure their parents will love us for it, but it'll make for a fun night," Dot said.

"I'll go with Mary to make sure we get the best kind!" Harper said.

Mary blew a kiss to her dad and ended the call.

"Let's make a list of what we want," Dot said.

"Why do you always need a list?" Mary was more of a wing-it kind of shopper.

"You'll thank me one day for the habit." She opened her notes app and asked, "What's your favorite candy? I think we should go old-school and get Snickers for sure."

"What about Milky Way?" Harper asked.

"I hate Milky Way," Mary said.

"Three Musketeers?"

"Oh wait, that's the one I hate." Mary couldn't stand the nougat.

"Anything Reese's is good," Dot said.

"Can't argue with that." Mary agreed.

"Twix?" Harper suggested.

"Definitely." Dot liked those. "Candy corn?"

"The worst!" Harper said.

"Raisins?" Dot tried one more.

"You want our house to get egged?" Harper said.

"Okay, okay. Just make sure to get some Starbursts for me. I may need them on election night."

"You got it." Mary and Harper headed to the Jeep.

"I'll keep Pippi here," Dot said, following them out. "I could use the company."

"Need anything else?" Mary asked.

"Don't forget your broom and cauldron," Dot said to Mary.

"That's what my brother Frankie always tells his mother-in-law," she said. "She laughs, but I'm not sure he's joking. Okay, put it on the list."

"Oh, now you need a list?" Dot teased.

"Ha! Just text it to us. We're going to run before Target closes." Mary got up behind the wheel.

"Don't buy any extras," Dot warned. They already had so much to pack after the election.

"Wouldn't dream of it." Harper hopped in the Jeep and closed the door.

DARKNESS CAME EARLY the last day of October. The temperatures plummeted when the sun went down, and parents braced themselves for fights about coats covering costumes. Those were battles they'd likely lose, with the kids fueled on adrenaline and their moms and dads bracing themselves for the sugar highs and lows to come over the next week.

The entire town of Cedar Falls had caught Halloween fever. Every house and business had joined in, with the streets filled with a carnival of pumpkins, witches, ghosts, and twinkling orange lights. Some ambitious families transformed their homes into mini haunted houses with tombstones poking out of their tidy lawns, and jack-o'-lanterns lit with candles on the steps of their front porches. On Main Street, the chamber of commerce led a contest to see who could make the best display, turning the tiny downtown into an enchanting Halloween village. There was a charming chaos to the decorations, which put even the most cantankerous and grumpy residents in a good mood as they prepared for the town's children to run from house to house to load up on their loot.

That day, Dot knocked on doors with campaign volunteers up until the last possible second before it got dark and the last thing voters wanted was a political canvasser rather than trick-or-treaters. She was going to take a couple of hours to pass out candy with Mary and Harper and then go back to the office and keep the team going on early voting with just days to go till the election.

The Crew was going to dress up and then hand out their full-size candy bars, courtesy of Mr. Russo. After tonight, there would be no time at home until election night the following week. Just seven more days to go. She touched her bracelet to remember to breathe.

FINALLY, IT WAS time for The Crew's costume reveal.

"Are you almost ready?" Harper called upstairs.

"Almost!" Mary called.

"Coming!" Dot said.

A few moments later, Dot and Mary nearly collided at the top of the stairs.

"Oh my gosh, you look *amazing*!" Dot said.

"And you're adorable," Mary said.

"Let me see!" Harper said.

They came down the stairs and started laughing.

"This is incredible!" Dot said.

Ever since Maddy had told her to click her heels three times to go back to New York, Dot had wanted them to dress up as characters from *The Wizard of* Oz. Mary was into it but insisted they had to be *sexy Wizard of* Oz costumes.

"Fine," Dot said, up to the challenge. And she'd risen to the occasion.

Dot was Dorothy, wearing a tiny blue-and-white-checkered miniskirt and matching crop top. She had on white netted stockings and red sequined platform shoes. Her hair was in curls and she'd put on a perfect Taylor Swift–red lip to finish the look. She twirled around while Harper took a video for social.

Mary took Harper's phone and recorded her sexy Scarecrow. She'd found a denim minidress and a checkered bustier, plus thigh-high boots, a floppy hat, and two big red circles on her cheeks. Pippi had a little sign around her neck that said, "Toto," and she was wearing a Kansas City Chiefs dog sweater. "It was all I could find," Harper said.

It was Dot's turn with the camera, and Mary didn't disappoint. The Wicked Witch was *very* bad, with a tiny, skintight dress that stopped just at the tops of her thighs. Then a sheer black skirt hung from the back, and her cleavage was . . . noticeable. She held on to a black broom, just in case people couldn't figure out who she was meant to be.

"Are we going to give these kids nightmares?" Dot asked.

"Nah," Mary said.

"But we might make their dads faint," Harper warned.

They gathered to take a selfie, and Dot posted it to her story. Her caption read, "Trick or treat, *Wicked* style." A second later it had already racked up a hundred views.

"Well done," Mary said, giving Dot a high five.

They passed out candy and had a wonderful time chatting with the kids in their costumes. Dot gave extra to the ones who'd made an effort with their costumes. She especially liked the political ones—twins dressed as red and blue waves, a cow covered in "VOTE" stickers, and a guy named "Bill" wrapped in white and with a replica of the Capitol on his head.

Dot pointed at that one and laughed. "Well done, Bill!" she called. Bill took a bow.

"Do you know him?" Harper asked.

"Oh no. That's just Bill—sitting on Capitol Hill. My dad used to play these really old cartoons he grew up with for my sister and me. Bill was 'introduced' in Congress but couldn't get a vote. It's how I learned how a bill becomes a law."

"Heck, I need to watch that now," Harper said.

Dot checked her phone and saw the time. "Yikes. What's happened to me? I need to focus. We have a race to win."

"I think you're going to win," Mary said.

"Me too," Harper said.

Dot appreciated their optimism, but she wasn't so sure. The race was neck and neck.

As the night wound down, fewer kids were coming by, the temperature was dropping, and the parents were ushering their children home. They still had school in the morning.

As they were about to close the door, Mary saw Tommy's truck on the other side of their street. Tommy rolled down the window and whistled.

"Hi, there—trick or treat, ladies?" he asked.

"What do you think?" Harper said.

Tommy and Jake got out of the driver's and passenger seats. And then the back door opened, and Danny stepped out.

"Definitely a trick," Mary stage-whispered to Harper.

Dot's heart caught in her throat. Danny, rugged, fit, and unforgettably handsome, but it was his wounded eyes that drew her right back in. She'd missed him so much but had tried to avoid thinking about him. She didn't think there was a point since she was going back to New York, and even though he'd shown up at the Lopez rally, she still had never responded to his text messages. She felt terrible about that. And now she felt embarrassed.

Jake walked up to the porch first. "Is it okay that he came, too, Dot?" He cocked his head back toward Danny.

"Oh, sure. Of course." Dot shot a look at Mary, knowing she probably had something to do with this little visit.

"Let's go inside, it's freezing out here," Mary said, Jake's hand on the small of her back. Tommy and Harper followed them in, taking Pippi with them.

And then Dot and Danny were outside together, alone for the first time in weeks, and face-to-face.

"Hi," he said.

"Hi." She made eye contact but nearly melted when she saw the sadness there in his big dark eyes.

"You look . . ." He didn't finish his sentence.

"Ridiculous, I know," Dot said, suddenly a bit embarrassed by her costume.

"I was actually going to say that you look more beautiful than ever."

"I've been meaning to write you back," Dot said in a rush.

"The silence has been deafening."

"I'm sorry. It was wrong. It's just that night—after being confronted by Maddy and . . ."

He interrupted. "By Maddy? Maddy Becker? What in the hell did she say to you?"

"She said that if I wasn't serious about staying in Cedar Falls that I shouldn't lead you on and possibly break your heart again."

"She had no business doing that," he said, an edge to his voice.

"I think she was just looking out for you, now that I've had time to think about it."

"I'm tired of everyone trying to look out for me. I can look out for myself," he said.

"I hear you. Loud and clear." Dot felt a little better knowing he felt that way about Maddy. "She's a bit . . ."

"Extra?"

That made Dot laugh. "Yes. She's extra."

"Now don't get mad at Mary and Jake, but they told me you think I was dating another woman? What gave you that idea?" he asked.

"It was the same night, right after Maddy and her friends had run into me at the Couture Closet. I started walking up Main and I saw you with a beautiful girl. At Cocoa and Cabernet. And since we'd not talked about being exclusive, I assumed I didn't have a right to be angry. So, I . . . I froze."

"Wait. Cocoa and Cabernet? Oh my gosh, Dot. Oh, Dot." Danny shook his head and covered his eyes.

"What?"

"That was Sadie's sister. We get together every year for a dinner on Sadie's birthday. She's just a good friend. We have leaned on each other ever since . . . ever since . . ."

"Ever since she died," Dot said gently, her foolishness becoming clear to her.

"Oh, Dot. I've missed you so much. And . . . . I was falling in love with you. I should have told you that. I should have demanded you listen to me. But I thought maybe you'd decided just to end things and go back to New York. I just couldn't let you go without setting the record straight. And without saying goodbye."

"Danny. I am so sorry." She was looking at her shoes, desperately sad she'd wasted her last month in Cedar Falls without him. Then suddenly she snapped her eyes up to meet his.

"Wait. Did you say you were falling in love? With me?" she asked, both hands over her heart.

"Yes. Yes, Dot. But I wasn't just falling in love with you. This time away from you has made me realize that I love you. Fully. And there. Now I've said it. I love you."

"Danny, I . . . I love you, too." She took a step forward and then she was right where she was meant to be—in his arms, kissing him, and trying to get as close as possible.

After several moments, Dot felt eyes on her. She turned to the window and saw half of Oz looking at them from behind the curtains.

"We're being watched," he said.

"Let them," she said, thinking of how apt that advice was now that she realized that the townies, and even her own stubbornness, almost kept her from knowing that Danny Dawson was in love with her.

He pulled Dot in close and rested his chin on top of her head.

"What are we going to do now?" he asked.

Dot touched her bracelet and breathed deeply.

"Can you hold that question until after election night? I have to see this through—I made a commitment to For the Win and to Senator Lopez—and it's almost over. And then we can talk?"

"That's a week from now," he said.

"Yes. Seven days. But who's counting?" she asked.

"I'll be counting."

"Me too," she admitted. "Me too."

Chapter 73

"Well, guys, we did all we could," Dot said to Fletcher and Rose at five in the morning on Election Day. Senator Lopez was in Milwaukee that morning, trying to drive up the Democratic vote totals in their biggest precincts. Governor Stone was in Detroit, then he'd hit Philadelphia before meeting back with Lopez in Atlanta, where they'd watch the returns together.

The Cedar Falls For the Win team all wore royal-blue cotton sweaters with red trim and white "FTW" lettering. Kitty Bell had made them for her team and all the volunteers of the office.

"We left it all on the field," Fletcher said. "That's a football reference, Dot."

"Oh, really? I thought it was some farming term I'd yet to encounter." She playfully punched him on the arm.

"I'm so glad you two were here this cycle. You made it fun, and your ideas helped make this race as close as it is. It's been an honor," Rose said, wiping a tear from her eye.

"Hey, don't cry yet, we can still win this thing!" Fletcher said, handing Rose a coffee.

"Oh, I think we could win. I'll just miss you," she said. "I'll be lonely without you."

"We'll stay in touch, Rose. Besides, I can't wait to have you on my new podcast. Gotta have my best girl on to explain to people how politics really works." Fletcher flattered Rose but meant what he said. He'd been all set to move to New York and had even come up with a name for his new podcast: *Left Unsupervised*. The plan was for it to air right after Thanksgiving, and he had major funding to help build an audience. He described his podcast as smart politics disguised with humor.

But plans had changed. While Dot had been offered the job with the American Progress PAC in D.C., she'd turned it down and instead recommended Fletcher for the role. She suggested they could get him to take the job if they let him do the podcast in addition to running communications. They ended up loving the idea, so instead of moving to New York City where Dot planned to be, Fletcher switched gears and had rented an English basement apartment on Capitol Hill. Dot admired his flexibility—but she knew that D.C. wasn't for her. She was a creature of New York.

And whether either of them would split the 20 percent of Kitty's win bonus remained up in the air. At this point, Dot thought she'd need it as a bridge since she didn't have a job to go back to in the city. But she wasn't counting on it. First, they had to win.

"Are you sure a seventy-something gray-haired grandma is what you really need?" Rose laughed off the idea.

"I'm positive," he said. "And Dot, you'll be a frequent guest, too."

Pretending to be a carnival barker, Dot said, "*Left Unsupervised*—the best podcast you'll ever hear. Give it a like, give it a share! I promise I won't miss an episode." She raised her coffee to offer a toast. "Here's to us. No matter what happens today, we'll always have each other."

Their favorite mixed set of ceramic cups met, and they each took a sip.

"Shall we get to work?" Rose said.

"Let's do it," Fletcher said.

Dot led the way; it was time to make sure their get-out-the-vote plan was executed perfectly.

"Let's take a pic for Kitty." Fletcher whistled and got everyone gathered outside of the war room. They lined up with the tallest in back.

"I've been in front my entire life," Rose joked.

There was a mirror in front of them. Fletcher held up his phone and took several shots from different angles, proving his Gen Z photographer status.

"You'll make someone a good Instagram boyfriend one day, Fletch," Dot said.

"I aim to please. I just texted you a bunch. Want to send one to Kitty and then we can post it on social? Polls open in thirty minutes. I have to monitor turnout numbers for the northern precincts."

"You bet." Dot started to scroll through the photos, looking for the best one.

Then it hit her. "Oh my gosh!"

"What's wrong?" Fletcher raced back.

"We can't post any of these," she said.

"Why? Who has their eyes closed? Rose!"

"It's not that." She handed him the phone. "What do you see?"

"I see all of us in our blue sweatshirts before dawn on Election Day."

"Nothing else?"

"No. What am I missing?"

"Fletch, look closer. When we're standing in front of the mirror, the sweaters don't have the initials for 'For the Win'—the reflection turns it around. So they say, 'WTF' as in . . ."

"Oh my gosh. Holy crap, Dot," he said, covering his mouth and laughing. "Thank goodness you caught that. We'd have never heard the end of it."

"Can you imagine? We'd be the laughingstock of the campaign trail." She was doubled over laughing. "What do you say I just delete these?"

"Well. Delete all but one. We may need it for comic relief in the future."

"Or blackmail." She winked at him and they started laughing all over again.

MEANWHILE, JOE TAYLOR called Mary and asked if she could meet up with him and Grace at Flour Power that morning.

"I have something to share with you. And I want to do it in person. Do you mind coming over around ten?"

"I'll be there." She set an alarm to make sure she left the house fifteen minutes before ten so that she wouldn't be late. She hoped Mr. Taylor didn't have bad news about the farm.

At Flour Power, Mary waved to Mimi and got in line behind the Taylors.

"Oh, there you are! What can we get you?"

"Cappuccino would be great," she said.

"What, no pumpkin spice for you? I thought all the young women liked that stuff."

"Not me, sir. Hard pass. Just give me an old-fashioned cappuccino, and I'm happy."

Joe ordered their drinks while Mary and Grace took over one of the bistro tables near the bakery's window. When Joe arrived and passed out the coffees, Mary dispensed with the small talk.

"Mr. Taylor, the suspense is killing me. What did you find out?" she asked.

"Well, Mary, I wanted to be able to look you in the eye when I told you how much Grace and I have appreciated your help in this matter. The farm means the world to us, and to our boys."

"Yes, I know. I admire that about you. You're determined to keep the family farm in your hands. Is it going to work?"

Grace reached over and placed her hand on top of one of Mary's, and Joe did the same to her other one. They squeezed.

"Mary," Joe said, "it worked. The government is backing off. The Agriculture Secretary, the guy I've known for years, said he heard about the law firm that didn't register even though they're working for Chinese companies. The feds have decided to walk away and try to find another site. They know the bad publicity to come from this would hurt the president and the governor and scare off the investors. So, as of now, it's over. And the farm remains in *our* hands."

"Oh, this is amazing!" Mary jumped up and hugged them both. "I'm so happy for you!"

Just then, the door to Flour Power opened and Jake and Tommy walked in.

"Hey, Dad, Mom, Mary. What's this all about?" Tommy asked. "We came as soon as we could."

"Sit down, boys. I've got good news to share." They were one seat short, so Mary gestured that she'd perch on Jake's lap while his dad repeated his story.

"And we've got Mary to thank," he said. "Grace, do you have the gift?"

"Right here," she said, handing Mary a large bag decorated in black and white, resembling one of their dairy cows.

"Oh, I didn't do anything," Mary said. "I just found a thread to pull." She gratefully accepted the gift bag.

"You were the key," Joe said. "We think you're brilliant. And we're going to throw a party at the Sin Bin for you, Dot, and Harper the night before you leave. Grace and I are handling all the details. Is that okay with you, Tommy?"

"It'll be an honor, yes, sir. I'm so relieved, Dad. Do you think I can build Alotto Gelato now?"

"I think we can talk about it, son." Joe Taylor laughed easily, something they'd all missed these last few months.

"Go on, Mary, let's see your present," Grace said.

Mary opened the card first and read it aloud, as she'd been taught by her Nonna. "Dear Mary, without you, we may have lost the farm. We are so grateful for your generosity in helping us—it took New York to save us here in Cedar Falls. We hope that you'll wear this when you're back in Manhattan and think of us often. Love, the Taylors."

Mary reached into the bag, pulled out a large box, and took off the lid. Wrapped in tissue was a pair of cherry-red Hunter boots.

"Water- and mud-proof?" Mary asked Joe.

"Exactly," he said.

"There's one more thing," Grace said.

At the bottom of the bag was another large tissue-wrapped parcel. Inside was a traditional Hamilton-brown Carhartt barn coat. So very Cedar Falls—so not New York. Still, she was touched.

"That's more appropriate for feeding the chickens than that beautiful black leather coat you wore the first day we met," Grace said.

"I've learned some valuable lessons—about life, as well as farm fashion. I love this so much," Mary said, putting the coat on and flinging off her flats to try on her new boots. "I'm really going to turn heads on Bleeker!"

Joe got his iPhone ready and took her photo as she stood next to Jake, their arms around each other, with Mary nearly clinging to him.

"We thought you could take a bit of the farm with you when you are back in the Big Apple," he said, snapping a pic.

"That's so kind of you. I'm really overwhelmed," she said, the tears spilling over—and they weren't just for the Taylors' kind gesture.

She was crying at the thought of saying goodbye.

But she didn't have a choice.

Did she?

Chapter 74

Election Day marched on.

"I've just realized that I've been wrong about something my entire life," Dot said.

"What's that?" Rose asked while she continued to double-check their targeted voter list.

"The summer solstice isn't the longest day of the year. Election Day is."

The hours dragged.

They were getting little bits of information from the field, but they were cautioned against listening to any of the exit polls.

So far, all the Democratic precincts were hitting their turnout targets. But so were the Republican ones. It was going to be very close.

IN THE MEANTIME, Harper and Pippi went to the Sin Bin to help set up for the watch party that Tommy was hosting that night. Jake stopped by to make sure the security that they'd arranged was up to snuff.

"Just be careful. You know how people can get," Jake said.

"I do," Tommy agreed. "But I think we'll have a good crowd, and I'm going to cut anyone off who gets out of control."

"Does that include Harper?" Jake joked.

"I hope so!" Tommy said. He was putting together a care package for her to take back to New York. All sorts of Cedar Falls mementos. She'd be taking Pippi with her, and he dreaded how sharply he'd miss them both.

AT TEN O'CLOCK that night, the election still wasn't over. A few states were yet to be called, and Wisconsin was one of them.

Dot, Rose, and Fletcher huddled together in the war room. Several TVs were on with the different channels trying to fill time with analysis though they still didn't have a result.

"It's all going to come down to turnout," one talking head said.

"We know!" they yelled in unison.

Dot said she was going to take a break. She went to her desk and noticed her calendar. She'd put a red line through every day that she'd been there since January. The November calendar picture was of Central Park in autumn, The Plaza Hotel in the background. It was almost time for her to cross out Election Day. And then what? Her stomach rolled at the thought. Or maybe that was the two slices of pizza she'd devoured after the Wisconsin polls closed at eight that night.

At 11:45 p.m., everyone was delirious. There were still five states to call. Arizona, Nevada, Michigan, Pennsylvania, and Wisconsin. Lopez won her home state of Georgia, plus the state of North Carolina. And Stone was looking like he could pull off Kentucky. Between those two, the Democrats had some hope that if two of these other states went her way—and barring any upsets they didn't imagine—that she'd win the election and become the first woman president of the United States of America.

Dot felt her phone vibrate. It was a text from Danny.

"I've been counting down these last few days," he said.

"Hi. Me too."

"How are you holding up?"

"I'm okay. Running on adrenaline and caffeine at this point."

"Have a moment for some fresh air? I'm outside."

"You are?" Dot mimed a gesture to Rose and Fletcher that she had to take a call outside. She texted, "I'm coming," and then pretended to put the phone to her ear.

She grabbed her coat from her chair on the way out. Danny's truck was across the street from the Democratic offices. A light snow had started to fall. He was standing outside, leaning against the driver's door. And he was gorgeous.

She ran over to him, and he picked her up, kissing her.

"I couldn't wait to see you," he said.

"I'm so glad."

"This has been a long seven days."

"Tell me about it," Dot said. "I've been torn in two wanting this to be over but mostly just thinking of you."

He pulled her into his chest, and she smelled his familiar scent of soap and shaving cream.

"When do you think it'll be over?" he asked.

"I'm not sure. It's very close. Could be a while yet. This could end up with an automatic recount," she said, wishing she had a better answer.

"I'll wait," Danny said.

"Here? It could be hours."

"That's fine. I'm not leaving without you."

Dot thought it over. And then she felt an impulse that fully clarified her mind.

"No. Don't wait. I mean. Wait. Wait right here for just a moment," Dot said. She took a step back and then dashed back across the street, snowflakes starting to melt in her hair.

Inside, she went to her desk and wrote Rose and Fletcher notes.

"I had to go. Please understand. I love you!" She signed with just a dot. They'd know who it was from. She placed the notes on their keyboards.

There was just one thing left for her to do.

Then she returned to her desk and picked up her red Sharpie.

Taking off the cap, she leaned over her desk and put a red line through Election Day. For her, the campaign was over.

DANNY PULLED INTO his drive, and he and Dot scrambled out of the car. The snow was falling more heavily by then and had already fully blanketed the ground.

They practically flew up his steps, hearts pounding. As soon as Danny got his key in the lock, he swung the door open and Dot's lips were on his, insistent and charged. His hands pressed firmly against her back, pulling her impossibly close. They barely paused to shed their coats, fingers tangling in each other's hair, lips retracing the well-worn paths they'd missed. Every brush of skin, every sigh, stretched the moment with powerful tension, the outside world fading away.

Yet, remembering what was happening across America that night and how important it was to Dot, Danny used one hand to search around for his television remote.

Opening one eye, but keeping up with her kiss, he aimed it at the TV and hit the power button.

Dot grabbed it and said, "No."

"Don't you want to see if they made any more race calls?" Danny asked.

"No." At this point, she didn't want another moment of politics. She wanted Danny.

"But you worked so hard . . ." he said, but was interrupted by Dot, who leaned forward and pressed her lips to his again. This time, she let her hands trace up his chest, tugging hm closer. Her kiss was insistent but playful, a little challenge. He responded in kind, hands tightening around her waist.

"We'll know when we know."

Danny closed his eyes. "So, if I have this right," he said, running feathery kisses down her neck, "I have you here and the politics is out there. This is like all my dreams coming true in one night."

"I accept the challenge," she said, laughing, then took his hand and started toward the staircase that led to his bedroom.

On the second step, Dot noticed that he glanced at the mantel and at the framed photograph of Sadie.

"Maybe I should put that away," Danny said, moving toward the picture.

Dot reached out her hand to stop him and said, "No." Then she maneuvered to be a step higher than he was. Now they could see each other eye to eye.

"Danny, listen. I know Sadie was an incredibly important part of your life. You don't have to hide her from me. I love you. *All* of you. For everything that's ahead and everything in the past."

He blinked rapidly to fight the tears that threatened to spill over. He pulled her closer to him. She rested her cheek just below his collarbone. Closing his eyes and breathing deeply into her hair, he said quietly, "Thank you. I love you, Dot."

"I love you, too."

She started to unbutton his shirt. "Let's see if we can make it up the stairs before I . . ."

They didn't make it up the stairs.

Chapter 75

"This has been a dream come true," Dot said to Mary and Harper as they finished a light bite of bagels and coffee on New Year's Day at Blackstone in the West Village in Manhattan.

"I can't believe we pulled it off. New Year's Eve in the city with our guys from Wisconsin?" Harper said.

"Wonder if they're freaking out about the prices," Mary said, watching Jake, Tommy, and Danny ordering for them at the register.

"They've been really good sports," Dot said. She'd planned the trip after Election Night—three days in Manhattan over New Year's Eve with Danny, Jake, and Tommy.

"We showed them a good time," Harper said.

"They'll never be the same." Mary winked at Jake as he looked back to check on her.

"How are you feeling about taking Jake to Sunday supper before his flight back to Milwaukee tonight?" Dot asked Mary.

"Ready as I'll ever be," she said. "I have a feeling everyone's going to love him more than me. He'll be the family favorite."

"Your Nonna is going to make him sit next to her," Harper said.

"I imagine she'll be pushing him to move to New York." Mary knew Jake was up for the challenge of running her family gauntlet. She just wasn't sure if she was.

"Tell me about it," Harper said. "I know my brother is going to hit it off with Tommy at brunch today. He's shocked that I'd date anyone who wasn't a hardcore lefty. I can just hear him gloating from across town."

"Danny was a hit at Christmas dinner in Providence," Dot said. "My mom and dad told me after that he seemed like an all-American boy with great manners. That's high praise, coming from them. And my sister said,

'He's the brother I always wanted.' They talked about sports most of the time. To be honest, I was happy to just sit and listen."

For Danny, visiting Rhode Island at Christmas was the first time he'd not been at the Taylor farm in many years. Dot wasn't surprised when Danny fit right into her family flow.

Over the visit, the Clarks mostly steered clear of politics, except to talk up Dot's work on the campaign and how much she got out of her Wisconsin adventure, both personally and professionally. When they'd left to travel south to Manhattan, her parents and Anne had gone to the train station to see them off and waved from the platform.

"You made quite an impression on them," Dot told him.

"It feels good to have them in my corner. And you next to me," he'd said as they held hands, sipped the Starbucks they'd purchased for the trip, and watched the New England coastline fly by.

For New Year's Eve, the six of them had gone to a special dinner and dance party at the Summit One building near Grand Central Station. They'd stayed out until after two in the morning, then all went back to The Standard, where they were staying. They'd really splashed out on the three-day trip, agreeing that it was worth the money to show them New York to repay them for the good times they'd had in Wisconsin.

The guys brought the coffees and bagels back to the table. They were short a chair, so Mary got up and then sat on Jake's lap to make room for him.

Danny made a toast. "To The Crew!"

"I'll drink to that," Harper said, grateful she'd had plenty of water the night before and hadn't taken an allergy pill. She had learned her lesson about drinking on Zyrtec during the Wisconsin tornado night fiasco. With everyone gathered, she decided now was the time to tell them about her plans.

"I have some news." Harper reached for Tommy's hand. Dot's eyebrows shot up in anticipation.

"Go on," Mary said, eager to hear it.

"Well, you gave me that little push of encouragement, and so I applied to a master's program in creative writing. And I just found out that I've been accepted. But here's the best part, it comes with *full* funding."

"Harper, that's amazing!" Dot said, grabbing her friend's hand. "Where is it?"

Harper smiled. "Well, you might be surprised. It's not here in New

York. It's in Iowa. My great Midwest adventure continues. It's about a four-hour drive from Cedar Falls."

"Four and a *half,*" Tommy said. "So it won't be that hard for me to drive across to see Pippi." He put an arm around Harper to show her he was joking and reached into the tote bag to pet Pippi, who was snuggled next to Harper's side. Harper leaned into him, glowing with a newfound self-assurance and contentedness.

"And the idea is that when I complete the workshop, the book should be done. Then I can try to find an agent who would be willing to take me on as one of their authors."

"Wow. Harper! That's incredible. I'm so proud of you!" Dot said, getting up to hug her.

"Me too! This has been an incredible year for you." Mary reached across the table and squeezed Harper's forearm, amazed at the transformation of Harper in just a year. "Kai, who?" she whispered and winked.

"Exactly! It's kind of amazing it's all worked out without any of my worrying or planning."

"What are you going to do until then?" Dot asked.

"A friend of mine from NYU teaches at a pod some parents put together in Brooklyn. She's pregnant and due any minute, so I'm going to take over for her for one semester. Then I'll figure something out for the summer."

"Why not come spend the summer with me? I'll dedicate your corner at the bar and give you unlimited Diet Cokes," Tommy said, and she cocked her head and raised her eyebrows.

"I just might," she said. They'd already talked about that idea, and it was a real possibility.

"Wait. Did you say, 'teaching pods'? I thought that was just some weird thing they did in Texas," Mary said.

"I thought so too, but I've learned it's becoming a lot more common even around here. It's less expensive than paying several tuitions. Instead, they just pay a couple of teachers very well and get better results. Win-win."

"Who knew!" Mary said.

"Well, here's to you, Harper," Dot said. "You're like a cat, landing perfectly on your feet."

The group raised their glasses to cheers.

"Well, we need to get going," Mary said, looking at Jake. "It's time for him to get the full Staten Island treatment."

"Think you can handle it?" Danny asked Jake.

"I'm up for the challenge," Jake said. "I'm prepared to answer every question and eat everything they put in front of me."

"Careful what you wish for!" Dot said. "The first time I went to Sunday supper at Mary's house, I couldn't move for hours."

"We're out of here, too," Harper said, putting on her coat and wrapping a scarf around her neck. "Next stop, Brooklyn. It's time for Tommy to meet the Adlers."

"Wow, Brooklyn," Mary said. "You're brave."

"Don't worry, Tommy," Dot said. "You'll fit in perfectly in the People's Republic of Park Slope."

"And Climate Change Denier got Rangers' tickets for himself, my dad, and Tommy. For once, my dad will be outnumbered politically."

"I'll be on my best behavior," Tommy said. "I need these guys to like me."

"At least you'll crush in the hockey trivia," Jake said.

"How are you getting to Brooklyn?" Dot asked Harper.

"Full New York city experience. All aboard the F train—as in effing slow."

"Yep, I'm bracing myself," Tommy said. "Kind of hope it's like the movies. Give me something to talk about at the Sin Bin."

"Well good luck with that, man." Danny stood and gave Tommy a bro hug with two slaps to his back. Tommy and Jake repeated the custom.

"All right. We should go," Harper said, standing to make herself actually get going. Pippi poked her head out of Harper's tote at the word "go." The little dog had loved all the new smells at Central Park and smugly looked at the bigger dogs who didn't get to go everywhere she did. "We're going to walk her in Prospect Park for a little while before we meet up with my family. My brother is so envious I have a dog. I'm going to make him pay me just to hold her."

"All right, guys. See you soon," Mary said. She, Jake, Tommy, and Harper headed toward Blackstone's front door, bracing themselves for the cold. Jake held the door for them, and Mary was the last in line to leave. Before she stepped out, she turned and said to Danny and Dot, "Love you. And I mean it. See you soon." She kissed her fingertips and blew them a kiss.

And then it was just them.

"So, what should we do now?" Danny asked Dot. And she braced herself for what was next.

Chapter 76

Mary's mother and Nonna had gone all out for Jake's Sunday supper visit.

"You didn't need to do all this," Mary said to her mother, surveying the appetizers. The Christmas decorations were still up, and the sideboard was filled with antipasti—asiago, provolone, and mortadella cheeses, plus olives, roasted peppers, mushrooms, and fried calamari. "You even used the good china? Ma, this is nuts."

"What? Can't I use the good china when my baby is bringing home her friend?" Christine Russo asked. "I can't send him home on an empty stomach."

"You're going to send him home weighing ten more pounds. He'll have to pay for extra baggage at the airport." Mary decided to lighten the mood and be happy her mom had gone to such lengths to make Jake feel welcome.

"Here, dear, I made you a plate. You look like you could use a few good meals," Nonna said to Jake, handing him a dish filled with Italian appetizers. He took it and stood while Nonna got herself settled on the sofa. "Such a gentleman!" She looked at Mary and nodded her approval.

When they'd arrived, Tony and Christine had treated Jake like a long-lost son. They asked about Grace and Joe Taylor and reminisced about their summer visit to the farm. Mary's brothers shook his hand firmly and peppered him with questions about the Packers, being a cop, and how Mary got around in the ice with her high heels.

"Very carefully," he'd said.

Mary's nieces and nephews wanted to show Jake their Christmas presents, and they all spoke at once trying to get his attention. If he felt overwhelmed, he didn't show it. Occasionally, he'd look for Mary, catch her eye, and smile to reassure her he was enjoying himself. She had to admit, he looked like he was doing just fine.

During the main course, Nonna insisted Jake sit next to her, and Christine was on her right. Mary sat across from Jake next to her brother, the priest.

Gabe led the table in saying grace and Jake complimented his prayer. "You know a way to a man's heart," Father Russo said.

"Yeah, through his stomach," Tony said. "Let's eat."

The dinner guests laughed and started dishing out the food.

All eyes were on Jake as he tried every dish they put in front of him. He especially liked the gnocchi, carbonara, and braciole. He asked Nonna for her secret ingredients, and she said, "I've never told anyone this, but it's . . ." whispering her secrets so quietly that no one else could hear her.

Mary's sister-in-law leaned over to Mary and said, "Home run."

"You think?"

"And he's hot!"

Mary smiled and took another bite of sausage and peppers. Yes, he is, she thought. Her foot found his and they linked ankles under the table.

When it was time for Mary to take Jake to the airport, the goodbye took close to an hour. Nonna had prewrapped treats in an insulated bag for him to take home and share with his parents. Mary watched as everyone gave him a hug, including a young niece who clung to his leg and said she was going with him.

"All right, all right. Enough. I'm going to take Jake to the airport," Mary said.

"You're driving?" Her brother Frankie was incredulous. "To the airport? No one does that anymore."

"It's a new tradition," Mary said. "It's kind of our thing." She walked out to her dad's Mercedes.

"Will you come back?" Christine asked Jake as they said goodbye at the front door of the Russo's home.

"If you'll have me," Jake said.

"I'll have you," she said. "You make her so happy. And you make a beautiful couple."

"Hey now, don't pressure him, Christine," Tony said. Turning to Jake, he put out his hand and Jake took it. They shook firmly. "You're a good man."

"You too, sir. And Happy New Year."

"Happy New Year indeed. Now get going. Don't want you to miss your flight." Tony and Christine wrapped their arms around one another, ignoring the cold, and watched them drive away.

"Well . . ." Christine said.

"Yep. I know," he said. "I know."

AS THEY EXITED the Staten Island Expressway, Jake let out the breath he'd been holding. "You are the classic New York driver," he said. "I'd have given you four tickets by now."

"Oh yeah? Hold on then." She stepped on the gas and merged within inches of two cars.

Jake grabbed his stomach with both hands and groaned. "Don't do that. I'm so full. I won't eat for days."

"Told you that you didn't have to eat all of that."

"How could I refuse," he said. "I felt like I was being hazed."

"Well, they loved you," she said.

"They did?" he asked.

"Yes. They love you more than me now."

"Well, I really liked seeing how you were raised. That's a tough house—but a loving one. I had a great time. You have a wonderful family." He reached for her hand, and she gave it to him. They rode the rest of the way in silence, dreading the next step.

An hour later at LaGuardia, Mary parked the car and went into the terminal with Jake.

"Wow. I've never done this before," Mary said.

"What, tried a long-distance relationship?"

"Well, yes, that." She half-smiled at his attempt to lighten the mood. She was rattled about having to say goodbye to him. "But usually I don't even park—I just shove people out while the car's still rolling. I don't like to get yelled at by security."

"I'm grateful to have some last moment with you instead of being tossed out at Departures," Jake said.

She cocked her head and raised one brow, a catch in her throat preventing her from answering. Instead, to fill the silence, he reached for her to put an arm around her. They walked slowly with their legs pressed tightly together, Jake nearly holding her up with one arm while shouldering his backpack and wheeling his overnight bag with the other. She matched his stride until at security, losing her composure, she wrapped her arms around his strong torso and turned her cheek to press against him as strongly as possible. Neither of them needed to say anything—their energy passed back and forth, speaking volumes.

They embraced for a long time.

"It's like in the movies," she said, trying to lighten the mood.

"But better than the movies. Because it's real," he said.

"But how does it end?"

"Maybe it doesn't end," he murmured, his lips hovering just above hers long enough to make her breath catch. Impatient for the kiss, she tugged him closer to her. Then he bent his head to reach her lips "I'll miss you, Mary." His whispered words made her shiver.

She nodded into his chest. "I'll miss you, too."

"But it's just three weeks until I'm back," he said.

"I'll be here," she said. They lingered in a hug for a long couple of minutes before she couldn't take it anymore. "Go. Or I'll chain myself to your carry-on."

Slowly, they disentangled, and Jake walked backward into the security line for a few steps before he turned around. He looked back a few times. When he could no longer see her, he stared straight ahead.

As he cleared the metal detector, he saw a poster that caught his eye.

"NYPD: Fighting crime, protecting the public." A recruiting number displayed prominently. Jake considered it for a moment.

Then he took out his phone and snapped a photo.

Chapter 77

With Mary and Jake and Tommy and Harper off for their family visits, Dot and Danny decided to walk the High Line in the crisp winter air. They grabbed one more piping hot coffee from Edith's, one of The Crew's favorite small cafés.

"I love that place," Dot said, as they headed out for their walk, steam swirling up and out of their to-go cups. "It was started by this woman after she got a divorce. Her ex said she'd never make it. And look at it now—it's super famous."

"Wow, you really know a lot about the local coffee shops," Danny said.

"I do! They have so much character," she said as they climbed the stairs to the High Line. "Especially the independent ones—they have personality . . . like the city itself."

They strolled along the elevated walkway with a few other New Yorkers breathing fresh oxygen into their lungs after ringing in the New Year the night before. Dot pointed out landmarks along the way, like Chelsea Market and the Whitney Museum of American Art.

"This is an amazing use of space," Danny said, checking out the design and admiring the construction.

"Isn't it? For a long time, it was overgrown and unusable. Then they made it into a kind of urban trail and now it's world famous. It's great for locals who want a quick way to get from one place to the next—unless it's overrun with tourists." Dot made a face.

"Hey, I'm a tourist," he said, elbowing her in the ribs.

"True," she said. "Though you're not annoying in any way. And the next time you're here, you'll feel more like a local. Promise me you'll come back here?"

"I will." He sealed that commitment with a kiss, until he realized they were blocking the path.

"Sorry!" Danny called out, waving to the couple who'd had to walk around them. He got a friendly wave in return.

Soon, they reached the end of the line and there was no more stalling. It was time to go. They dropped down to street level and Danny hailed a taxi.

It was going to be so hard to say goodbye.

AS THEIR DRIVER turned left off Central Park West onto Sixty-Seventh, Dot craned her neck to look toward the Buckley.

As always, there he was. Albert Hawkins, her friend and loyal doorman. She couldn't wait for him to meet Danny.

Dot and Danny got out of the taxi and stepped under the Buckley's awning. She hugged Albert fiercely.

"There she is," Albert said. "My little ray of sunshine. I missed you so much, kid."

"I thought of you every day," she said. "I missed you, the park, the coffee shops. The subway. Even the guy with a food cart on Fifty-Eighth who'd shout out a compliment if he liked my outfit." Dot's words tumbled out. She had so much to tell him. "I knew I loved New York, but I didn't realize how much until I was away for a year."

"Well, nothing changed much around here. Oh! Except remember Mr. Schaztman in 5D? He's engaged! Met a gal who was widowed after being married for over fifty years—she was working as an usher at a lecture at the 92nd Y. Three months later, he put a ring on it. They're getting married downtown on Valentine's Day. I'm going to be one of the witnesses!"

"That's amazing! I guess it's possible to find love anywhere," Dot said, gesturing for Danny to come closer. "Speaking of meeting someone—Albert, this is Danny. He and I met in Cedar Falls."

Danny stuck out his hand. "Mr. Hawkins, Danny Dawson. I've heard a lot about you."

Albert gave him a hearty handshake.

"So, she didn't forget about me then?" Albert asked as he winked at Dot. "She's a special young lady. But I can see you already know that." He gripped Danny's shoulder and held him there looking him up and down, as if the young man was on inspection.

"I do," Danny confirmed, hoping he was making a good impression on Dot's friend.

"Hey, I'm just going to check my mail—be right back," Dot said, popping into the lobby.

When she was out of earshot, Albert leaned into Danny. "Son—be ready for what's coming. I've known her since she was a girl. She can be very stoic, but under that tough New York exterior, she's a sensitive soul. Parting is going to be hard for her."

"Yes, sir. I'm prepared for that." He gave a sharp nod of his head to confirm he understood.

"Good man."

Dot came back out and stopped when she saw Albert and Danny in conversation—and the words she'd planned to use to say goodbye caught in her throat.

DANNY EXCUSED HIMSELF to take a quick call from one of his employees who was about to demolish a kitchen for a remodel they were doing back in Cedar Falls.

"He's a fine young man," Albert said, watching him go. He turned and rested his arm around Dot's shoulders.

She was grateful for his approval. "I agree," she said, giving Albert a squeeze.

When Danny returned, Albert hailed a taxi. Time slowed and Dot's vision blurred. The vehicle stopped, and the driver got out to put the bags in the car's trunk.

Dot turned to Danny and met his deep brown eyes.

This was it.

IN THE TAXI, the taxi driver made eye contact with Dot in the rearview mirror.

"Where to, love?"

She reached for Danny's hand, met his gaze, and said, "Home."

Epilogue

When they landed in Milwaukee, Dot felt butterflies stirring in her stomach—a swirl of eagerness for her new chapter, worries she'd live anywhere but New York, and wonderment about how her life had changed so much in a year. But the emotional thread that made her butterflies fly in formation was because she was deeply in love with Danny Dawson. And with him, this new adventure felt not only possible but nearly perfect. She pushed down thoughts of how she'd suddenly rejected her chosen career in high-tech PR and shunned a D.C.-based job in national politics so that she could be with him. But, some questions nagged at her. Who was she without the work that helped define her? What would happen when she let go of her plans and rode the wave of whatever life had in store for her?

Well, she was about to find out.

After landing in a frigid Milwaukee, Dot and Danny held hands as they made their way to his truck. It occurred to her that she'd have to renew her license and get used to driving. She was already dreading the parallel parking test.

As Danny drove them to Cedar Falls, they listened to the country music channel playing softly in the background. "Oh, I love this song," she said, surprised how even her Spotify algorithm knew her new musical preferences.

So much had changed.

When they drove into town, Danny said, "Mind if we stop at the bookshop for a moment?"

"No, that would be great. I'd love to start the new year off with a bunch of new reads, anyway."

Danny nodded and took a right onto Main Street.

"It's truly the cutest town," she said, looking around, the Christmas decorations still framing the storefronts.

"It is," he agreed, letting his eyes sweep over Main Street.

Danny parked across the street from the store and saw that Dot hadn't noticed yet. He hoped she liked surprises.

He got out and came around to her side to open her door.

"Welcome back, Dot." He used both hands to gesture toward the store.

She looked at him quizzically, not understanding. So, he spun her around. And then she saw it.

A new sign was affixed above the store—it no longer said "Reader Falls Bookshop."

It was now: "Dot's Bookshop & Second Cup Café."

"Wait. What?" She still hadn't registered what she was seeing.

Then, Ted and Jeanie Jankowski, Grace and Joe Taylor, Mimi and Rose, and several of Danny's employees came out of the store and started chanting her name. "Dot! Dot! Dot!"

Danny put an arm around her shoulders and squeezed her tightly into his torso.

"Happy New Year, Dot."

And then it finally sunk in.

"Oh my gosh. Danny. Wait. You didn't. Wait. You did! You bought the store from the Jankowskis? For me?"

"I did. And it's in your name, not mine. I wanted you to have something of your own here in Cedar Falls. But it's not just the bookstore. My guys spent the holidays fixing up the empty space next door. They knocked down a wall and put in a full coffee bar. And Mimi has signed on to be your pastry partner."

"Danny!" she exclaimed and threw her arms around his neck. "Oh my gosh. I love it! I love it! I love you! I love Cedar Falls!" Adrenaline took over her body and she did a little dance in the street. "And 'Second Cup Café'? That's our thing!" She recalled when he'd first said that to her the morning after the first night she'd spent at his place.

"All the good stuff happens during the second cup, right?" Danny said.

"Always." Dot tore her eyes away from Danny for a moment and looked for the Jankowskis. Spotting Ted and Jeanie, she went to them. Ted grabbed both of her hands.

"Dot, we couldn't have asked for a better outcome." He was teary. "And we're not going far. We'll be here to help. Though you have great instincts and are good at whatever you turn your hand to."

"I'm so happy for you," Jeanie said, wrapping Dot in a big hug and then whispering into her ear, "Welcome back to Cedar Falls. I promise that it's a good place to call home."

Dot hugged her back. "Thank you for helping me realize what I could have lost."

"I've learned a thing or two over all these years, dear."

Danny joined them and they basked in the love of their small-town friends and the feeling of a new adventure.

"Ready?" Danny said, gesturing to the front door.

"Ready!"

"Let's do this the right way." He carried her across the threshold to cheers.

"Welcome home, Dot," he said, planting a kiss on her lips.

"I love it. And you," she said, leaning her head against his chest and letting herself be carried.

A wave of serenity coursed through her body, and she knew in her heart that after all the worry about what she was going to do with her life, she had finally made the right choice.

Acknowledgments

The number of people I want to thank for their support would double the size of this book, and my editor has had enough. "Wrap it up, Dana." He's right, as always. Sean Desmond is brilliant and the best editor of his generation. While our previous work together was in nonfiction, there was no one else I wanted to work with on *Purple State*. Thank you, Sean, for traveling virtually to Cedar Falls with me. What a trip it's been.

My gratitude also goes to his junior editor, Jackie Quaranto. She has an incredible eye for detail and an ear for story. I enjoyed learning from her. Join me as we watch her rise.

The entire team at HarperCollins Publishers shines brightly. A special thanks to the CEO, Brian Murray, who loved the character Mary Russo from the start. My appreciation extends to the talented team supporting this book, including Elizabeth Catalano, Theresa Dooley, Amanda Pritzker, and Leah Wasielewski.

I benefited greatly from the guidance of CAA—especially Rachel Adler, Cait Hoyt, and Mark McGrath. Cait and Mark both welcomed babies into the world during the writing of *Purple State*, and I am excited to see them grow up.

The leadership at NewsCorp has given me more chances to grow and experiment than anywhere else. I am grateful to Rupert and Elena Murdoch and to Lachlan and Sarah Murdoch. I especially cherished the moment my fellow reader Sarah learned of the book—her enthusiasm gave me quite a boost.

My family at Fox News cheered me on yet again, and their encouragement is deeply appreciated. Thank you to Suzanne Scott, Jay Wallace, Irena Briganti, Kim Rosenberg, Lauren Petterson, Jonathan Glenn, Jessica Ketner, Jennings Grant, Nicole Cooper, Kristy Cappiello, Charlie Horan, Amy Fenton, and Brett Zoeller.

A special thanks to Megan and Scott Quimby of FNC, and to Megan's mom, Joy Albano. They were the first to hear about my idea—Scott is from Wisconsin, and Megan has found love and joy there, too. Joyce is a big reader, and I delighted in her feedback on an early draft. They answered many questions and steered me in the right direction.

My coanchor of *America's Newsroom*, Bill Hemmer, and his assistant, Molly Harrigan, had my back throughout the process. I also found creative inspiration from my cohosts of *The Five*—Greg Gutfeld, Jesse and Emma Watters, Jessica Tarlov, and Harold Ford Jr. Even though Greg hates romantic comedies, he said he'd read this one.

Paul Mauro—a man who is good at everything he turns his hand to—edited early versions and got me on track. His wife, Joan McNaughton, jumped in to encourage me. They believed I could do it before I did.

People who follow me on social media will be familiar with Kate DePetro. Her first day as my assistant was the night of the debate between President Biden and President Trump. Late that night, as we said goodbye, I asked how she'd feel about spending two extra days in Wisconsin after the RNC convention. "I'd love to," she said and clapped her hands together. From the start, she immersed herself in each character and invested in their stories. I've loved every minute of being on this journey with her. When no one knew about the book, she and I would see a situation in New York City and say, "Oh, that's so *Purple State*." Kate is going places, but she will always be in my heart.

I've loved everyone I've ever met from Wisconsin, including former Rep. Mike Gallagher, who put me in touch with Kelsey Fenske. Kelsey took Kate and me on a whirlwind tour of Wisconsin in July 2024. Cedarburg was our last stop, and as we pulled into town, she said, "I think this is going to be your favorite." She nailed it. Thank you, Kelsey, for answering all of my questions. Your future is so bright.

A special note of thanks to President George W. Bush, who gave me the opportunity to serve as his press secretary. It was the experience of a lifetime, and not a day goes by that I don't give thanks for it. Through him, I also developed deep friendships, especially with Jeanie Mamo. Jeanie read *Purple State* with cheer and enthusiasm and cried with pride at the end. What a friend she is.

My efforts to write *Purple State* were supported by my Michigan, New Jersey, and Texas crews. Thanks especially to Becki and Jose Patino, who traveled to Cedarburg with me. And to my Bay Head family—thank you to Gina and Ava Hayes; Barbara, Kimmy, and Lauren Fritts; and Jenny and Erin Landers. All the rest of you—drinks on me at our next adventure.

Dear friends, including Ingrid Henrichsen, cheered on The Crew from the start, and I thank her for her attention to detail. My previous assistant, Caroline Sherlund, was there at the beginning and the end of the writing process, and I don't know how I'd ever live without her. Misha Randelovic, Dakota Pizzi, and their baby Rae listened to me talk about this book between ballroom dance rounds and helped me more than they could ever know.

Kelly Coyle and I bonded over our love of fiction at her store, The Little Point Bookshop, in Point Pleasant Beach, New Jersey. She is a beautiful writer in her own right and runs one of the most important businesses in any community—the bookstore. Not only did she encourage me every step of the way, but she also runs the Second Cup Café and let me use that name and the story behind it in *Purple State*. I look forward to the book she has inside her.

While my admiration for novelists knows no bounds, three writers were especially helpful. While on a walk, Andrew Graff nudged me to start writing. Patti Callahan Henry and Siobhan Fallon read early versions, and their feedback reassured me. They are all so talented, and I remain in awe of how they ply their craft.

As I thought about these acknowledgments, I especially wanted to thank my first-grade teacher, Joan Rittenbaum. In 1978, she spotted me as a reader and gave me a lifelong passion that has meant so much to me. Sadly, when I looked her up, I learned she had died in 2008. I shouldn't have waited to express my gratitude. Lesson learned—thank your teachers now.

Purple State is dedicated to my sister, Angie Perino Machock, who was so excited when I learned to read that she told everyone about it. She was a champion for this book and kept asking if she could read every draft. I adore you, Angie.

Then there's the crowd favorite, my husband, Peter McMahon. As the writing process ended, I overheard him telling friends all about the book. His pride in me was fuel in my tank. I loved how Harper became his favorite character. Once he understood why I was explaining what cigarette pants were, he became the book's biggest champion. Thank you, Peter, for all you do, especially taking care of Percy and me with such care and attention.

Finally, but also primarily, to my mom and dad, Leo and Janice Perino. They never told me to get my nose out of my books, and I'll never forget their relief when we found that secondhand bookshop on Colorado Boulevard. It saved them a fortune as I chose stacks of books on every visit. My mom read the drafts and said, "I can't believe my daughter wrote this." Same, Mom, same.

And to all my readers, especially those young women coming through their quarter-life crises and finding all that life has to offer—thank you for being in my life. I am so much better for it.

About the Author

Dana Perino is a Fox News anchor, cohost of *The Five*, coanchor of *America's Newsroom*, and one of the channel's key election analysts. She's the #1 *New York Times* bestselling author of *And the Good News Is . . .*; *Let Me Tell You About Jasper . . .*; *Everything Will Be Okay*; and *I Wish Someone Had Told Me . . . .* She also hosts her own podcast, *Perino on Politics*. Dana is the former White House press secretary for President George W. Bush—the first Republican woman to hold the job. She grew up in the Rocky Mountain West and now lives in New York City with her husband, Peter McMahon, and their dog, Percy.